Praise for *Felicity George*

'The perfect mix of dramatic, sexy, emotional and
deliciously romantic'
CRESSIDA McLAUGHLIN

'An enthralling, emotionally satisfying story with an
unforgettable heroine who has the courage to fight for
what she believes in – even if it breaks her heart'
EMMA ORCHARD

'Oh what fun! Take the perfect hero, filthy rich &
"frightfully rude and a dreadful grouch" add a spirited
do-gooder heroine determined to separate him from his
cash & send them on a poignant search & rescue through
the underbelly of Regency London. It's a treat!'
JANE DUNN

'A gorgeous, captivating Regency romance'
SOPHIE IRWIN

'A smart story, compelling writing and a big smile on
any reader's face when they finish'
JODI ELLEN MALPAS

'A scorching romance combined with a very satisfying
mystery. Readers are in for a treat'
JESSICA BULL

Felicity George is a writer and teacher from Toronto, where she lives with her husband, her two teenage children, a large cat, and a tiny dog. A lifelong devotee of Jane Austen and Georgette Heyer, Felicity adores a happily-ever-after. *A Debutante's Desire* is her third novel.

Connect with Felicity

X Felicity George @FgeorgeRomance
f Felicity George, Author
@FelicityGeorgeRegencyRomance
Felicity George @felicitygeorge_romance

Also by Felicity George

A Lady's Risk
A Courtesan's Worth

A
DEBUTANTE'S
DESIRE

FELICITY GEORGE

ORION

First published in Great Britain in 2024 by Orion Fiction,
an imprint of The Orion Publishing Group Ltd,
Carmelite House, 50 Victoria Embankment
London EC4Y 0DZ

An Hachette UK company

3 5 7 9 10 8 6 4 2

A CIP catalogue record for this book
is available from the British Library.

ISBN (Paperback) 978 1 3987 1884 5
ISBN (eBook) 978 1 398 71046 7

Printed and bound in Great Britain by Clays Ltd, Elcograf S.p.A.

For Jessica Bull and Suzy Vadori

with gratitude

and in memory of Annie

Prologue
January 1808

Oakwood Hall emerged from the snowy Yorkshire countryside, grey stone blending with grey sky. As John Tyrold cantered out of the ancient oak grove fronting the manor house, the mist creeping over the moors seemed to seep into his bones. Ever since his parents' letter had arrived in London with news of Helen's death, he'd anticipated a gloomy return to his childhood home; evidently even the weather wished to ensure his expectations were fulfilled.

A legion of familiar figures fanned out from the house to stand at attention, as if even the scullery maids had been summoned to greet John's arrival. Which was a damned nuisance, of course. He'd hoped to slip in undetected to see his grieving parents, at least initially. Every servant knew the reason he had not returned home in eight years, and their minds no doubt dwelt upon that now. In general, John was indifferent to the opinions of others, but, oddly, here at Oakwood, he wasn't.

The servants arranged themselves like statues, their breath clouding around their noses, their black clothes stark against the grim, grey vista. Everyone wore mourning for Helen, and, as his horse drew closer,

John grew conscious of his brown hat and green great-coat, realising for the first time that he ought to have acquired black attire before leaving town. It had been an oversight on his part, for he rarely thought of his clothes, but perhaps it would look like disrespect.

He tightened his numb fingers around the reins and halted Thunder in front of the formidable company. As he dismounted, his parents stepped forwards, his father tall with long white hair and his mother weeping, her arms outstretched.

'My boy is home at last,' Mrs Tyrold cried, enveloping John in a warm embrace. 'But you're not a boy any more, are you?' Tears pooled along her lower lashes as she stroked his unshaven cheek. John was seventeen when last he'd seen her; he was five-and-twenty now. 'All the same, how good it is to see my son. If only Helen were alive and well, then I could be happy again.'

John held her close. 'There, there, Mother. All will be well,' he said with as much conviction as he could muster. 'I can't stay long, but while I'm here I shall help in any way needed.' Even a short absence from London was a strain because of the incessant demands of his ever-expanding fortune, but John loved his parents too well not to have cast aside business to return home when he'd received their heartbroken letter.

He glanced at his father, who looked careworn, his face lined, his eyes weary. 'When is the funeral?' John queried, his voice flat.

'Tomorrow. We shall bury her in the Tyrold vault.'

'Naturally,' John responded curtly.

The wrinkles on his father's forehead deepened. 'Son, Helen was like a daughter to your mother and me.'

Mrs Tyrold buried her face into John's chest, her sobs muffled against his greatcoat.

'I know, Father,' John said, more kindly. He rubbed his mother's back. Dammit, now there was a lump in his throat, but John wouldn't reveal any weakness here, in front of the entire household staff. 'Come, Mother, let's go inside. It's far too cold to stand about, especially when there has so recently been illness in the house.'

Mrs Tyrold sniffled and broke the embrace to thread her arm through John's.

A groom stepped forwards to lead Thunder to the stables, and John patted his horse's neck before relinquishing the reins. 'Take care of him, please,' he said. 'He's been on the road for three days.'

'Shall we expect your luggage by carriage later, sir?' the groom asked.

'No, no carriage follows,' John replied. He'd packed his few changes of clothes in the saddlebags.

'But, John, you will need a carriage to return to London,' his mother said. She hung heavily on John's arm, and her tread was slow as their feet crunched the icy gravel on their walk to the front door.

'Thunder does very well,' John reassured her.

The fashionable world scratched its head that he kept neither carriage nor any other trappings of a gentleman despite his nearly unparalleled wealth, but it suited John to have everyone believe him a miser. In truth, he *did* despise the unnecessary waste of money, and his horse did the job as well as a carriage, with much less expense.

His mother tightened her hold on his elbow. 'I'm certain Thunder is a good horse, but the child cannot make such a long journey on horseback.'

John frowned as they stepped over the threshold and into the vaulted medieval hall, as oppressively cold and grey as the outside despite the crackle of logs in the vast stone hearth. 'Whatever do you mean, Mother?'

It was his father who replied. 'Flora will return with you, my son.'

John drew back, astonished his father would make such a request about Helen's young daughter, but his reply withered on his lips as he noted movement by the hearth. Emerging from a makeshift construction of blankets and pillows was a slip of a mite wearing a black frock and clutching a large leather book to her chest.

The child's appearance froze John, for the mass of burnished copper curls, the rosebud lips and the small nose were the spit of her mother − yet the owl-like eyes that returned his gaze with frank regard weren't blue like Helen's, but the unadulterated green of an oak leaf.

'John, this is Flora,' his mother said, her voice sounding muffled in John's ears.

The servants filed in behind his parents. Aware that dozens of eyes watched, John disguised how the child's appearance affected him. 'Good day, Flora,' he said, his bootsteps echoing as he approached the hearth. He knelt, facing her on her level. 'I'm John.'

'Yes, I know,' she whispered, before pressing her lips together, as if sealing her mouth.

A dull ache throbbed in John's chest. Helen had been an effervescent child, a ray of sunshine, but Flora was sombre beyond her years.

He tried again. 'I'm pleased to make your acquaintance at last, although I'm terribly sorry it's under such dreadful circumstances.'

She blinked, studying him.

Then her large eyes gleamed, abruptly animated. 'What's your favourite bird, John?'

John hid his surprise at her transformation. Birds were clearly a topic that interested her, and he knew from his own childhood experiences that she expected a proper answer. In such cases, nothing was worse than an adult who laughed, so he replied solemnly with the first bird that came to mind. 'Owls.'

'Tawny, barn, long-eared, or short-eared?' she queried, her green gaze intense.

'All owls,' John replied and, suspecting she'd want him to justify his answer, he fabricated reasons, although it was the child's appearance that had inspired his response. 'I admire their solitary nature, their keen observational skills and the effectiveness of their hunt.'

Flora nodded approvingly. 'If you wish to observe one in nature, look for their pellets. An owl's nest will be nearby. Tomorrow, let's search together. If we find a pellet, we can dissect it, for inside will be the tiny bones of mice and shrews, and we can reconstruct their skeletons.'

With that pronouncement, she marched out of the hall, still clutching her book. For a moment, John stared after her, marvelling at her obvious intelligence, but then the deep ache stirred again within his chest. The child had witnessed her mother's slow death; what dreadful thoughts would invade her young mind as she sorted mouse bones?

John stood and turned to his parents, who gazed after Flora with misty eyes. The servants had dispersed, allowing him to speak candidly. 'I cannot take that little one to London. She's better off here, scampering over the moors in search of owls.'

His father shook his weary head. 'Regardless, she must go with you. You're her guardian now, per Helen's will.'

'Helen left you this.' Mrs Tyrold extended a folded paper. 'To explain, presumably.'

John took the letter and ripped the seal, his heart thudding at his name rendered in Helen's familiar script. After all these years, what had she written?

As it turned out, very little, for only a few lines crossed the page.

My dearest John,

I leave you my precious doll and I trust that in your heart of hearts you know why. Flora has never known a papa's love, although your own father did well by her. Love her, Johnny, for the sake of all which was once dear between us.

Helen

6

John's hand shook, causing the written words to waver. Helen trusted his heart of hearts to know why? What the devil did she mean by that? Good God, if there had been a reason, why had he not received this letter years ago? Why hadn't Helen . . .

Swiftly, John buried this disturbing new thought in the same deep hole where he concealed his old resentment, and refolded the paper. Her word choice likely meant nothing; Helen had been feverish for months before her death, according to his parents. 'I shall act as the child's guardian, but Helen writes nothing about London. It is best Flora remain in the only home she has ever known.'

'I disagree, son.' His father delivered his contradiction in a tone much firmer than John had ever heard from the quiet man. 'This has been no life for her, especially during Helen's long illness. Oakwood is too remote. You had Helen and Arthur to keep you company growing up, but Flora has always been alone. She needs other children—'

'School, then,' John said. 'I shall find a school, for I am in no position to raise a child, nor would she be around other children in my company.'

'But it's time you settled down,' his mother urged. 'A proper home, a wife—'

'I have no inclination towards fortune hunters, Mother. And women only want my money.'

'Helen didn't,' his father ventured softly, looking at the floor.

John snorted. 'You know how that turned out.'

7

Mrs Tyrold shot her husband a scowl before addressing John again. 'Son, what happened with Helen is in the past. You have a full life ahead of you. Don't you feel lonely?'

John shrugged. 'I'm considering a dog.'

'Be serious, John.' His mother was evidently unamused for there was exasperation in her voice. 'You must have a son to inherit this estate after you.'

'Flora will inherit,' John replied.

His father's head snapped up from observing the flagstones. 'You well know that Flora cannot inherit an estate entailed through the male line.'

'As legal heir, I can change the entail. I shall be the first Tyrold heir ever to do so, but I assure you it can and will be done.' John shoved Helen's letter in his pocket. 'And, as Flora's guardian, I believe it is best if she remains here—'

'No,' Mrs Tyrold said with finality.

John lifted his brows, for it was the first time in his recollection in which either of his parents had told him no.

But his mother stood resolute. 'Frankly, she is too much for us. We are not young, John – we were not young when we were blessed with you, our only child, but we grow old now.'

John felt the truth of her words. Lines that hadn't been there eight years earlier were etched on her face, her red–gold hair was streaked with grey, and his father's shoulders stooped with age. Mrs Tyrold's slow and heavy tread John had attempted to dismiss as grief, but the truth was, his father had passed seventy and his mother was not much younger.

'Flora is a handful, John,' Mrs Tyrold said with a sigh. 'Not without justification, mind you. She's lived a difficult life in her few short years. Death, illness, more death, and now you suggest she continue to live with two aged people in this remote corner of Yorkshire? No, she needs youth and vitality. She needs firm but loving guidance. She needs you, and all you can provide her.'

John tossed aside his hat and ran his fingers through his long hair, his thoughts in turmoil. He couldn't return to London with Flora in tow. If he wasn't ready to face the explanation he'd have to offer his friends, he certainly wasn't ready to parent a child who was the spitting image of the woman who'd broken his heart . . . except for those damnable green eyes.

And there was another concern. John had long ago made Flora the primary beneficiary in his will, and his arriving in London with a child people would suspect – quite rightly – of being the heiress to the Tyrold millions would cause a sensation. It was one thing for John to be hounded – he knew how to throw off fortune hunters – but a little girl? Flora would be a target of incessant toad-eating and flattery, if not worse. It was no way to grow up.

Yet John couldn't disregard the only request his parents had ever made of him. It was simply a matter of managing the situation properly. Naturally, Flora must reside at a school. A sensible, homey institution where she'd receive a well-rounded education, perhaps with the daughters of prosperous shopkeepers.

That way, none amongst his circle of acquaintances need know of her existence until John decided they should.

John applied himself to locating such a place that very evening, writing a dozen inquiries by candlelight after Flora and his parents had gone to bed. Within a fortnight – despite spending every afternoon being pulled across the icy moors by a little red-haired wildling – he reached a satisfactory arrangement with a Miss Crayford at the David Street Girls' Seminary in Mary Le Bone.

He described what he knew of the school as he left Oakwood Hall in a post-chaise a month later, Flora snuggled against his side. 'It's a small school, with about a dozen girls to be your friends. You will live there, but I shan't be far away.'

'I like to learn,' Flora said. 'And I think I shall enjoy having friends.' Wrapped in blankets and furs, she swung her little legs on the bench seat, her gaze fixed on the icy moors outside the carriage window. In her lap rested the large leather volume she was rarely without, *The Birds of Britain* embossed on its cover. 'Will you come and see me, John?'

'On occasion, yes. I can visit, although I must be discreet when I do.'

She peered up at him, her owl-like eyes piercing. 'Why?'

John tugged at his shirt collar, loosening its hold. 'I'm rather well known.'

'Mama said your fortune has made you famous. She showed me whenever your name appeared in the papers.'

John's mind conjured a vision of Helen and Flora together, reading about him as if he were a fairy-tale character in a bedtime story, but he erased the imagining swiftly. It probably hadn't been anything like that. Helen had perhaps mocked and ridiculed him, silently if not aloud. Had she hated him, even?

He despised these wonderings, which had come to him frequently in the last fortnight. He hadn't wanted to resolve things when Helen was alive, so why did he care now?

Because now you have seen her child, a disturbing thought whispered.

Swiftly, John silenced it by returning to his conversation with Flora. 'It's not a nice thing to be famous.'

'Why not?' she asked in her solemn manner.

'Because people constantly bother me. They fixate on me and pursue me relentlessly unless I am dismissive and rude. Even then, they attempt to force my attention in all manner of ways. I rarely go into company because I find it so . . .' John hesitated, searching for the word which best described his sentiments. Exhausting wasn't quite right. Nor was grating. It was something more complicated than that. Interacting with society *confused* him because he could never trust people's motives. Except for his few close friends, when people were kind or attentive or acted as if they found him interesting, it was because they wanted something. 'Because I find it difficult to discern who I can trust, Flora,' he concluded at last. 'If others learn of your connection to me, I'm afraid unkind people might treat you in confusing ways. I don't want you to experience that until you're ready.'

'When will I be ready?'

John exhaled, considering. 'You're seven now?' He knew the answer.

'Eight in April.'

That gave John a decade, at least. Surely, within the next ten years, one of his friends would marry a lady John could trust to oversee an heiress's coming out. 'When you've completed school at eighteen, you will be ready.'

Flora studied him carefully. 'And then I shall live with you?'

'Perhaps.' The girl's eyes narrowed, as if she intended to question him further, but John changed the subject. 'There's one matter more to discuss, little one. I believe it's best if you're called Flora Jennings at school.'

Flora tilted her head. 'But I'm Flora Tyrold.'

'Yes, yes,' John said quickly. 'But that surname will connect you with me, whereas Jennings protects you from the unkind people I mentioned earlier.'

Flora's lips turned down, but at last she nodded. 'Very well. Jennings was Mama's name, and I shall like that.' Her green-eyed gaze fell to her book. 'Do you have a pencil?'

'A pencil? I believe so, yes.' John reached into his coat pocket and shuffled round his pipe, his tobacco pouch and his coin purse until he felt the wooden cylinder.

He extracted it, checked its tip – well sharpened enough for writing – and handed the instrument to Flora.

After opening her book, she wrote the name *FLORA JENNINGS* in careful block print *with her left hand*.

John's breath hitched. The green eyes and now this? What did it mean that he and the child shared such a rare peculiarity? But scarcely had the question formulated before he scolded himself for thinking it. Surely it meant nothing other than his parents had imparted upon Helen their belief that it was cruel to tie back the hand of a left-handed child. If others were so sensible, left-handedness likely wouldn't be so uncommon.

All the same, John's chest ached with a profound sharpness, as if wounded anew. He drew Flora close and placed a kiss on her copper curls. She sighed, contented, closed her book, and soon fell asleep in his arms.

I

1st April 1816

London

Georgiana Bailey strolled on the arm of her father's wife, drawing courage from the beauty of the day. Hyde Park was a brilliant burst of opulence and colour during the late afternoon hour when the *beau monde* emerged, to see and be seen. On the fashionable bridle path Rotten Row, young bucks atop high-bred horses cantered past barouches and curricles, their occupants on display, while a sea of silk parasols, plumed bonnets, and tall-crowned hats navigated the tree-lined walkways. To Georgiana's right, the Serpentine sparkled blue, dotted with swans and toy sailboats, and the laughter of the boys and girls playing along its edge lent a festive air.

The sight of the children warmed Georgiana's heart. She promised herself for the thousandth time that somehow, one day, she'd purchase a garden for the residents of Monica House, the refuge she ran for women and children in distress. The garden would be a place for children to run and play amongst trees and flowers, and for the women, a sanctuary of beauty and peace, offering healing and hope to those who had suffered.

Today was the renaissance of all her dreams after months of despair; it was also her unofficial debut into the world of the *haut ton*, which was why she felt alert and tense, like a deer facing a pack of wolves. Georgiana knew that she appeared to fit the part in an indigo-blue redingote adorned with gold braid, but all the trimmings on earth wouldn't long disguise the fact that she was the natural daughter of an opera singer, whose father had hidden her like a shameful secret, until now.

Regardless, for the sake of everything she held dear, Georgiana simply must make the *ton* accept her. The odds were stacked against her, as always. Society never looked kindly on illegitimacy, and the discovery that the moralist Duke of Amesbury had a bastard had already caused a stir. Never mind that Georgiana's conception predated her father's marriage by a few months; Amesbury's hypocrisy was raising eyebrows and setting tongues wagging. The smallest misstep on Georgiana's part would destroy her chance of acceptance, for the *ton* would judge her far more harshly than other young women. Like the deer amongst the wolves, the slightest falter could be her demise.

Yet failure wasn't an option. The wellbeing of too many people depended upon her success.

'These first few appearances will be the most challenging for both of us, Georgiana,' said her father's wife. Fanny Bailey, the Duchess of Amesbury, was an exceedingly pretty blonde lady in her mid-forties, a leader of high society for more than two decades and yet, now, on this all-important afternoon, there was a quiver in her rather girlish voice. She offered a smile as she smoothed the walnut-brown curls peeping from Georgiana's bonnet brim, but the action was one of nervous energy rather than necessity. Georgiana had dressed herself, and she knew not a pin was out of place nor a hair astray. 'You look lovely,' the duchess continued, 'and despite your protestations, I *do* want you to attempt to secure an advantageous match this Season. Have fun, dearest. Flirt – demurely, of course. As pretty and clever as you are, you'll have a husband in no time, for everyone is thinking of marriage since Princess Charlotte's engagement last month.'

Georgiana blinked, incredulous that the duchess was rehashing this dispute. For years, she'd remained steadfast against her father and his wife's arguments for her marriage. The only reason she'd finally agreed to enter society this Season was because Monica House had recently lost a valuable benefactress, depriving the charity of much of its income.

All Georgiana's thoughts were bent upon helping Monica House. She must raise a substantial sum of money for the charity to operate without a deficit, not to mention find funds to pay an arrear of debts and to restore her dream of establishing a school and the garden. Her successful debut into a social world filled with wealthy potential sponsors wasn't coming a moment too soon.

'No more talk of marriage, ma'am,' Georgiana said firmly. 'As I have said many times before, I am entering society to find sponsors for Monica House, not to find a husband.' She squared her shoulders and lifted her chin as she surveyed the crowds before her, like a soldier facing the battlefield. 'So with that in mind, please introduce me to the most charitable souls of your acquaintance.'

A tightness formed at the corners of Fanny's lips. 'First, make an effort with some eligible gentlemen, Georgiana. You underestimate the benefits of marriage to a man of breeding and fortune, both for yourself and your charity work. In fact, ready yourself now, dearest. Sir Ambrose Pratley-Finch comes your way. He has ten thousand a year, and he's looking for a wife.'

An old man with wispy white hair weaved towards them, a leer on his florid face and a black armband tied round the sleeve of his mauve tailcoat.

Georgiana's eyes widened. 'You cannot be serious, ma'am! Pray, let us walk in the other direction before he approaches.' She turned – intending to escape whether or not the duchess joined her – but Fanny clasped her hand, restraining her, and then it was too late to leave without appearing impertinent, a misstep Georgiana couldn't afford.

'Good afternoon, Sir Ambrose,' Fanny said, responding to the baronet's bow. 'I'm pleased to see you looking well. Naturally, the duke and I were devastated to learn of the death of Lady Pratley-Finch in the autumn.'

The baronet, whose watery eyes scaled the length of Georgiana's frock before peering at her face, dabbed his bulbous nose with a purple handkerchief. 'Yes, yes. But life goes on. May I beg an introduction to your protégé, Duchess?'

With effort, Georgiana set her face into a pleasing expression while the introductions were made. After all, Sir Ambrose was a rich man and therefore it was worth her time to encourage him to donate to Monica House.

Her composure almost faltered when the baronet planted a raspy kiss on her gloved hand.

'Stroll with me, my dear,' Sir Ambrose said, speaking in a deep voice he must imagine was alluring. He tucked her hand into the crook of his elbow and manoeuvred her away from Fanny. 'I don't mind admitting I'm already quite in your thrall. I didn't know Amesbury had a daughter until last week when Lady Frampton told me. Everyone's talking of it, many not so kindly, but it doesn't matter to me if you were born on the wrong side of the sheets. A duke's daughter is a duke's daughter, and I expect your papa intends to do well by you, eh?'

Still hoping for a donation, Georgiana formed her lips into what she hoped resembled a genuine smile. 'My father is extremely good to me, sir,' she said sweetly. The truth was, the fortune her father had bestowed upon her four years earlier was long spent on renovations to Monica House and other charitable deeds, but neither the duke nor the duchess knew that. 'I am so truly blessed that I try to give a little back by running a charity house for women and children. Perhaps you might like to sponsor—'

The baronet pressed close, his sour breath on Georgiana's cheek. 'A bit of do-gooding is well enough for a lady, but a gentleman has bigger concerns, doesn't he? I hear your mother was Anna Marinetti, *La Grande*

Bellezza. Saw her perform countless times. By God, what a voice. What a figure, what a face. There never was anything more exquisite. You resemble her, you know. Haven't got her shape, more's the pity, but you're still a handsome thing. Besides, you might yet put some meat on your bones. And you're more of an age for me than most debutantes, eh?'

At six-and-twenty, Georgiana was old for a debutante, but that didn't mean she was 'of an age' for an ancient lecher like Sir Ambrose.

If the baronet didn't wish to donate to Monica House, Georgiana was done with his company. 'Excuse me, Sir Ambrose,' she said as prettily as she could muster. 'But I must beg to return to the duchess.'

Sir Ambrose's expression darkened, his bushy brows drawing together. 'Don't be so dismissive, my girl. There won't be many as tolerant of your birth and as willing to make you an honourable offer as I am.'

Georgiana repressed a retort, for she couldn't afford to give offence. 'I do not intend to be dismissive, sir. I merely wish to be at the duchess's side, as is right and proper for a debutante.' Without giving him a chance to protest more, she curtsied and then darted to Fanny, who stood blinking innocently under a tree some distance away. 'That was a cruel trick, ma'am,' she hissed against the duchess's plumed hat.

Fanny drew her lips into a circle. 'You didn't *like* Sir Ambrose?' As Georgiana glared her response, the duchess shook her head, as if in disbelief. 'I can't think why, dearest. He's rich and likely to die soon.'

Georgiana couldn't help but smile. 'Ah, now I know you're only teasing.'

Fanny's blue eyes twinkled. 'About dreadful Sir Ambrose, yes. But I am quite serious about your finding a husband, so show me who you *do* like.' With that pronouncement, the duchess swept her closed parasol towards Rotten Row, as if it were a fairy wand able to grant Georgiana her pick of husbands.

Exasperated, Georgiana followed the arc of the parasol over the promenading crowds as she readied her argument against marriage, for the thousandth time. 'Ma'am, my work at Monica House consumes me . . .'

The rest of her words withered away as her attention was captured by a man approaching from the west with determined strides, his hands shoved deep into his pockets, a pipe dangling from his lips and a lanky black wolfhound at his side.

Georgiana drew herself up, raising on her tiptoes as she studied him, for he was none other than John Tyrold, one of the wealthiest men in Britain, and at the very top of Georgiana's list of people to approach about Monica House. An introduction to Tyrold could change everything if she played her cards well; he was rich enough to reverse Monica House's troubles by tossing out his pocket change. It was unimaginably good fortune to spot him on her first day out with Fanny, especially since he was famously a recluse.

'*Him?*' Fanny asked, having evidently followed Georgiana's gaze. 'Good Lord, child! Do you know who that is?'

Georgiana dropped down from her tiptoes, grinning. 'I live at a charity house, not under a rock! All of London knows the legendary "King Midas" Tyrold on sight.'

It was said that everything Tyrold invested in multiplied its value manyfold, so that the man was hounded by every venturer and capitalist in the kingdom. It was also said that Tyrold was eccentric, brusque and unapproachable. That despite possessing the wealth of a king, he'd skin a flint if he could.

He certainly *seemed* to wear the evidence of his parsimony with apparent pride; as always, the same shabby brown hat shaded his stubble-darkened face, his olive-green frock coat was years out of fashion, and he must be the only gentleman under seventy in London who still sported long hair tied back into a queue, as if he were too cheap to visit a barber. Even his pipe was terribly outmoded, for the fashionable set had long preferred snuff.

'Georgiana, you won't succeed,' Fanny cautioned. '*Everyone* has tried to catch Tyrold for years; he's considered the prize of the marriage market, for although his fortune is largely self-made, he comes from an ancient family and is heir to a vast estate in Yorkshire. He never shows interest in debutantes.'

That didn't deter Georgiana. She wasn't *truly* a debutante and she only wanted his attention to ask for a substantial donation. But it wouldn't do to tell Fanny that, as determined as the duchess was for her to find a husband, so she continued her pretence. 'You told me to find someone eligible. I might as well aim for someone worth catching.'

Fanny gazed again at Tyrold. After some moments, she shook her head. 'It's no good, dearest. You must set a more realistic goal. Quite honestly, I can't fathom how I'd initiate a conversation with the man. Although I was introduced to him some time ago at a ball of Lord Holbrook's – for he's a good friend of the marquess's – I'm too terrified to approach him. He's frightfully rude and a dreadful grouch.'

Georgiana raised a sceptical brow. 'He won't ignore a duchess, surely?'

Fanny scrunched her face. 'I wouldn't put it past him, and I'm far too frightened to find out. If your father were here, it would be a different matter, but, alone, I shan't attempt it. Only look at him, my dear! Observe how he walks amongst the most fashionable company in London – he barely acknowledges anyone and only gentlemen when he does. Not a word to a lady.'

The duchess wasn't wrong. Tyrold bore swiftly through the crowds, people parting before him like the waters of the Red Sea. Occasionally, he nodded to an acquaintance or two – always a man – but he conversed with no one. When a courtesan threw a glove in his path, he kicked it out of his way and didn't even spare her a glance as he and his wolfhound walked on.

As Georgiana narrowed her eyes to focus more closely, a smile played on her lips. She noted with amusement that dog and master were two of a kind: both gangly, with tousled black hair, their dishevelment rather endearing, as if they simply needed someone to take care of them . . .

A hot wave of embarrassment swept over Georgiana. Lord! What was she thinking, letting her imagination take her down such a dangerous path? She couldn't let herself be *attracted* to Tyrold. Imagine the disaster if she blushed or giggled like a schoolgirl as she asked for a donation.

He'd think her a fool!

No, she must retain her composure and speak intelligently – and *not* flirtatiously – with him. Georgiana knew she possessed intelligence in abundance; she drew upon it now, her thoughts bent on getting her introduction.

She scanned the scene before her, her mind rapidly proposing options of how she might capture Tyrold's attention and discarding them as ridiculous just as quickly, until she was half tempted to emulate the courtesan and throw her own glove. Perhaps the oddity of two kid-leather missiles within such a short span of time might startle Tyrold into noticing her.

Thankfully, fortune smiled before she was driven to such desperation for as she watched, Tyrold fell into a conversation with Lord Edward Matlock, a gentleman she knew well.

Lord Edward had been her friend during her schooldays and although she hadn't spoken to him in years, the moment it became clear that *he* and Tyrold were on congenial terms, Georgiana knew she'd found her opportunity for an introduction. If she could engage

Edward's attention, he would certainly bring her into his conversation with Tyrold. But for her plan to succeed, she had no time to waste – and to convince Fanny to participate, she must pretend she was still husband-hunting. Edward would do perfectly for that as well.

She clasped the duchess's wrist. 'The gentleman currently conversing with Mr Tyrold is another with whom I am willing to make an effort,' she said urgently, indicating the handsome chestnut-haired exquisite, dressed to the nines in skin-tight pantaloons and a pale blue tailcoat.

Fanny tapped her closed parasol thoughtfully against her skirts. 'Lord Edward Matlock? Why him?'

'I was friends with his sister, Lady Henrietta, at school.' Georgiana offered the simplest explanation. No need to add 'before you even knew I existed', because the words already hung like a deadweight between her and Fanny, as always happened when Georgiana mentioned her childhood. 'I was infatuated with him, once upon a time,' she added quickly, hoping to ease the discomfort. 'And he's eligible, as you requested.'

She spoke only partial truth. Georgiana *had* thoroughly enjoyed a flirtation with Edward during one sun-soaked summer holiday at the Matlock estate in Sussex, in the naïve days of her youth. When her high spirits had aroused passionate urges in her body. When she'd craved attention and lapped at any offered. But, of course, Lord Edward wasn't truly eligible. Georgiana would rather marry a tomcat than the rakish artist, but at least Edward was someone with whom she could flirt to appease Fanny with no real danger of engaging his fickle heart.

Georgiana tugged at Fanny's wrist. 'What say you, ma'am?' she asked, desperate to move towards the men, for Edward had thrown an arm about Tyrold's shoulders and they had resumed their eastward progression. If Georgiana didn't hurry, they'd be out of the park and she'd miss her chance.

'*Well*,' Fanny said frustratingly slowly, drawing out the word while seconds ticked away, 'Lord Edward is a shocking rake, but so are many men before they marry and come to their senses.'

Although the duchess likely didn't mean to refer to her own husband's past, the words still cut Georgiana deeply. The Duke of Amesbury was a faithful husband to Fanny and devoted father to his five legitimate sons, but that didn't erase the fact he'd impregnated Georgiana's mother and left her to bear a bastard at Monica House while he married a proper lady.

But the opportunity to meet Tyrold was too critical for Georgiana to waste time dwelling on her father's betrayal, so she dismissed those thoughts. 'Lord Edward's parents always appeared agreeably married,' she said emphatically. 'Surely he will be the same.'

Fanny brightened. 'Yes, that is very true. Lord and Lady Lockington are as happy as your father and me. In fact, now that I reflect, I think this an excellent plan, dearest. Start with Lord Edward, for practice, if nothing else, and if it comes to anything I believe your father will consider it an unobjectionable match, since Lord Edward's father is his particular friend.'

'And it appears as if Mr Tyrold is Lord Edward's particular friend,' Georgiana added with a grin. 'So I shall get my introduction after all.'

Fanny blinked before bursting into laughter. 'You're incorrigible, but you're correct. Lord Edward and Mr Tyrold lodge together on Half Moon Street.'

Better and better. 'Shall we walk over? We must make haste if we are to overtake them.'

Fanny nodded, her eyes sparkling, and together they scurried towards the retreating backs of the millionaire and the artist. Georgiana's spirits soared; perhaps she'd acquire that school and garden for Monica House's residents sooner than she thought. Of course, it was madness to hope, but if anyone could make her dream come true, it was John Tyrold.

Georgiana merely needed to convince him he wanted to.

But Tyrold and Edward walked quickly and when she and the duchess made little progress with their quarry, Georgiana threw manners to the wind, cupped her hands beside her mouth, and called, 'Lord Edward!'

Fanny hissed a reprimand, but Georgiana had achieved her purpose. Edward pivoted, no doubt attuned to stopping the moment a feminine voice called his name.

Fanny halted just as abruptly. 'Stop walking, dearest!' she urged, out of breath. 'We must stand now. We cannot appear to be pursuing them!' And with that proclamation, the duchess popped open her parasol and twirled it over her head, staring towards the sky as if they hadn't been almost running a second earlier.

Edward still scanned the crowds, so Georgiana waved to assist him. The instant he noticed her, a brief recoil crossed his face, swiftly replaced by a wide grin. He called to his friend and, to Georgiana's delight, Tyrold stopped and glanced over his shoulder.

After a short, rather agitated exchange between the men, they both approached, although Tyrold lacked Edward's enthusiasm. He shoved his hands in his pockets and stared at his boots, his countenance obscured by his hat brim and pipe smoke.

'Here is an enchanting face I haven't seen in an age,' Lord Edward exclaimed when they neared. 'Georgiana Marinetti, you outshine the springtime. Does she not, Tyrold?'

Georgiana smiled her brightest smile, but Tyrold appeared not to have heard Edward, for he gazed to the side, as if lost in his own thoughts. Georgiana suppressed a flicker of frustration, reminding herself that engaging with the famously reclusive man wouldn't be easy. But armed with intelligence, noble purpose and her well-prepared speech about Monica House, she was confident of her ability to succeed.

'Good day, Lord Edward,' she said cheerfully.

Edward put a hand to his heart. 'Darlingest Gee, I haven't seen you in years! How can you offer a mere "good day"? Where have you been, my lovely scamp?'

In fact, Edward had seen her a number of times since her return from Italy four years previously. He simply hadn't *recognised* her, for she'd been in costume. But Georgiana couldn't say that with Fanny present.

She chose not to answer his question. 'I'm called Georgiana Bailey now, my lord.'

Edward's eyes darted to the duchess and back again, no doubt understanding everything. 'Ah, I see!' Collecting himself, he made a formal bow to Fanny. 'Good day, Duchess. Please forgive my familiarity with Miss Bailey. She and I knew each other as children – old habits and whatnot. I trust you are acquainted with my friend, Mr Tyrold?'

'Naturally,' Fanny said, still catching her breath. 'And, Mr Tyrold, if I may introduce you to my . . . to my husband's relation, Miss Bailey.'

Georgiana boldly extended her hand, knowing this was her opportunity to create a favourable first impression.

But the moment Tyrold faced her directly, she made a fool of herself.

By *blushing*, of all things.

Deeply, judging by the scalding heat of her cheeks.

And for no better reason than because she hadn't realised John Tyrold was a surprisingly handsome man.

His eyes were a brilliant oak-leaf green, startling next to his black lashes and the long strands of inky hair that had escaped his queue. He wore his collar and cravat looser than most men, displaying a strong neck and a hint of his Adam's apple. His days–old dark stubble – inexcusably untidy but rather devastatingly masculine – defined a firm jaw.

A jaw that was clenched, perhaps to hold his pipe between his teeth, but more likely because he didn't enjoy introductions to blushing debutantes.

Georgiana cursed silently. Her face was most certainly scarlet and she could do nothing about it other than hope he attributed her blush to the warmth of the sun – but she doubted he did because his brows drew together in a manner worryingly like a scowl.

Taking a deep breath, Georgiana decided to be forthright and bold, no pretence, no façade. She couldn't help the blush, but she *could* draw upon her courage.

'Mr Tyrold, I have long desired to meet you.' She grasped his hand firmly, gave it a vigorous shake, and his scowl dissipated into vague surprise. 'Indeed, I confess I called my old friend over hoping for an introduction to *his* friend. If you have a moment to spare, may I tell you about the charity home I manage? We are in desperate need of sponsors, and I believe it would touch your heart to learn of the positive impact your patronage could make.'

Fanny's head snapped round, her blue eyes flashing. 'Georgiana!'

But Georgiana didn't care.

For the sake of Monica House, she couldn't let this opportunity pass.

The friend Edward had begged John to meet was a diminutive young woman. Pretty and delicate. Not really John's style, but he noted her voice from the moment she spoke. It was exceptionally beautiful. It possessed *presence*. There was a complexity to its timbre, an unusual richness, depth and control.

It intrigued John.

His attraction to that voice alleviated some of the annoyance he typically felt during forced introductions. In fact, he found himself contemplating how to engage her in a bit of conversation to discern if she possessed at least some of the intelligence her voice seemed to suggest, without giving her false hope. But that was always an impossible balance, which John had never learnt to navigate. Displaying the slightest interest in a young lady linked her name to his so instantly that John hadn't attempted to converse with a debutante in years. He didn't want to raise expectations he had no intention of fulfilling and he had enough business to attend to already, without fighting fraudulent lawsuits claiming a breach of promise.

Not that John was opposed to matrimony as a rule. He believed marriages could be extremely happy when two partners united in mutual love and respect. His friends, Nick and Meggy, and Sidney and Kitty, as well as his own parents' decades-long union (evidently still as strong as ever, although John rarely returned to Oakwood), provided proof that the institution could be joyful.

But his distrust of others prevented him from choosing it for himself. He refused to marry a woman drawn to his wealth, yet that was what they all wanted. He'd long since resigned himself to bachelorhood, deeming loneliness preferable to partnering with someone who valued only his fortune.

Yet he frowned when Miss Bailey offered her hand, no doubt displaying his curiosity despite his best intentions. There was something familiar about her heart-shaped face, her tanned complexion, her small but shapely lips. She blushed, as young ladies often did when introduced to him, but she met his gaze boldly with a pair of captivating dark eyes – long-lashed, expressive and, like her voice, seemingly intelligent.

His curiosity escalated into genuine surprise when she commenced her bold appeal for her charity home. People weren't usually so honest about wanting his money.

Her frankness was commendable. As was her confident approach. Furthermore, she seemed to possess something of independence and strength of will, for she was clearly acting against her sponsor's wishes. The Duchess of Amesbury trembled like a displeased hummingbird, looking as if she wished to swat her protégé with her parasol.

Yet John smoked his pipe impassively, concealing his intrigue behind a composed countenance. It wouldn't do to let Miss Bailey know he admired her gumption, but he was curious if her appeal would match her bold beginning. He decided to hear her but determined to receive her in a brusque manner. It was best to keep both a figurative and literal distance from debutantes.

He spoke without removing his pipe. 'Be aware that efforts to engage my sponsorship are rarely successful, Miss Bailey, but I shall nevertheless grant you two minutes to present your appeal.' He extracted his watch, flipped its lid and noted the position of the second hand. 'Begin now.'

Her dark eyes gleamed as if she relished the challenge. 'I manage a charity home situated off Soho Square. Monica House. I doubt you've heard of it?'

'Never.' John glanced at the second hand. 'Begin stronger if you wish to secure my investment in your project, Miss Bailey. Time's ticking.'

Edward shot him a reproachful glance.

Miss Bailey, evidently undeterred, began to speak rapidly. 'We are more than a project, sir. Monica House has stood for over a hundred years, but our roots extend further. We are a refuge for women and their children, if they have any, who need a place where *certain people* won't find them.' As she spoke, she caressed a gold locket that glinted against her blue gown, tracing the etching of an *A* and an *M* with her finger. 'We protect them from cruel husbands and vicious fathers. Controlling brothers. Uncles, stepfathers. Thieves who keep them as molls and force them to steal. Their pimps or bawds.'

That made John withdraw his pipe. Edward coughed to hide an exclamation of surprise and Miss Bailey paused to support the duchess, who emitted a strangled sound and looked as if she might wilt to the ground.

'It's a sanctuary, then,' John said, encouraging Miss Bailey to continue once she retrieved a silver bottle from the duchess's reticule. 'And you want a sponsorship from me, to assist in the cost of meals and other necessities?'

'Exactly, sir,' Miss Bailey agreed. She uncorked the bottle and held it to the duchess's nose, prompting a recoil and a return of colour to the noblewoman's

32

cheeks. 'And in strengthening my networks to find women who need my help,' she continued cheerfully, leaving the restorative vinaigrette in the duchess's hand. 'I'm skilled at locating women in trouble, but there's always room for improvement. Some women are so oppressed as to be nearly imprisoned, and many of my sponsors are comforted to hear of the relief I'm able to give with their donations. I believe you would find the same. While you go about your impressive business, sir, it might brighten your day to recall, as you can spare the thought, that I shall be tirelessly using your generous donation to make this world a better place for women and children to whom life has been cruel.'

John stuck his pipe back in his mouth, unimpressed by the end of her speech. 'I despise flattery, Miss Bailey, and it makes you seem silly to attempt it.'

'Oh, no, Mr Tyrold,' she replied with sunny self-assuredness. 'I assure you, I'm not *silly* to attempt a tactic that works like a charm with most rich people.'

'But I am nothing like most rich people,' John replied, matter-of-factly. 'I am without parallel, which is why your appeal to me should be impeccable. At this point I might consider giving you two pounds a month. If you'd like more money, try another approach.' He glanced at his watch. 'I'll grant you another thirty seconds.'

Miss Bailey hesitated, but only for a moment. 'Very well,' she said with renewed vigour. 'Since you are without parallel, I shall tell you about a venture only you could support. There is a leasehold available for an adjacent property – a house with a beautiful garden

– in which I want to open a school for the children. I was close to achieving my goal when the family of a long-time donor contested her will successfully, and we lost a great deal of expected income. If I could move your heart to give a one-time donation of two thousand pounds, plus a generous monthly subscription of your choosing after that, I could begin to resurrect this dream. A man of your wealth wouldn't notice the absence of five times that, and, since you are peerless, you might wish to declare so to the world. Be the school's patron and make an éclat of your philanthropy. The Tyrold Seminary, if you wish. I shall steward your donation with the greatest of—'

He snapped his watch shut. 'Time's up.' Her appeal was still too obsequious. She was performing to whatever she imagined he expected, employing the same affectation and pretence most people used when they wanted something from him. 'Five pounds a month, take it or leave it.'

She hesitated, mouth slightly ajar. 'In addition to the one-time donation of two thousand?' she ventured hopefully.

John snorted. She was bold, he'd give her that. 'Of course not. Your appeal about the school was weak.'

She drew back, colour draining from her cheeks. 'So only five pounds *in all*?'

'Approach me in the autumn to show me what you've done with my donation and I'll consider offering more – but sixty pounds per annum is nothing to scoff at. Managed wisely, it could provide a year's worth of basic necessities for thirty individuals.'

'Basic necessities?' She shook her head, as if in disbelief. 'Mr Tyrold, perhaps you aren't aware of the power for good which your wealth holds? It could reverse the fortunes of thousands of people.'

John slipped his watch into his fob pocket. 'There are twelve million people in Britain, many of whom are poor. I cannot help them all.'

She lifted her chin, meeting his gaze undaunted. 'No, but you can do more than provide enough coal and oats for thirty people to shiver around the same hearth, supping upon watery gruel. If I were you, I would welcome every opportunity in which a knowledgeable charity worker offered to distribute my wealth for the betterment of those in need.'

John raised an incredulous eyebrow. Was this tiny woman now telling *him* how to manage *his* money? 'With such a foolish attitude, you wouldn't have any money to give to others – and now you've made me quite determined not to give you more of mine. Anyone who'd carelessly donate to the first supposedly needy person who asks shouldn't oversee charity subscriptions. My request that you prove yourself isn't unreasonable, Miss Bailey; everything about your appearance indicates that you don't know the value of money. I doubt it's your fault; hardly anyone here' – he waved his hand over the fashionable crowds – 'does. Your gown, bonnet and the other frivolities you wear likely cost twenty or thirty pounds from whichever high-priced shops you and the duchess patronise, but a working-class family lives for a half a year on that same amount.'

'I say, John,' Edward objected. 'A bit much, old man.'

The colour rapidly returned to Miss Bailey's cheeks. In fact, they blazed scarlet, revealing a previously hidden temper. The sensation that there was something familiar about her features returned in force, along with the rather disturbing discovery that she was an exceptionally handsome woman.

'With all due respect, sir,' she declared defiantly, 'you know nothing about me.'

'If my possessing such knowledge would have strengthened your appeal, then you should have told me about yourself. But that is a moot point now. Besides, while I may not know *you*, I do know business, and one doesn't start a *second* charity when one's first charity isn't yet self-subsisting, which is what you propose doing with your school. Investments of whatever principal you possess is what you need, not more people throwing more money into an ever-expanding pit. I've been exceptionally generous in offering you five pounds for what is no doubt a charitable hobby—'

'A *hobby*!' Miss Bailey exclaimed, aghast. 'Mr Tyrold—'

John held up a hand to interrupt. He needed to draw the conversation to a close, for he was beginning to feel the danger of giving her too much attention, of spending too much time looking at her lively dark eyes and wondering why she looked familiar. 'Yours is not the first charitable appeal I've heard from ladies who dabble in this sort of thing, Miss Bailey. If you decide you want my subscription of five pounds, send your direction to Twenty-Nine Half Moon Street, and I shall arrange for the money to be delivered quarterly.'

As Miss Bailey held his gaze, the fire vanished from her eyes. 'Thank you for the five pounds, Mr Tyrold,' she said in subdued tones. 'However, Monica House isn't a hobby. It's a serious and noble endeavour in desperate need of assistance. When I send you my direction, I shall request another audience to show you my ledgers, for I have nothing to hide. Please consider granting me a second interview sooner than the autumn, sir.'

John puffed on his pipe, finding himself moved by her even-tempered resilience. 'State a stronger appeal in a letter and perhaps I shall,' he said, employing a kinder tone.

The Duchess of Amesbury, who had been fretting and twisting her parasol for some time, looked greatly relieved. 'Well, well, now that's settled, do let's talk of other matters. Lord Edward, Mr Tyrold, will we have the pleasure of seeing you at Lord and Lady Holbrook's garden party on Easter Monday?'

After replying in the negative, John let Edward assume control of the conversation, as he had no interest in further small talk with the duchess. It was a mercifully brief period of time before Miss Bailey bid him a polite good day, and the interaction was thankfully over.

John glanced at her retreating form as she and the duchess strode away, wondering if he'd been unnecessarily harsh. But the incongruity between Miss Bailey's plea for sponsorship while dressed expensively and clearly enjoying the patronage of a wealthy aristocrat soon eased his conscience. It *hadn't* been unreasonable of him to insist she demonstrate responsible use of a small donation, before considering giving her anything more.

Clicking his tongue to his wolfhound, Jolly, he walked on.

Edward caught up shortly. 'Where have you been today?'

'I had business in Kensington and now must see someone south of Knightsbridge.'

As he walked towards the French *automatiste* who lived on Cross Street, his thoughts wandered to his ward, Flora. Her sixteenth birthday was four weeks away, but the present he'd ordered months ago was finished and he wanted to have it delivered early. Their relationship had grown strained in recent years, yet John had reason to hope that would soon change.

Flora had been a near-constant source of stress since around the time of her thirteenth birthday, when she'd turned into the most impetuous child imaginable. Scarcely two weeks had passed in the interim without notes from the headmistress lamenting Flora's deliberate overturning of inkpots, her habitual lateness for morning prayers, or her propensity for engaging other girls in disruptive tussles during dinner.

But of late, according to Miss Crayford, Flora had become thoroughly sweet-tempered, and John was pleased. It was a surprisingly rapid alteration from Christmas, when she'd told John she despised school, life, and John most of all, but Flora had always been an unpredictable child.

He'd long lamented their uneasy relationship – and her words had often hurt him more deeply than he cared to acknowledge – but surely when he visited her on the morrow to show her the glorious birthday present, she'd no longer have any doubts about how much he loved her.

'Georgiana is quite something, isn't she?' Edward asked.

John had forgotten his friend's presence. 'I'm not going home yet, so why are you following me?' he asked, ignoring Edward's question.

'Because I have nothing better to do,' Edward replied. 'Did you know, Johnny, that Georgiana remains, to this day, the only lady to whom I ever proposed marriage?'

'Indeed?' John asked, more astonished than he let on.

'Indeed. And at the moment, I'm rather regretting that it didn't work out,' Edward said as they crossed Knightsbridge at the turnpike. 'Gee is a delightful scamp. Vivacious, full of fun, and pretty, as you can see. Sings like a nightingale, too. Got her voice from her mater, who was a famous opera singer. *La Grande Bellezza*. Sir Joshua painted her. The full-length portrait of a lady in blue hanging at the Royal Academy – you must know the one I mean.'

This revelation utterly astounded John. 'Do you mean to tell me Miss Bailey's mother was the soprano Anna Marinetti?' he asked, no longer hiding his surprise. But even as he spoke, he knew it to be true. *That* was why Miss Bailey looked familiar, for John knew the portrait of which Edward spoke. Recalling the *A* and *M* on Miss Bailey's locket, a heated sensation crawled over his skin, as if the day had grown uncomfortably warm. If

Miss Bailey possessed even a fragment of her mother's talent, she must be something, and her lovely speaking voice held a great deal of promise . . .

Edward interrupted his thoughts. 'You know of Anna Marinetti, then?'

'I saw her perform, in fact.' The memory was etched deeply in his mind, for watching his first opera on a trip to London as a young child had been the foundation of John's lifelong love of music. The performance had ignited a fervour, leading him to beg his father for voice and pianoforte lessons. His father, always indulgent, had located the best master in the North Riding and paid him handsomely to travel to Oakwood twice a week.

'What happened to Anna Marinetti?' John asked. He'd wondered about her fate. It seemed no one knew what had become of her – only that *La Grande Bellezza* had been the greatest soprano in London prior to the King's Theatre fire in June of 1789, but that by the time the opera recommenced, she had vanished.

'I *think* she died when Gee was an infant,' Edward replied. 'But all I know for certain is that Gee's father wanted to hide his by-blow, so he put my father in charge of supervising her education. Pater placed her at school in Brighton with my younger sister, Henrietta, and Gee spent her summers with us at Deancombe. Before then, she was fostered at that charity home she spoke of.'

John rubbed his stubbled chin as he walked. Edward's revelations changed matters. If Miss Bailey was raised amongst the desperate women and children she spoke of, there must be far more to her life experience than her elegant appearance had suggested. It spoke to the depths he'd suspected were hidden within her – the depths she disappointingly hadn't revealed.

'Perhaps my judgement *was* too hasty,' he admitted. 'I shall grant her a second interview.'

Edward's blue eyes gleamed. 'Impressive that she squeezed some money out of your tight fist already, but Gee is clever. And admit it, it didn't hurt that she's pretty, eh?'

John lifted his brows. 'Since when has a pretty face ever swayed my actions?'

Edward shrugged, his smile fading. 'True, true,' he said, conceding the point. 'Why have we come here?' His gaze took in the cramped terraces of the streets south of Knightsbridge.

'I must speak with someone inside. Wait with Jolly.' John gestured for the wolfhound to sit. Jolly obeyed, lowering his lanky bottom to the pavement, but he whimpered, as if asking why he must remain outside. 'It's your tail, sir,' John explained kindly. 'Wags far too much. You'll destroy the shop.'

Jolly sighed, resigned to his fate, especially once Edward began to scratch his ears, and John stepped into the *automatiste*'s home.

He was pleased from the moment he saw Flora's present. The life-sized mechanical swan was a work of art, so exquisitely detailed as to appear real. With feather-like metal plates covering its cogs and clock-work, the swan moved its slender neck to preen and feed itself as an internal music box played.

Walking around it, studying it from every angle, John grew confident the swan would change matters for the better. This masterpiece was more than a mere gift; it was a declaration of what John felt in his heart. A way for him to express that though he watched from afar, he recognised Flora was growing into a young lady. This gesture, combined with Flora's newfound maturity since Christmas, would hopefully restore their relationship to what it once was, when she was younger and understood why they must live apart.

John arranged for the swan to be delivered to Flora's school the next day and left the shop feeling happier than he had in months.

John's optimism lasted less than twelve hours.

Just before midnight, a frantic knocking upon the door of Number Twenty-Nine Half Moon Street shattered his slumber. With a groan, he raked his fingers through his hair, donned his banyan and trudged down the stairs. His manservant, Smith, clad in a nightcap and holding a candle aloft, had already unbolted the door.

Standing before them was Miss Gertrude Crayford, the younger sister of Flora's headmistress. 'I must speak with you at once, sir.'

John's heart pounded. 'By God, what's happened? Is she injured? Ill?'

Miss Crayford dabbed a handkerchief to her swollen eyes. 'Worse, sir. Ever so much worse. She's run away – and with a *man*.'

2

On Easter night a fortnight later, John paced the length and breadth of his study. Gone was his assured bluster. Gone was his confidence. His peace was shattered, his life tottered damnably near disaster, and he could do little about it other than *wait*. In stockinged feet, he marched back and forth past shelves of leather-bound books, hands clasped behind his back, as Jolly perched peak-browed on a sheepskin bed. Every dozen turns, when John reached the far wall, he pulled aside the drapes of one of the two large windows. And every time, his stomach sank, for no horseman rode hellbent towards his townhouse door.

John narrowed his eyes at the mantel clock above his fireless hearth. As the hands ticked closer to eleven, it grew increasingly unlikely that the express from Scotland would arrive tonight. He glanced out the window again. Half Moon Street stretched below, nearly deserted, the streetlamps casting a gold river along the rain-slick cobblestones. No doubt due to the holiday, the only traffic consisted of a few sedan-chairs lugged by hunch-shouldered carriers, a single hackney and an arm-linked couple wavering down the street.

John left the window and stalked past his mahogany desk, knotting his fingers in his hair, loose from its queue and falling past his shoulders. At the opposite end of the room, he collapsed onto the bench seat of his pianoforte, slumping more than the sedan-carriers.

Good God, where was Flora? And why had she willingly put herself in harm's way?

Grinding his teeth, he resumed pacing as the shortest candle on the mantel flickered out. His thoughts reverted to the past dreadful fortnight. From the moment Miss Gertrude arrived to tearfully explain that Flora had run away in the company of a mysterious young man, John had placed a discreet but thorough watch on every road leaving London in an effort to save both Flora's reputation and her life from utter ruin. Yet a fortnight later, all but one had ended in naught.

The remaining piece of information was only moderately promising, but it was likely John's last hope to swiftly, and secretly, recover Flora. When he'd received word that an 'auburn-haired chit' named 'Miss Tyler' had boasted to an innkeeper in St Albans of intending to elope to Scotland, he'd sent his best investigator north, although neither the timing nor the description perfectly fit. The last John had heard, days ago, Starmer was hot on that couple's trail, but, as of yet, there had been no express confirming the investigator had found his quarry.

It was driving John to distraction. All Easter, he'd listened hopefully for a knock upon the door, jumping at the slightest noise, but otherwise pacing his study in his shirtsleeves, occasionally flipping through Flora's journals, although he'd nearly committed them to memory. They offered no clues to her abductor's identity.

What would he do if this last lead resulted in nothing? The longer Flora was out of John's protection, the more power her abductor held. If the fortune-hunting villain married her or got her with child, he'd have the upper hand.

John clenched his jaw, seething. He wanted to rip the man from limb to limb.

Footsteps upon the outside steps roused him from his fury. He hurtled out of his study and bounded down the stairs, but, as he arrived in the entrance vestibule, a key turned in the lock, confirming that it *wasn't* a messenger with the longed-for express.

Instead, Edward stumbled over the threshold with a buxom woman clinging to him, her exceptionally full lips greedily sucking his earlobe.

'Johnny!' Edward's blue eyes sparkled from under his chestnut curls. 'Meet Lise. She's to model for the erotic series Lord Hetherington commissioned. Lise, this is Mr Tyrold. He won't like you, so no scheming, sweetheart.'

Lise's lips slid off Edward's ear with a pop. 'Good evening, sir,' she purred, batting her lashes as if a gnat had flown into her eye. 'It's *such* a *pleasure* to make the acquaintance of the famous Mr Tyrold.'

She pursed her plump lips and played suggestively with a ribbon upon her low-cut bodice. Against John's will, his gaze lingered, and her eyes gleamed, as if in triumph. She thought he wanted her, and irritation prickled John's nerves. *Of course* he wasn't immune to her open invitation, but he didn't embroil himself with scheming women.

Edward tugged at his woman's chin. 'Eyes on me, Lise, you gold-digging minx.'

'But he's *Mr Tyrold*, and rich as a prince.' Lise tittered, peeking at John even as Edward held her chin. 'Mr Tyrold, will you join his lordship and me tonight? I've got more than one way to please a gentleman. Or, for the right price, you can have me all to yourself, for as long as you want.'

John's irritation flared into anger. It was constantly thus with Edward's endless stream of models, one after the other hoping she could entice John to make her his acknowledged mistress, and shower her with riches. Not that it was only the women; nearly everyone in the kingdom hounded him for his money. No interest in him, only what they could get from him.

John hurried back upstairs, Edward's merry laugh echoing behind him. 'I told you he wouldn't like you, Lise. But don't pout, sweetheart, because *I* like you exceedingly well.'

As soon as Jolly lumbered over from the study, John closed his bedchamber door. He stripped off his clothes before falling into bed, shoving his massive pet to one side. John's stomach growled. Perhaps he hadn't eaten since yesterday. He couldn't remember. His servants, the Smiths, were celebrating the holiday with family in Hampstead.

He buried his head in his pillow. What had his life become?

Edward and his model traipsed upstairs, laughing, and their footsteps soon resonated above John's head. John flipped on his side, throwing one arm around Jolly's snoring form. Best just to sleep. Mrs Smith and her niece, Ellen, would be back in the morning, so there would be breakfast, and surely the express would arrive tomorrow. Perhaps the holiday had delayed the rider, for some reason.

But sleep didn't come, because the noise upstairs escalated.

And *escalated*.

Off and on all night long, Lise shrieked her pleasure, each time accompanied by a great deal of thumping furniture. John squished his head between two pillows, which muffled but didn't silence the exuberance. Poor Jolly whined with every scream.

John called out once for silence, which resulted in a moment's pause before the woman called, 'Come and join us if the noise bothers you.' A burst of laughter followed, and the activity recommenced.

John pressed his pillow tighter to his ear and passed a restless, miserable night.

The following morning brought unseasonable heat for mid-April. John opened his study windows wide to catch the breezes and was attempting to work at his desk when Edward poked his head round the door around noon.

'Leave, you jackass,' John ordered, applying himself with more vigour to a canal proposal he held. Despite having read the report multiple times, he hadn't retained the particulars, because his attention was primarily focused on listening for the arrival of the express rider. 'You are the most insufferable housemate since time began, and I despise you.'

'Nonsense, John.' Edward sauntered into the study. 'Get away from your desk and come with me to Nick and Meggy's garden party.'

John cast a critical eye over his friend. Edward had adorned himself in an apple-green tailcoat, a daffodil-yellow-striped waistcoat, and white pantaloons. 'You look like a box of Webb's confectionary, you damned fop.'

Edward looked as pleased as Punch. Evidently, he thought John had complimented him. 'Quite dashing for Easter, isn't it? Will you come with me?'

John returned to the canal report. 'Absolutely not.'

'But I need a friend,' Edward pleaded, looking rather like Jolly begging for a bone. 'Aunt Agatha was waspish at Easter dinner yesterday. Said she'll revoke my allowance unless I behave myself and court respectable young ladies this Season. Mater tried to intervene on my behalf, bless her, and even Pater spoke up in my defence – wild oats and all that, *he* understands, for he had his day too, before Mater attached the shackles. But Aunt Agatha dug in her heels and refused to budge. So now I must go a-courting.' Edward approached the desk, stood behind John's chair and peered over his shoulder.

After a cursory glance at the canal report, he smiled down at John. 'That seems dreadfully dry reading, old man, and you know what they say about all work and no play. Do come with me instead and divert yourself at my expense. You've been even more foul-tempered than usual of late.'

'Perhaps because I didn't sleep a damned wink last night, thanks to you. I have half a mind to toss your paints and easels out your studio window and evict you. You might spare a thought for me the next time you shag a woman *that* vocal.'

Edward patted John's back patronisingly. 'Impossible, my dear boy. You couldn't have been further from my thoughts if you'd been on the other side of the world. Last night quenched my thirst after my longest drought yet. Six weeks, John! It was as if I'd given it up for Lent.'

'However did you survive?' John's words dripped with contempt.

Edward threw an arm around John's shoulders. 'Don't be bitter, my boy. You have only yourself to blame if you miss the companionship of the fairer sex. You could snap your fingers and have almost any woman in London as your wife or mistress. As a matter of fact, you're the reason for my drought. I made no progress with my last model because her head was full of *you*.'

John shrugged off his friend's embrace. 'Her head was full of jewels, expensive frocks and all manner of things that she thought I'd lavish upon her in exchange for her favours. No thank you.'

49

'Ah, yes.' Edward deepened his voice, mockingly. 'I'm King Midas Tyrold, richest fellow in England, and if a woman won't adore me for my growly, unpleasant, unshaven self, with my patched clothing and smelly dog, she's not the woman for me.'

John bristled. 'Jolly doesn't smell.'

'*That's* the part of my speech you object to?'

John shrugged. 'The rest was true. I never object to the truth.'

Edward threw his head back, his laughter filling the room. 'You never cease to amuse me, my dear friend. If you come with me today, I can amuse you in turn. I intend to court Georgiana Bailey.'

John nearly dropped the canal report in his surprise. 'The tiny charity worker?' he asked, his mouth oddly dry as he tossed the report on one of the many stacks of unanswered correspondence cluttering his desk. 'Is she aware of your intentions?'

Edward grinned mischievously. 'Not yet. Come and watch me propose the notion to her.'

John grunted. 'Do you anticipate it will please her?'

'Not at all!' Edward replied, his grin broadening. 'That is what makes my choice so clever. Aunt Agatha will be pleased if I court her, but I know with certainty that Gee wouldn't marry me if I were the last man on earth. She told me so when I proposed years ago, even though we were quite good friends. She also called me a villainous profligate.'

John chuckled outright. 'Sensible woman.'

'Oh, Gee's an imp.'

'Is she, indeed?' John asked, raising an eyebrow. 'Seemed rather angelic.'

'A damned fine woman is both, old boy.' Edward laughed. 'Do come with me, John. I can't bear to face the ladies alone, lest they eat me alive.'

Hooves drew John's attention before he could reply; instantly, all thoughts but of Flora left his mind. He jumped to his feet to lean out the window and was rewarded with the sight of the express carrier just as he halted his slick-sided horse at the door.

John's heart leapt to his throat; a flurry of sensations – hope, dread, fear, longing – wreaked havoc on his gut, but he didn't have long to wait now until he had answers. His servant Smith – bless the man – must've been waiting, for he retrieved the missive before the rider could dismount.

Edward peered over John's shoulder. 'What is it?'

'Never mind.' John dashed towards the door. Smith entered before he'd crossed the room; John snatched the letter and handed his manservant two gold coins. 'Give the rider this for his troubles, have Mrs Smith feed him well, and take the horse to the stable yards for care.'

The moment Smith closed the door, John ripped the seal. With shaking hands, he held the letter to a beam of sunlight.

His eyes ran over date and location . . .

The Black Bull Inn, Trongate, Glasgow
Saturday, 13th April 1816

. . . to the opening line:

Dear Sir,
Unfortunately, our hopes have come to naught . . .

The edges of the paper crumpled under John's tightening fists. He cursed violently before forcing himself to continue. As he'd dreaded, the auburn-haired girl who'd boasted of her elopement hadn't been Flora, which meant the trail was cold. Furthermore, it appeared Flora had never left London at all, as they had now investigated all leads on red-haired females taking stagecoaches, post-chaises, or the Mail before John put the watch on the tollgates.

John's stomach twisted violently as he read the conclusion of the letter:

I shall place watches at critical points along the Great North Road before I return to London. Expect me no later than Friday. In the meantime, I shall be so bold as to suggest you contact the Bow Street Runners. I know you wished for this search to remain a secret to protect Miss Tyrold's reputation, but, as you are aware, London is rife with danger, and it is worrisome the young man isn't attempting to marry your ward. It is my experienced opinion that every moment is critical.

I remain, sir, your obedient, etc.
Jas Starmer, Investigator

John crushed the paper with a white-knuckled fist, sank onto a leather armchair and squeezed shut his eyes.

Waves of anger thrashed his body and he fed his fury. When he got his hands on the bastard who'd seduced Flora, he'd destroy him.

But as for Starmer's advice to engage the Runners, well, John wasn't ready to capitulate yet. If he could think of a way to find Flora without word spreading, he might yet bury this whole incident as if it had never happened. That would be the best possible outcome: recover the girl and put her in an even more secure school, preferably outside of London. Or return her to Oakwood with a legion of staid governesses to guard her from men.

'Here, old man.' Edward's voice invaded John's daydreams of retribution.

John blinked. He'd forgotten his friend's presence, but Edward stood at his side, two brandies in hand.

John took a deep breath, trying to steady himself, but refused the drink. He clamped his hand over his eyes and rubbed his temples. Dammit – all his hopes had rested on this last lead. How the devil was he to find Flora in London? No place in Britain offered easier concealment and more danger than the kingdom's crowded, warren-like urban heart.

'Come, Johnny boy,' Edward cajoled, sitting across from him and placing one of the brandies on a table. 'What's troubling you? Tell Edward all about it.'

John let his hand fall to the armrest. He might as well tell. Alone, the burden was suffocating, and twenty years' friendship had proven that whatever faults Edward had, he didn't break confidences. 'It's a girl.'

Edward's brows rose over the rim of his glass. 'Indeed!'

'A fifteen-year-old *child*, Edward.' John paused. 'Helen's daughter. I've been her sole guardian since Helen's death.'

Edward nearly dropped his drink. '*Helen?* The girl you were in love with when we were boys?'

Deep inside John, a soreness throbbed, as if Edward had poked a bruise. 'Helen Jennings, yes.'

'Damn, John,' Edward breathed. 'I'm sorry to hear that. When did she die?'

'The twenty-third of January in oh-eight,' John replied, reaching out to take his brandy. 'I'll have that drink after all.'

Edward handed it over. 'Eight years! And you've been her daughter's guardian all this time?'

John quaffed the brandy, its fiery warmth burning his throat. 'Yes.'

'Good Lord, man. We've lived together all the while! How have I not heard of this before?'

'Because I had no need to tell you.' John placed his empty glass on a side table. 'It's not that I don't trust you, it's just that I realised the more people who knew of her connection to me, the greater the danger she'd fall victim to fortune hunters.' That's what John had told himself and Flora over the years, anyway. 'Flora's a beautiful girl, far too impetuous for her own good, and she's my primary heir.'

Edward's jaw dropped. 'Well, this is a day of surprises! Helen Jennings's daughter is your *heir*? Does Nick know? Surely you told Sidney?'

John cradled his scalp, rubbing his head until his hair loosened in its queue. It did nothing to alleviate a throbbing ache, which seemed to come from his brain itself. 'No. No one knows. No one in London, anyway. And my parents live in such a remote corner of Yorkshire, no one could discover Flora's connection to me without the awareness of my parents' servants and tenants. But it's been more than two years since there were any suspicious enquiries into my past.'

Edward shook his head. 'Yes, well, if a beautiful young heiress to the Tyrold millions exists, as you say, I don't blame you for safeguarding the secret. She'll draw every fortune hunter in Britain – no, by George! – she'll draw every fortune hunter in Europe when she comes out. I assume you keep her under lock and key?'

'I *tried* to, but she ran away from her school on the first of April. Or rather, some villain abducted her – although by all accounts she went willingly with the wretch. I shall kill him when I find him, of course.'

'I should imagine, yes. They've eloped to Scotland, I assume?'

'I assumed the same. But this letter' – John lifted the crumbled parchment, which had fallen beside him on the armchair – 'has seemingly proven otherwise. It's likely she's still in London, which means he cannot have married her at all.'

Edward frowned as he sipped his brandy. 'That makes no sense. The girl may be pretty, but the blighter must want her fortune as well. Unless he doesn't know about it?'

'He knows. Amongst the possessions Flora left behind was a love poem addressed to Miss Tyrold.' The poem was beautifully written out on fine paper in India ink, but it was unsigned. Not that John could blame the author for not wishing to put his name to drivel, for the composition was utter rubbish, with no sense of rhyme or rhythm. John scoffed for the hundredth time as he recalled the opening line: *I will when in a grove with my Flora meet* . . . But shaking off the memory, he returned to the conversation with Edward. 'The poem confirmed my suspicions that he knew Flora's true identity. The other students know her as Flora Jennings, to keep her connection to me a secret.'

Edward gazed at Jolly, who sat before the fireless hearth, his ears perked and alert. 'Do I understand correctly that Helen Jennings's daughter's proper surname is Tyrold?'

The query chafed, but John answered. 'It is.'

Thankfully Edward didn't ask the question that hung heavy between them, because John had no wish to discuss what had happened with Helen, ever, and there were some questions he'd never be able to answer, as much as they plagued him.

The street noise blowing in from the open windows grew deafening.

Edward cleared his throat. 'Er, and has Miss Tyrold a fortune of her own, or merely the expectation of yours, one day?'

'In addition to having Helen's fortune, which is significant, I've given Flora assets and investments worth at least a half a million pounds, ever increasing.'

A strangled sound emerged from Edward. 'A half a million pounds!'

Edward's reaction didn't surprise John. It was a colossal amount, which any sensible girl would've appreciated. But the last time John had visited Flora, she'd narrowed her green eyes and snapped, 'Your money brings me nothing but misery.'

'However' – John lifted his index finger – 'I hold everything in trust until she marries with my consent or turns one-and-twenty, whichever happens first. Now do you suspect, as I do, *why* the bastard hasn't married her?'

'Because that's six years away?'

'Precisely.' John ground his teeth. 'He wants to force the payment now.'

'Good Lord, John. He'll wait until he gets her with child before approaching you.'

John nodded, seeing red. 'He'll think he has his boot firmly planted on my bollocks then. And the damned cursed thing is, he very likely will.'

Edward grimaced. 'What will you do?'

John shoved the crumpled letter in his pocket. 'I must scour London and locate them, immediately, although I haven't the foggiest notion where to begin.' He stood, slump-shouldered. With one hand still in his pocket, he strode to the hearth and tousled Jolly's ears.

Jolly rustled his tail, but his peaked eyebrows revealed that he knew something was amiss.

Behind John, Edward cleared his throat. 'Perhaps Georgiana could be of assistance. Didn't she mention she knows how to locate women in distress?'

'What! The charity worker again!' John exclaimed with a derisive snort. 'She's your answer to everyth . . .'

But the rest of his words died on his lips as he absorbed Edward's statement in its entirety, and, as he did, he straightened his slumped shoulders. Edward was correct; Miss Bailey had emphasised her skills in locating women trapped in oppressive circumstances.

She'd claimed to have a network that helped her find women.

Edward observed John closely. 'Ah, you mocked me and now you realise I may be right. At any rate, it seems rather prophetic that you subscribed to Gee's charity on the very same day Flora ran away, doesn't it?'

'A coincidence,' John muttered, stroking his chin. 'But a timely one, indeed. And such things are never to be disregarded.'

John firmly believed in maximising every worthwhile opportunity the moment it presented itself. He hadn't amassed his vast fortune by ignoring prognostications, indications and warnings. Quite the opposite, in fact.

Edward drained his brandy. 'Georgiana will be at the garden party. Get ready, and you can ask her.'

John yanked out his hair ribbon, ran his fingers through his hair, and retied the queue at the nape of his neck. 'I am ready.'

Edward cast his eyes up and down John's figure. 'There's a reason barbers and tailors exist,' he said mournfully.

Ignoring his friend, John strode to his desk. 'On second thought, I need five minutes to write a reply for my investigator,' he declared. 'But I shan't change my clothes.'

He proceeded to compose a brief response to Starmer, to be sent off with the express rider. Then he whistled for Jolly and left his study with Edward, grabbing his brown hat in the entrance on the way out the door.

John descended his steps, pulling his hat low to shield his eyes from the sun. With Edward at his heels, he marched south on Half Moon Street, laying his plans. He was in no mood for a party, but his business needn't take long. He'd simply arrange to meet Miss Bailey later, for he couldn't discuss Flora surrounded by listening ears.

3

Sunlight drenched the grounds of the Marquess of Holbrook's London residence as hundreds of elegant guests gathered under canvas pavilions, sipping chilled champagne and fanning flushed faces. A fountain's rainbow spray soared high into the cloudless sky. A string quartet played Mozart. Conversation hummed. Children shrieked as they ran races on the lawn.

And Georgiana promised herself yet again that one day, Monica House would have its school and garden, even if that insufferably condescending Mr Tyrold hadn't responded to the heartfelt and carefully crafted letter she'd pored over for hours after their Hyde Park encounter.

Over the last fortnight, she'd finally admitted to herself that she'd failed with Tyrold.

She couldn't fail Monica House again.

She stood amongst a throng of ladies and debutantes, and wrote a name and sum in her small notebook while a breeze waltzed with her muslin skirts. Despite the discouraging reality that so far only three ladies had offered monthly subscriptions, each amounting to only one guinea, Georgiana refused to lose hope. There were five hundred people in attendance; if she could convince half of them to contribute a guinea a month, she could save Monica House.

With that bolstering thought, Georgiana smiled as she displayed her notebook to the middle-aged baroness seated nearby, who held a plate piled with pastel confectionaries. 'Ma'am, you see here that I've entered your name, The Right Honourable The Lady Frampton, and here I've written the amount of one guinea to be donated monthly to Monica House. If you will perhaps put a signature to the subscription?'

Lady Frampton popped a raspberry-coloured bonbon into her mouth. 'No need for that, Miss Bailey,' she said while chewing, her teeth stained pink. 'You have my word.'

Georgiana bowed her head, hiding a quiver of unease. 'On behalf of the women and children of Monica House, I thank your ladyship for your generosity.' She slipped her book and pencil into her reticule and smiled at the debutante beside Lady Frampton, a lovely child with golden curls and a porcelain complexion. Perhaps only seven years separated Georgiana from her in age, but Miss Frampton's face shone with an innocence Georgiana had long since lost. 'God's blessings upon your beautiful daughter, my lady.' *And if she marries, may he be a kind man*, she added silently.

Lady Frampton dusted sugar off her shelf-like bosom. 'A word of caution, Miss Bailey. It's all very well to be a bit of a Samaritan, but if you come at it terribly strong, blessing people here and there, it smacks of sanctimony. Might make *some* people wonder what you are compensating for.'

Beneath her silk bonnet, Georgiana's ears burned, for Lady Frampton's comment hit uncomfortably close to the truth. But while Georgiana could play a *rôle* when needed, that wasn't what she was doing now. All her thoughts today were focused on helping Monica House.

However, she couldn't alienate a new benefactress by defending herself, since her words might be construed as impertinence, so she plastered on a smile. 'Thank you, ma'am. I shall heed your advice.'

Lady Frampton glared, as if she suspected impertinence anyway. 'I remember your mother, Miss Bailey. She was quite the sensation in her day.' The baroness's piercing eyes scaled Georgiana's frock before returning to her face. 'You have something of her look, particularly around the mouth and the shape of your face, but it is your air of innocence that is most like her. Your mother possessed the same virtuous appearance. She never ventured anywhere without her maid, and everyone said she was as pure as the new-fallen snow.' Lady Frampton lifted another bonbon, her little finger extended. 'And yet, here you are, living proof that appearances can be deceiving.'

The baroness's words were a knife to Georgiana's heart. Lady Frampton was utterly correct; she was no more a lady than her mother had been. She had lived a worldly existence far beyond the comprehension of those present at this garden party, and she carried the pain of her past with her every moment of every day. In fact, it was the weight of her grief that fuelled her unwavering dedication to Monica House. Only by seizing every opportunity to do good for others could she ease the secret anguish that threatened to consume her.

Lady Frampton watched her keenly. 'Have my words given you pause for reflection, Miss Bailey?'

Georgiana swallowed hard, trying to steady herself. 'Your ladyship is wise and I'm grateful for your counsel.' Despite her best efforts, her voice wavered. 'However, I am merely what I say I am – a charity worker determined to make the world a better place, in whatever small ways I can. Thank you for your generosity.'

As Georgiana turned away, she fought back tears of hurt – and of anger. She was furious at herself that she must pander to selfish rich people because she'd depleted her own fortune, which was all her father could spare with five sons and several nephews to provide for.

But she couldn't give in to her emotions, so she clutched the handle of her well-worn guitar case and strode purposefully across the pavilion, drawing upon her resolve with each step.

Fanny was engaged in conversation with the widowed Duchess of Gillingham, who was Georgiana's father's sister. Despite her inner turmoil, Georgiana greeted the two duchesses with a smile. They made a charming pair, with Fanny in pink silk and Aunt Clarissa in lavender.

'I successfully achieved a third subscription,' she announced. 'Will you introduce me to another lady with a charitable soul?'

Fanny swirled the champagne in her fluted glass. 'Dearest, you are spending far too much time speaking with ladies when there are many eligible bachelors present. You can't know that you don't want to marry if you don't *try* to like someone. Your father and I are united on this matter, as we are in everything.'

Aunt Clarissa pulled a face. 'Nonsense, Fanny, and if my brother feels that way, I shall give him a set-to.'

Fanny pouted. 'There is no greater joy in life than a husband and children of one's own.'

The ever-present wound in Georgiana's chest throbbed.

Aunt Clarissa came to her rescue by casting her trump card. 'And there is no greater agony than marriage to a monster.'

Fanny scowled but conceded the point without an argument. Everyone had breathed easier since the old Duke of Gillingham's death five months earlier.

Clarissa drew Georgiana's hand into the crook of her elbow, enveloping her in lily-of-the-valley scent. 'Come, my dear niece, I have friends I shall introduce you to.'

She directed Georgiana back towards Lady Frampton's side of the pavilion, where a cluster of debutantes and their mothers had now gathered around the baroness and her daughter. Georgiana felt Lady Frampton's eyes bore into her as she returned, and she wondered if she formed some part of the whispered conversation occurring behind fans.

Three kind-looking ladies who sat in another corner of the pavilion – near but not too close to Lady

Frampton's cluster – turned welcoming countenances towards Georgiana and her aunt as they approached.

'My dear Clarissa,' said the stunning brunette beauty Georgiana knew to be the Countess of Eden. Lady Eden had famously once been a courtesan and would certainly know something of the trials of women, but, from what Aunt Clarissa had said previously, Lord and Lady Eden already gave a great deal of money to charity, despite the earl's constrained financial circumstances. Georgiana had no hope of a tremendous sponsorship, but she experienced true pleasure in Lady Eden's kindness as her aunt made the introduction.

'Your aunt called upon me when I arrived in town last week,' the countess said. 'Ever since that visit, I've longed to meet you. She mentioned you manage a charity home for women, with no aim other than to provide safe and hidden shelter. That you care for these women lovingly no matter their background, and yet you do not attempt to reform them or alter the path they wish to tread. I cannot tell you how profoundly moved I am by this mission.'

Tears sprang to Georgiana's eyes, and before she knew it, she and Lady Eden were embracing tenderly.

Aunt Clarissa drew them apart. 'I knew you'd adore each other. But you must meet Meggy and Rose as well, Georgiana.'

'Meggy' was the garden party's hostess, the Marchioness of Holbrook, a young and pretty woman with golden-brown curls. She started to rise, placing one hand upon a swell under her primrose gown's high waist.

'Pray, stay seated, please, my lady,' Georgiana urged.

Lady Holbrook sat at Georgiana's bidding, but she laughed merrily as they shook hands. 'I will remain sitting as you request, but only because of the heat. The baby's not due to arrive until September, and this isn't my first. My son, Freddy, is there, playing with his father and the other children upon the lawn.'

Georgiana glanced politely at the marquess and his toddler son, and admired the boy's dark curls to his mama, but her thoughts were on a village in the Italian Alps, and a heartbreak that could never heal. Yet she swallowed the lump in her throat and tucked her pain back into its spot deep in her chest. She was here today because of that heartache. She was alive on this earth to do good, and so she must be strong.

But at the introduction to the third lady, the wound threatened to open again. Lady Holbrook's sister-in-law, Lady Rose Edwards, was dressed in ebony crêpe and a black Mary Queen of Scots cap.

A widow. And a recent one, at that. It was surprising that she was out in company at all.

Aunt Clarissa – also a recent widow, although she was rather gaily clad, with amethysts and diamonds sparkling at her throat and ears – smiled as if nothing were amiss as she made the introductions. 'Lady Rose will want to hear all about Monica House, Georgiana.'

Georgiana was mortified that her aunt would suggest she solicit a new widow for a subscription. 'I am honoured to make your acquaintance, Lady Rose,' she said, clasping the bereaved woman's hand. 'But I wouldn't presume to intrude upon your grief with talk of my charity.'

A pause followed as the three friends and Clarissa exchanged glances.

Then Lady Rose spoke. 'Please dismiss any such reservations, Miss Bailey, for if others waited for my mourning to pass to speak with me on important matters, they would have to wait for ever. My grief is not new; my husband is two and a half years dead.'

Clarissa spoke quietly in Georgiana's ear. 'Not all widows are ready to put off black after four months, like I was.'

Heartbreak for the widowed Lady Rose overcame any mortification Georgiana might otherwise have felt about her faux pas. She looked deeply into Lady Rose's eyes. 'Time doesn't heal all wounds.'

Rose smiled gently. 'You must see much grief and sorrow at your work.'

Georgiana did, but it was not that experience that made her internalise the widow's pain. In Rose she sensed a kindred spirit, someone for whom grief didn't pass on a timeline ordained by society, but instead wove itself into the very fibre of one's being.

Lady Eden drew Georgiana from Rose by asking to introduce her daughter, Ada–Marie, and, upon reflection, Georgiana was grateful for the conversation shift. She didn't wish to dwell upon her pain. Her grief *fuelled* her. Everything good in her life was built from her heartache and only by pushing forwards incessantly and without pause could she soften the pain.

Georgiana smiled as her gaze fell on the blonde girl brought forwards by her mother, holding a plaited wreath of daisies. 'My mama says you have a guitar,' the child said, her blue eyes sightless. 'May I touch it, please?'

'Most certainly,' Georgiana replied warmly. 'In fact, my dear, would you like to learn some chords?'

John hesitated when he and Edward rounded the corner of their friend Nick's palatial residence. He puffed the pipe dangling from his lips and scanned the crowds for Miss Bailey, reluctant to enter until he'd found his quarry. There were hundreds of people, and his presence at a society event would cause a stir. It would be ideal if he could speak to the charity worker quickly and then leave.

'How can one find a particular lady in this sea of bonnets?' he grumbled after his preliminary search was unsuccessful.

'Gee's not wearing a bonnet.' Edward jutted his chin towards a pavilion sheltering several of their friends, including John's dearest friend, Sidney, the Earl of Eden, his wife Kitty, and a crowd of fashionable people.

Miss Bailey was not amongst them.

'Where is she?' But even as John asked, he found her, seated on the grass, surrounded by the soft folds of her apricot skirts and snuggled next to Sidney's daughter, Ada-Marie, who held a guitar in her lap. 'Ah, excellent. Let us not waste more time.'

He set off with Edward and Jolly following, ignoring the acquaintances who called out as he progressed across the lawn, but, as he neared his target, he slowed his pace, the better to observe Miss Bailey teaching Ada-Marie guitar chords. The difference between the Duchess of Amesbury's protégé and other young ladies struck him. There were dozens of debutantes at the garden party, and whether prim and proper or blushing and giggling, they all gave the appearance of being on display . . . yet Miss Bailey sat on the grass, tucked out of sight, playing an instrument with a blind child as if only the two of them existed in the world.

It was an enchanting sight.

Miss Bailey's bonnet rested on the grass near her feet and she wore a daisy crown in her thick brown hair, matching one that adorned Ada-Marie's flaxen curls. As John watched, she guided the child's fingers into a chord. 'Hold these down and strum with your right hand.'

A smile spread across Ada-Marie's face as the music sounded. Miss Bailey beamed in response, as radiant as the sun. 'What chord, Ada-Marie?'

'It's A minor,' came the reply.

'Well done!' Miss Bailey praised. 'Will you sing it with me?'

Ada-Marie strummed again, singing a sweet, clear A. Miss Bailey joined in, softly blending her voice a third above with stunning purity – and, without thinking, John removed his pipe and found himself joining in an octave below Ada-Marie, creating a three-part harmony.

He realised his mistake immediately, for two dozen pairs of astonished eyes turned towards him, and he might've found himself inundated with unwanted attention had not Ada-Marie saved the day. 'It's my Uncle John,' she exclaimed, removing the guitar strap and springing to her feet.

John caught her in his arms and planted a kiss on her cheek. He had a special fondness for Sidney and Kitty's daughter, and, knowing that her path in life would be far from easy, he'd long since been growing investments specifically intended for her. No matter what, she wouldn't lack for financial resources.

Conversation resumed under the pavilion. John's friendship with Sidney and Kitty was well known, so (thankfully) everyone appeared to assume he'd joined the singing for the sake of their child. That was ever the worry when John went into company: if he showed the slightest interest in socialising with anyone other than his few established friends, he'd be besieged. Everything from investments proposals to bedroom proposals would follow before he could escape again, hours later, his ears ringing from incessant conversation, his person violated by unwanted touching.

While he exchanged greetings with Ada-Marie and the rest of his friends, John observed Miss Bailey tying on her bonnet and settling herself into a nearby chair, her guitar cradled in her lap. He needed to speak with her, but he must be discreet, so others didn't notice . . .

Meanwhile, the Duchess of Amesbury flittered around Edward like a pink butterfly. 'Georgiana and I were so hopeful you would attend today, my lord. Do sit with us, and listen to her play, won't you?' She gestured towards a vacant chair beside her protégé.

'Indeed, I shall, ma'am,' Edward said, plopping himself merrily in the seat beside Miss Bailey. 'And so must Tyrold, for he is a true connoisseur of music and no doubt would like a guitar lesson himself.'

'Good God, Edward,' John muttered, but he didn't mind much, for Edward had provided an opportunity for him to speak with Miss Bailey. He glanced around the pavilion as he seated himself, noting gratefully that most of the revellers were engrossed in conversation, eating or drinking.

'Are you here to critique my performance as you did the in the park, Mr Tyrold?' Miss Bailey asked, tuning her instrument. 'Will I again be allotted two minutes in which to attempt to impress you?'

'No, not at all,' John said hurriedly, removing his pipe. He wasn't certain if she was teasing, flirting or merely trying to bring the conversation round to her charity house again, and he had no time to attempt to assess. 'In fact, I'm unable to listen to you perform, as I have pressing business elsewhere, but first I wish to speak with you about . . .' He hesitated, scratching Jolly's head and wondering how to mention Flora with so many people nearby. If *anyone* overheard, it would be disastrous.

'About Monica House?' she asked, clearly hopeful. 'My letter moved you after all?'

'Your letter?' John repeated, momentarily baffled. He thought of his piles of unanswered correspondence – he'd opened letters only to see if any contained demands for ransom or a word from Flora or her abductor, which none had – but he now remembered that there had been

71

one from Miss Bailey so thick Smith had commented on the extra charge. He'd received it the day after their meeting, when his mind was most frazzled, and opened it only to ensure it was indeed from the charity worker, before tossing it unread onto his desk.

The letter was a perfect pretext for a private conversation. 'Ah, yes, your letter. If you are available later today, bring your ledgers to Half Moon Street and we'll discuss a potential donation.'

She gasped, as if he'd offered her the world. 'Truly, sir?'

'Yes, yes.' John nodded, feeling awkward. But he hadn't completely lied; he would give her money if she could find Flora. He jammed his pipe between his teeth and stood, determining to leave since he'd concluded all the business he could at that time.

Miss Bailey's hand on his stopped him; he looked down at her dark eyes. 'I cannot call upon a gentleman, sir. May I request that you meet me at Maria DeRosa's coffeehouse in Soho Square at seven o'clock, instead? It will be more discreet than Mayfair, but still proper.'

'Of course,' John muttered, shoving his hand in his pocket, the feel of her soft touch lingering on his fingers.

He intended to walk away – he truly did – but her brown eyes gazing up at him as if he'd granted her heart's desire turned his feet to lead and before he could force them to move, Miss Bailey smiled, their gazes still locked, and began to strum a complex opening motif on her guitar. 'I know you must attend to your business, Mr Tyrold, but please allow me to play you on your way, as a gesture of gratitude.'

But by that point, her musicality had so entranced John that he couldn't have moved if someone had shoved him. Her fingers flew effortlessly over her instrument, sending delighted tingles along his spine. Then she opened her mouth to sing and the most exquisite vocal note struck his ears, electrifying him with its purity. As Miss Bailey's voice grew in volume, it filled the pavilion with a brilliance and warmth far surpassing the spring day.

John was captivated.

The ghost of a smile played at the corners of her lips as she sang, as if she'd known he would stay, which meant she knew how good she was. Her self-assurance was powerfully attractive to John, who admired confidence in others when it was well warranted.

He drank in the sight and sound of her with more appreciation than he'd felt for a woman *or* a performer in a long time. She perched elegantly on the edge of her chair, with her clingy skirt draped over her crossed legs like a toga, singing perfectly on pitch, each note crystal clear. Nothing artificial or decorative. A sublime mastery that declared John was in the presence of a paragon.

The song was poignant, a tale of the trials of women, no doubt fitting to Miss Bailey's cause, but the words were really beside the point to John, who was drawn in by her talent and her proficiency. She sang with a *voce di petto* – a robust voice from the chest, as rich as molten gold – until the end of each verse, when the tune leapt an octave, and she switched effortlessly into a *voce di testa*, or head voice, as clear and high as a flute.

The effect raised the hair on John's arms and the nape of his neck – and likely not just his, because conversation fell silent and dozens of heads under their and neighbouring pavilions turned.

And although the last thing John needed was to embroil himself publicly with a debutante, he settled himself again in the chair across from Miss Bailey, with his eyes glued to her face, her voice penetrating his soul. Yes, *this* was the feeling he had experienced years ago, grasping his father's hand as he'd listened to *La Grande Bellezza* perform, his little body rigid, too mesmerised to breathe. It had been the very moment he'd fallen in love with music.

4

Georgiana didn't remember her mother, but she'd seen her portrait. Despite what others said, she believed she bore little physical resemblance to the famed soprano besides her thick walnut-coloured hair and a complexion that tanned easily, even under a mild English sun. Anna Marinetti had been beautiful and voluptuous, with eyes as blue as the Mediterranean Sea, whereas Georgiana had inherited her father's slight build and stature. The Duke of Amesbury had also gifted his eldest – and only illegitimate – child with features that were pleasing but unremarkable, except for the velvety darkness of their brown eyes.

But *La Grande Bellezza* had given Georgiana her voice, which was a gift far greater than physical beauty.

And Georgiana gave that voice back to the world.

She'd done so all her life, in one way or the other. As a small child, she'd realised her voice had a power that could attract even the most scornful adult's attention – that it could change their view of her as a scrawny, motherless illegitimate unworthy of notice to something of breathless wonder. As she had shed childhood and developed the first curves of womanhood, her voice had brought different attention: wariness and jealousy from other girls, but something thrilling, which she couldn't quite understand but which had made her feel powerful, from men, young and old. She'd thrived on this, understanding that it must've been a power her mother had possessed, in Anna Marinetti's brief but spectacular glory days – and Georgiana had determined she'd learn to harness that power fully, one day. It had become her dream to be the top-billed soprano of Covent Garden. The toast of London. *Everyone* would love her, and she'd make her father proud.

But then her heartbreak had changed her irrevocably, so that when Georgiana had at last taken up her long-desired formal voice study in Italy, under the tutelage of a great master, her motive had been only to ease the sorrows of others through her song. To do what little she could to bring joy to a hurting world.

That was the only power worth having, for using her talent for her own gain had brought nothing but devastation.

After a lifetime of experience, she knew what would happen when she began her song, so she chose an old folk ballad about the sorrows of womankind. As she'd expected, everyone within earshot listened. Supercilious Lady Frampton's eyes bulged. The cluster of debutantes stopped giggling. Beautiful Lady Eden and golden-haired Lord Eden tilted their heads together, and precious Ada-Marie clasped her hands over her heart. Edward smiled tenderly and genuinely. Aunt Clarissa dabbed a handkerchief to her cheeks. On the other side of the pavilion, Georgiana's father, the duke, turned from conversation with a parliamentarian, his expression half pained, while the MP raised a quizzing glass in Georgiana's direction, his brows lifted to his hat brim.

And Tyrold forgot his pressing business.

It was always this way. Once Georgiana's voice left her, it belonged to her listeners. It seeped into their hearts, their minds, their emotions. Her music brought healing tears when needed, sparked the embers of perishing passions, conjured phantoms of loved ones long dead. She'd heard teary-eyed praise for as long as she could remember: *you bring back memories*; *you soothe my soul*; *you give me hope*.

Georgiana gave her music to everyone, but, at that moment, she sang primarily for Tyrold. Above all else, she wanted to touch his heart and align him with her cause before their meeting that evening, so *he* was the one she projected her voice towards. She even let her gaze linger more on him than anyone else, although it was rather disconcerting to do so. His dishevelment, his handsomeness, and, yes, even his arrogance stirred something deep inside her, as much as they had two weeks earlier.

And her effort was not in vain, for it appeared she was succeeding in her goal. Tyrold loved music, as Edward had said. His unwavering eye contact confirmed this. He leant forwards, his elbows resting on his widespread knees and his fingers interlaced, as he studied her intensely, his green eyes alert.

When Georgiana at last let her voice fade and strummed her final note, a full second of silence followed. Then Tyrold clapped resoundingly, leaving no doubt of his appreciation. Others joined in, but Tyrold clapped the loudest.

'Miss Bailey, that was magnificent,' he said. 'A sublime performance.'

The compliment was so immensely satisfying that Georgiana gave him her brightest smile. 'Thank you, sir,' she said, unable to hide the confident swell of her voice. Once he saw her carefully kept ledgers and her dedication to her work, perhaps her dreams would yet come true.

He returned her smile with a grin which utterly transformed his face. 'You know how splendid you are. That is an admirable trait when justified.'

'God – or Nature – gave me talent,' she replied modestly. 'All I did was honour that gift through hard work.'

Tyrold's smile deepened. 'Ah, but of course that's false modesty, Miss Bailey. You and I both know that tenacity is even more commendable than talent.'

'*Perhaps* there's truth to what you say,' she admitted.

'About tenacity? Or your magnificence?'

She grinned in turn. 'Both.'

He laughed, his eyes gleaming with obvious admiration, and her cheeks warmed against her will. To her mortification, she realised that not only was she starting to blush, but surely everyone who still watched her after her performance would notice. She looked down, letting the poke of her bonnet shield her face as she put her instrument back in its case, hoping if she made it clear she wouldn't perform again, people would return to conversation and refreshment.

But there was a prolonged, uncanny silence under the pavilion, and once Georgiana had secured the latch on the case, curiosity compelled her to glance up again. What she saw compressed her chest.

Tyrold still gazed at her, leaning back in his chair now with one ankle crossed over his knee, rubbing his stubbled chin as if lost in thought, pipe between his teeth. There was nothing wrong with that, per se. It was good, even. The more she intrigued him, the better her chance of getting a sizeable donation. The trouble was that nearly every *other* set of eyes under the pavilion darted between Georgiana and the millionaire, and the bitter scowls of Lady Frampton and several other matrons were pure poison.

Georgiana had experienced looks like those before, so she knew what they meant. They expressed revulsion, abhorrence, rejection – and jealousy. The tolerance she'd briefly perceived that afternoon had been only the thinnest of veneers. Underneath it, everyone was prejudiced against her, although only Lady Frampton had been vicious enough to hint at it. Even public recognition by the Duke of Amesbury didn't alter society's hatred of a bastard, when that bastard flaunted the talents of an immoral mother to draw attention from a man others desired. This was precisely the reaction Georgiana had most hoped to avoid as she entered society, because if the *ton* despised her, she'd never raise the necessary funds to save Monica House, much less establish her school and garden.

Lady Frampton hissed something to a companion and within a moment, the debutantes' mothers congregated around the baroness's chair like a swarm of angry wasps.

Georgiana's throat clamped; they were talking about her. Her momentary triumph in impressing Tyrold had come at the cost of losing a dozen or more potential sponsors who now viewed her as a rival for their daughters. Furthermore, malicious gossip would spread like wildfire, setting more people against her. Georgiana's mind raced, desperately searching for a way to convince these influential matrons she posed no threat.

But before she could formulate a plan, Lady Frampton rose from her chair and propelled her beautiful blonde daughter between Georgiana and Tyrold. 'I didn't know you enjoy singing so much, Mr Tyrold. You simply must hear my Lettice.'

The swarm of mothers followed, thrusting *their* daughters between Georgiana and Tyrold, until a wall of women blocked her view of the millionaire. When Georgiana attempted to lean back, hoping to avoid the tip of a closed parasol, a matron seized the opportunity to squeeze herself between Georgiana's knees and a neighbouring mama, grinding her heel into Georgiana's satin-covered toes. Pain pierced before Georgiana yanked her foot back, but she still found herself pinned against the back of her chair, with the silk-clad posterior of the offending matron directly in her face. Trapped with a table at her back, there seemed to be no escape, and the relentless matrons had cut off her access to Fanny.

Desperate, Georgiana shifted her weight, but to little avail. As Miss Frampton began a pleasant but unremarkable aria, Georgiana glanced to her side. Lord Edward was equally imprisoned but appeared in good humour, for he waggled his eyebrows.

'Why do you give me that look?' Georgiana demanded, her voice low so as not to be overheard.

'Because it's amusing to watch you scheme,' Edward whispered back. 'Admit it, you want my friend.'

Georgiana glared. If she'd still been the impetuous youth she'd been when she and Edward had carried on their flirtation, she would've no doubt smacked the artist. 'I want his donation,' she corrected sternly. 'Nothing else. My life is dedicated to serving Monica House. It's the only thing that brings me happiness.'

Edward drew back, shedding his playful manner. 'Only thing that brings you happiness? Surely not, Gee?'

'It's the solemn truth.' She placed a hand over her heart. 'Every minute of every day, I serve those women.'

'I don't like to hear that, Georgiana,' Edward exclaimed. 'Not at all. It's all very well to do good things for others, but there's no harm in thinking of yourself too, you know. What happened to the wild girl who had such magnificent dreams? She told me countless times that one day she'd be so famous, I'd beg to paint her portrait, as Sir Joshua begged Anna Marinetti.'

A flame ignited in Georgiana's breast, for what did a libertine like Edward know of life? Those dreams were long dead. 'That girl grew up, Edward. You might try it yourself sometime.'

Edward studied her, then shrugged. 'Well, I wish you luck getting your donation from my friend, but in case you have *other schemes*, a word of warning. No one succeeds with Tyrold. He's made of steel where women are concerned. Which reminds me, in a rather improper manner, of something I wanted to ask you. I gather the mystery of your paternity has finally been resolved. The Duke of Amesbury is your pater, eh?'

The matron in front of Georgiana shifted, pressing Georgiana's guitar case into her chest. Fitting, really, for an emotional weight pressed there too. 'He is, but I don't wish to discuss that.'

'Then shall we limit our discourse to reminiscences of our past ardour?' He grinned rakishly. 'You're more beautiful than ever, my love.'

'You're a ridiculous man.' Georgiana stuck out her tongue, which elicited a laugh from her old friend. They exchanged knowing grimaces as a second debutante commenced a mediocre performance of a challenging ballad beyond her vocal abilities, and, in those moments of shared playfulness, a solution to Georgiana's troubles with the matrons formed in her mind.

Edward couldn't help but flirt. It was in his nature, but it meant nothing. As the fifth son of a marquess, dependent upon a great-aunt's allowance and income from his art, he was an eligible bachelor, but no stunningly remarkable catch that would incite jealousy. The close friendship between his father and Georgiana's father would render a courtship between them unexceptional; a fifth son paired with a natural daughter was exactly the sort of uninspiring match the *ton* would permit Georgiana. Therefore, if she pretended to be in love with Edward, no one would suspect her of aiming for Tyrold, and gossip would quickly dissipate.

Pleased with her ingenuity, she laid a hand on the artist's forearm. 'Edward, I've such a plan. These ladies won't contribute to Monica House if they believe I have designs on Tyrold's affections, so, for old time's sake, will you engage in a pretend flirtation with me? Rest assured, it'll be temporary. You need only exert yourself until I secure the necessary donations.'

Edward's eyes gleamed; it appeared he enjoyed a lark as much as he ever had. 'Why, this is perfect, Gee. In fact, I was about to propose the same plan to you, because Aunt Agatha's hounding me to court respectable ladies. Let's you and I pretend to be desperately in love, and both our problems will be solved. Shall we shake on our deal?'

As Georgiana shook his offered hand, she reflected on Edward's earlier statement about Tyrold's resistance to women. She was intrigued, because the casual comment might explain quite a lot about the reclusive millionaire, and Georgiana could adjust her approach to getting a sponsorship accordingly. 'What did you mean when you said Mr Tyrold is made of steel where women are concerned? Do you refer to *respectable* women?'

'I mean *all* women. He's simply not interested.'

'Oh!' Georgiana put her fingertips to her lips. So Tyrold was like her Prozio Pietro in Roma. It made perfect sense now that she thought about it. The lack of interest in debutantes, the absence of any rumours linking Tyrold to a mistress or lover. The way he disdainfully kicked aside the courtesan's glove at the park, and how he only engaged in conversations with gentlemen. It also explained his reserved, reclusive nature; he didn't want others to guess at his preference for men. Not that the criminal repercussions of following such an inclination would ever touch a man of Tyrold's position and wealth, but society was so condemnatory. Perhaps if it were common knowledge, his business dealings would suffer.

Well, Tyrold's secret was safe with Georgiana and there was no point in discussing the matter further with Edward, who likely imagined she didn't know of such things, so she let the subject drop and listened to a third debutante begin a performance of a love song from *Fidelio* in horrific German.

As she shared another grimace with Edward, Tyrold's voice rang out, interrupting the aria. 'Enough, for the love of God. Move. All of you, *move*! I cannot stand another moment of this torture.'

The flock of mamas gasped, but they scattered back from Tyrold and his wolfhound as the duo rose, allowing Georgiana a clear view of the action, at last. Some debutantes giggled. Others pouted. The young lady closest to Tyrold covered her face with her hands and burst into tears.

Tyrold appeared astounded by her reaction. 'There's nothing to blubber about, child. You're no worse than the others, but your butchery of German is too much to be borne.' When the girl's sobs escalated, Tyrold lifted his eyes upward in an exaggerated expression of suffering. 'Good Lord, stop whimpering, girl! Simply learn to sing before you inflict performances on others. Take lessons and if you want my advice, you and your friends should ask Miss Bailey to supply them.'

Georgiana froze, horrified, as the mothers glared at her with blatant hostility. They wanted to rip her apart. Destroy her. Leave her torn carcass to the vultures.

Evidently unaware of the vitriol he'd unleashed, Tyrold turned his back and stalked across the lawn with his dog loping beside him.

And Georgiana realised she must persuade him to give *substantially* to Monica House when he met her later, or the bloodthirsty enemies he'd inadvertently created could unravel all the progress she'd made over the last four years.

Failure wasn't an option.

5

John stalked furiously across the lawn, desperate to return home. The debutantes' performances had served to reinforce why he rarely ventured out in company. He'd known something like this would happen if he came to the garden party. Society's damned relentless insistence on forcing his attention drained and frustrated him. Why couldn't other people respect that if he didn't seek their company, he didn't want it?

He hadn't wished to be cruel, but the singing had continued incessantly, one debutante after the other, despite John adopting a stony face and crossed arms to display his utter lack of interest. The third girl had been the final straw, since she was singing to him in German about, well, *ardent marital love*. The child had barely been older than Flora, bringing the fact that his ward was at the mercy of her abductor forcibly to John's mind.

'Mr Tyrold,' a man's voice called out. 'A minute of your time, please.'

John glanced over his shoulder to find the Duke of Amesbury two paces behind. Amesbury was an intelligent man in his mid-fifties, famed for his amiability and graciousness, but, at the moment, his eyes blazed.

Amesbury's conversation was tolerable; had John's mood been better, he would have wanted to discover what had altered the duke's composure so significantly. Perhaps there was a distressing matter of state and he sought John's opinion on its economic repercussions. Such a discussion could be mutually advantageous, as it naturally benefitted John to keep well abreast of politics, to better inform his investments.

But John was in a foul temper and the duke was yet another person attempting to force his attention, so he continued walking. 'I haven't a minute to spare. Write to me instead and I shall answer when I can.'

'You will hear me now, Mr Tyrold!' Amesbury spoke with what others would undoubtedly consider awe-inspiring aristocratic authority. 'In the future, don't bandy my daughter's name about.'

That forced John to an abrupt halt.

Miss Bailey was the duke's *daughter*? Of course, the surnames were the same, but John had assumed a lower-ranking Bailey had sired her, perhaps the duke's uncle or cousin. The revelation otherwise was shocking. Had Amesbury, who was an outspoken and prominent proponent of morality, truly got himself a bastard with *La Grande Bellezza*? And then ignored the child for years, leaving her in the Marquess of Lockington's care not because he was a single man too preoccupied with business to care for her himself, but because he didn't want to raise her with his legitimate children?

John faced the duke squarely. Now that he knew, he could certainly see the resemblance. The duke possessed masculine versions of Miss Bailey's dark eyes and slight build, characteristics she hadn't inherited from her mother, and John resigned himself to the fact that Amesbury was yet another hypocrite. He oughtn't to be surprised, of course. People were rarely as good as they pretended to be, which was something he should keep in mind about Miss Bailey, herself.

He looked down his nose at the irate father. 'I *complimented* her, Amesbury.'

The duke's normally placid countenance creased into a scowl. 'After she performed, yes. But when you compared Miss Frampton, Miss Lawrence and the other debutantes' singing unfavourably with hers, you made my daughter enemies amongst those who are all too eager to consider themselves her superiors. You are a man of the world, Tyrold. You know an illegitimate young lady can ill afford adversaries.'

John narrowed his eyes, his hackles rising that the duke would dare accuse him of harming Miss Bailey. 'You exaggerate the situation, Amesbury. I merely spoke a truth that anyone with half a brain would recognise, but which most people are too spineless to voice. Your daughter can sing exquisitely. Those *children*,' John waved his hand at a cluster of debutantes, although he had no idea if they were the ones who'd sung, 'cannot. It's best for them to hear the truth, and for each to determine if she has the tenacity to improve. Besides, your daughter strikes me as clever enough to outwit a few jealous harpies. Now you've had your minute of my time. Good day.'

John turned his back, but, as he proceeded across the lawn, emotions warred in his chest: a combination of indignation that the duke should chastise him like a schoolboy and an uneasiness that there was truth to what Amesbury had said. But it was of no consequence. Even if he had injured Miss Bailey's good standing, gossip would soon find a new outlet.

In the end, his anger won over his uneasiness. Throughout the afternoon, as he attempted to work at his desk, the storm raging inside him intensified. He dwelled on the injustices done to him of late: Flora's disappearance; Edward keeping him up all night; the fortune-hunting matrons not permitting him to enjoy even a single bloody song without inflicting him with their daughters.

Above all else, he was irritated to find himself anticipating his appointment with Miss Bailey with the eagerness of a child at Christmas. His leg tapped involuntarily, he constantly checked the mantel clock, the hours seemed to drag endlessly, he could barely eat his dinner. He attempted to convince himself it was his desperation to find Flora and the hope he'd laid at Miss Bailey's feet that caused his restlessness, and likely part of it was, but the cursed full truth was that after their brief but enchanting interaction at the garden party, he *wanted* to spend more time with her. And it had been a long time since he'd felt that way about a woman.

It was a dangerous thing, especially in his current distraught state.

His propensity to like and admire Miss Bailey was something he must suppress and until he'd conquered it fully, he must conceal it. He admiration earlier had been too obvious; he couldn't afford another misstep. After all, she was simply another woman after his money, albeit *evidently* nobler in her motivations than others, and the last thing he needed in his life right now, with the situation with Flora, was to develop a *tendre* for anyone.

The metal sign of a coffee pot swayed in the evening breeze on the east side of Soho Square as John stood on the pavement, his pipe clenched between his teeth. He took a deep breath, savouring the rich tobacco, exhaled slowly, and mentally reviewed the plan he'd decided upon during his walk from Mayfair.

As he did so, a surge of confidence swelled his chest. This meeting was strictly business and in business matters, John was self-assured and *always* triumphant. He knew how to control his mind, how to avoid traps. He had resolved to resort to his customary brusqueness tonight, to prevent any potential misunderstandings. If Miss Bailey endured it well, he would eventually reward her with a handsome donation to her charity – and with an even more substantial sponsorship if she succeeded in finding Flora.

With his mind now regimented, he shouldered open the oak door. The aroma of roasted coffee greeted him as he stepped into a chamber filled with wooden tables and mismatched chairs. Men occupied a few seats, conversing or reading newspapers by candlelight. Several heads turned at John's entry, and chatter quietened as he surveyed the establishment's occupants.

Miss Bailey wasn't there.

John removed his watch from his fob pocket and flipped its lid. Five minutes past seven. Miss Bailey's lateness surprised him, but he'd use it to his advantage. Whenever she deigned to appear, he would commence the meeting with a lecture on punctuality. That would establish his dominance from the onset.

An older woman wearing a frilled cap – Maria DeRosa, presumably – scurried over. 'Good evening, sir,' she said in accented English. 'I took the liberty of preparing you a private parlour. You'll find your *coffee* already waiting.'

Oh.

John was the unpunctual one.

He removed his pipe, dismissing a damnable heated sensation crawling over his neck. 'Lead on, then,' he barked. He would still manage to assert his dominance with brusqueness, even if he no longer had reason to commence with a scold.

Maria DeRosa bobbed a curtsy before waving John into a dim corridor. As he followed the proprietress down the passageway, a door opened, illuminating the shadows with sudden brilliance, and Miss Bailey stood before him, haloed by golden light. She was attired in a simple blue gown cinched under her bosom by a chatelaine belt, with her hair pulled into a heavy chignon. Her gold locket nestled above her modest neckline, shining against her tanned skin.

'Good evening, Mr Tyrold.' Miss Bailey stepped closer and the chains of her chatelaine chimed. Even with the tobacco smoke between them, John caught a whiff of a delicious floral scent.

He tightened his teeth over his pipe stem, willing himself to reveal nothing of his attraction. Aloofness, that was the key. Or was it brusqueness?

'Well?' he snapped, deciding upon the latter. 'Are we to talk in the corridor?'

'Not at all. Maria and I have prepared this parlour for your comfort.' Miss Bailey held his gaze unfalteringly as she waved him through the door and into a small parlour with white-plastered walls and exposed dark beams. A sturdy table, laid out with a coffee tray, stood before a fire crackling in an iron hearth. Beside the tray rested a leather-bound ledger.

With her hand upon the door, Miss Bailey smiled at the proprietress. '*Vi ringrazio*, Maria.'

The older woman's lips thinned. She looked at John as if he were an especially loathsome insect. '*Non ha buone maniere, mia cara.*'

John stifled his amusement. Signora DeRosa spoke the truth. He didn't have good manners.

Miss Bailey kissed the proprietress's cheek. '*Va tutto bene. Fidatevi di me.*'

All is well, John translated in his head. *Trust me.*

Miss Bailey's voice was even more beautiful in Italian.

Signora DeRosa mellowed. '*Come desiderate, mia vita. Ma niente trucchi, eh? Mi avete promesso che non lo avreste fatto mai più.*'

John frowned. His Italian was imperfect, honed only for understanding opera, but he thought the proprietress was reminding Miss Bailey of a promise not to play tricks.

Miss Bailey's laughter chimed, accompanied by Italian reassurances, while John's skin prickled. What tricks did Miss Bailey play that concerned the older woman?

When Signora DeRosa left, Miss Bailey slid the wooden door closed.

John tossed his hat on a peg set into the plaster, all too aware of their seclusion. '*This* is what you call a proper way to meet a gentleman?' he asked gruffly. 'A private parlour with a closed door, down a dark corridor in a rather dubious coffeehouse?'

Miss Bailey lifted her shoulders, evidently unruffled. 'After your public praise of me earlier today, it is quite as impossible for us to converse in the coffeehouse as it would be for me to call at your residence. You will simply have to trust me not to endanger your virtue, for Maria is too busy to serve as chaperone.'

'I never trust anyone, Miss Bailey – and you might as well know at once that I shall not have my hand forced with claims I've compromised you, even if they are bought forwards by the Duke of Amesbury himself. I have the means to best your father in any suit.'

She gazed at him steadily, her hand resting on the lever fastening the door. 'I would never seek to force any man into marriage, Mr Tyrold. Furthermore, I know you are a confirmed bachelor, and I perfectly comprehend your reasons. Edward explained and your secret is safe with me. You see, my mother's uncle, with whom I resided in Rome for a time, is the same.'

John furrowed his brow, not understanding. 'Your mother's uncle is a confirmed bachelor?'

'Yes, except for his dear friend, Stefano, with whom he's shared a household for forty years.'

John stared blankly until, suddenly, the significance of her declaration dawned on him. 'Good Lord!' he exclaimed, nearly choking upon his pipe. 'I can't imagine what Edward told you, Miss Bailey, but let me assure you he and I share a residence and nothing more.'

She waved her hand. 'Oh, I know *Edward*'s not your companion, in that sense. As for what he told me, he merely mentioned you have no interest in women, respectable or not. If it weren't for my experience living with my uncles Pietro and Stefano, I doubt I would have understood. I assure you, I shan't breathe a word to anybody.'

John hesitated, contemplating correcting her before realising it was much easier to let her believe what she wished. If she thought him uninterested in women, there could be no misunderstandings. 'Well, then, see that you don't,' he said, but he softened his tone considerably.

She motioned towards a chair. 'Please, be seated. I shall pour your coffee.'

John grunted, feeling somewhat off-kilter after their exchange. 'No milk in mine.'

As he sat, Miss Bailey lifted the coffee pot with a scrap of wool and poured some into a sturdy mug.

'A lump of sugar?' she asked, her eyes dancing. 'In general, it is my belief that a little sweetness makes all the difference.'

John suppressed a twitch of his lips. 'I manage without.'

She offered him the filled mug, handle forwards; when her fingertips grazed his, John's breath hitched involuntarily. More damnable yet, he held her gaze too long as they touched, possibly ruining all his efforts to appear indifferent.

A devilishly lovely rosiness tinted her cheeks, giving rise to a suspicion that she, too, wasn't expressing all she truly felt.

John's wariness rose as she sat on the chair across from him, and he determined to keep vigilant. With his eyes on Miss Bailey, he tested the coffee. It was surprisingly good, its flavour complex and robust, unlike the brown-tinted swill one usually received at coffeehouses.

Miss Bailey opened her ledger, displaying pages of neat writing in precise rows, with numbers in three columns to the right. 'Sir, two weeks ago, in the park, you expressed concern over my management abilities. I hope to prove myself to you tonight.' She paused, meeting John's gaze steadily. 'I confess I *have* mismanaged some funds in the past, but it was all my own money and—'

'You can save your breath, Miss Bailey,' John interrupted. 'I'm not here to discuss Monica House's finances.'

She tilted her head. 'But at the garden party, you said . . .'

'I said what I did because I couldn't speak openly with so many people around us, but the truth of the matter is, I require your assistance, and if you provide it in a satisfactory manner, I shall compensate you for your time. What you do with the money is of no account to me once you've achieved my task. Spend it however you wish; you'll owe me no explanation.'

She furrowed her brow. 'Then how can I assist you?'

John scraped his chair closer to the table. 'I need to find a girl. A girl in a great deal of trouble, whether or not she realises it.'

'What girl?' she asked, clearly surprised.

John hesitated. 'Miss Bailey, from this moment forwards, you must hold everything I say in the strictest confidence. You do not wish to cross me, so don't think of mentioning this conversation to anyone.'

'I wouldn't consider it,' she responded with indignation. 'No more than I'd discuss your reasons for bachelorhood. I don't break confidences.'

John held her gaze as he drank more coffee, but she didn't falter. She studied him back with unblinking sincerity, and he rewarded her with a nod. 'Excellent. I shall hold you to your word. I'm looking for my fifteen-year-old ward, Flora Tyrold, or Flora Jennings, as she is sometimes called to keep her connection to my fortune secret. She has run away from her school in Mary Le Bone.'

'Run away?' Miss Bailey exclaimed, her eyebrows snapping together. 'Why? Was she mistreated?'

'Of course not! She ran away because she is an impetuous child who has often been difficult to manage, but that's neither here nor there to the matter at hand.

Since you boasted of your ability to find females in trouble, your task is to locate Flora with the utmost swiftness. You should know she appears older than her age, but, I reiterate, she is a child, and she is – or was – innocent of this world's evil.' John paused to consider, briefly studying the steam wafting from his coffee. 'Except grief; she has known grief.' Not wishing to dwell a moment longer on that, he continued briskly. 'I haven't got a portrait, but her looks are distinctive. She is beautiful by anyone's measure, with a mass of copper-coloured curls in ringlets like corkscrews. And she has,' his voice caught, damn it, 'she has green eyes.'

'Like yours?' Miss Bailey queried.

John looked up, hope rising. 'Have you seen her?'

'Oh, no, no.' Miss Bailey waved her hands as if pushing away his words. 'Forgive me if I gave that impression. I asked because your eyes are' – her face flushed – 'well, uncommonly green.'

John grunted. After draining the last of his coffee, he relayed to Miss Bailey the entirety of what he'd told Edward. 'I do not fear for Flora's life,' he concluded, 'because she's far too valuable alive, but I shan't have my hand forced by a villain. I must find her before she is in a condition where she imagines herself obligated to marry, yet I cannot go to Bow Street and initiate a formal search without risking a spread of gossip ruinous to her reputation.'

Miss Bailey stared intently, as she had throughout his recitation. 'Would you feel she's obligated to marry a man who impregnated her, Mr Tyrold?'

He shifted his weight in his seat. 'All I feel right now is a desire to have Flora back in my protection immediately, upon which point, I shall lock her away until she proves to have sense. The only other course of action I've decided upon is castrating the bastard who abducted her.'

Miss Bailey closed the ledger and set it aside. 'I'm sympathetic to your plight and I'm certain you're immensely worried.' She clasped her hands on the table, fingers entwined. 'But if I find Miss Tyrold, I shan't force her to return to you unless she wishes it.'

'She's fifteen,' John snapped. 'Her wishes have nothing to do with anything.'

Miss Bailey pursed her lips. 'Are you her sole guardian? Where is Miss Tyrold's mother, for example?'

Helen.

'Her mother is dead. And, yes, I am Flora's sole guardian. Her only relation at all, apart from my aging parents who never leave Yorkshire.'

Miss Bailey studied her folded hands. 'Poor child. She must be lonely.'

John's pulse rose. 'I've done my duty by Flora. The only area in which I fell short was my failure to realise the ungrateful impulsivity of a fifteen-year-old girl—'

'Or, potentially, her overwhelming unhappiness. You said the other girls at the school believed her to be in love with her mysterious admirer?'

'What can that possibly signify?' John threw up his hands. '*Love?* Bah! What she feels is mere infatuation at best. A fifteen-year-old knows nothing of love.'

Helen had taught John that.

Miss Bailey regarded him steadily. '*Infants* know love, Mr Tyrold. But even more, they know the lack of it. Humans are not meant to be unloved; it drives us to despair. It drives us to seek it wherever, and however, it's offered. Was Miss Tyrold happy at her school? Did she have friends?'

Flora's anger-twisted features leapt to John's mind, along with her venomous outburst: *Your money brings me nothing but misery*. His stomach coiled, but he merely grunted. 'That's immaterial to the matter of how to recover her.'

Miss Bailey's gaze was penetrating. 'I see,' she said curtly. 'Well, I shall look for her and if I find her, I shall ensure her comfort and safety, but I can promise no more.'

John leant forwards, bringing his face closer to hers. 'You'll return her to me if you find her, Miss Bailey,' he said, although his mouth went dry at her proximity. What *was* the scent she wore? Rose, perhaps, but with something else deeply aromatic, like incense. 'I command it.'

Miss Bailey shrugged. 'I shan't follow your commands, Mr Tyrold.'

'Because you can't?' The nagging worry that approaching Miss Bailey would yield no results had plagued the back of his mind. 'Because your proclamations about your ability to find and help women in trouble were empty boasts?'

She leant forwards too until her nose was mere inches from his, an assertive move that surprised *and* disarmed

John. 'Not at all, Mr Tyrold,' she said firmly, narrowing her dark eyes. They were so close he could see the depths of their velvety layers; her irises were chocolate brown, without a hint of green or gold, and her lashes were thick and black, curling upwards at the ends. 'I am adept at what I do and I have connections who constantly watch for women in need of refuge. Once I spread the word, I'll discover leads, if your ward is in London. Certainly, I cannot guarantee I will find her, but I'm confident I will find out *something*.'

John growled as he reclined, stretched his legs, and crossed one booted ankle over the other. He needed to put distance between himself and those beautiful eyes, made all the more attractive by her self-confidence. 'And you will tell me everything you discover? And bring her to me if you find her?'

'Not necessarily. I shall exercise my judgement as the search progresses, but you need to understand that I'll protect women at all costs.'

'At all costs, indeed.' He laced his fingers over his abdomen. 'In fact, you'll find that such a stance will cost you dearly, for if you don't return Flora immediately upon locating her, you'll never see a penny more of my money beyond what I rashly promised you at the park.'

'Then so be it,' she responded boldly. 'My concern is for your ward's peace of mind and wellness of spirit, not for your demands, Mr Tyrold. My principles are not for sale.'

John scoffed. 'Principles are always for sale.'

She crossed her arms. 'I shan't budge on my stance regarding Miss Tyrold, so it appears we have nothing more to say to each other. I trust you can see yourself out.'

Miss Bailey was a damned good negotiator, John would give her that. He tapped his fingertips as he studied her stubborn expression. She was putting up an excellent fight – he hadn't been this frustrated by an adversary in a long time – but she'd given him the tool for her capitulation two weeks ago. It was time to cast his trump, so they didn't keep arguing in a circle. 'Miss Bailey, you said you need two thousand pounds to open a school.'

Again, she narrowed her eyes. 'No, I didn't,' she said after a pause. 'Two thousand pounds merely allows me to purchase the leasehold. The lease is three hundred per annum after that; in addition, the school would have significant operating costs.'

Even still, it was a pittance to pay for Flora's safe, quiet return, if Miss Bailey could do it. The trick now was to make her want to return Flora without all this nonsense about principles. If he controlled the house, he controlled her dream. If he controlled her dream, he controlled Miss Bailey. 'And this house is located where?'

'On the south side of Oxford Street, across from the Boar and Castle,' she replied. 'But that information does you no good, for I shan't—'

John held up his hand to silence her. 'I shall absorb that leasehold tomorrow. How I then choose to use the property – whether, for example, I sell the lease for a profit, or divide the house into lodgings or, say, let you run a school from it for no rent at all – will depend entirely on whether you find *and return* Flora to me.'

She hesitated, and her eyes lost some of their fire, yet her gaze never faltered. The tip of her tongue flicked across her lips; then she nibbled her bottom lip, staring at John all the while. 'Under these terms,' she said at last, 'I shall agree to notify you if I find her, but only if you write a signed declaration that you won't seek to remove her without her consent—'

'Oh, come now, enough of that,' John said, thoroughly exasperated. 'No more negotiations. Of course, you will accept this offer, and you will accept it under my terms, or I shall walk out of here and find someone else who wants my money.'

'Then I bid you a good evening, Mr Tyrold,' she said, and pressed her lips together.

Only the crackle of the fire sounded as they faced each other, eyes locked.

Then John sighed heavily, but he sweetened the damned deal. 'Very well – I shall also have the house renovated to your specifications, and I shall pay your school's expenses, including the hiring of masters and staff. Now, be sensible, Miss Bailey! I'm not usually so generous in my business dealings.'

She frowned. 'So you seek to tempt me with terms almost impossible to decline . . .'

'Precisely.' John threw his arms up in praise. 'Thank God, I'm glad you finally realise that. I take it you agree?'

'Of course not,' she said, as cool as a cucumber. 'I already told you that I shan't yield on a matter of principle.'

'Good Lord, woman!' He clasped his hands to his scalp, wanting to tear out his hair. 'You would try the patience of a saint.'

'Forgive me, sir,' she said, as sweet as honey. 'But it is precisely because I humbly try to perform the work of a saint that I must decline your terms.'

Against his will, John's heart softened. The cursed thing was that she did, in fact, look saintly, for now she'd cast down her eyes like a damned Madonna. Perhaps she *actually* suffered some moral quandary.

John racked his brain for a solution. As always, that organ didn't fail him. In fact, the solution it presented was surprisingly pleasing, although it meant the venture wouldn't be as inexpensive or as untroublesome as he had hoped.

'I have a proposal, Miss Bailey.' He kept his voice level with great effort. 'That would allow you to find my ward, release her to me, and get your school without compromising your principles. Instead of searching for Flora, lead me around London to the places where you might search for someone in Flora's position. That way, when we find her, you needn't struggle with your conscience.'

Miss Bailey's cheeks reddened. 'You want *me* to lead *you* around London? The two of us, alone? Are you determined to ruin my reputation, then, sir?'

'I've no intention of doing anything of the sort. Others won't find out unless you tell them – and that would be your fault, which I shan't rectify.'

She snorted derisively, not breaking eye contact with him. 'Mr Tyrold, you are recognised in every part of London. Any female spotted alone in your company, at night, unchaperoned, will naturally be the object of such speculation that my identity would eventually be discovered. Furthermore, after your damaging praise of me earlier, you and I cannot afford *any* gossip.'

John ignored the vexatious reminder of his afternoon behaviour. 'I can disguise my appearance.'

She pursed her lips and studied him as the fire crackled. Then she stood, smoothed her skirts, and paced the short length of the room.

He found himself holding his breath. Somehow, Miss Bailey had got the upper hand despite his best intentions. If she didn't agree to this solution, he'd have to capitulate to all her demands. What other recourse did he have, apart from the Runners? Besides, he *would* do anything to know Flora was safe – even if it meant relinquishing his right ever to see her again.

Miss Bailey pivoted, her skirts swishing about her legs, and put her hands on her hips. 'Very well, Mr Tyrold. I shall cut your hair and you must shave. That will work for tonight.'

John blinked, surprise overpowering his relief. 'You will cut my . . .'

She patted the scissors on her chatelaine. 'Your hair, yes. Everyone knows you have long hair. Without it, at night, you'll look like *any* gentleman somewhat down on his luck, wearing an unfashionable coat and boots that need resoling.'

He ignored the slight on his appearance. 'So you agree to my proposition?'

She extracted her scissors from their sheath. 'I shall personally mediate between you and Flora when we find her, for it would be both pointless and cruel if I allowed her to return to an unhappy situation. But, yes, I agree. We'll start tonight' – she hooked her fingers through the shears' rings – 'setting out at ten, which gives us slightly over two hours to ready ourselves. But considering the amount of hair you possess, we haven't a moment to spare.'

She stood directly behind him and, without another word, yanked the ribbon holding back his queue. When she threaded her fingers through his locks, spreading his hair loose over his neck and cheeks, John's shoulders tensed again. He was *not* prepared for the electric sensation elicited by her fingertips on his scalp.

'Yes, that's better,' Miss Bailey said. 'Sit up straight. I'm less likely to botch this.'

John growled low in his throat, masking his attraction with gruffness. 'Have you ever cut hair?'

'I frequently give the boys at Monica House haircuts.' There was laughter in her voice. The first snip of the shears released a chunk of hair, which Miss Bailey held out before dropping to the floor. 'Remove your coat, Mr Tyrold, or your valet will never brush this out.'

John rose, glaring down at her as he wrestled out of the garment. 'I don't keep a valet.'

Her eyes twinkled. 'I never would've guessed. You must break your back over the care of your wardrobe.'

He tossed his coat to the floorboards, and her amused gaze rested on the crumpled heap. 'Ah, yes, I can see you do.'

He pressed his lips together to keep from laughing as he sank into his chair again. 'Are you cutting my hair or not?' he asked brusquely, steeling himself for her touch.

When she threaded her fingers into his hair again, John set his jaw. He'd resisted attractions before, so he could resist this one . . .

Even if Miss Bailey *had* just added to her charms by being the best negotiator he'd ever had the pleasure and frustration of dealing with.

6

For all Tyrold's supposed skill at negotiating, it hadn't proven difficult for Georgiana to get exactly what she wanted once she'd realised how desperately he needed her. And she'd even got him to agree to *help*, a first step in his acknowledging an emotional responsibility to his ward – something he seemed to deny.

Certainly, Georgiana genuinely sympathised with the girl; after all, she vividly recalled her own loneliness at Flora's age. But her protestations were primarily a ploy to salvage the garden-party disaster by extracting everything she could from Tyrold. Despite what she'd initially said, she always knew she would've returned Flora once she'd mediated a satisfactory arrangement for the child, because Tyrold seemed more of a distant and detached guardian than a cruel one, whereas the man who'd abducted Flora was undoubtedly a predator. Honourable people didn't lure children away from their rightful guardians.

Georgiana now had her work cut out for her, but she was up to the challenge. She needed to save Flora, she needed to convince Tyrold of his emotional responsibility and she must succeed in using this opportunity to get her school. A chance like this wouldn't come again, so failure wasn't an option.

Just as she wouldn't fail with this haircut.

Wanting to impress upon Tyrold that she excelled at everything she put her mind to, Georgiana worked carefully from the top of his forehead to the nape of his neck. His thick hair was soft and clean, smelling of cedarwood soap, as Georgiana isolated neat rows between two fingers of her left hand and snipped. Section by section, segments pooled on the worn floorboards. Tyrold sat impassive and straight-backed, which allowed Georgiana to concentrate, except when she brushed against his jaw to angle his head one way or the other, and his leaf-green eyes cut to hers and held her gaze until the chamber felt suffocatingly overwarm.

Each time, it was difficult to avert her eyes and attack a new section of hair, but she did, wondering at her attraction to the man. Was it his celebrity that excited her? Or his self-made millions, the envy of princes? Maybe it was his growly gruffness, the way he projected an air of unattainability. Or perhaps there was a foolish part of her that imagined that, if he were inclined towards women, she could melt his curt crust and reveal something tender beneath?

It was a thrilling, if ridiculous, thought, and one which had the potential to distract her from her true purpose but for the fact that Tyrold couldn't possibly return her attraction. Knowing there could be nothing physical between them would allow Georgiana to act pleasingly through their partnership without giving Tyrold a wrong impression.

Georgiana *did* want to please such a valuable potential sponsor, which was why she intended to make the most of their intimate and secluded setting. In her experience, men – regardless of their romantic inclinations – were often susceptible to someone taking care of them. Thus, Georgiana gently ran her fingers through Tyrold's hair, allowing her fingertips to graze the sensitive skin of his scalp. As she continued her ministrations, she softly sang a north country ballad, since he was from Yorkshire.

But rather than succumbing to relaxation as she had anticipated, Tyrold tensed, his body stiffening. When their eyes met again, his gaze seemed hostile. 'If you focus on your task rather than singing, perhaps you'll finish this damned haircut before midnight.'

The lyrics withered in Georgiana's mouth as Tyrold looked away, taking up the account book and glaring at its pages. An intensity of emotion crackled about him. He acted as if he was angry, but Georgiana wasn't convinced.

Oh, well. So, he didn't want her to sing, even though he'd loved her performance earlier. Georgiana shrugged it off and concentrated on her task, but she continued to rake her fingers through his hair on occasion. He hadn't objected to *that*.

Tyrold flipped a page. A few moments later he said, 'Your total on this page is miscalculated,' and Georgiana perceived a note of triumph in his voice.

She paused the haircut to look over his shoulder. 'Where?'

He pointed to the numbers at the bottom of the page. 'Should be eight-and-twenty pounds, seventeen shillings and five pence.'

Georgiana frowned, indignation rising. True, she frequently dashed through the accounts – there was so much more *important* work to be done and she was often called from her desk to attend to everything from a colicky baby to a smoking stove – but she prided herself on her ability to calculate with accuracy. And even if she had made a mistake, how could Tyrold have noticed it when he'd barely glanced at the page? 'I doubt there's an error, Mr Tyrold, but if there is, it's impossible for you to spot it so quickly.'

He extracted a pencil from his pocket, and with his left hand, scratched *28-17-5* at the bottom of the page. 'Check the sum later,' he said, as he carried his calculations to the next page. 'You'll see I'm correct.'

Frustrated, Georgiana bit her tongue and returned to her work, attempting to ignore his scribbles as he flipped pages and retotalled her sums. Within a quarter of an hour, he snapped her account book closed and tossed it upon the table.

He returned his pencil to his pocket. 'Off by nine pounds, thirteen shillings and ten pence in the end. I've seen much worse, but I find your miscalculations especially frustrating because they are mostly mistakes of inattentiveness – carrying the wrong total to the top of your next page, for example. It speaks to your lack of business sense, as I suspected when we first discussed Monica House in the park. I recommend you not hurry so much over your books if you wish to attract serious sponsors.'

'*You* hurried,' she retorted, before she thought the better of it.

'Because I can,' he replied, gratingly arrogant.

Georgiana held back another retort. After all, she *did* rush through the books. The business side of her work was unfulfilling. Ledgers were paper and ink, while people were alive. People *needed* Georgiana. Account books did not.

'*If* I'm off,' she asked, 'is it in my debit or credit?'

He folded his arms over his chest. 'You are poorer than you thought.'

Fantastic, Georgiana thought with a heavy sigh. She hoped Tyrold was mistaken, but she began to suspect he wasn't. After all, there must be *some* explanation for his unparalleled ability to grow a fortune.

'So you're a mathematical prodigy, are you?' she asked as she tidied the top of his head, where she'd left the hair longer. 'Is that the secret behind the Tyrold millions?'

He grunted, but Georgiana perceived a hint of pink round the edge of his ears. 'For as long as I can remember, I've been able to compute rapidly and with perfect accuracy. Numbers fall into place in my mind, like soldiers at drill. But my fortune grew only because I applied that skill with rigour and determination. Whatever talent Nature gave me, I chose not to waste, like you with your singing.'

'That would be admirable if you were willing to share the fruits of that unwasted talent with the world, as I am with my voice.'

He jerked his head round until his eyes bored into her. 'Again, I shall throw your own words back at you, Miss Bailey: you know nothing about me.'

'True, I don't,' she admitted, ceding the ground. She of all people ought to know not to judge based on rumour and speculation, no matter how much Tyrold's appearance and behaviour appeared to support the general perception of the millionaire's miserliness. 'Let us speak no more of it.'

After all, she gained nothing by angering the man.

Georgiana continued her task, and, at last, she evened out the line from one sideburn, round his neck, and to his other ear, before returning her scissors to her chatelaine.

'There.' She smoothed her hands over Tyrold's shoulders to brush the last snippets of hair off his waistcoat and shirtsleeves, applying pressure to ease his tension. She *would* succeed in charming him. 'I've finished, and you look well. Quite handsome.'

He looked *very* handsome, in fact. His shortened hair revealed his strong jawline and defined his smooth forehead, and his green eyes were more noticeable than ever, no longer partly hidden by long strands of loose hair.

But his brows drew together. 'Handsome, am I? Kindly recall that flirting won't get you anywhere with me, Miss Bailey.'

Irritation prickled Georgiana's skin. 'I'm not flirting. I'm being *pleasant*, but I suppose you wouldn't—'

She pressed her lips together rather than finishing. Insulting him wouldn't get her a school.

Tyrold snorted. 'Please don't stop, Miss Bailey. You were about to say I wouldn't know pleasant behaviour if it hit me in the face.'

'Pleasant behaviour doesn't hit one in the face, Mr Tyrold. It seeps into the heart and soothes the soul.' And with that rebuttal, she turned on her heel and marched out the door, instructing him to wait as she procured shaving items from Maria.

When she returned bearing a rather tarnished mirror, razor, bowl, soap and hot water, he was drinking another mug of coffee, which he'd evidently managed to pour himself.

'This coffee is excellent,' he said as she laid out the shaving items. His voice was less gruff, as if he were attempting to behave more agreeably. He wasn't hopeless, Georgiana decided. He could learn manners if he set his mind to it – or if he had a good teacher.

She rewarded his pleasantness with a smile. 'Thank you. I shall tell Maria you said so. It will please her greatly.'

Leasing and refurbishing the coffeehouse for her old nanny had been one of the first ways Georgiana had spent the fortune her father had given her when she'd returned from Rome four years earlier. It had helped the older woman forgive Georgiana for running off to Italy alone four years before *that*, something Maria assumed had been an act of youthful rebellion. She didn't know the truth, and she didn't know the terrible price Georgiana had paid for her actions.

Georgiana flipped open the razor. 'Would you like me to shave you?'

Tyrold cocked an eyebrow. 'I most definitely do *not*.'

Georgiana lifted the mirror. 'I'm afraid there's hardly any untarnished reflective surface left.'

'Ah, a looking glass so I can inspect the damage you inflicted.' Tyrold grabbed the frame, his fingers covering Georgiana's as he pulled her hand and the mirror closer. She leant over his head and peered with him into the glass, her elbow resting on his shoulder, the heat of his body mingling with hers, their breath rising and falling in tandem.

'It's not terrible, is it?' She brushed his hair forwards over his forehead, as was the style. 'Quite good, in fact, and you can't object to the price, even with your tendency towards, er, careful money management.' She smiled cheekily, determined to break through his gruffness.

Within the mirror, his narrowed eyes met hers. 'It's not horrific, but it may yet be the most expensive haircut I've ever had. Hold the mirror for me and I shall shave, since you insist.'

Georgiana moved a chair beside Tyrold's as he poured steaming water from the kettle into the bowl. As she held the looking glass, she watched him roll up his sleeves, exposing hair-darkened forearms. He untied his cravat, laid it aside, and unbuttoned the fastening in the hollowed dip of his throat. When he spread out the opening of his shirt, it revealed the defined ridge of his collarbones and a smattering of dark curls at the top of his chest.

The room suddenly felt stifling – and the warmth only increased when Tyrold again placed his hand over hers to reposition the looking glass until the angle satisfied.

'Don't move,' he said gruffly, with his palm still enveloping her fingers. 'Not even a waver.'

Then he smiled a stunning, eye-crinkling grin, like the one he'd given her after her performance that had so transformed his face. Already overheated, Georgiana responded to it like a moth to a flame. Her lips involuntarily parted and her cheeks flushed hot. To her further dismay, *he* responded to *her* a fraction of a second later, for his eyes darted over her face, as if seeking an answer, and his fingers tightened over hers and his smile vanished, his mouth softening as if he intended to ask her something. Something *intimate*. Something personal.

Horrified, Georgiana realised Tyrold perceived the attraction she couldn't conquer, despite knowing he wasn't interested in women, despite her proclamations that she wasn't flirting. He was on the verge of questioning her about it, and she must do everything in her power to convince him she knew theirs was a business partnership only. If he believed she had romantic aims, he'd never take her aspirations for Monica House seriously. She would be another woman throwing herself at him, imagining she could change him and make him admire her, desire her.

To salvage the situation, she tried to laugh dismissively, although her lingering blush likely continued to betray her, and her laughter sounded too shrill to her own ears. 'Concern yourself with the steadiness of your own hand, Mr Tyrold. *You're* the one holding a blade to your neck. A neck, which, I might add, has suddenly become immensely valuable to me.'

There was a fleeting moment when Tyrold's expression softened further, into something breathtakingly tender, as if Georgiana were an object of wonder . . .

But then that look vanished.

'Two thousand pounds of value, you mean?' he asked, his tone steely.

'Of course,' Georgiana replied with a tenuous smile, hoping to lighten the tension.

He set his mouth in a hard line, released her hand and reached for the bar of shaving soap. Georgiana wasn't certain what had transpired between them, but it seemed that Tyrold had now reverted to his brusque manner, which was decidedly less attractive.

Sadly, it wasn't unattractive enough to cool the flickers of ardour already incited in her mind. As Tyrold lathered the soap, a piney, masculine scent pierced her nose, which did nothing to help matters. He smoothed the suds over his skin, and she kept the mirror steady only with great effort, for sitting beside him as he performed such an intimate task infused her senses. The smell of the soap combined with the rich aroma of pipe tobacco still clinging to Tyrold's person, the sound of the razor against stubble mixed with the crackle of the fire, and the proximity of Georgiana's body to his strong forearms, aroused her profoundly.

Which was something that hadn't happened in years, perhaps because she didn't generally sit alone in small rooms with virile, handsome millionaires.

Nothing would come of it, of course, but Georgiana secretly relished the excitement, provided she could keep her feelings better hidden in the future. Imagining what it would be like to take over the job of shaving, perhaps straddling him as she worked and kissing his smooth, soap-fresh neck once she wiped away the last of the lather, made her body tingle.

She'd remember that later tonight and perhaps she'd be tempted to take out her leather dildo, which had been a farewell gift from her seasoned Italian lover, Domenico, who'd taught her body to feel pleasure again and thankfully never attempted to capture her wounded heart. Their unemotional arrangement had been perfection – one she could have in Italy, but never in England, where with a whiff of scandal, Monica House's sponsors would flee.

The dildo had lain unused in her bedside table drawer, for it had become easier to ignore sexual urges. But Tyrold's proximity aroused them, and Lord knew Georgiana could use a little tension release. The knowledge that Tyrold's preference for men would ensure nothing ever came of her forbidden fantasy made it all the more titillating . . .

Tyrold's voice startled her out of her reverie. 'Are you laying plans?'

Georgiana's face flamed. 'What?' she asked, rather breathlessly.

Tyrold lifted his chin, stretching the skin of his neck, and shaved down over the swell of his Adam's apple. Heavens, but the man had an attractive neck. 'For our search tonight,' he said, swishing the blade clean in the bowl of water.

'Oh!' Georgiana's heart calmed, grateful he hadn't perceived the turn of her mind. 'No. My thoughts were . . . on something else entirely.'

Tyrold grunted a response as he applied the blade to the last lathered section of his delicious neck.

Georgiana adjusted her elbow, which rested on the table. Now that she'd taken her mind out of the gutter, she realised her hand ached from holding the mirror. 'I don't need to plan. I know exactly where to start the search.'

'Where?' His freshly shaven Adam's apple bobbed as he spoke. With effort, Georgiana resisted the urge to wipe away an errant sliver of lather upon the lower edge of his earlobe. 'I assume she's been taken to a private residence.'

Georgiana shook her head as Tyrold dabbed his shaved face with the towel. 'If her captor wishes to keep her location secret – which I assume he must, if he wants to force you to relinquish control of her fortune – it's unlikely he took her to his home.' Georgiana put down the mirror and flexed her fingers. 'It's too risky. He'll worry that you might yet manage to discover his identity. Furthermore, a private residence will have servants, and even the most loyal servants might whisper a word or two about something as salacious as an abducted heiress. For that reason, it's only slightly less unlikely that your ward is at an inn, or even a boarding house. If her captor is attempting to wait out what could be months before she gets with child, he will want to hold her somewhere discreet, with people who are accustomed to securing young girls, whether with or against their will. A place the Runners won't care about, even if a servant does talk. A place where *everyone* wants secrecy.'

'And what sort of place is that?' he asked.

'A brothel,' she replied.

Tyrold frowned as he fastened the button at his collar. 'That's hardly likely. As a prostitute, Flora has no more value than any other pretty girl.' He wrapped his cravat around his neck. 'Control of her fortune must be her abductor's goal; thus, he's certain to want to marry her.'

'I don't mean to imply he's pimping her, Mr Tyrold.' The millionaire botched the knot at his throat, so Georgiana offered to substitute her hands for his fumbling fingers. 'Here, let me,' she said, knowing it was best his neck was well covered in her presence. He drew in a sharp breath but lifted his chin to provide easier access. As she untied and reset the knot, Georgiana continued. 'Although Flora went willingly with this man, I suspect she'll realise soon enough that his goal is your fortune, and she's likely to begin to object at that point.' Georgiana spoke from a place of experience, but she didn't say so to Tyrold. 'If she doesn't object to *that*, she'll dislike being kept out of eyesight, especially as the weather warms. Or there will be something else. My point is, eventually she'll grow restless. Thus, I'd wager ten to one he's got her at a brothel where escape will be nearly impossible.'

'If what you say is true, how will you find her?'

Georgiana finished the knot, tilted her head to view the results, and nodded, satisfied. 'As I said earlier, I have connections throughout London. I costume myself and venture amongst them.' She rose and picked Tyrold's coat from the floor, dusting it off with her palm. 'Tonight, we shall first go to my most valuable contact, a Covent Garden resident who is aware of much that happens in the most notorious brothels. She is likely to know if a young girl with a unique appearance is being kept somewhere. If she has heard nothing, I shall then enquire amongst the streetwalkers and the pimps, as we work our way through the streets south of the Piazza and ultimately move towards the brothels of St James, which tend to be more reputable and therefore are less likely to imprison your ward. Still, it'll be worth a search if we discover nothing in Covent Garden.'

Tyrold cocked an eyebrow. 'This is what you do at night, Miss Bailey?' he asked, something like disbelief in his tone.

Georgiana met his gaze. 'Amongst other things, yes, Mr Tyrold.'

'And what sort of costumes,' he gestured with his fingers towards her simple gown, the same as all women at Monica House wore, 'do you wear?'

'Tonight I shall dress as a procuress, and we'll pretend you are my customer.'

Tyrold coughed. Or choked. One or the other.

Georgiana grinned, holding out his coat. She suspected he was at last beginning to believe her claims. 'I've shocked you terribly, but don't be frightened. Not *really* my customer. You needn't even touch me, beyond, oh, perhaps an arm about my shoulders.'

Tyrold took his coat, staring as if horrified as he struggled into the garment. 'An arm about your . . .' He faltered, paused, and shook his head before continuing. 'Does your father know you do this?'

Georgiana clapped her hand over her mouth, unable to repress rising laughter. 'Does my father, the Duke of Amesbury, know I skulk about Covent Garden pretending to be a bawd? Good Lord, no. Of course not. Can you imagine? And the duchess! Why, Fanny would take to her bed with a year-long nervous spell.' Georgiana giggled, imagining the horror amongst her father's household if ever she were discovered – but then she grew serious, because if she *were* discovered, the repercussions for Monica House might be serious. 'No, Mr Tyrold, my father doesn't know. Nor will he, ever.'

She grabbed Tyrold's hat from the wall peg, intending to return it. But she hesitated. Its slightly conical silhouette was some years out of fashion, and its brown shade was distinctive.

It was unmistakably John Tyrold's hat.

'This is far too recognisable.' She returned the hat to its peg. 'Maria probably has something a customer left. Not likely in the first stare of fashion, but,' she winked, 'you're accustomed to that. Which is a shame because a tall-crowned black beaver would become you well. I suggest you purchase one tomorrow.'

He lifted his eyebrows. 'You do, do you?'

'Yes, and a new coat as well. You'll need another disguise if we don't find Flora tonight, and no one would suspect a *well-dressed* gentleman of being Mr Tyrold. Now, come, we haven't time to waste, for I must dress as well.'

She instructed Tyrold to wait at the back door. As she strode quickly into the coffee shop to enquire about a hat, she reflected with amusement that the miserly millionaire was more malleable than he pretended. He'd demonstrated so by acquiescing to all her demands so far, and by tolerating the haircut and shaving. His appearance was already improved.

If Georgiana could make a proper, presentable gentleman of him, it would greatly satisfy her sense of order and neatness. Additionally, her efforts would provide income for a tailor, a barber, and perhaps for a valet.

Georgiana smiled, relishing yet another opportunity to do good.

Every bit helped.

The old-fashioned, three-cornered cocked hat was overlarge, falling to John's eyebrows, but Miss Bailey laughed his protestation away, her palm resting on his sleeve as they stood near the coffeehouse's back door.

'It's perfect because it casts your face into ominous shadow,' she said teasingly, deepening her velvety voice. 'A dark and mysterious man. No doubt dangerous. Possibly a pirate or a highwayman.'

John spoke through a thickened throat – not the only part of his anatomy that responded to her bedroom voice and the heat of her hand searing through his coat. 'You sound as if you enjoy such men.'

She flashed a roguish grin – one that made her eyes sparkle, and her nose crinkle, giving John a hint of the impishness to which Edward had alluded. 'How improper, Mr Tyrold! Naturally, I simply mean that no one will trouble us.' She slid her hand down John's arm, wrapped her warm fingers around his and pulled him towards the door. 'Let us go to Monica House so I can change. Male visitors upset the residents, especially at night and without warning, so I shall take you the back way, directly into my bedchamber.'

Her *bedchamber*?

John's pulse quickened, but he allowed her to pull him through the coffeehouse's back exit and into the murky alley-warren east of Soho Square. The plan to find Flora had been his, so why was he surrendering control, letting Miss Bailey cut his hair, exchange his hat and lead him to her bedchamber? Was it, in fact, a curiosity to discover Miss Bailey's *tricks*?

Shuffles and rattles arose from blackened alley corners as they progressed. Babies' cries filtered out of dimly glowing windows towering above, followed by deep grumblings and shrill retorts. Carriage wheels rumbled from Oxford Street and Soho Square, but the traffic noise quietened as they delved deeper into the lanes, still hand-in-hand. Above them, lines of washing criss-crossed the paths, ragged grey flags hanging slack in the dank air. The smell of rot mingled with urine, stale ale and boiled cabbage.

John stumbled on an uneven cobble, and Miss Bailey took the hand she'd clasped and tucked it under her upper arm, pressing the back of his fingers against what was most definitely an unbound breast. 'Allow me to steady you.'

Her sensual softness aroused such an intense jolt of desire that John quickly withdrew his hand and stuffed it deep into his pocket.

Grateful for the dark, he stopped walking and closed his eyes, reminding himself that Miss Bailey was a young lady, a debutante. Whatever her designs, and despite the warnings he'd issued earlier that he wouldn't be tricked into marriage, John had a gentlemanly responsibility to avoid any behaviour that would compromise her.

'I can steady you,' she repeated, evidently assuming he'd frozen because of the uneven passage. 'I'm well acquainted with these lanes.'

He gritted his teeth. 'Lead on. I shall manage.'

She did so, gliding along the dank paths, and John raked his gaze over her slender back. Good God, but he needed a woman – and *badly*, judging by his reaction to the feel of Miss Bailey's breast.

His long-term, casual affair with a former opera singer had ended eleven or twelve months earlier, when she'd married another of her lovers, and John hadn't even attempted to search for companionship since. There had been an equality to his relations with Galatea that John despaired of finding with another woman. In fifteen years, she'd asked only for sex and financial advice, which he'd liberally given to her great advantage. Moreover, she'd respected his desire for privacy. No one but the two of them had ever known of their affair.

As they turned the next corner, Miss Bailey side-stepped two cats copulating beside discarded wooden crates. The male, evidently unconcerned about company, merely lifted his head, his eyes glowing in a sliver of light, but the female screeched and disengaged herself, nipping at her mate's tail before he ran into the dark.

Miss Bailey shrugged her shoulders. 'I guess he didn't impress her.'

John snorted with laughter, though in his current state, he felt some sympathy for the tom. 'Good Lord,

Miss Bailey,' he said, both diverted and perplexed by her unconventionality. 'When I first met you standing at the park with a duchess, I expected a debutante, but you're not like any other I've ever met.'

'I'm only a debutante in the strictest since of the word.' She led him further along the narrow alley. On one side, the windowless back of a large building rose. The other side was comprised of a high brick wall, beyond which the sky opened and a nearly full moon provided some illumination through a haze of cloud cover. 'My father and the duchess want me to marry so I'm no longer an embarrassment to the Bailey family, but I only agreed to go amongst society to find new sponsors. I have no interest in matrimony. I'm as confirmed a spinster as you are a bachelor.'

John couldn't repress a sound of derision. This was a game of some sort, surely. 'Oh, come, Miss Bailey! Women say that, but they don't mean it.'

She glared over her shoulder. 'Women say it and *do* mean it, as well. Besides, I believed you, so it is only fair that you believe me. I haven't the time or energy to devote to a husband when I have dozens of women and children who require my attention, and a city full of desperate souls in need of assistance.'

John frowned, still doubtful. On the surface, her argument seemed plausible, but it didn't hold up, at least not in relation to a man of wealth, which clearly was the duchess's aim. With more money, Miss Bailey wouldn't need to devote so much time and energy to her charity. She could employ others to do it for her.

But he remained silent, and soon Miss Bailey halted before a solitary metal door set into the high wall. She laid her hand upon it as tenderly as if she pressed her palm to her heart. 'This is Monica House,' she said with reverence. 'It mayn't seem like much, but it's the most wonderful place in the world to those who need it.'

She extracted a key from her chatelaine, inserted it into the lock, and gestured for John to enter a cramped and barren yard. While Miss Bailey secured the door behind them, John observed the moonlit brick building set in the centre. It rose four squat storeys and contained no ornamentation other than flower-filled jardinières under many of the regularly spaced windows. Behind some of those windows, soft lights flickered through white curtains.

From a corner of the yard, a lantern held by an unseen hand steadily approached, casting a circle of warm glow upon the pavement.

'Good evening, Ben,' Miss Bailey said as the light neared.

The lantern-bearer lifted his light higher, revealing the countenance of a handsome young man. He appeared no more than twenty, yet he was broad-shouldered and muscular. He jutted his square jaw at John. 'Who's he, Georgiana?'

'My guest. I shall lead him to my quarters by the back door, so as not to upset anyone.'

Judging by Ben's expression, John's presence had already upset someone. The young man glowered and edged close, blocking John from following Miss Bailey towards the building.

John extracted a coin from his waistcoat pocket.

Ben sneered. 'Put your money back, man, and know I'll rip out your throat if you lay a hand on *anyone* here.' As if to prove his point, he raised a sizeable fist.

John bristled. No one treated him in such a manner. If not for John's disguise, this boy wouldn't dare. 'Calm down, Ben,' he said in a dangerous voice. 'I'm not here to play fisticuffs with a boy, but I'll engage to your detriment if you don't remove yourself from my path.'

The boy held his gaze, but John didn't waver, and at last Ben retreated. John stalked across the yard towards Miss Bailey, who was inserting a key into a door on the far side of the house.

'Quite the bulldog you have,' he said, when he arrived at her side.

She turned the lock. 'Ben? He's a sweetheart. He grew up at Monica House, but, unlike most boys, he stayed past the age of apprenticeship. He maintains the property and studies in his leisure.'

'Studies what?'

Miss Bailey opened the door. 'Metallurgy. Steam engines. He's brilliant.'

John felt an unexpected flare of jealousy. Miss Bailey hadn't seemed particularly impressed by *his* show of brilliance at the coffeehouse when he'd recalculated her sums. 'Tell me, Miss Bailey – do the other men you take to your bedchamber agree with your assessment of Ben's amiability?'

Miss Bailey's tiny form straightened like an arrow. 'I do *not*,' she said icily, '*normally* bring men to my bedchamber. The current circumstances are extraordinary, and I rely on your discretion as much as you rely on mine. If you have difficulty comprehending that, Ben can show you out at once.'

John grunted his reply, but he hid a smile as he followed Miss Bailey up a flight of narrow stairs. Her indignation proved her sincerity, although it baffled him why he cared if she took other men to her room. Wasn't he concerned about walking into a trap? Yet he put one foot before the other on the wooden steps, undeniably fascinated by this woman who surprised him every few minutes.

At the top of the stairs, Miss Bailey opened another door, lit a candle, and ushered John into an orderly bedchamber wallpapered in ivy-leaf print. As he stepped onto the plank floor, Miss Bailey's floral scent flooded his senses, which did nothing to calm his unsettled mind.

'Put your hat upon the trunk and have a seat.' Miss Bailey's voice retained some frostiness as she indicated a sitting area on the one side of the room – two green wing chairs facing each other near an unlit hearth. 'I shall ready myself swiftly.'

The trunk upon which John threw his hat gleamed as if recently oiled. Besides it and the armchairs, the only other furniture was a fabric-panelled screen and a spindle-legged table next to a narrow four-poster bed.

John averted his eyes from the bed and strode to a chair. Staring at Miss Bailey's tidy green counterpane and fluffed pillows wouldn't help him in his mission to be a gentleman.

Neither did the rustle of fabric coming from behind the screen as Miss Bailey presumably changed her clothes. John adjusted himself in the seat. He really ought to wait in the alley, but the prospect of asking burly Ben to unlock the gate didn't appeal as much as listening to Miss Bailey's soft movements and melodic humming.

He regretted his decision not to leave as soon as Miss Bailey stepped from behind the screen wearing only her chemise and stays, holding her laces behind her back. 'Will you tie these up for me, Mr Tyrold?'

John remained sitting, since a rigid reaction in his breeches rendered standing inappropriate as long as Miss Bailey stood before him in her underclothing. 'Er, tie them up?' he repeated, rather inanely.

'Please,' she replied. 'If you weren't here, I'd ask my friend, Amanda, for assistance, but I want to keep your presence a secret. Unfortunately, I don't have any that tie in front, since I rarely wear stays. I don't have enough up top to need them.' She indicated her breasts, which were tucked into the two half-moon cups, their upper halves fully displayed.

They looked sufficiently plentiful to John.

'Mr Tyrold?'

John realised he was staring – fully staring – at her bosom. Horrified, he swiftly drew his eyes up.

Her head tilted as she returned his gaze. 'I didn't think you'd mind, given your . . . well, I mean to say, my great-uncles never minded helping me dress.'

Ah, yes, she still mistakenly assumed – or *pretended to believe* – that John was attracted to men.

'Of course,' he said, the words sticking in his throat, because for the love of all things *unholy*, he wanted to take her damned stays *off* rather than tie them up – and enquire if Miss Bailey would like to make use of her bed rather than go out quite yet.

But he couldn't . . .

And besides, she *wouldn't* . . .

On occasion, Miss Bailey had appeared to return the attraction John felt for her, like when she'd gasped, pink-cheeked and mouth parted, when their hands had entwined on the shaving mirror. But, like everyone, she was *self-admittedly* only after John's money. If she was playing a game – one of her *tricks* – with these intimate interactions, she was playing a dangerous one.

'Come here and turn around,' John said, and he didn't arise until she stood with her back to him. He couldn't otherwise hide the bulge in his breeches.

Lacing the stays wasn't the last trial John suffered. Miss Bailey also requested he lace up a low-cut, wine-coloured velvet gown, instructing him to cinch it tightly under her breasts. She glided her stockinged feet into heeled slippers in front of John's chair. Then, glancing into her above-mantel mirror, she removed her locket and pinned a posy of red silk flowers, such as street-walkers sometimes wore, on her bodice.

'Nearly ready, Mr Tyrold.'

Still at the mirror, Miss Bailey lined her eyes with kohl, rubbed rouge into her cheeks and dabbed her lips with blood-red carmine. The effect, although lurid, wasn't settling matters in John's trousers. Miss Bailey was unquestionably more handsome *without* cosmetics, but her breast-bearing gown, smoky eyes, and ruby lips were designed to make a man think of hot, torrid sex.

It was a convincing costume.

The last additions were long black gloves and a garish hat with crimson plumes and a lace veil. 'The idea,' Miss Bailey said, adjusting the veil in the mirror, 'is to disguise my appearance, but not so much that it looks like I'm hiding anything. Does it work?'

She stood for inspection, with red lips pursed. The lace veil obscured her features, but John could still read invitation in her kohl-rimmed eyes, and he had no damned idea how he was going to survive an evening in her company.

'It works,' he said curtly.

Miss Bailey tucked a key into her bodice and adjusted her breasts until they nearly spilled from her gown. 'Dressed thusly,' she purred into her looking glass, 'I've passed old acquaintances, my cousins, my father and the duchess, and our mutual friend Edward, who looked me up and down quite thoroughly. None have recognised me.' She spun towards John, with her black-gloved palm outstretched. 'Let's begone. First stop: my contact in Covent Garden.'

John took her small hand and she lifted her chin to meet his gaze. As if adventures energised her, she displayed her roguish grin, her smoky eyes gleaming. Despite the garish cosmetics, to John she was still unmistakably the elegant young lady who'd mesmerised him from their first moment of meeting.

Standing before him now, she was utterly ravishing.

Which settled matters. John must inform Miss Bailey he was neither harmless to her virtue *nor* susceptible to her tricks. In a public place where matters couldn't possibly progress too far, he'd demonstrate where his sexual attractions lay . . . but he'd have to take care not to reveal how much he liked *her* specifically, or she *would* set her cap for him.

Then John would face a formidable foe, indeed.

8

Tyrold was pleasant during the walk, playing the role of Georgiana's fancy man admirably, with his arm tucking her securely against his chest, and Georgiana delighted in it more than she should. She breathed in his scent of pipe tobacco and shaving soap, as intoxicating as drink, and pressed the side of her face against his upper chest, relishing the feel of broadcloth on her cheek, telling herself she was playing a part.

The walk between Soho and Covent Garden was treacherous at night. Rodents scurried amongst the filth littering the dark streets, and unsavoury characters lurked in the shadows of dilapidated buildings. There were pawn shops and rag-dealers, their doors dim and barred, but most of the area's business occurred under the cover of darkness. Usually, Georgiana took a hackney to the Piazza because of the danger, but no one accosted her on Tyrold's arm.

A woman could grow accustomed to something like this, she thought, sighing softly against his coat as they arrived at last at the Piazza, which was bustling with noise from riotous merry-makers and gleaming with the brilliant blaze of countless streetlamps and torches.

A woman other than *her*, of course.

Tyrold glanced at the clock on the portico of St Paul's Church. 'Why did you wish to venture out so late?'

'Because Covent Garden awakens at half past ten. Keep your arm about me, please. I shall lead you.' Georgiana pulled Tyrold's lapel like reins, directing him into the undulating crowds that smelled of liquor and ale, damp wool and sweat. She passed between two street musicians: a violinist and a ballad girl, delighting everyone with *different* tunes. A foppish, drunken lout with shirt collars to his cheekbones attempted to accost the singer, while another dandy assigned himself the role of her champion. Prostitutes and young men called to each other, their voices mingling with the songs of peddlers pushing wheelbarrows of pies, and the cadences of fruit and flower girls selling oranges and posies. After edging to the periphery of the action, Georgiana navigated Tyrold around a mountain of pungent horse dung and other debris the street sweepers had piled to the side of the Piazza, ready for the cartman to shovel up. 'We're heading towards Russell Street,' she said as they continued through the jostling pedestrians. 'But hold me even tighter and keep your head down. Anyone here could recognise you, even with your short hair and that hat.'

'I thought, Miss Bai—'

'Shh!' She stopped walking and placed a hand on his chest. 'Don't use my real name.'

He leant close and whispered, 'What should I call you then?'

Georgiana met his gaze. Since he was looking down, and they stood in a half-embrace, her hand on his chest, and no more than a hairsbreadth between them, she realised they must look like two lovers about to kiss. Her eyes trailed involuntarily to his lips before she forced them up, her heart racing. 'Call me Georgie.'

'Georgie?' he said, and then he repeated it, slowly, as if savouring the word, and something changed in his voice. It was huskier, deeper. It reverberated in Georgiana's core, like a throbbing in hidden places.

'Yes.' She licked her lips. Her mouth was as dry as the desert. 'Georgie.'

Tyrold lifted his hand, cupped her neck and ran his thumb along her jawline. 'How adorable.'

The unexpected caress robbed Georgiana of the ability to breathe, and she found herself leaning into his embrace for support. Lord, but Tyrold was acting his part extremely well. 'And excuse the liberty,' her voice emerged hoarse, 'but I shall call you John.'

He cocked an eyebrow, his eyes gleaming under his hat's shadow. 'John? You get a nickname and I do not?'

He continued to stroke her cheek with his thumb. He might as well have poured whisky down her throat, so strong was the effect. 'There's no need for you to have a nickname,' she replied, their eyes locked as she murmured the words. 'John is a disguise in itself. One man in five is called John.'

He brought his mouth to her ear, lifting her lace veil so nothing came between their faces. 'I could be Jack, a roguish fellow, if you like. Isn't that more fun?'

'Fun? Since when are we having fun?' Georgiana murmured against his cheek, the feel of his skin against hers every bit as sensuous as she'd imagined while he'd shaved.

'Oh, my sweet dear.' Tyrold chuckled, long and low, his thumb caressing her jaw, his lips against her cheek. 'Jack is having a great deal of fun right now. Surely you are beginning to understand that he's a scoundrel when he holds a lady of pleasure in his arms. He wants you, Georgie. In the way a man wants a woman when there are no societal constraints to hold them back from pleasure.'

'He wants me?' Georgiana repeated, her mind as muddled as mud. She could make little sense of what was happening, other than that Tyrold was playing his role very well indeed, and her body was happy to respond, for she was melting like wax in his arms. 'You needn't pretend this thoroughly, sir. No one is watching us *that* closely.'

'I couldn't care less what others are doing.' Tyrold's voice rumbled low in her ear, but his tone had changed. No longer did his words caress her like hot silk. Now there was a hard edge, a sharpness. 'I'm thinking only of you.'

Georgiana stiffened. 'You're a better actor than I realised,' she said, trying to make light of what suddenly felt uncomfortable. 'Anyone would think I'd *actually* aroused your interest.'

His hand slid over her shoulder blades and down, coming to rest in the dip at the small of her back, and, when he spoke, his lips were on the curve of her ear, his breath hot against her skin. 'Press closer and you can judge my state of arousal for yourself.'

Georgiana froze, her heart thumping so violently she felt its vibrations in her throat, her mind swirling. 'But you . . . but Edward said . . .'

'Good God, woman,' Tyrold snapped in her ear. 'Forget what you think Edward said and use your considerable intelligence to assess the current situation. Otherwise, I shall know beyond doubt that this is a game to you.'

'A game?' she asked, baffled. 'Finding your ward is not a game, sir—'

'It had better not be,' he interrupted. 'But to ensure there's no more confusion, let me explain: when a woman – any tolerable-looking woman, so don't let this go to your head – undresses in front of me or fondles her own breasts or asks me to hold her as if we were lovers, my reaction will be the same as any man who is wholly and *only* attracted to women.'

Then realisation fully dawned, and Georgiana's stomach heaved. She had utterly, horribly, and dreadfully mistaken matters. Mortified, she squirmed against his embrace.

Tyrold released her instantly and shoved his hands into his pockets. 'That's a clever girl,' he growled. 'Keep your distance from now on. Much safer for both of us.'

Blazing fury conquered Georgiana's humiliation. How dare he be so patronising after he'd purposefully let her continue in her misconception? Yet she bit back the impulse to unleash a violent reprimand for his boorish behaviour, because, although no one in the packed Piazza paid them any mind, the middle of Covent Garden on a busy spring night was hardly the place to make a scene.

So she contented herself with something short and sweet. 'Go to the devil.'

And then she turned on her heel and stomped across the square towards her destination, fists clenched and not giving the least damn whether Tyrold followed her. She'd find his ward on her own, and he could go hang, for all she cared . . .

Except he couldn't.

Because Georgiana needed his money.

No humiliation was too great to bear for Monica House.

She stopped hunch-shouldered in a deserted corner under the colonnade and hugged herself as she waited for him to catch up. The noise of a drunken crowd emanated from a nearby tavern, but no one stood close. When Tyrold's booted footsteps sounded behind her, she glanced over her shoulder. 'Answer me this: what did Edward mean when he said you were not interested in any women, at all, ever?'

Tyrold shrugged. 'I assume he meant that, unlike him, I don't give in to the wiles of every woman willing to shake her breasts in my face – and there are *many* willing to do so, not just you.' Georgiana's face burned. That *wasn't* what she'd done. She simply hadn't wanted her key to slip out. 'Besides,' Tyrold continued. 'Edward is my friend, but he is an idiot.'

Georgiana bristled, but rather than snap the infantile reply that popped into her mind ('Better an idiot than an asinine prick'), she faced Tyrold, chin high. 'He's not. In fact, he's much cleverer than he lets on. And he's one of the most honest men I've ever known.'

Tyrold snorted. 'He's a jackass, and the least moral man in London.'

'He seeks pleasure and pleasure only, but at least he doesn't pretend to be what he's not. You, on the other hand, encouraged my false impression, which led me to assume a level of comfort with you I would never otherwise assume. Why did you do that? Did you find it amusing to silently mock my mistake?'

'I had my reasons,' he growled. 'And at least I mentioned it before you asked me to undress you and tuck you into bed, or whatever you had in mind for later tonight. Now *you* answer me *this*: did you think you'd trick me into marriage with this evening's pageantry? Is that what your coffeehouse friend meant?'

Georgiana frowned, not comprehending until she realised Tyrold must've understood her conversation with Maria DeRosa. Then her fury resurged with newfound force because Maria's 'tricks' referred to the very thing that had caused Georgiana's heartbreak. 'You're a vile, contemptible man,' she said, her voice shaking with anger. 'And you ought to be ashamed of yourself.'

Tyrold's brows shot up. 'Me? Ashamed of myself?'

'Yes!' Georgiana put her hands on her hips. 'Because you imply I was lying when I told you I don't want to marry.'

'Well, perhaps you were.' Tyrold shrugged. 'You certainly wouldn't refuse *me* if I offered.'

Georgiana drew back with a furious gasp. 'Are you truly so conceited?'

'No, but unlike Edward, I'm not an idiot,' he replied, with maddening nonchalance. 'Your account book shows how desperately Monica House needs money, so to refuse me would be foolish, and I have a higher opinion of your intelligence than that.'

'What nonsense,' Georgiana countered. 'Such a ridiculous conclusion shows me that you know nothing about anything.'

He gave a vexing little chuckle. 'Are you suggesting I misjudged your intelligence?'

'I'm suggesting you're the fool, sir! Marrying you would be the worst possible thing I could do for Monica House.'

'Indeed?' he asked, but Georgiana noted with satisfaction that he no longer seemed quite as amused.

'Yes,' she said, feeling her triumph. Tyrold obviously considered himself perfect and desirable, and it would do him good to hear the truth. 'I would feel sorry for any woman who married you. No doubt you'd dispense her pin money in driblets and force her to account for every penny of the household expenses. I have no interest in such a life, sir, nor do I need it. I shall get all the money I require once I find your ward, because you all too easily capitulated to my demands during negotiations. I'd rather scour London on my hands and knees than marry a parsimonious bully like you. You're hateful and horrid, and not nearly as clever as you think.'

A dangerously dark scowl descended upon Tyrold's face. 'Well, if that's your opinion, madam, it's fortunate I shan't ask. And if you mean to scour London, you'd better get on with it. We accomplish nothing arguing; meanwhile, my ward is at the mercy of a villain.'

That was true, and Georgiana's fury retreated. Somewhere in London was a girl who needed her help. The children of Monica House needed a school. Their wants were far more significant than a quarrel with an irritating man.

She'd tolerate Tyrold for their sakes.

'Follow me, *Jack*.'

Georgiana strode out of the Piazza and east along Russell Street. At the first junction, she turned south, away from Bow Street and onto Charles Street, which was lined with relatively reputable brothels catering to wealthy clients on the west side.

She stopped before Number Six. Music spilled from an open window on the ground floor, meaning that performances were underway at Galatea's House of Opera Buffa, a word play on comic opera and the state of undress in which the women performed.

'We begin here,' Georgiana said, climbing the first step.

Tyrold didn't follow. He hung back, silhouetted against a streetlamp.

'Well? Are you coming with me or not?' Georgiana asked.

Tyrold cleared his throat. 'Why here?' he asked, his tone subdued.

'Because Galatea is the contact I mentioned earlier. She is a kind and honest woman who knows much what of happens in Covent Garden. I know this establishment looks disreputable,' Georgiana acknowledged, for Galatea's sign depicted a nude opera singer with prominent hips and breasts. 'But it's not a brothel. It's a theatre, only performed—'

'Yes, yes. I know what it is.' Tyrold put a hand to the back of his neck. 'However, since you wish to keep our connection secret, be aware that I can't go in without being recognised. Even with the haircut.'

'Oh!' Georgiana exclaimed, understanding at last. So Tyrold patronised Galatea's establishment. She certainly couldn't blame him; she'd watched two or three performances herself over the years and found them excellent. Most of the women were actresses, dancers, and chorus girls in London's best theatres, who wished to earn extra income without *having* to resort to prostitution – although Georgiana suspected many of them chose to have arrangements with regular patrons.

'It will be fine,' she concluded after a moment's reflection. 'We shan't venture into the theatre. Simply keep your head down in the entrance vestibule and on the stairs. The footman knows me. He'll lead us to Galatea's private sitting room immediately, and we can trust Galatea not to utter a word to anyone.'

There was a brief pause.

Then Tyrold waved his hand, ushering her forwards. 'In that case, lead on, Georgie.'

With his hat brim shadowing his face, Georgiana couldn't see the millionaire's expression. But she thought she detected amusement in his voice.

9

John suppressed laughter as he followed Miss Bailey through Galatea's steamy entrance hall and climbed the stairs, keeping his head low and shielding his face with one hand to his hat brim. It amused him that, of all the places in London, Miss Bailey was beginning their search at his former lover's establishment.

It was also immensely satisfying, because when Miss Bailey witnessed the warm manner in which Galatea was certain to receive John, she'd realise that not *all* women found him horrid, vile, and contemptible.

During their first meeting in Hyde Park, John had wanted Miss Bailey to speak to him without sycophancy or flattery. Well, she'd certainly done that tonight by giving him a tongue-lashing such as he'd never received from any woman. As a result, John no longer suspected her of having motives towards him. She'd made it sufficiently clear that she despised him, and she certainly wasn't cowed into deferential behaviour by the enticement of his wealth.

It was oddly refreshing – *but* it also made John determined to prove she'd misjudged him.

When the footman closed the door to Galatea's private receiving room, leaving John alone with Miss

Bailey, every nerve in his body was alert, heightened, aware of the growing complexity of his sentiments towards her. The gold-and-black chinoiserie chamber was a room John had associated with carnal pleasure for fifteen years, and seeing smoky-eyed Miss Bailey grace it in her revealing gown did nothing to calm his attraction to her.

She perched primly upon an ebonised bamboo chair, her lips pursed.

John leant against a Chinese dragon carved into the black marble mantelpiece and extracted his pipe and copper cleaner from his pocket. 'I wasn't aware that Galatea is a Covent Garden spy,' he ventured, wanting to clear his mind of inappropriate thoughts with conversation.

'There's much that Galatea's gentlemen patrons don't know about her,' Miss Bailey replied, her manner still frosty. 'For example, her name is Betty Brown and she's from Northumberland.'

This was news to John. He busied himself with tapping his spent tobacco into the fire, hoping Miss Bailey couldn't perceive his surprise. 'And how did the daughter of the Duke of Amesbury become acquainted with Betty Brown from Northumberland?'

'Betty is my godmother.'

'*Your godmother*?' John exclaimed, with no attempt to hide his astonishment.

'Yes.' Miss Bailey folded her hands in her lap. 'Thirty years ago, my godmother arrived in London, a girl with nothing to her name but a beautiful voice and dreams of the stage. She met a woman at the coaching inn who claimed to work for a stage manager.'

John grimaced as he withdrew his tobacco pouch from his pocket. 'A procuress?' he queried, though he knew the answer.

'Of course,' Miss Bailey replied. 'But Betty was an innocent and trusting fourteen-year-old from a country village who knew nothing of such matters. She happily followed that woman, and soon found herself imprisoned at a brothel.'

'Good God,' John muttered, feeling deeply for his former lover. He'd had no idea of her sufferings.

'Betty's story ends far better than most. She escaped almost immediately, though she had nothing but the clothing on her back. She was too innocent to realise that a girl with no money and no character reference alone on the streets of London is in even a more precarious situation than in a brothel, but, by tremendously good fortune, she soon heard of Monica House. She went there for a short recuperation; not many months later, she took the stage name Galatea and became a chorus singer at the King's Theatre in the Haymarket, where she worked for almost two decades.'

'That part I *did* know,' John said, tamping fresh tobacco into the oak burl bowl of his pipe.

'Do you also know that my mother was a soprano at the King's Theatre for a few years?'

John acknowledged that he did.

'Betty and my mother became friends. After my mother's death, I was raised at Monica House, and

Betty visited me often, always bringing me little gifts, like marzipan and roasted chestnuts. She even provided my earliest singing lessons.'

Miss Bailey looked down at her folded hands, a smile playing on her lips, as if lost in childhood memories. It was some time before John realised he was staring at her inanely, his forgotten pipe and tobacco hanging listlessly in his hands.

As he hastily returned his tobacco pouch to his pocket, his conscience twinged. Galatea was a mother figure to Miss Bailey. The charity worker might find it decidedly awkward to learn the nature of her godmother's relationship with John, if sprung on her without warning, while in company with both of them.

John fiddled with his unlit pipe. 'Er, Miss Bailey, perhaps I should mention something before your godmother arrives—'

But the door handle clicked before he could finish, and Galatea entered the chamber, her back to John. She was attired with her customary extravagance in a gown of dark blue silk spangled with faux constellations. Diamond star brooches sparkled on her turban and cerulean-dyed ostrich feathers curled over her head.

'Ah, Georgiana, my heart's delight,' she crooned as she closed the door. 'I've not seen you in weeks.' Her voice had a decidedly Northern accent, which John had never heard before. 'Where have you been, pet?'

She stretched her arms wide and swept across the room as Miss Bailey rose to meet her and nestled into her embrace.

'I've a new scheme for fundraising which consumes much of my time,' Miss Bailey explained when they'd kissed cheeks.

'Any success?' Galatea asked.

'Soon, Betty,' Miss Bailey replied, her eyes moving towards John and drawing Galatea's gaze with them, so that John felt the scrutiny of both women upon him at the same time.

Even as intimately as Galatea knew John, a cloud of confusion washed over her face for a moment before her jaw dropped. 'Why, it's *John*!'

John swallowed hard and glanced at Miss Bailey. Her dark eyes met his, darted to Galatea, and then a deep blush rose from her bosom, over her neck, and up her rouged cheeks. Of course, as exceptionally intelligent and observant as she was, she'd realised *everything* the moment Galatea used John's given name.

Meanwhile, Galatea flew to John's side, threaded her arm around his and raised herself on tiptoes. 'It is the greatest pleasure to see you, lovey,' she whispered, low so only he could hear, her lips tickling his ear. 'I trust you read my letter?'

'Your letter?' John repeated, rather stupidly. 'I, er, I'm behind with my correspondence.'

''Tis of no consequence! I wrote to inform you that I did as I promised I would.'

'As you promised?' John queried, his mind unchar-acteristically dull.

'Regarding your new lover.'

Only then did John recall that when Galatea had

informed him of her upcoming nuptials, she'd laughed away his surprise by telling him she'd find him a discreet new lover. He'd feigned interest in her assistance, but only to disguise the fact that the abrupt end to their affair had affected him more than he could have imagined. But many months had passed since that day, and he'd long since forgotten about her promise. He'd tried not to think of Galatea or lovers at all, the better to pretend he hadn't missed her casual but comfortable presence in his life.

'It just so happens,' Galatea continued, 'that the woman I wrote of is performing later tonight. I shall introduce you—'

John hastened to step back. 'No, no,' he said, glancing across the room. Miss Bailey no longer looked at them. She'd sat again, eyes down, and was picking at an invisible thread on her velvet skirts. 'No, thank you, Galatea. I-I don't require that, er, service any more.'

Something tugged at John's heart as he observed Miss Bailey. At the moment, she had little of her usual confidence. In fact, she seemed almost vulnerable – a young lady dressed to appear as if she belonged to the world of prostitution for the sake of their search tonight, but unmistakably not of it.

John's failure to disclose his connection with her godmother had put her in an awkward position, and he regretted his actions immensely. The best thing now would be to remove himself from the room, to allow godmother and goddaughter freedom to talk intimately without his presence adding an uncomfortable element.

John spoke to Galatea. 'I should go. Georgie can explain our business better without me here.'

'Ah, I understand now,' Galatea said, although what she understood, John wasn't certain because he'd shifted his attention back to Miss Bailey.

She was watching them, her dark eyes alert, and John crossed the room in a few long strides, arranging his expression into what he hoped indicated his regret in putting her in an awkward situation. 'I shall wait for you outside, Georgie. You don't need my assistance here.' A sudden stroke of genius inspired him to add, 'After all, you *are* the better negotiator.'

Her smile illuminated the room, and John felt a warm rush of satisfaction in knowing his compliment had delighted her.

'You admit that?' she asked.

John stuck his pipe in his mouth. 'Unreservedly.'

She nodded, her expression as pleased as a cat in the cream. 'I'm pleased to hear it. Now, take that pipe out of your mouth. You mustn't smoke while you wait for me.'

John blinked, uncertain if she was teasing. 'You cannot be serious?'

'Oh, but I am.' She extended her hand, palm up. 'I shall keep your pipe, to reduce temptation.'

John protested. 'Why on earth may I not smoke?'

She stood, boldly plucked the pipe from his mouth, and spoke with authority. 'Because this pipe is distinctive. Besides, you're the only gentleman in London under the age of sixty who still takes a pipe rather than snuff. It's as much a declaration of your identity as was your old-fashioned queue or your dreadful brown hat.'

John's lips twitched, but he kept his laughter at bay. 'So I should procure snuff instead while I wait for you?'

'Of course not,' Miss Bailey scolded. 'All tobacco is a deplorable habit. Purchase an orange from a fruit seller in the Piazza. And overpay her.'

John shook his head in mock despair. 'Good God. I don't recall agreeing to let you dictate my pastimes.'

She sat again, folding her hands around his pipe, and smiled prettily. 'I hope you enjoy your orange, Jack.'

When John stepped out of the room a moment later, having bid Galatea a good evening, he allowed himself a moment's pause against the closed door, a smile on his own face, before dashing down the stairs.

That hadn't gone quite as planned, but he suspected he'd redeemed himself somewhat – even if only a *very* little – after his abhorrent behaviour in the Piazza, when he accused her of trickery.

Georgiana stared at the door after Tyrold left. She squeezed the bowl of his pipe, the smell of his tobacco tickling her nose, and wondered if he truly had been – as she suspected – trying to make amends for his reprehensible actions in the Piazza, when he'd teased her with tender caresses and sweet murmurings before falsely accusing her of wishing to shackle herself to him in exchange for his beastly gold.

She cast an exasperated look at her godmother, who'd lifted her meticulously groomed brows to her turban's edge. 'So. You and King Midas, eh?'

Betty raised her hands in a gesture of surrender. 'Not for over a year, pet. And although he is lovely, ours was never an affair of the *heart*. He appreciated my discretion; I profited immensely from his financial advice. But I ended everything with John when Mr Robinson proposed.'

'*John.*' Georgiana rolled her eyes, bristling despite herself. She knew her godmother could be trusted with confidences – of course, Betty would keep her affairs with prominent men secret, if the men wished it. Still, for some reason it rankled that she hadn't known of her godmother's connection to Tyrold.

'Forgive me, Georgiana.'

'Oh, no need for that,' Georgiana said, suddenly ashamed she'd let her feelings get the better of her. 'Truly, I have nothing to forgive, Betty. Naturally you may do as you please, and it's no affair of mine. I was merely surprised.'

Betty grimaced slightly. 'I was asking for forgiveness for what I said to him. Before he tells you, 'tis best I confess – I offered to introduce him to a performer whom I thought he would like. Naturally, I wouldn't have mentioned it if I'd known he is your lover.'

Georgiana choked. '*My lover?*' she repeated, equal parts appalled and diverted. 'John Tyrold isn't my lover, of course.'

Betty pursed her lips, blinking as if she didn't believe Georgiana.

'He's *not*.' Georgiana reiterated this with a note of finality. Finding it difficult to continue to meet her godmother's gaze, she traced a swirl in the oak burl with her gloved finger and thought over what Betty had said. 'Out of curiosity, why did you think he'd like that *particular* performer?'

Betty seated herself in a chaise longue, her silk skirts rustling as she settled. 'Well, he's looking for a mistress, but a man like him requires a certain level of discretion. And a very specific understanding.'

'What understanding?' Georgiana asked, unable to control her curiosity.

Betty shrugged. 'Desire. He deems it important that there be real desire, on both sides, as well as mutual affection and respect. He rejects women who approach him expecting gifts or money, no matter how beautiful they are.'

Georgiana scoffed. 'No wonder one doesn't hear his name linked with any lovers. If he wants women to desire him, he really ought to make himself more likeable.'

'But that's just it, pet.'

'What is?' Georgiana asked, frustrated. 'You're speaking in riddles.'

'I merely mean that he improves on acquaintance, but one must go to considerable, determined effort to gain that acquaintance. And, lest you mistakenly think him stingy, once he became my lover, I only ever found him immensely generous, in *every* way a man can be.'

Georgiana recoiled with a grimace. '*Phah*! Tyrold between your legs is *not* an image I need in my mind, dearest godmother.' But secretly, she felt a little thrill imagining Tyrold's generosity as a lover.

A knowing glint come to Betty's eye, as if she guessed the turn of Georgiana's thoughts. 'Are you aware that he likes singers, as a rule? The performer I hoped to introduce him to is quite good. Nothing like your ma, of course, but no one is. No one except *you*,' she added with a sly smile.

Georgiana's tingling feeling intensified. Tyrold did like her – specifically *her*, despite what he'd said in the Piazza about 'any tolerable-looking woman'. She hadn't imagined the mutual attraction which had seemed to sizzle between them multiple times. It was a very real thing.

But that wasn't *good*, she realised, for it would make working together more challenging than it already was. She fiddled with the velvet folds of her skirt, aligning them neatly, as if making order of the fabric would ease the agitation of her mind, and wondered how she'd repair matters.

Betty's voice drew Georgiana from her reverie. 'Are you in love with him, pet?'

'*What?*' Georgiana asked, truly appalled that Betty had arrived at such a fantastical conclusion. 'Of course not! I only met him a fortnight ago, and we've barely spoken until tonight.'

Embarrassed by her heated face, she lifted her skirts to her knee and tucked Tyrold's pipe into her garter for safekeeping, as if her godmother's words had no effect on her. She licked her lips, readying herself to ask about Flora.

154

But Betty spoke first. 'It's clear as a silver bell that you want him. Are you trying to catch him for a husband?'

'I'm not trying to *catch* him,' Georgiana said primly. 'I'm *helping* him. In exchange for his support for Monica House. Which brings me to why I've come.'

As Georgiana delved into the details about Tyrold's ward, Betty sobered and listened attentively, maintaining complete silence; at Georgiana's description of Flora, she gasped.

'Well, now,' she exclaimed, pressing her hands to her mountainous bosom. 'Copper curls, you say? Don't be getting your hopes up, but evidently, there is a girl fitting that description at Mother Harris's establishment on Tavistock Street. But I didn't write to you about it because I didn't hear that she was in any trouble.'

The news elevated Georgiana's hopes, though not without reservations. Mother Harris ran a brothel notorious for providing deviant forms of sexual gratification, and she despised Georgiana, believing her to be a meddling rival who stole girls. It would be difficult indeed to make enquiries at her establishment.

The more information Georgiana could gather beforehand, the better, so she urged her godmother to reveal everything she knew.

'There's little to tell,' Betty replied. 'If you hadn't mentioned copper curls, I wouldn't have thought of it. A week or so ago, I overheard Lord Murden and Mr Hawkins inform a group of my gentlemen patrons that Mother Harris's whore, Maud Whiplash, isn't working right now because she's protecting a ladylike virgin with copper curls. They reckoned there was either going to be an auction or that Mother Harris intended the chit for a gentleman's mistress. Mind you, I suspect it's coincidence – they said the girl was a high-spirited, cheery, friendly thing. I wasn't in the least concerned.'

High-spirited was *exactly* Georgiana's impression of Flora, based on Tyrold's description. And the girl might indeed be cheery – at least initially – after escaping from school with a young man she fancied. 'It's too coincidental for me not to enquire, although it's a shame it's Mother Harris.' Georgiana worried her bottom lip, wondering how best to approach the investigation. 'She won't let me talk to any of her girls.'

'You've got a partner, haven't you? Get John to enquire.'

Georgiana arched an eyebrow. 'Easier said than done. A vicious old busybody like Mother Harris would know John Tyrold at a glance.'

Betty dismissed her concern with a wave of her hand. 'By this time every night, that bitch is on the opium or well into the bottle. Her footman handles the business after that. He's a nasty sort but none too clever. John simply needs to pay up as a customer and glean what he can from whichever girl he gets. You likely won't want him playing sweet with a whore, jealous little kitten that you are—'

'To clarify, I'm *not* jealous,' Georgiana objected. 'I'd have to like Tyrold to be jealous and I *don't* like him.' *Not much, anyway.* 'He's curt and rude and abominably conceited.'

'And yet he permitted you to take his pipe, and I'd wager he's outside eating an orange right now.' Betty laughed. 'As I said, he improves on acquaintance – when he wishes to. And, anyway, have some compassion for the poor dear. He must be distraught. I reckon the girl's his daughter.'

Georgiana recoiled, thoroughly shocked. Despite their sharing a surname and eye colour, it had not previously occurred to her that Flora might be Tyrold's daughter, but, then again, until half an hour ago, she had believed him uninterested in women.

'I don't know about that, Betty. It's quite clear that she's a relation, but he referred to her as his ward, not his daughter,' she remarked pointedly, as if doing so would ensure this wasn't another case of a father neglecting his parental responsibilities.

Betty raised a knowing eyebrow. 'This surprises you, of all people? Weren't you eighteen before your father's family found out about *you*?'

'Yes,' Georgiana replied, her heart heavy.

'There you have it, then. Men often conceal such matters for as long as possible. But mark my words, she is indeed his daughter, born of that lady he mourns.'

Georgiana's surprise grew. 'What lady? Another secret mistress?'

Betty leant forwards, clearly relishing the opportunity to share her gossip. 'No. She was a *lady*. A Miss Jennings, I understand. Of considerable fortune.'

Georgiana tilted her head, considering. 'That *is* the other surname Tyrold gave for his ward.'

'Ah, I knew it!' Betty exclaimed, as if that alone proved Flora's paternity. 'When I first made his acquaintance fifteen years ago, he was only just becoming the marvel that he is. Some hailed him as a prodigy, but most said his success would not stand the test of time.' She sat up straight, her eyes glittering. '*I* knew he was remarkable, however. I knew because of how he watched the opera. He never missed an opening night, and he'd sit on one of the first benches in the pit, oblivious to those around him – the drunkards, the jeerers, the catcallers. I had just come into a little bequest from a dearly departed lover, and one evening, after the performance, I approached him, asking if I might call at his lodgings, to hear his opinion on how I should invest my newfound wealth. In those days, John wasn't yet wary of such approaches. He was kind, warm, complimentary of my performance, and, well, one thing soon led to another, for I found myself very attracted to him, despite his youth. But, that first time, I expected . . .' She trailed off, waving her hand. 'Oh, a schoolboy. Someone I would have to teach, someone who'd need instruction. That wasn't the case. John knew exactly what to do with a woman's body – the beginning, the middle and the *multiple* ends. No fumbling, no searching, no mistaking one hole for another, no touching this place or that, thinking it was something else altogether.'

When her godmother paused, Georgiana realised she'd been holding her breath. Heated embarrassment crept over her skin. She didn't want to hear these intimate details about Tyrold, and yet she did.

Betty continued. 'Afterwards I said to him, "Who taught you how to do *that*?" And, pet, he went pale. "The young lady I loved," said he, after a time. Or something to that effect, rendered in a tone so mournful it broke my heart. "We learnt together, she and I" – those words he most certainly said. And – remember, he was hardly more than a boy – he hugged himself, his whole body shaking, like he was holding back tears. "She's dead?" asked I, and he looked so sorrowful I worried he'd be ashamed later. I didn't wish to frighten him away. "I shouldn't have asked," said I then. "And I shan't ever again." And so I never have.'

'How then do you know the lady's name?' Georgiana asked, still sceptical.

Betty chuckled. 'I made enquiries of his friend Lord Edward, when that darling scamp was in his cups one night. "A Miss Jennings, of considerable fortune," his lordship declared, before hastening to tell me – no doubt remorseful that he'd broken his friend's confidence – that it was a trifling matter, a calf-love, long over and never of any significance. But I knew it couldn't be so. I knew she was the lover John mourned at eighteen, and now you tell me – fifteen years later – that he has a fifteen-year-old ward who bears his name, with eyes like his, whose mother is dead, and whose surname is both Jennings and Tyrold.'

Georgiana rubbed her palms on her velvet skirts. The revelation that Flora was likely Tyrold's daughter did not fill her with warm feelings, even if he mourned her mother. Perhaps it was common practice for wealthy men to hide secret daughters at schools, but that was no excuse. Tyrold should love the girl. Every day, he should give her the tender, protective embraces that would help her to know she mattered, that she was his darling. He should soothe away nightmares when they came, so she learnt that nothing could hurt her when her father was nearby. Make her a home, laugh at her jokes, listen with rapt attention to her hopes and dreams . . . and all the things a father *ought* to do with his motherless, lonely daughter.

She swallowed back a sudden, hard lump in her throat. 'Well, whether or not she's his daughter matters little to my search. I should get on with it, for the poor child's sake.' She stood, steadying herself as she rose because her legs felt shaky. 'Thank you, Betty.'

Betty stood as well, taking Georgiana's hand in both of hers. 'Thank *you*, pet. You know I think you're an angel.'

'I'm not so remarkable,' Georgiana replied. She had to do what she did, for peace of mind and heart.

Betty enfolded her into her motherly, perfumed embrace. 'Ah, yes, you are, pet. Bless you for the work you do. Your ma's heart must burst with pride up in heaven.'

When Georgiana stepped onto Charles Street two minutes later, the cool air provided relief from her godmother's stifling drawing room and disconcerting conversation. Feeling unsettled, she held on to the railing and took deep breaths as she scanned Charles Street for Tyrold, but he was nowhere in sight.

'Did you find out anything?' Tyrold's voice sounded in her left ear, making her fly out of her skin.

She pressed her hands to her hammering heart. 'Oh, Lord! You gave me a fright.'

He stepped up from the servants' stairwell and joined her on the pavement, his face furrowed with concern. 'Forgive me,' he said, brushing the back of her shoulder. 'I lurked in the shadows because a few acquaintances have passed by. Besides, I didn't think anything frightened you.'

His words inspired a flicker of pride, but the truth was she was flustered after the confusing events of the last hour. Betty's unsettling conversation replayed in her mind, making it difficult to meet Tyrold's green-eyed gaze.

Yet she didn't want to appear missish. 'You're correct.' She lifted her chin. 'I chose my words poorly. You *startled* me.'

'So, *did* you find out anything?' His flat tone indicated he had little hope of a positive answer.

'Perhaps,' Georgiana said, shifting her weight.

He brightened. 'Truly? There's hope?'

Georgiana held up a finger. 'I said perhaps. I need your assistance to discover more.'

'As it happens, I excel at following your commands, woman.' Tyrold grinned as he extracted an orange and a penknife from his pocket. 'I already ate one, so this orange is for you. I shall peel it as you tell me what I must do.'

Though still unsettled by his agreeableness, Georgiana relayed what she'd learnt from Betty.

'So I am to pretend to be the sort of boorish man who'd frequent Mother Harris's?' Tyrold asked, tossing the peel into the gutter.

'You are more likely to succeed than I, but if you truly don't want to—'

'I don't.' He handed her an orange segment. 'But I will, of course. Believe it or not, I'd do anything for Flora. And I already have boorishness perfected.'

It was gratifying to hear him say he'd do anything for Flora, but why then hadn't he made the child a home? Georgiana chewed the orange and considered. Perhaps helping Tyrold and Flora become the family they ought to be was something else she could do to help. Because every opportunity she found to do . . .

'Good?' Tyrold asked.

She looked up. 'What?'

'The orange.' He gave her another slice.

'It's lovely, yes.' She popped the segment in her mouth, observing him closely as she considered asking him to explain his relationship to Flora. But she didn't; not yet. She'd wait until she thought him ready to talk about it, ready to be receptive to advice.

It wasn't until Tyrold handed her another orange slice that she realised she'd been staring intently at him all the while. 'A penny for your thoughts?' he asked with a half-smile.

Georgiana shook her head. 'I don't charge for my thoughts, Jack. I dispense them for free, but only when I choose.' She gathered the rest of the orange from his hand, her fingers brushing his. 'Which is fortunate for you, because if I *did* charge, I'd decide my fee according to ability to pay. *Your* rate would be one hundred guineas per idea.'

His half-smile spread into his eye-crinkling grin, once again disarming Georgiana with its sweetness.

To counter its effects, she teased. 'But since you enquired *nicely*, I shall share some of my thoughts. I understand there's an opening, for lack of a better word, for the position – my heavens, there's another unfortunate word choice – of your mistress.'

He visibly started, and then either choked or coughed. While he was recovering his breath, Georgiana nibbled the edge of an orange slice. 'Provided,' she continued, 'said mistress adores your unpleasant disposition and has no interest whatsoever in your millions.'

'Good Lord, woman,' he muttered. 'You don't mince words, do you?'

She swallowed her orange. 'You *did* ask for my thoughts.'

He stuck a finger under his cravat, tugging upon the knot she'd set. 'Mistress isn't the word I'd choose. It implies an inequality I'm uncomfortable with.'

'And is there not always an element of inequality between a man like yourself, who possesses all the world's advantages, and *every* woman, in our society?'

'I didn't always possess all the world's advantages, as you say. I worked for my money.'

'I doubt the heir to an ancient Yorkshire estate worked for his money the way most women do,' Georgiana countered. 'Rather than speak of equality, you'd do better to acknowledge your advantages, and then use them to help others.'

Tyrold drew his brows together fiercely. 'Although it's none of your business what I do with my money, allow me to assure you I give thousands every year to relieve the sufferings of the poor, although I don't empty my pockets into the hands of every single charity worker the moment that she accosts me in Hyde Park with her demands.'

Undaunted, Georgiana persisted. 'But you can afford to give *more*. With your resources, you could open training schools and fund businesses allowing women opportunities to earn a living wage in employment that doesn't put their lives at risk from disease, childbirth and violence. There are precious few such options available.'

She concluded her speech by popping her last piece of orange in her mouth.

Tyrold scowl deepened. 'Evidently, you're determined to be displeased with everything about me,' he said angrily. 'So be it, then, because I shan't defend my stance on charity, just as I shan't defend my stance on the women with whom I choose to consort, and on what terms our arrangements stand. Besides, other than getting myself a wife – which you've implied would be nothing short of torture for any lady – what would you have me do better?'

Georgiana grabbed his right wrist and held his hand aloft. 'You could use this. That's what spinsters do.'

Tyrold's brows shot skyward.

Then he snorted with laughter and, despite herself, Georgiana felt a desire to smile. But she dropped his hand and covered her mouth with the back of hers, so he couldn't see her amusement while he gave vent to his.

'The difficulty with your *precise* suggestion, Georgiana,' Tyrold said at last, her real name falling softly from his lips, and his voice without a trace of vitriol, 'is that I'm left-handed.'

Georgiana blinked as she registered his meaning, and then her pent-up laughter bubbled over. She turned her back to Tyrold, trying to stifle her amusement so as not to draw attention from passers-by on the street, but, in turning, her high-heeled shoe slipped on the top step of the servant's stairwell, and she stumbled.

Broadcloth-clad arms enveloped her before she fell.

'Have a care, my dear,' Tyrold said, still chuckling as he steadied her against his chest. He looked down at her, his eyes twinkling. 'And tell me, is that truly what spinsters do?'

Georgiana's cheeks burned, but surely her veil and the shadows hid her blush. 'Spinsters feel sexual desire as much as bachelors.' Her voice emerged husky, for her breath had gone odd from the moment Tyrold caught her stumble, although he held her loosely, quite unlike the embrace in the Piazza. 'But both societal and personal consequences require us to exercise self-control. Why should not men be held to the same standards?'

He studied her for several moments.

'What?' she asked at last.

'I've never met a woman like you before.' His lips curved into a slow smile. 'Do you truly despise me? Irreversibly so?'

'Why! I don't . . .' Georgiana faltered, unsure how to continue. Confused by his tender manner, she'd impulsively started to say she didn't despise him, but that wasn't true, was it? He was conceited and irritating. He'd ruined her society debut, making her scores of enemies. He'd humiliated her in the Piazza. He'd wanted to embarrass her in front of Betty, and only changed his mind at the end.

But yet . . .

There was something, sometimes.

The way he praised her singing. That grin which rendered his face so endearingly sweet. The spark she'd felt when their hands had entwined over the mirror. And now, as they embraced on the street, their breath rising and falling in unison.

He drew her closer, but oh-so-gently this time, and his eyes – heavy-lidded now – trailed to her mouth. Georgiana raised on her tiptoes, her lips drawn to his, thoughts of why she was letting John Tyrold embrace her vanishing from her mind as Betty's words replayed in her head: he likes singers; he improves on acquaintance; he deems it important for a lover to desire him as much as he desires her; he's searching for a mistress . . .

If he weren't already considering Georgiana for the role, she knew it would be within her power to bend his thoughts in that direction. She imagined kissing him. Her frustration could so easily switch to fierce passion for this infuriating man. She would bring him down, make him pant, let a physical act give her a satisfaction she hadn't achieved through their arguing. The heat of their mouths' union would enflame her, burning though her conflicted feelings, swelling her lust until she took Tyrold back to her bedroom at Monica House and . . .

Monica House.

Georgiana pulled back within Tyrold's embrace. Monica House needed her, and *that* was the only thing that mattered. She couldn't do anything that might involve her in scandal and though an affair with Tyrold might be consensual and hurt nobody, society would never, ever allow the bastard daughter of the Duke of Amesbury to go unpunished for it. Not here in England. Not with a man everyone wanted.

She disengaged from his arms and stepped away. Without observing his reaction, she spoke over her shoulder as she began to walk towards Tavistock Street. 'I despise your *manners*, Jack, and I suggest you continue to make an effort to improve them, not merely with me, but with everyone. But beyond that, what I think of you is irrelevant. We simply have a task to accomplish. So do everything I say and try – if possible – not to be loathsome.'

For four years, Georgiana had dedicated herself to establishing a fulfilling life in England. A life that kept her heartbreak at bay. If she fell to scandalous temptations, if she fell for *him*, she ruined everything, for herself and for others.

She could not allow herself to desire John Tyrold.

IO

John's stomach churned with revulsion as he studied the stone façade of Mother Harris's notorious establishment on Tavistock Street, the darkened windows and unsavoury surroundings amplifying his dread. If Flora was indeed held captive within these walls, the devil alone knew what horrors she had faced.

'I shall wait here,' Georgiana said, drawing him from his thoughts.

They stood together in front of a bagnio. Two women, nude but for gauzy skirts, danced in the bathhouse's bow window, waving colourful scarves above their heads.

John glanced at the sign, a turbaned man luxuriating in a steam bath under the inscription *The Turk's Delight*. His scrutiny shifted to Georgiana; he cast a sceptical eye over her wine-red gown and garish hat. 'You intend to wait *here*, on the pavement before this place, dressed like *that*?'

She crossed her arms under her bosom. 'Yes, I do. While you enquire next door.'

John surveyed the street. Men were everywhere, especially congregated around a boisterous tavern with a sign displaying a crude portrait of the first King Charles. He needed to find Flora, but he disliked leaving Georgiana alone on a dangerous street.

'Do you doubt my ability to take care of myself?' she asked, as if she could read his mind. 'How do you suppose I've managed for years without your protection?'

'Luck?' John ventured.

She thinned her pretty mouth and pointed a black gloved finger at Mother Harris's shadowy entrance. 'If there's any luck to be had, I pray that it's finding Flora safe in that hellhouse. Go. I'll be fine.'

John drew in a deep breath and braced himself to enter Mother Harris's. As he approached the door, his gut twisted with the realisation that he *hoped* to find Flora at the notorious brothel, rather than face a cold trail again. Above all else, his priority was her safety. He'd deal with the consequences of whatever she had faced once she was again in his care. Somehow – some impossible way he couldn't yet fathom – he'd ensure she hadn't ruined her life at fifteen. Because what would Helen have said about how John had bungled—

John shook his head, surprised by the thought. *He* hadn't bungled anything regarding Flora. The child had brought this disaster on herself.

Freshly resolved, John climbed the steps. Noise from the tavern pervaded the night as he knocked on the door. No one answered, so John knocked again. While he waited, he glanced over his shoulder at Georgiana, who watched the bagnio dancers intently, for all the world as if she were appreciating their performance.

John couldn't help but smile. He infrequently spent time with ladies other than Meggy or Kitty, so he really couldn't attest to the typical behaviour of the elegant female – but, still, he was fairly damn certain that there wasn't another young lady in London even remotely like Georgiana Bailey.

John knocked a third time, banging with the side of his fist.

No answer.

He looked over his shoulder again, hoping to catch Georgiana's attention for advice, but she was conversing with a young prostitute. As she spoke, she brushed her fingertips over the girl's face, touching dark smudges that looked disturbingly like bruises.

Something deep in John's chest ached. Georgiana truly was as tender-hearted as she claimed – a rare trait, indeed.

But the dark bruise reminded John of the urgency of finding Flora.

He knocked again, the loudest yet.

This time, the door opened, revealing a slender woman with handsome features, clad in ill-fitting attire a quarter century out of fashion. Her tattered gown possessed a long-waisted bodice attached to a floral chintz overskirt, open in front to display soiled petticoats. Her auburn hair was lightly powdered, with a single, thick curl cascading over her shoulder and down her bosom. A wide necklet of lace and ribbon adorned her throat.

The prostitute's grey eyes gleamed. 'Why, you're not who I was expecting, but that makes you all the more welcome.' She grabbed John's cravat and pulled him forcibly into a shadowy entrance hall where only a handful of tallow candles sputtered in tarnished sconces, their rancid meat smell mingling with stale tobacco and other sour stenches. 'I thought it was *another* when Mother Harris told me to gown myself this way. I didn't realise there's two men what likes the old styles.'

She slammed the door and pressed herself against John. Although her musk perfume suffocated him, he overcame an urge to pull away. 'Are you Maud?'

She slipped her arms around his waist, under his coat. 'No, handsome. I'm Lucy. Didn't you request me?' She jutted her chin at John's hat and he comprehended at last. Because of his three-cornered hat, she'd assumed he had a fancy-dress fetish.

'No. I'd like to speak to Maud, please.'

Her lips turned down. 'Maud's claimed for the night, but I can use a whip, if you like.' Then she gasped, one hand flying to her mouth. 'Oh, but! No, no! If you didn't ask for me, then . . .'

She drew back, cowering against the wall, her eyes glued to the front door. 'You stupid girl, Lucy,' she muttered. 'Gettin' your hopes up that the devil's not coming when you know he is.'

Seeking to ease her terror, John laid a hand on her trembling forearm. 'My dear, we can help each other. I can pay for your night's work so you needn't see whomever it is you expect, and you tell me if Maud's been guarding a copper-haired girl.'

'Oh!' Lucy breathed out, extending the sound. She stood straighter, supporting herself with a hand against

171

the grimy wallpaper. 'You're *him* – that man they all talked about. You've come for Flora. I thought you looked familiar.'

'Yes,' John said eagerly. Thank God – Flora was here, and she was safe. 'Yes, Lucy. I'm Tyrold.'

Lucy's eyes widened. 'Gads, and so you are! The very man himself. I can see it now, although you look different. You cut your hair.'

John bristled, annoyed he'd foolishly given information she clearly hadn't known. 'Then what did you mean by saying I look familiar, if you didn't already know my name?' he asked, his tone more cross than he'd intended.

Lucy threw her hands over her face. 'Don't be angry, sir! I only meant you look like Flora. At least, your eyes do. I knew the girl had a wealthy relation, but I never imagined it was *you*, what everyone says is richer than the King himself. No wonder Mother Harris wanted Flora guarded like she was the Crown Jewels, even though Flora said you wouldn't come 'cause you don't care tuppence for her.'

'No, that's incorrect.' John stepped closer. 'I—'

Lucy quaked as he neared, hands still protecting her face. 'Don't hit me, sir. I didn't mean to get it wrong.'

'I won't hit you, Lucy.' John outstretched his arms, hoping the gesture would reassure her when she uncovered her face. 'Believe me, I'm extremely concerned about Flora, and I shall reward you generously if you bring her to me.'

Lucy peeked through her fingers. 'But I can't, sir.'

'Name your price, my dear.' John kept his voice level with difficulty. He was so close. He couldn't misstep. 'I shall give you five guineas if you merely point me to her room.'

''Tis not that.' Lucy removed her hands from her face at last. 'I can't show you because she's not here any more. She was here only two nights.'

John's hopes plummeted, a devastating feeling after thinking himself on the brink of success. 'Where did she go? Where is she now?'

A clock lost to the hall's murky depths began to chime the hour. Lucy's eyes darted in its direction. 'I . . . I . . .' She looked towards the door and trembled.

John tried again. 'Who brought her here, Lucy? Please tell me whatever you can.'

The clock finished its twelfth chime before Lucy spoke. 'I can't talk now.' Her voice was hushed and urgent. 'Meet me tomorrow evening. Nine o'clock at the Bolt in Tun on Fleet Street. But I want a hundred pounds so I can . . . oh, sir, so I can go *home*.'

'I can't wait until tomorrow,' John snapped, his concern for Flora mounting 'If you won't reveal what you know now, I shall send for the Runners to tear this place apart – and then you won't get a penny from me, Lucy.'

A knock sounded upon the door.

Lucy inhaled sharply. 'That'll be him.' Her grey eyes darted into the depths of the hall, as if she was searching for someone. 'Don't bring the Runners, sir. They won't find any trace that she's been here and it might let her captors know how close you are, if they come to hear of it.'

'How do I know you're not a part of the ploy?' John asked, furious. 'You might alert them yourselves tonight.'

Lucy drew back. 'I'd never! Your Flora was kind to us girls, never looked down on us, though she could tell we weren't ladies like her. Treated us like we're humans, and there's not many what do that.'

John felt a sudden swell of pride in Flora, but he quickly suppressed it. Lucy might be lying, attempting to trick him into trusting her. After all, Flora seemed incapable of making friends at school. 'I have no reason to trust you, Lucy.'

'I swear it's true.' Her face fell. 'But, yes, why would the likes of you believe a whore like me without proof?' She raised her hands and untied her lace necklet. Purplish bruises in the shape of handprints marred her throat. 'This is all the proof I have of my sincerity. Do you think I want this life?'

John drew back, horrified. 'My dear girl, why do you not walk out the door?' he asked, softening his voice. 'There's no one to stop you.'

'With nothing in my pocket and no character reference to find honest work?' Lucy retied her necklet. 'I'll get worse than this on the streets. With a hundred pounds, I can leave this wicked city—'

The knock sounded again, loud and sharp, metal on wood.

Lucy wrung her hands. 'The footman ain't here, so I must answer now. I can't upset this one, or I'll pay for it. I swear I'll tell you all I know tomorrow. Please meet me. Don't desert me. Your coming is God's grace, at long last, for I shan't see *him* ever again after tonight.'

An interior door opened farther into the house, in the deep shadows of the hall, and Lucy snapped to attention, shoving John aside as a footman swaggered from the gloom. Behind the manservant, a girl fumbled with loose bodice laces.

'Lud, Joe, so you've been fucking in the storeroom.' Lucy addressed the footman in a strident voice. 'Answer the door. I can't open it, for he likes to pretend I'm a lady, and ladies don't open doors, do they? And as for you, Sally, Mother'll tear you apart if she knows you was screwing Joe when you ought to be out on the street, bringing in customers.'

Sally stuck out her tongue.

Joe adjusted his breeches as he eyed John with a leery gaze. 'What country hole did you emerge from, man? Girls here is at least two guineas for the night. You'd better try your luck at the bagnio next door. There, you can get a blow for half a crown.'

John bowed his head, debating what to do. If he alerted the Runners, the news that John Tyrold's heir had been abducted would spread over London. Quite apart from ruining Flora's reputation, the rumours would likely expose her to even more danger, driving her abductors to desperation as well as alerting *other* opportunists to her vulnerability. Yet if he trusted Lucy, he'd lose another one-and-twenty hours waiting for a costly appointment in which he might or might not receive useful information.

Neither were good options, but there was also the matter of Lucy's vicious bruises. If John didn't help, what would become of *her*?

'God, stupid as they come, ain't you?' Joe shoved past John. 'Move out of the way, you lug, while I attend to the door. Don't let our customers see a country bumpkin like you, eh?'

John slunk into a dark corner as Joe opened the door. Perhaps seeing Lucy's tormenter would clarify matters and decide a course of action.

'About damned time,' said a gentleman's voice, cold and clipped, with consonants as sharp as cut glass.

It was a voice John thought he recognised.

'Forgive me, m'lord.' Joe bowed. 'Lucy awaits your pleasure, as you can see.'

'She's to be called Rosamunde. I've said so countless times.'

'Rosamunde awaits your lordship's pleasure,' Joe responded, not missing a beat.

John peered from under his hat brim as a straight-backed, long-nosed, silver-haired man strutted into the corridor, holding his gold-handled walking stick aloft with his littlest finger in the air. John swiftly looked down again. Yes, it was as he'd thought: Viscount Wingrove, a sunken-cheeked cadaver of an old rakehell. The septuagenarian aristocrat, who'd supposedly killed men in duels and driven his own wife to madness, amongst other salacious rumours, had come to John two or three years earlier for advice on the repair of his fortune. It had resulted in naught, for Wingrove hadn't wished to curtail his gambling or alter his extravagant lifestyle. In fact, the old man had been so unreasonable, John had questioned his sanity.

The force with which Wingrove grabbed Lucy's arm and yanked her close exhibited a strength surprising for his advanced years. 'By God, Rosamunde, you beautiful bitch. You hoped to make both me and the duchess jealous, flirting with Devonshire so outrageously tonight. Now I must teach you a lesson.'

John curled his lip in disgust. The viscount *was* mad, recreating events decades in the past. The current Duke of Devonshire was a bachelor. His mother, the famous duchess, was ten years dead.

Lucy faltered, as if unsure what to respond. 'I . . .'

Wingrove pushed her against the wall. 'Don't speak unless I tell you what to say, girl! It ruins the effect.'

Revolted by Wingrove's cruelty, John tightened his hands into fists and advanced from the shadows. He'd deal with this now – save Lucy from Wingrove and then get the Runners to tear this disgusting house apart. Never mind that he had no evidence. Never mind that . . .

But Lucy's frightened eyes caught his and, as if she guessed his thoughts, her eyebrows peaked, pleadingly. She gave a slight shake of her head while motioning John towards the door with a flick of her fingers.

Wingrove grabbed her hair. 'You have eyes only for me, Rosamunde. Say it. Say, "I have eyes only for you, my lord. Frederick and Devonshire and the others are nothing to me.'"

'I have eyes only for you, my lord. Frederick and—'

Joe the footman shoved John's shoulder. 'Why are you still here?' he hissed over Lucy's quivering voice. 'If you plan to get off on watching this, it'll cost you two bob. Otherwise, leave.'

All at once, John knew exactly what he should do: tell Georgiana everything so she could advise him on the best course of action. Resolved, he threw open the door and bounded over the threshold, gulping in night air as if it could cleanse himself from the horrors he'd beheld. But it was to no avail, for his skin crawled and his stomach still turned. As Joe slammed the door shut, John stood on the steps, revulsion overpowering him. God, that Flora had lived in that house of horrors! He clamped his teeth together until his jaw ached. Disgusting and vicious, that's what it was. That vile doorman must've looked at her, men like Wingrove slaked their deviant lusts in rooms near her . . .

John's hand tightened on the railing.

Yet Flora had said John wouldn't care. That he wouldn't come. That he wouldn't seek to save her from such a nightmare.

Could she truly believe that?

As the truth became all too clear, John's grip loosened and his arm slumped to his side.

Eight years ago, immediately after Helen's death, John should have cast aside his hurt and made a home for the girl. He had the money to give her all the best. A house on one of the grand squares. Trips to Yorkshire so she could spend summers and Christmas at Oakwood Hall. A governess for lessons at home. Ponies and pets and dolls and friends and books and all the things Helen's daughter would want.

And, most importantly, those two things that Helen had wanted above all else: love and companionship.

Flora believed John didn't care. And, as Georgiana had suggested, the lack of love had driven the child to despair. It had driven her to seek it however it was offered.

John was thoroughly disgusted with himself.

'Jack?'

A soft voice, warm as velvet, came from the pavement, and the grateful yearning that arose in John's chest angered him. On top of everything else, his damned heart was reacting to a whispered word from Georgiana Bailey. He wanted to pour out his distress and let her comfort him, hear her say all was not yet lost, yet the last thing he needed in his life was to lose a heart he'd guarded for a decade and a half to a woman who only wanted him for two thousand pounds.

A fresh wave of anger crested and, this time, it was directed at Georgiana. Why had she taken so damnably long to ready them both this evening? If she hadn't been threading her fingers through his hair for an hour, making him fall half in love with her, he'd have his answers from Lucy already.

'Jack, what is it?' Concern laced Georgiana's voice.

John faced her. 'Why the *devil* didn't we start earlier this evening, woman?' he asked, though his churlish fury did nothing to improve his feelings towards himself.

What a damnable bastard he was.

No wonder Georgiana only wanted his money.

Georgiana sat next to Tyrold on the filthy step of a doorway across from the oyster bar on Maiden Lane, the salty scent of shellfish heavy in the night air. In these shadows, they were two nobodies on the London streets, ignored by everyone walking past. Tyrold was hurting, and frightened for Flora, and so Georgiana dismissed his judgemental harshness as he relayed what had happened at Mother Harris's.

He concluded with a pathetic attempt to justify his anger. 'If we'd started earlier, I could've spoken to Lucy tonight and saved a day's time and a hundred pounds.'

'You aren't angry about that, Jack. You're angry because you feel helpless.'

He stiffened, as if he intended to argue.

Georgiana placed her hand on his shoulder. 'Don't,' she said softly. 'Don't argue with me. You know I'm correct.' He sighed, his muscles loosening under her touch. 'Focus on the progress we've made. And think of Lucy, who will get a chance at a new life starting tomorrow.'

'Or she may become a bawd herself, funded by my money,' he growled. 'Do you know how many honest lives I could help with a hundred pounds?'

Georgiana leant closer. 'You cannot count lives like that. You must instead be grateful for every life you save, whatever the cost. Some years ago, *The Times* reported that five thousand London prostitutes die annually of disease, brutality or poverty. The number is so staggering that I cannot breathe when I think upon it. Five thousand,' she repeated, willing him to understand. '*Five thousand* a year, Jack. That means every day . . .' She hesitated, dividing in her head. 'Five thousand by three sixty-five makes . . .'

'It makes fourteen deaths a day, rounded up,' Tyrold said gruffly.

'Yes, and rounding up is *exactly* what one must do, because you and I both know more die than are found or reported.' Georgiana tightened her grip on his shoulder until her nails dug into his coat. 'Fourteen a day, Jack! Don't you see?' she urged, her eyes prickling. 'All we can do is take advantage of every single opportunity to help. Some girls can be saved by procuring an apprenticeship with a seamstress for five pounds. Lucy requests one hundred. Some – like Flora – may cost two thousand or more. But every life – every single life saved or transformed is one more life. Do you understand? It's one more life. One more life held back from the overwhelming sea of poverty and despair . . .'

Against Georgiana's will, imagery she constantly fought inundated her mind: the dead, the thousands and thousands and thousands of forsaken dead, a ghostly legion of mournful souls calling out to her, begging her never to let another woman or child or infant die of hunger or violence or hopes lost or illness a doctor could heal . . . and Georgiana hugged herself as the darkness closed in, rocking as she attempted to fight the horrible vision.

'Georgiana.' Tyrold's voice was muffled, as if he were in another room.

'Don't you see?' she asked, far more viciously than she'd intended. 'Don't you see?'

Tyrold furrowed his brow. 'See what, exactly? I understand you care deeply—'

'Don't you see that every time I can save a life, I give whatever I must?' The words caught in her throat, choking her. 'Whatever I must, to my last penny.'

Tyrold looked at his hands. 'Er, yes, I do see that now. But surely you understand such spending isn't sustainable? This is the reason your charity can't support itself.'

Georgiana shook her head in dismay. 'Even still you don't understand. You think I care about money, but I don't. I care about human lives. So, as long as I live, I shall do whatever I must for Monica House, because *there is no pain*,' she emphasised the last four words, although speaking now hurt because her grief was surging so forcefully, 'like knowing you could've saved a life – that you held a life in your hands – and you *didn't* save it in time. That you failed the ultimate failure.'

With that, Georgiana stood, needing to get away from him. 'We've done what we can for tonight.' She spoke fiercely, disguising the sorrow tearing her apart. 'We must wait until tomorrow evening to speak with Lucy, so goodnight, Jack. I shall make my own way home and you should do the same.'

Tears moistened Georgiana's eyes as she marched away from Tyrold. She didn't want him to see her cry, if the tears fell. Because now the image in her mind was of a smile that existed only in her memory and when Georgiana wept for this grief, she allowed no one to witness her tears. No one else knew.

Tyrold's bootsteps grew closer.

Georgiana walked faster. With all the preparations for the Season, too many weeks had passed since she'd combed the streets herself, searching for women in need. There was nothing else she could do for Flora until they spoke with Lucy, but there were others who needed hope tonight. She'd find as many as she could before the sun rose, and she didn't need or want Tyrold around as she did so.

'Stop, please, Georgie.' Tyrold's pace increased. 'Allow me to see you safely home.'

'I told you I can take care of myself.' And with that, Georgiana hitched her skirts and ran for the Piazza. She'd lose him amongst the throngs. She'd weave through the crowds, seeing what good she could do. Whispering, 'If you ever need help, come to Maria DeRosa's coffee-house, Soho Square, and ask for Monica,' into the ears of those who wanted to listen.

That, and that alone, would ease her pain . . .

II

The next morning, after a short and restless sleep, Georgiana combed through the ledgers in her study. To her chagrin, Tyrold's calculations were correct, bringing her total arrears to over five hundred pounds for the months she'd run a deficit. Additionally, even with the donations of the day before, she still needed to raise subscriptions of fifty pounds per month to avoid accumulating more debt.

The numbers were staggering, but Georgiana persevered. She set aside the letters threatening legal action and recalculated her stack of creditors' bills to ensure she hadn't made hurried mistakes. As she rechecked her sums, a rap at the door drew her from her calculations, making her lose her total.

She sighed. *Interruptions*, not carelessness, were the root of her business troubles – although she doubted Tyrold would understand. Likely no one ever interrupted *him*.

She put down her pencil. 'Come in.'

Her friend and assistant, Amanda Bellamy, entered. 'This just arrived,' Amanda said, placing a letter on Georgiana's desk. 'One of your father's footmen delivered it, and he's waiting in expectation of your reply.'

Georgiana broke the seal. A second letter fell out, landing upon her ledger. The enveloping parchment bore lines of Fanny's feathery hand.

Dearest Georgiana, come to me the moment you've read the enclosed invitation. I know for certain that Lord Edward will be present and the more I think upon it, the more pleased I am with the prospect of that match. I saw his great-aunt, Lady Agatha Matlock, in Hyde Park yesterday after the garden party, and together we've decided you will be the making of him. Do bring your songbook collection, lovely; in her letter to me, Lady Eden said her sweet daughter must hear you perform again. FB

Georgiana sighed as she ripped the wafer of the other letter.

No. 17 Curzon Street
Tuesday, 16th April 1816

My dear Miss Bailey,

My daughter Ada-Marie can talk of nothing but you since yesterday. If you aren't dreadfully busy, could you spare an hour of your time for my salon this afternoon? I'm afraid it will be a horrid squeeze (Lord Eden has invited everyone he hopes to persuade to support the reforms on the wheat bill), but I think it would be a perfect occasion to find more sponsors for Monica House — and, selfishly, I would so love if you might sing a song or two. It delights me and my

little girl, and I believe it will move others to your
worthy cause. With many warm wishes, I remain,
Your friend,
Kitty Wakefield (Lady Eden)

Georgiana tapped her fingers on her desk. Her accounts would have to wait, but if she could raise funds at Lady Eden's salon, the day wouldn't be wasted. Besides, she and Edward needed to continue their pretend courtship to dispel any rumours about her and Tyrold. Of course, one day she'd have to extract herself from *that* mess, as Lady Agatha and Fanny had got their hopes up – but those were worries for another day.

Monica House's needs came first, and Lady Eden – who, as a former courtesan, must know something of the troubles some women faced – might be the perfect person to help.

John slept for four fitful hours and woke at five o'clock. After his customary morning tasks – including, *unusually*, yet another shave, he departed Half Moon Street with Jolly and strode northeast. He had a great deal of business to accomplish.

When he arrived at the Boar and Castle Inn, John surveyed the row of houses across Oxford Street, scratching Jolly's ears as he considered. The terrace was of relatively recent construction, with each house possessing a pleasing stone façade and a gabled fifth storey. John narrowed his eyes to look down the busy street towards the new Circus. Oxford Street had been rising in prosperity for thirty years, but the gentry largely ignored it, especially this close to the St Giles Rookery. Still, with Mayfair full to bursting and hordes of people eager to live and shop near London's most exclusive residences, there was a great deal of potential for development.

John stroked his dog's neck. These buildings would do. He could make them lucrative. This morning, he'd absorb the leasehold for the house Georgiana desired. This afternoon, he'd write to the Earl of Oxford and offer something his lordship couldn't refuse to purchase the land encompassing the entire row. Then John would renovate his new buildings, turning them into stylish shops and genteel lodgings, amongst other things, as well as giving Georgiana her school, *if* she succeeded in finding Flora. But as Georgiana already had progressed the search far more than anyone else had, John had some faith in her abilities.

An hour later, after purchasing the leasehold, John travelled with Jolly into the City. Amongst other dealings, he procured one hundred pounds in coins at the Bank of England. He didn't want to pay Lucy in banknotes traceable to him.

Their next stop was Old Bond Street, where John purchased a new coat. Then he ventured into St James's, where he bought a tall-crowned hat and had his boots polished to a gloss.

Satisfied with his morning's accomplishments, John crossed Piccadilly towards home, eager to write to Lord Oxford.

Edward was leaving Number Twenty-Nine Half Moon Street as John approached and when they met upon the steps, Edward's jaw dropped.

'Catching flies?' John asked gruffly as he attempted to shoulder past his housemate.

Edward jutted the tip of his walking stick into John's chest, staying his progress. 'Steady on, my boy. Steady on for a moment.' He tapped John's lapel with his stick's ivory handle. 'This devilish fine coat is like the one in Weston's window. Thirty guineas he wanted for a copy. When'd you order it?'

John glanced at the new garment, a dark green, double-breasted tailcoat with a silk velvet collar. 'I bought the coat in the window. It was all Weston had ready-made that fitted.' He'd questioned the style, but the great tailor had insisted it was à la mode and presented recent gentlemen's fashion plates as proof. That Edward liked it spoke to the veracity of Weston's claims. At least Georgiana wouldn't complain it was old-fashioned.

Edward rubbed his chin while giving John a sceptical glare. 'Weston doesn't let gentlemen purchase ready-made. One must always bespeak a copy. Besides, that fits you like a glove.'

John shrugged. 'He made some adjustments.'

Edward's eyes widened. 'Ha! The great Weston bent to the even greater Tyrold. Nicely played, but you must be fifty or more guineas poorer this morning, especially with that first-rate new topper, as well. What's the occasion?'

Rather a lot more than fifty guineas, John reckoned, thinking of the house on Oxford Street, the coins for Lucy and the letter he would soon write.

But he growled dismissively at Edward. 'I don't need an occasion to purchase a coat and hat. Now, if you'll step aside, perhaps Jolly and I can enter our own home?'

Edward held up a finger. 'Not so fast, old boy. You can't wear that fine coat with such a beastly waistcoat. Come with me.' And, pushing with his walking stick, he conducted John through the door and upstairs into Sidney's old bedchamber, which Edward now occupied.

Ellen was dusting when they arrived, but she bobbed a curtsy and departed.

Edward threw open the doors to a cedarwood wardrobe. 'Stand there,' he said, pointing towards a large looking glass, 'with your coat and waistcoat off.' He cast an eye over John's legs. 'Breeches off too. Lord, why *do* you wear such old-fashioned things during the daytime? You can borrow these.' He handed John a pair of ivory-coloured pantaloons.

John complied out of curiosity, kicking off his boots and breeches, and sliding on the pantaloons, which clung to his legs like a second skin.

John tucked in his shirt, buttoned up the front fall, and tightened his braces, but he grimaced when he looked at his reflection. 'I can't wear these, Edward.'

Edward popped his head round the wardrobe door, his arms full of waistcoats. 'Why not? They fit beautifully. You have damned nice legs, John.'

'It's not *that*, it's *this*.' John indicated the fall front.

189

Edward focused on John's crotch. 'What's your concern? You fill it out fine.'

John looked again. Although all the gentlemen who followed Brummell's style wore pantaloons as tight, if not tighter, John had never done so. The fall front provided extra capacity for the – er – natural parts, yet there was still unmistakable bulging. 'But, it's . . . obscene.'

'No, no.' Edward laughed. 'Not obscene. A mere suggestion at best. Besides, is it obscene when ladies display their bosoms in low-cut gowns? No? Well, it's a gentleman's duty to return the favour. Show a lady what one has to offer. It's benevolence. Consideration. After all, ladies must have their fun as well. Now, try this.' He tossed a waistcoat to John.

Several minutes later, after a succession of waistcoats, Edward sat on the edge of his bed and cleared his throat. 'John, I've been thinking about something . . . oh! Which reminds me, was Lise quieter last night? I asked her to be, but then I forgot to pay attention to how much noise she made. Caught up in the moment, you understand.'

John grunted as he buttoned an ivory-on-gold-figured damask waistcoat, the tenth garment he'd donned. 'I was hardly home.'

'Yes, I noticed you came in late. Stop – don't take that off,' Edward said, referring to the waistcoat. 'That's the one. It'll be perfect with those ivory pantaloons and this gorgeous green.' He stood, bringing John his coat. 'I suppose you were searching for your ward?'

John grunted an affirmative reply as Edward helped him into his tight new garment.

'Was Georgiana any help?'

'We'll see.'

'I'm certain she will be,' Edward said. 'And as it happens, it's Georgiana who occupied my thoughts much of last night.'

Irritation prickled as John pushed his coat's velvet-covered buttons through their trim slits. 'While you shagged your model?'

'Of course not. Right *after*, when I was trying to fall asleep.' Edward folded his arms across his chest, his expression thoughtful as he paced towards his window. 'Yesterday evening, I received a message from my Aunt Agatha. Seems she and the Duchess of Amesbury have decided I should be yoked to Georgiana. In fact, Aunt Agatha considers the matter quite settled, which is positively mediaeval since neither Gee nor I had our say, *but* − and this is the material point, John − as I tried to sleep last night, I had a sort of . . . change of mindset. Marrying Gee mightn't be such a bad thing.'

John scowled, but he said nothing because there was nothing to be said. Why should he object to Edward turning his mind to developing some principles, at last? There was no good reason why it should annoy him, provided Edward intended to honour and respect Georgiana as much as she deserved . . .

'Gee's an agreeable scamp,' Edward continued, pulling his curtain edge as he peered outside. 'And Aunt Agatha wrote that I shall get four thousand a year upon marriage, on top of whatever Amesbury settles on Gee. It would be a sort of marriage of convenience, of course, but I don't think I could choose better. Gee can run her charity or sing or whatever she wishes to do, and I can continue to pursue my painting.'

'And your models?' John couldn't help but ask as he extracted his watch from the breeches he'd worn earlier. 'Would you continue to pursue them as well?'

'I don't know.' Edward rubbed his chin thoughtfully. 'I'll ask Gee, but I can't imagine she'd mind much. She's not like other ladies, John.'

John's hand shook as he shoved his watch into the fob pocket of Edward's pantaloons. 'Dammit, Edward, don't marry Georgiana or any woman when all you truly desire is your inheritance from your aunt.'

Edward looked surprised. 'But why not?'

'Because the only sound foundation for a marriage is strong, mutual love and respect between two people.'

'Come now, old boy.' Edward laughed. 'Easy for to you deliver such a sermon; you don't need to marry for money or capitulate to the will of a tyrannical great-aunt. I must try my hand with Gee no matter what you say, because I'll starve to death if Aunt Agatha disowns me.'

Thoroughly furious, John pulled on one of his boots. 'No, you won't. You'll simply have to purchase fewer waistcoats.'

'But I don't want to purchase fewer waistcoats,' Edward said simply. Then he cocked his head. 'Your barber did an excellent job, by the by. I say, are you busy this afternoon?'

'Extremely.' John had had enough of his friend for the day.

'Ah, well, if you happen upon a spare moment, Kitty's hosting a salon for Sid's sake – to help him raise support for those wheat bill reforms – and you know how Ada-Marie loves music, so Kit plans to encourage performances from some of the young ladies—'

'I had quite enough of that yesterday,' John said, grabbing his other boot.

'I mention it because Kitty says Georgiana will be there. I thought you might enjoy hearing her again.'

John's hands stilled, with his boot halfway up his calf. He paused. How odd to think of mingling with Georgiana amongst society after the rather unbelievable misadventures of the night before – one night at a brothel, the next afternoon at a countess's salon. Did he *want* to see her? After a moment's reflection, he realised he did, if only to ensure no harm had befallen her after she'd disappeared into the Piazza the night before.

John finished pulling up his boot. But what would he say?

Perhaps he should wait until the evening . . .

On second thoughts, he couldn't wait until the evening because he didn't know her plans for their meeting with Lucy. He'd followed the only orders she'd given by purchasing the coat and hat, but beyond that, what? Should he seek her at the coffee shop? Or weave through the alley-warren, searching for the metal door in order to escort her to Fleet Street? Or did she wish to meet him at the coaching house?

The uncertainty settled matters. John *must* go to Kitty's; it was essential for the search.

'Perhaps I'll call in if I can spare a moment,' he said, hoping no tremor of anticipation betrayed him. He leant towards the mirror, tightened the knot of his cravat and dusted the dark green sleeves of his coat. Superfine was a lovely fabric, a wool as soft as silk. Somehow it moulded to the body without being constrictive. There really was some truth to Weston's reputation, wasn't there? Not merely trumped-up praise, simply because the Prince of Wales and Brummell patronised him.

John smoothed the hair at his temples, admiring Georgiana's efforts for the dozenth time. He attempted to mimic her styling by combing his short, thick waves forwards with his fingers. While doing so, he met his friend's gaze in the mirror.

John's hand stilled.

Edward was grinning from ear to ear.

Georgiana regretted her decision to attend Lady Eden's salon soon after her arrival.

Not that there hadn't been lovely moments. Lady Eden herself had been warm and gracious, greeting Georgiana like a cherished friend, and then Georgiana had passed a pleasurable half hour teaching Ada–Marie more chords on the guitar. But when Georgiana had left the little girl to practise a simple melody so that she might approach potential donors, the trouble had begun.

No one had wanted to talk to her about Monica House.

The truth was, no one had seemed to want to talk to Georgiana much at all, although she'd suspected from the glances cast her way during whispered conversations that she'd formed at least a portion of the discourse of others. Not that she'd received the cut direct, but those who had spoken to her limited their comments to banalities about the weather or music. Only Mrs Lawrence, a friend of Lady Frampton's, had been forthright enough to give a hint of what others were thinking; when Georgiana had approached her about a donation, the lady had laughed. 'Clever of you to adopt this saintly demeanour so the gentlemen won't think of your illicit birth. I *do* hope you succeed in catching a husband, but a word of caution, my dear: it won't be Tyrold. He could marry *anyone*.'

So, within an hour of her arrival, Georgiana found herself squashed between Lady Rose and Lord Edward on a sofa, wondering what she was going to do to salvage matters. Even now, when she was merely sitting quietly amongst friends, Lady Frampton and her cronies cast hostile looks from the opposite side of the drawing room.

Georgiana realised she wouldn't succeed with her subscriptions until she convinced the *ton* that she was smitten with Lord Edward Matlock, and that John Tyrold's green eyes and knee-weakening embrace formed no part of her thoughts at all. Therefore, the next time Lady Frampton set eyes upon her, Georgiana turned in her seat to smile brightly at Edward.

He'd been dull since his arrival twenty minutes earlier, tapping his fingers on his thigh and glancing frequently at the door, as if their pretence already bored him. But it wouldn't do for him to look as if he wished to escape, or their scheme would never work. 'Have you any interesting commissions this Season, Edward?' she asked cheerfully.

Her query seemed to enliven him, for his blue eyes twinkled. 'One interesting commission, indeed, but I'm afraid it's not intended for a lady's eyes. Beyond that, only a few portraits of men. They pay well enough, but grow tedious. For some reason,' he added with a cheeky grin, 'I'm rarely asked to paint young ladies.'

Lady Rose shifted her attention from watching Ada-Marie play the guitar, surrounded by a cluster of singing children, which included her own red-haired girls. 'I would be delighted to commission a portrait of my daughters, Edward. Perhaps situated around a cameo bearing Thomas's likeness or gazing over the sea towards the setting sun.' She turned to Georgiana with a sorrowful look in her grey eyes. 'My husband died in the Battle of Lake Erie. A terrible defeat; so many officers and sailors lost their lives . . .' As Rose began to sob quietly, Georgiana noticed the three red-haired girls stop singing, lyrics withering on downturned lips as they glanced at their mother.

Georgiana ached for the family.

The widow's sorrow, and that of her daughters, pulled Georgiana away from her mission to engage Edward. 'Tell me about him, please, Lady Rose,' she said, pressing her handkerchief to the distraught lady's pale cheek.

'Truly?' Rose clasped Georgiana's hand. 'Do you *truly* wish to hear about my Thomas?'

Edward checked his watch, evidently already losing interest, but Georgiana nodded at Rose. 'You must miss him terribly.'

'Oh, Miss Bailey . . .' And, as if a dam had been opened, Rose's words gushed out, but with them, her tears stopped and the faces of her daughters brightened as they joined their voices with Ada–Marie again.

Normally, Georgiana would've given her whole-hearted attention as Rose enumerated the late sea captain's perfections, but, as it was, she could only half listen. Edward's foot-tapping and tuneless humming distracted her, and Lady Frampton's scrutiny from across the room bore into Georgiana's side. After a time, the baroness held up her fan and whispered something to her neighbours. One companion laughed as she glanced at Georgiana; the other observed Edward through a quizzing glass with narrowed eyes.

Georgiana traced her locket's etching as she racked her brain for a way to help Rose and still appear to be falling in love with Edward.

'Sometimes,' the widow was saying, 'I have a brighter day, and I laugh at the children's antics or consider wearing grey instead of black, but then guilt consumes me and the pain returns with the strength of a thousand horses . . .'

The words pierced Georgiana's soul. She understood the widow's sentiments so much that she'd once written a song . . .

She sat up straight, suddenly aware of how to comfort Rose and further her own cause simultaneously.

'Lady Rose,' she said when the widow next paused. 'I once wrote a song about finding joy and purpose after terrible grief, which I believe might resonate with you. I have it here in my portfolio. With your permission, may I play it?'

Rose tilted her head, her eyes soft. 'I'd love that.'

Ada-Marie stopped strumming the guitar, as if she'd also been listening to the conversation while singing with her friends. 'Do you want your guitar, Miss Bailey?'

'No, thank you, Ada-Marie. I'll play on the pianoforte.' She reached for Edward's hand. 'And Edward will sing duet with me.'

Edward slumped. 'Oh, Lord, Georgiana, I'm no more than tolerable—'

Georgiana squeezed his palm. 'Edward,' she said firmly. 'I need your help.' Her plan wouldn't work if he remained aloof. He must sing with her for all to see.

He sighed, but he arose.

Georgiana clasped her leather portfolio and together they weaved through the room.

Lady Eden sat near the pianoforte with Lady Holbrook and Lords Eden, Holbrook and Lockington, and a smattering of other politicians, including Georgiana's father. As Georgiana and Edward approached the instrument, the countess jumped to her feet. 'Do you mean to play, Miss Bailey?' she asked, her beautiful face aglow. 'How delightful! My lords, politics can wait. Miss Bailey and Lord Edward will perform for us.'

Georgiana smiled, filled with gratitude because Lady Eden's exuberance had brought the attention of the room to her and to Edward. Although he muttered something about his poor musicality, a weight lifted from Georgiana's chest. Singing with her old friend would help put the rumours to rest about her and Tyrold, and it was all the better that Edward wasn't a strong performer. Others wouldn't view Georgiana as flaunting her talent today.

She perched on the pianoforte bench, smoothed her blue skirts around her and extracted the song from her portfolio.

'All you must do, Edward,' she explained in a low voice, 'is to—'

A collective gasp filled the drawing room, interrupting her instruction. Georgiana glanced up from her music, expecting that a servant had overturned the tea or some such thing, but what she saw instead filled her with cold horror.

Across the drawing room, a hardly recognisable John Tyrold stood framed in the doorway, a stunning green tailcoat and beautifully tailored ivory pantaloons moulded to his tall figure, the whole effect as elegant as a fashion plate. He was staring directly at Georgiana and the moment their eyes locked, a smile spread across his handsome face.

Georgiana ignored an intense fluttering deep in her chest, for there were more important concerns at hand . . . like working out how she would *ever* salvage matters now.

Upon his arrival at Kitty and Sidney's salon, John scanned the company, searching for Georgiana.

He smiled when he located her, seated at the pianoforte in a cornflower-blue gown, her thick hair piled high with tendrils framing her heart-shaped face. What an astonishing alteration from the night before! Each of her variations captivated him, from graceful debutante to chatelaine-wearing housekeeper to rouged bawd. And, especially, chemise-clad innocent clasping the laces of her stays, trustingly asking assistance, an image seared into John's mind even as he locked eyes with her now, all elegant simplicity in a room full of silk and feathers.

She broke their eye contact to speak with Edward, but Edward didn't deserve her attention because he was an unprincipled scoundrel who intended to marry her to gain an inheritance, with no intention of being faithful. John would cut in, he decided, and tell Edward to go to the devil when he did so.

Kitty approached John, presumably welcoming him, but he patted her hand without attending to her conversation. He noted with relish that Georgiana and Edward appeared to be quarrelling, because Georgiana glowered as she pointed repeatedly to the music. Meanwhile, Edward slouched, a sullen air about his downturned lips.

John disengaged his hand from Kitty and crossed the room to investigate.

Edward sprang to his feet as he approached. 'Ah, John, you're precisely the man needed. Georgiana wants me to sing, but you know I struggle to carry a tune.'

'It's not a challenging song, Edward,' Georgiana said, sounding vexed.

John glanced at the score, written in the same precise hand that had recorded the Monica House accounts. 'I would be honoured to play and sing with you, Miss Bailey,' he offered, delighted to be given such a simple way to oust Edward and claim Georgiana's attention for himself.

Edward clapped his hands. 'It's settled then – to the relief of all.'

John couldn't have agreed more and, as Edward scurried away, he happily claimed his friend's vacated space on the small bench seat. Georgiana stared resolutely ahead, no doubt concentrating on her music, as if she didn't notice that John's shoulder and thigh pressed against her on the narrow seat. But John noticed. He noticed that her hair was so close to his nose that he could smell its floral fragrance. He noticed that her locket shone at her breast, nestled amongst rising and falling lace. He noticed the whisper-softness of her breath.

And her proximity rendered him speechless.

But, evidently, *she* wasn't.

'Why are you here? And dressed like that?' she hissed under her breath.

Her tone shook John from his stupor. 'I'm here to discuss our plans for this evening. And what's wrong with how I'm dressed? You told me to purchase a new coat.'

'Yes, but I never imagined you'd purchase one in the first stare of fashion. That's a Corinthian's coat.'

John's heart sank. 'You don't like it?'

She hesitated, then sighed. 'It's an extremely handsome coat, Mr Tyrold,' she said, her voice kinder. 'But it's distinctive, and still more distinctive now because you wear it. I meant for you to purchase something nice, new – but unremarkable.'

'You didn't specify that,' John countered, dejected, although her poor communication ought to anger him. He'd thought she'd be pleased. On the short walk from Half Moon Street, he'd noticed women turn to observe him (and not in the *usual* way women looked at him, but rather, with something more of genuine appreciation in their expression), and he'd wondered if Georgiana would find him attractive. Now he felt ridiculous, dressed like a damned fop, with everyone staring *except* the only person he cared to impress. 'You instructed me to purchase a coat, and I did.'

Her dark eyes sought his, and he met her gaze from under drawn brows, his lips pressed together as he willed himself to disguise his hurt. But, despite his efforts, she appeared to see beyond his bluster, and her gaze softened.

'Forgive my harshness, Mr Tyrold,' she said gently. 'It was indefensible. Thank you for following my instructions. But I worry . . .' She glanced about the room. 'No, it is of no consequence now. What's done is done. We should perform this song because I promised it to Lady Rose, and then both speak to other people for the remainder of the afternoon.'

'But I only came here to make arrangements with you for this evening,' John said, still hurt and humiliated. He certainly didn't possess the wherewithal any more to make small talk, and heaven forbid anyone ask about his damned coat. 'You cannot expect me to exchange banalities with others as if nothing were wrong when Flora is lost and possibly hurt.'

'I'm sorry, but now that you've come, you *must* talk to other guests, or there will be gossip. As for this evening, I shall meet you outside the Bolt in Tun at quarter to nine. Please don't wear your lovely new coat. Dress in your most nondescript attire and . . .' She hesitated, looking flustered. 'Oh, I don't know. Powder your hair, I suppose.'

'Powder it?'

'Yes, at the temples, as if you were going grey. I can think of no other disguise. Now, you play and sing as written, and I shall sing and play harmony.'

John directed his attention to the score, placing his fingers on the ivory keys next to Georgiana's. Once he began to play, the music consumed him, and the unpleasantness of moments earlier slipped away. The song was a folk lament, and Georgiana's soprano swelled beside his own tenor as their close-pressed bodies swayed in unison to the rhythm.

'*All night and each morrow awash in her sorrow,*' they sang.
'*Her lonely heart only felt pain.*
Alone and forsaken, she longed to be taken,
To feel the pain never again.
With longing she sighed, tears fell from her eyes,

And watered the mountain like rain.
But as her heart ached, some hope did awake,
As green grew the alpine again.'

Emotion stirred in John's chest, fed by the poignant lyrics and lush melody, especially as the song swelled into a crescendo with the refrain:

'With joy and woe, still forth we must go,
Whatever befalls us today.
Of grief is born purpose, of gladness comes pain,
'Twas ever and always the way.'

Yes, this was music to nourish hope, to cultivate faith, to make one believe *something* beyond understanding moved through this hurting world. Something so profoundly good that it could ease even the deepest sorrow.

When the song finished some verses later, and Georgiana's voice diminished, John stole a glance at her face. Her eyes glistened with unshed tears as she looked at Rose, who gazed back with equal intensity.

'That was . . . powerful. Poignant,' John ventured, although neither word described all he felt. 'I haven't heard it before.'

Georgiana began to gather her music. 'You haven't heard it because I wrote it.'

'Indeed?' John asked, astonished. 'It's about a love lost.'

'Very observant, Mr Tyrold. Yet you sound surprised. Is it so incredulous that I might have some complexity to my life?' She tied up her portfolio. 'Are you astonished that I might be more than merely a trickster who begs important people like you for money for my silly charitable hobby? Does it surprise you, Mr Tyrold, that someone other than yourself might've lost a great love?'

Her words startled John. He'd said nothing about Helen other than that she was dead. He'd certainly never mentioned love. How had Georgiana perceived sentiments he kept well hidden, if he'd ever felt them at all? 'Mine was no great love story, Miss Bailey. Not in the end, at any rate.'

She studied him, as if seeking to read his mind. 'Well, mine was,' she said at last.

An odd and uncomfortable feeling lodged in John's chest. 'And he forsook you, as the song says?' But though he asked, he knew that wasn't what had happened.

'No, Mr Tyrold,' she said quietly. 'My beloved is dead, like yours. Forever gone. And yet,' she touched the gold locket at her breast, 'always here.'

John recalled what she'd said the previous night about her great failure. 'Is his . . .' He hesitated, but curiosity pushed him to enquire. 'Is his the life you couldn't save?'

Her eyes brimmed with sorrow. 'I shall see you tonight.'

She hadn't answered his question in words, but John knew all the same.

'Remember,' she continued. 'Don't speak to me again while we are here. But please do converse with some of the young ladies, especially with Lady Frampton's daughter. She's a lovely girl.'

She rose, and John followed suit, and she was gone before John could breathe again, leaving him no opportunity to object. She crossed the room and sat next to Rose, who withdrew a miniature portrait from her black reticule. Georgiana examined it, murmuring something while Rose leant against her shoulder, but – John noted with interest – Georgiana didn't share whatever memento of her lost love she carried in the locket that bore her mother's initials.

So, she'd known love, John mused, whereas he sometimes believed he had no understanding of it at all. His feelings for Helen hadn't been what he'd thought they were, had they? If they had been, wouldn't he see in Flora all that was left of her mother's spirit, rather than viewing the girl as the embodiment of his own selfishness and shortcomings? Nor had Helen's feelings for him been what he'd believed, because if Helen had loved him, surely she wouldn't have left him with an aching, burning question, so that sometimes John loathed himself when he looked at Flora, with her appearance so like her beautiful mother except for her green eyes.

John's eyes.

Or maybe not.

Either way, a torturous reminder of how much he'd disappointed Helen. Of how much he'd lost because he'd wanted to live unencumbered, continuing to amass his unmatched fortune, rather than be the man Helen had needed.

A young lady approached John, propelled forwards by Lady Frampton, the vile wife of an innocuous baron.

If John wasn't mistaken, the chit was one of the debutantes who'd sung to him the previous day. Presumably, she was also the Miss Frampton with whom Georgiana wanted him to speak.

Alert to his danger, John tensed. He wished to flee, but Georgiana's command echoed in his mind. He'd failed her last directive miserably. Should he even attempt her latest request?

Miss Frampton curtsied. She possessed an exquisite porcelain countenance, and a smile teased the corners of her plump lips. 'Will you play while I sing, sir? I'm much better when I have accompaniment, and I'd appreciate the chance to redeem myself.'

John hesitated, thick-tongued and uncertain. She was a beautiful girl, and clearly inviting his attention, a perfect example of the sort of fresh-faced, high-born debutante John could have his pick of, should he wish to marry.

But he could see only that Miss Frampton was barely older than Flora.

Flora, who John too frequently dismissed as a troublesome child, but who had needs and hopes and thoughts, just as this child who stood before him must. What did Miss Frampton desire in life? Did she even *want* to marry, or were there other paths she dreamed of taking, were it not for society's expectations? And what had been *her* experiences at the age of fifteen, which must've been only a few years earlier?

John braced himself. If Georgiana wished for him to converse with Miss Frampton, he'd do so – but only because perhaps it would help him understand Flora better.

Yet even as he formed his resolution, a sentiment that had long been dormant within him stirred. *No, you're doing this only because Georgiana asked it of you*, it seemed to whisper. *You're doing this because you desire her good opinion.*

And John acknowledged its truth.

12

As Georgiana listened to Lady Rose, she watched Tyrold and Miss Frampton perform from the corner of her eye. They sat together at the pianoforte, bathed in golden sunlight that streamed in from a tall window.

Georgiana wasn't surprised at Tyrold's technical proficiency on the pianoforte, as mathematics and music were related, but his *talent* astounded her. His fingers played with an energy that could not be mimicked even through hours of practice. He sang in an exquisite tenor, as rich and fluid as silk, a voice to lift one's soul above the stars.

When he and Miss Frampton finished their song, Georgiana applauded with the other guests. Lady Frampton smirked triumphantly as the performers stood for a bow, side by side. They formed an elegantly matched pair: Tyrold tall, dark, and handsome; Miss Frampton fair and statuesque. She was a charming size for Tyrold's height, her golden curls level with his chin, unlike Georgiana, who wasn't as tall as his shoulder, even in heeled slippers.

Lady Rose touched her arm. 'He's exceedingly talented, is he not?'

Georgiana managed a smile. 'Yes.'

Fanny, who now occupied Edward's vacated place, spoke unnecessarily loudly. 'Lady Rose, are you aware that Georgiana made a most favourable impression on Mr Tyrold at your brother's garden party yesterday?'

Georgiana's face flamed. 'Ma'am, *please.*' Goodness, what if one of Lady Frampton's friends overheard? The baroness was feeling her triumph right now, simpering as she watched Tyrold escort her daughter to the tea service.

'But, dearest, his alteration is for you.' Thankfully, Fanny lowered her voice. The widow likely could still overhear, but hopefully no one else could. 'I can scarce credit it, but it is so. I perceive it in the way he looks at you.'

'Nonsense,' Georgiana said under her breath. 'He's devoting more time to Miss Frampton than to me.' Tyrold and the beautiful blonde carried their tea towards a small sofa on the far side of the room. Miss Frampton conversed animatedly, her face vibrant, and Tyrold appeared genuinely interested, nodding and responding intermittently.

A part of Georgiana wondered if she should triumph. Perhaps Tyrold spoke so charmingly to Miss Frampton only because *she* had asked it of him. But there was another part, deep inside, where a green monster reared its head.

Especially when Tyrold laughed heartily at something Miss Frampton said, and she joined him, pressing her hand to her mouth not unlike how Georgiana had on the stairwell the night before . . .

'Don't despair, dearest,' Fanny whispered in her ear. 'What is a baron's daughter to a duke's daughter? Her fortune is little more than yours, and you sing much better than she does.'

A baron's *legitimate* daughter, with an intact fortune and an intact something else, as well. Not that Fanny knew Georgiana had given away both her wealth and her virtue . . .

Of course, Tyrold would marry someone as lovely and fresh as Miss Frampton, if or when he decided to abandon bachelorhood. In fact, perhaps this was another opportunity for Georgiana to do good. Just the day before she'd wished a kind husband upon Miss Frampton. Well, Tyrold required significant guidance still, but Georgiana suspected that underneath his arrogant bluster he possessed a kind heart. She could mould him into husband material, convince him that marriage would increase his happiness (he *clearly* needed someone to take care of him, after all), and encourage him towards Miss Frampton . . .

For once, however, the prospect of a good deed didn't lift Georgiana's spirits.

Quite the opposite, in fact.

Fanny patted Georgiana's forearm. 'I shall wave Tyrold over if I catch his eye.'

'No,' Georgiana said, too sharply. 'Don't call him over.'

'But he likes *you*. Look, he glances your way.'

It was so – he did, and there was *something* in his look. A barely perceptible wink, followed by an arrogant lift of his brows and an amused twist of his lips before he faced Miss Frampton once more.

Perhaps it was merely Georgiana's silly imagination, but it *seemed* as if the look communicated, 'You see, woman? I excel at following your commands,' in the teasing manner he'd employed the previous night, over oranges outside Galatea's.

Georgiana's chest compressed. A mutual infatuation with Tyrold wasn't a distraction she could allow herself. She couldn't risk an affair and whatever Fanny thought, Tyrold wouldn't marry a ruined woman, even if Georgiana were in the market for a husband . . . which she most definitely was *not*, because she'd dedicated her life to Monica House.

It was best Georgiana nip Tyrold's attraction in the bud.

She'd do it tonight.

She'd make herself as unattractive as possible.

That evening, Georgiana didn't dress as Georgie the bawd. Instead, she attired herself in an over-large brown wool frock. The garment hung heavy and shapeless, its skirts a tent over her body. She tied a coarse apron under her bodice and covered her hair with a massive mob cap.

She laughed when she inspected her reflection; she resembled a walnut, which was perfect. Tyrold couldn't possibly find her attractive tonight.

The Bolt in Tun, the most notorious of London's many coaching inns, was a four-storey structure with a yellow front along busy Fleet Street. The sun had set when Georgiana arrived, but gaslights illuminated the green sign above the main door and the open carriageway into the court.

She recognised Tyrold at once. He'd dressed inconspicuously, as she'd asked, in a plain coat, his new black hat and a pair of dark trousers. His hair was powdered at the temples, so a quick glance suggested an exceptionally trim-figured middle-aged man, and he leant against the inn's front with one booted foot against the wall, staring at the ground. A long clay pipe dangled from his mouth.

Georgiana almost laughed. The pipe was ridiculously old-fashioned, such as ancient men puffed in hazy corners of coffeehouses. It wasn't the short oak pipe Tyrold commonly smoked, but, still, something about his stance was so unmistakably the tall, brooding, aloof millionaire that Georgiana swallowed her laughter, marched to his side and snatched the pipe away.

He jolted upright.

Then recoiled when he recognised her.

His gaze trailed over her cap, down her body and back to her face. 'Good Lord! What's this? Why are you dressed in a moth-eaten blanket with a petticoat on your head? Where's my enticing Georgie?'

Georgiana's breath caught – *his* Georgie? – but she waved a dismissive hand. 'I'm dressed as your servant. Call me Ginny tonight.'

Tyrold's eyes twinkled. 'Why is my servant Ginny snatching all my pipes?'

Georgiana looked away, hoping shadows concealed her flushed face. His oak pipe lay on her bedside table and she'd put her nose to it after returning from Lady Eden's party. And then once more as she'd dressed for their adventure tonight. Both times, she'd imagined what it would feel like to nestle her face into Tyrold's neck, skin on skin, and breathe him in as deeply as the aromatic tobacco. 'Smoking is a filthy habit and you should stop. You'll ruin your singing voice, which would be a shame.'

He smiled his eye-crinkling grin. 'You liked my singing?'

'You're excellent,' Georgiana said primly. 'Miss Frampton was exceedingly impressed.'

'Who?'

As if he didn't know. 'The beautiful young lady you sang and conversed with for half an hour.'

Tyrold scoffed. 'Oh, that child.'

Georgiana fought to suppress her delight at his casual disregard. Surely, he was pretending indifference. He couldn't possibly be immune to Miss Frampton's loveliness. Unable to resist determining the degree of his attraction, Georgiana defended the girl. 'That *child*? She's an exquisite young lady and she'd make you an excellent wife.'

'*Wife?* Ha! If ever I go in search of the Mrs John Tyrold you said I'd make miserable, I shan't be looking in cradles. I'm three-and-thirty, which is far too old for any woman a day younger than . . .' He paused, looking her up and down carefully as Georgiana's heart leapt to her throat. 'Nine-and-twenty, perhaps.'

'*Nine*-and-twenty?' Georgiana repeated, appalled. 'I've only just turned six-and-twenty.'

He raised his eyebrows and blinked. 'Why! Did you think I meant *you*?'

Georgiana's cheeks flamed. 'Oh. N-no.' Feeling foolish, she grasped at how to salvage her dignity. 'How silly. I-I thought you were enquiring as to my age in a circumvent sort of way.'

'I assure you, when I wish to ask you something, I'll enquire forthright.'

Georgiana found she couldn't breathe, although she wasn't certain if he'd intended to imply anything. What a ludicrous conversation they'd got themselves into, skirting dangerously near flirting. Rather than embarrass herself further, she said nothing more. The silence lay weighty between them despite the bustling activity of Fleet Street.

'By the by,' he said after a time. 'I hope you noticed the effort I made with your Miss Frampton.'

'I did,' Georgiana responded, although she wished he'd chosen a different subject. 'Thank you. I think it went some way towards alleviating gossip about us.'

'Ah, was that your reason? I had a different one. I wanted to know if she attended school — which she did — and if she enjoyed it.'

'You were enquiring about her schooling?' Georgiana asked, surprised.

He studied his feet, his expression pensive. 'Apparently other schoolgirls can be quite cruel? Was that your experience as well?'

Miserable memories flooded Georgiana, but she answered calmly. 'I was an opera singer's bastard whose father didn't claim her. Of course, they were cruel.'

She'd been subjected to endless taunts – *like mother, like daughter; such is the seed, such is the harvest*, and others much crueller – and in her terrible last year at school, her friend Henrietta had no longer protected her.

'I'm sorry to hear that,' Tyrold said, his eyes darting to hers. 'Miss Frampton had a stammer and the other girls teased her mercilessly. She's mostly overcome it now, although there are hints at times. I told her it was charming, which I think you'll agree was well done of me.'

'Indeed,' Georgiana said. But she didn't *quite* mean it.

'It *was* somewhat charming, truth be told. She impressed me to a degree I wasn't expecting when she spoke of her resilience in overcoming her impediment. Singing helped, she said.'

'Musical instruction is beneficial for many reasons,' Georgiana agreed, her tone terser than she'd intended.

'Yes.' Tyrold frowned, still looking at his boots. Clearly, he'd had them polished that day, and they shone in the gaslight. 'The conversation made me think a great deal about Flora and what she might've suffered at school. I wish I'd asked her about it. I wish I'd more often taken half an hour to speak with her, as I did today with Miss Frampton.'

Georgiana's heart warmed. 'You can ask when we find her.'

'I don't know. I doubt she'd answer me. After all, I did try, on occasion. She was never as receptive to my questions as Miss Frampton was.' Tyrold glared down Fleet Street. 'Besides, who knows if Lucy will even come.'

'She will,' Georgiana said, sounding more convinced than she was.

Tyrold slumped against the inn wall with a sigh.

'Did you go to school?' Georgiana asked, to turn his thoughts as they waited.

He didn't answer immediately, but his eyes narrowed as he watched a coach rumble into the inn's carriage entrance. 'Yes, to Eton for a few years. There was cruelty there – worse for some than for others – but no one bothered me much because I would fight. Nick – Lord Holbrook, I mean – and I were a formidable pair. We protected Edward and Sidney, who were younger and more vulnerable.' He paused, then continued more pensively. 'I stopped attending classes altogether at fourteen. I felt I'd surpassed them. Why should I care for classics or philosophy when my mind could run countless figures and predict outcomes flawlessly? Perhaps that's some of what Flora felt; she's clever, the teachers said, although she despises her lessons. She loves birds. And *books*,' he added, with a chuckle. 'Her room was full of them, stacked in crooked towers on every surface.'

He stopped suddenly, as if startled. 'Good Lord. I apologise. I can't imagine why I rambled on.'

Georgiana was accustomed to people sharing intimacies even when they hardly knew her, like Lady Rose had earlier. At separate times, both Amanda and Maria DeRosa had explained that she emitted a comforting spirit, which led others to trust her instinctively. But since Tyrold wasn't accustomed to vulnerability, she reassured him by squeezing his hand. 'I'm honoured you shared that with me.'

Tyrold didn't release her hand when she loosened her squeeze; instead, he caught it in his own, and it was *his* turn to hold tightly. 'I worry Flora turned to books in lieu of friends,' he mused, grazing Georgiana's palm with his ink-stained thumb, which sent tingles up her arm. 'I think perhaps I didn't do as well by her as I should have.'

Georgiana edged closer, her body brushing against his sleeve. Tyrold was trying to change for Flora's sake, which was immensely gratifying. How different things would be for the girl when they found her.

'It's not too late, Jack.'

'Unless it is,' he replied mournfully. 'Perhaps I'll never find her, or I'll find her de—'

'No,' Georgiana interjected. 'Don't say it. Don't even let the thought cross your mind. We shall find her.'

Tyrold closed his eyes and drew her hand to his chest. Georgiana leant against his upper arm, willing him to derive strength and comfort from her presence. His body was tall and firm, his tobacco scent warm and masculine, and Georgiana closed her eyes as well. The moment was perfect in their shared closeness. Together, they would find Flora. They must – failure wasn't an option.

'Er, sir?' A feminine voice sounded nearby, startling Georgiana out of her reverie. She snatched her hand away, suddenly recalling that she stood on bustling

Fleet Street, exposed to the prying eyes of count-less passers-by, her costume her only protection from identification. Stepping back from Tyrold swiftly, she directed her attention to the young woman who stood near, wrapped in a woollen cloak. Under a deep hood, large grey eyes darted from side to side like a terrified rabbit. 'You got my money?'

Tyrold stood tall, planting both boots on the ground. 'Of course, Lucy. But you'll need to convince me you've earned it.'

Lucy's eyes narrowed, although her haunted fear was still discernible under a defiant veneer. 'First buy me an inside ticket for the night coach to Gloucester. It departs in twenty minutes. That's why I didn't want to escape last night – I want gone from this city, on my way home, before Mother Harris knows I've fled.'

Tyrold crossed his arms. 'Tell me what you know first,' he said sternly.

Sensing the extent of Lucy's terror, Georgiana inter-vened, tugging at Tyrold's sleeve. 'This is no time to negotiate. Purchase the ticket. Whether or not she assists us, we'll help her.'

He released a weary sigh, but he didn't protest further.

Once he'd entered the inn, Georgiana spoke to Lucy, hoping to reassure the young woman's fears away. 'Stay close to me while he purchases the ticket. I promise I won't let anyone hurt you. From this moment, you are safe.'

Lucy's lips trembled, her gaze shifting between Georgiana and the inn's sign as tears welled in her eyes. 'This was where I first come, when I arrived in London two and a half years ago.'

Georgiana understood. 'Someone stole you from here, didn't they?'

The tear-filled eyes widened. 'How did you know?'

'Because it's all too common a tale.' Georgiana reached for Lucy's hand and pressed it gently between her own. 'Was it Mother Harris?'

'No,' Lucy said bitterly. ''Twas her sister, Mrs Coleman, what acts as her procuress.'

Ah, this was valuable knowledge. If only Georgiana had more money at her disposal, she could pay trustworthy people to keep a watch on stagecoach inns such as the Bolt in Tun to ensure that young women didn't leave with criminals. 'I'll find Mrs Coleman, Lucy, and see what I can do to prevent her stealing other girls.'

Lucy wiped away a tear. 'She's a wily one. I was supposed to be maid to my mother's old mistress, and the bitch said she'd been sent by her. She seemed to know all the particulars, and I believed her . . .'

Yes, Georgiana thought. It sounded like many of the stories she'd heard. The circumstances from one poor country girl to another were so similar that it wasn't difficult for a cunning procuress to pretend she'd been sent by a prospective employer.

Lucy was still talking. 'I know now they wanted me for my appearance. They'd been looking for a tall, slim girl with dark red hair and grey eyes. *He'd* ordered it, you see.'

'Viscount Wingrove?' Georgiana asked, recalling what Tyrold had told her.

Lucy nodded. 'He pretends I'm some lover from his past. I don't know what happened to her, if she's dead or if she spurned him, but whatever it is, he . . . hates her, like. Hates her and loves her, you know? But it's a poisonous love, like he can't decide if he wants to possess her or kill her.'

Georgiana's stomach turned. Poor women – both Lucy and her predecessor. 'Do you know who she was?'

Lucy shook her head. 'No, but a grand lady, to be sure. Her name was Rosamunde. She was married to someone. *Not* Wingrove. Her husband's name was Frederick, and Wingrove hated him too. Lord knows I'll be glad to think no more of them. They've haunted me for years.' She shuddered violently, as if trying to purge her memories. 'When I first come, Wingrove wanted to buy exclusive rights to me, set me up somewhere so I could pretend to be her all the time for him. I reckon if he'd done that, I wouldn't be alive today.'

Georgiana pressed Lucy's hand tighter. 'Thank God you are delivered from this, sweet child.' Clearly, Georgiana needed to keep a closer eye on Mother Harris. With this in mind, she continued to question Lucy, hoping to learn more about the inner workings of the establishment. 'Why didn't Mother Harris allow Wingrove to keep you exclusively? Because you hate him?'

Lucy scoffed. 'You think Mother Harris cares that I hate him? Of course not – she don't have a drop of human kindness. She'd turn me over and never ask about me again if the price was right. Five thousand is what she demanded, but he didn't have the money, did he? Mother Harris says he's in tremendous debt, and no one loans to him any more, even with him being a lord and all. So, she only lets him have me once a week, but I *hate* it when he comes. Sometimes I take days to recover from what he's done, and then Mother Harris won't let me eat because I'm not earning.'

Georgiana wrapped her arm around Lucy, drawing her close. 'They won't trouble you again, Lucy. You're finally free.'

Lucy sniffled against her shoulder. 'Why are you helping me?'

Georgiana reached into the high bodice of her gown and extracted her locket. After releasing the clasp, she paused, gazing at the pencil drawing on one side. She touched the curl of thick golden hair, tied with a snippet of white ribbon that had once decorated a baby gown Georgiana had sewn herself, first used for a christening, then for a shroud.

Then she showed Lucy. 'This was my daughter, Annie,' she said, her voice as heavy as her heart. 'Everything I do in this world, I do in her memory.'

It was the only way Georgiana could assuage her guilt.

Lucy traced the drawing with the tip of her finger. 'I was with child once,' she said, sniffling. 'But Mother Harris made me drink a tincture and the baby came away. I guess I'm a wicked girl, for I'm glad I didn't bring it into this world.'

'You're not wicked, Lucy. It is never easy for an unwed girl to have a child, but my circumstances were better than yours.' Or they *should* have been better – if Georgiana hadn't been too wilful and proud to ask for help. She'd been so *angry* at her father. So livid with white-knuckled rage at his betrayal that she'd run away from anyone who might've helped her, including Fanny, Maria DeRosa and the community of Monica House. If only she'd stayed, borne her daughter in safety . . .

The intense pain came again and tears threatened. To prevent them, Georgiana drew Lucy close. She was helping this child. *That* was what she needed to think about.

A familiar voice drew her attention. 'Your ticket,' Tyrold said to Lucy, but his eyes were on the still-open locket cupped in Georgiana and Lucy's entwined hands.

Georgiana drew in a deep breath to settle her emotions as she clasped the lid and tucked the necklace inside her bodice. Then she kissed Lucy and wiped away the girl's tears. 'Let me take you to your coach, dear child, and you tell me all you can about Flora so there's not another who has this pain.'

John followed Georgiana and Lucy into the bustling, galleried coaching yard of the Bolt in Tun.

Georgiana's extraordinary compassion amazed him. No, more than that. He was astounded, astonished, in awe. What kind of duke's daughter kissed away the tears of prostitutes? Moreover, it seemed she'd confided in Lucy, revealing the mysterious locket's contents, which she hadn't disclosed to Rose. John realised there was much more to Georgiana than he could fathom, and he felt an overwhelming desire to unravel her enigmatic layers.

His mind thus occupied, he trailed behind as Georgiana manoeuvred Lucy through the chaos of luggage-burdened stagecoaches, sweat-drenched horses, and weary travellers. They dodged fast-moving grooms and beer-swigging drivers and drew into a secluded corner, shielded from the hustle by a low-hanging gallery.

When John arrived, Georgiana was querying the girl. 'Lucy, was red-haired Flora for Wingrove, as well?'

John clenched his fist, instantly enraged by the thought, but Lucy swiftly shook her head. 'Lud, no,' the girl said, and John could breathe again. 'Wingrove didn't have nothing to do with Flora. She was with a young feller of her own, who was scheming with Mother Harris for a portion of *his* fortune.' She cut her eyes to John. 'What is she, your baby sister?'

'Never mind the relation,' John said. 'Tell me who this fellow was.'

Lucy pursed her lips. 'I ain't saying nothing until I have my money. I got too much at stake here. It was all I could do to get away and I wasn't able to bring a thing with me – I can't go back there for I'd rather die, and I can't go home without something to live on, can I?'

John withdrew a heavy leather pouch from his coat pocket. The coins inside – a mixture of small gold guineas and larger silver five-shilling crowns – weighed near four pounds, but Lucy whipped the bag from his hand and clawed hungrily at its opening. Her eyes grew enormous as she peered inside. 'Lud! To imagine such riches.' She crouched, her cloak billowing about her, and lifted her skirts to deposit the bag in some undefined location. 'There,' she said as she stood. 'I'll tell you what I know. Your girl, she arrived a fortnight ago on the arm of her feller—'

'Who is he?' John asked.

'Lud, if I knew that I would've said. All I can tell you is he was a gentlemanly boy—'

'Boy? Young man, you mean?'

Lucy shook her head. 'No more'n a boy. If a razor has ever touched his cheek, it didn't come away with much on it.'

It was surprising news, but John had seen cruelty in boys. 'Very well, continue. Had you seen him before?'

'Never. Maud, she watched Flora but she don't know more'n what I do – nor would she tell you if she did, for she and Mother Harris are as thick as thieves. All I know is your girl, she came in happy. I think she thought he'd taken her to a boarding house, at first, but she learnt quick enough.'

'How?' John demanded, sick to his stomach. 'What happened to her?'

'Nothing so bad. But she was downstairs with Maud one day – middle of the afternoon – and these two swells come by. Wanted Maud, but they liked the looks of your Flora. Chatted with her for a while, all easy-like, and then asked Maud outright what she'd cost.

Maud says Mother Harris is saving her. One of them – Lord Murden, if you know him – he said he'd pay a hundred guineas for her maidenhood. Your girl's eyes near popped from her head, but Maud took her out the room quick, before she could say nothing. Your girl's feller was out at the time and when he come back that evening, she threw a fit like a banshee. Broke near everything in her room. Mother Harris said she caused fifty pounds of damage, and said she'd get her money off the boy. I had to take a customer then, so I don't know more other'n that the next morning, your girl and her boy were gone.'

Lucy stopped talking.

'That's *all*?' John asked, outraged. 'That's what you can tell me? You've shared nothing of value beyond the fact that she was with a boy.'

Lucy pouted. 'I ain't finished. His name was William. That's what she called him, at least. Also, I was looking out my bedchamber window some days after he left, and I seen him going into the King's Head, the public near Mother Harris, though your girl wasn't with him. So enquire there if they know him.'

'Enquire at a public house if they know a lad named William?' John seethed. 'Good God! Useless.'

Georgiana furrowed her brow. 'Think, Lucy, what else can you tell us of the boy? What did he look like? What did he wear? Was there anything distinctive in his attire, in his address?'

'He wasn't nothing special to look at. Light brown hair, lean build. Neither tall nor short. His eyes were

226

uncommonly pale – blue, but like the sky on a hazy day – and he was as timid as a mouse. Jumped at everything. But he talked genteel, like you do, and his voice was kind.'

'Did you see how he arrived?' Georgiana asked.

'A hackney, same as you see all over London.'

John's shoulders slumped. It felt as if the weight of the world had descended upon him. This interrogation was going nowhere and he'd lost all hope of finding Flora based on Lucy's information.

Georgiana glanced towards the courtyard and nibbled at her bottom lip. 'Lucy, how do you know he was the same gentleman you saw going into the public house? There must've been *something* distinctive for you to distinguish him from an upstairs window across the street.'

'Yes, there was!' Lucy cried, brightening. 'I seen his limp.'

John perked up. 'A limp?'

'Aye. One of his legs is shorter than the other. Not so much that you would easily notice, but rather than swinging his walking stick, like most young gentlemen do, he *leant* on it. Discreet-like, but you started to notice after a bit.'

Nearby, a stagecoach guard blew a long tin horn. 'Gloucester departure!'

Lucy clasped her hands together. 'Oh, that's my coach leavin'. If I don't get on it, Mother Harris might find me. I can't go back. I can't.'

'Is there *anything* else you can tell us?' John asked, although he'd given up hope already. A distinctive walk was something, but not nearly enough in a city of well over a million people.

Lucy seemed to consider, tilting her head and scrunching up her features. 'There was another person,' she said at last. 'At least one other person in the hackney – but they didn't get out.'

'A man?'

'I don't know,' she responded. 'I didn't see them. I just seen the boy, William, talking to someone inside the cab. He was arguing, looked like. When William turned away and came inside with your girl, his shoulders drooped as if something was bothering him, much like yours are now.' Lucy glanced anxiously at her coach, where the driver was taking his seat. 'Now that's all I know, I swear. *Please* let me go home to my ma. I have a granny as well, leastwise, she was alive when I left. They must've thought me dead this whole time. Let me go, please. I want to go home.'

Her grey eyes pleaded with John, and, although his heart sank that they'd get nothing else from her, he nodded. 'Go.'

'And thank you,' Georgiana added, kissing the girl's cheek. 'God's blessings go with you, Lucy. Find happiness.'

Lucy threw her arms around Georgiana and squeezed. 'Thank you, ma'am. Oh, thank you.' She released the embrace and fled across the yard, holding her skirts in her haste.

John slumped onto a bench and cradled his head in his hands.

Georgiana sat beside him.

'A waste of a hundred pounds,' he said with a huff.

She rubbed his back, which comforted him, despite everything. 'I know you don't really regret the loss of the money,' she whispered, her breath sweet against his cheek. 'Just like I know you aren't as stingy as the reputation you like to cultivate.'

John's eyes met hers, mere inches away. 'You do, eh?'

'Yes, I do.' She held his gaze. 'What you're actually feeling right now is intense sorrow about Flora.'

John stared at his folded hands.

'Don't despair, Jack, for neither your time nor your money was wasted. You've saved Lucy from a vicious life, and we've learnt a great deal in the process.' She hooked his chin with her finger until he again met her gaze. 'Flora is fighting,' she continued, a smile on her lips. 'All that rebellious energy you despaired of is now serving her well. We've learnt that she didn't know what she was getting herself into. I strongly suspect that she was lonely and unhappy, and a sweet-talking boy made her believe he was the cure to that despair. It's a story as old as time, I'm afraid. But she's no one's fool, any more than you are.'

'Oh, but I feel a fool now,' John confessed.

Georgiana leant close and pressed her lips to his cheek.

John's heart leapt to his throat.

She sat back, but the phantom imprint of her kiss lingered.

'Thank you, Georgiana,' he said when he found his voice. And lest she think he was thanking her for the kiss, he swiftly added, 'For your guidance, I mean. And your wisdom. I could not begin to do this without you.'

Her dark eyes widened. 'Oh! I-I . . . Yes . . .' Her words trailed off, and after a short hesitation, she nodded briskly. 'Yes, of course. You're welcome. Now, come; let us walk to the King's Head.'

She left John's side and marched across the yard, a purposeful swiftness to her straight-backed gait, somehow dignified even in her drab gown, making her way through the dung-and-straw littered yard of a filthy coaching inn.

And John was left on the bench, marvelling at the wonder of her.

She hadn't kissed him. Not on the mouth, that is. Not in *that way*.

She'd wanted to, when he'd surprised her with those beautifully sincere words of appreciation. But she hadn't.

And that was good.

Or so Georgiana tried to tell herself as she strode towards Covent Garden with Tyrold a silent but pleasant companion just behind her shoulder, as if he were her protective shadow. Tonight, she didn't mind; in fact, she found his presence supremely comforting after years of walking dangerous streets alone. Naturally, she didn't need a man to protect her, but that didn't mean it wasn't nice to have one.

When they arrived at the King's Head, Tyrold opened the door and ushered Georgiana through with a lingering but silent gaze. A rush of steamy air greeted her as she entered the beam-ceilinged taproom, filled with working-class men swigging pewter tankards at mismatched tables. In her unattractive attire, Georgiana fortunately drew little attention as she weaved her way to the bar counter, where a red-faced man pulled the taps.

He grew shifty-eyed when she enquired about a William who limped. ''Ere, love, how am I supposed to see how they walk from behind this counter? Now, I don't like women in my taproom, so either get out or go back to my kitchens. We're short-handed, so I'll pay you a shilling for an honest night's labour.'

'She's with me,' Tyrold growled, standing close and sliding a half-crown across the wooden counter. He placed a firm hand on the small of Georgiana's back – another protective-type gesture she found she didn't mind in the least. 'We'll have two ales. Let the woman be and you can keep the change. I shall give you more if you decide you remember aught of William.'

The tavern owner pocketed the half-crown with a snort. 'I already said I don't know nothin' about him. Now, if your woman behaves proper and modest, fine, but, otherwise, go to the bagnio across the street and rent a bathing room. There's no whoring allowed here, even in our rooms upstairs. I run a respectable establishment.'

'I doubt the respectability of this tavern,' Georgiana said several minutes later, after other enquiries resulted in similar dismissive replies. She nodded over her tankard at a waiter ushering a group of fashionable gentlemen towards a back door. Money was exchanged – gold coins by the look of it – and the gentlemen disappeared down a dark stairwell. 'I suspect there's prize-fighting or a cock pit in the basement.'

'This is a useless endeavour anyway,' Tyrold grumbled.

Georgiana considered. It did seem hopeless, but the night was still young. 'Let's discuss our options.'

She led Tyrold to a back table, where they sat side by side on a bench, and she leant close, her lips at his ear so as not to be overheard. 'We could go to the Runners, but that's the last resort. I think you should infiltrate the cock pit, or whatever it is, and enquire amongst the spectators. Perhaps William, like other young gentlemen, visited here to view a fight—'

'I recognised two of the gentlemen who went down.' Tyrold's cheek rested against hers as he whispered. He glided his hand behind her waist, gently pulling her closer so she could hear better, and she placed her hand on his far shoulder, sliding her fingers under his coat collar to stabilise herself, trying to ignore the tantalising feel of her breasts against his upper arm. 'They will recognise me as well,' Tyrold continued. 'Aren't we trying to avoid that?'

'Yes, you have a point,' she murmured, his cedar-wood-scented hair tickling her nose. Knowing she must resist the urges swelling inside her, she pulled back so their faces were no longer touching. 'Perhaps we should ask Edward,' she suggested. 'For then there would be no connection to Flora—'

'Hey,' a voice interrupted loudly, startling Georgiana so that she jumped back in her seat, releasing her hold on Tyrold's shoulder.

A freckled lad carrying a tray of pewter mugs stood before them.

Tyrold adjusted himself on the bench, his hand sliding slowly across Georgiana's lap before dropping. 'Yes?'

The waiter sucked his teeth. 'I seen that lad you're lookin' for.'

Georgiana squeezed Tyrold's forearm. 'Sit, sit, please,' she said to the lad, waving her free hand at the space before them. 'Please tell us what you can, Mr . . . ?'

'Name's Dick.' The waiter placed down his tray and sank into a chair. 'The rest, they won't talk to you, for somethin' was unsavoury 'bout the 'ole deal, but I'm not scared. That young William, he stayed upstairs for several days with his father and his sister. Left on Saturday.'

Tyrold deflated next to Georgiana, so she tightened her hold on his arm. 'What did the sister look like?'

Dick's eyes gleamed. 'Prime piece. Cheeks like roses, hair like a copper penny. Curls all about her face.'

Georgiana pressed on, ignoring a growl from Tyrold. 'What else can you tell us, Dick?'

The boy glanced ruefully at his ales. 'Can you buy these off me first? I've got to sell 'em.'

'Of course.' Georgiana gestured to Tyrold, who rolled his eyes but reached into his pocket. He slapped a handful of small change on the table as Georgiana handed the lad a tankard. 'Here's one for your troubles, Dick. Now, tell me, how was the girl's health? Her wellbeing?'

'It's the gal you're curious about, is it?' Dick tossed back his mug, his Adam's apple bulging as he drank. He slammed down the tankard and wiped froth from his upper lip. 'I only seen her on the last day, but I heard her a'right on the first morning, yelling like a wild thing from her room, driving old Sam over there,' he nodded at the barman, 'to distraction. The man – not the boy but his father — said she was mad. Sent for some laudanum and she got quiet after that.'

Tyrold squeezed his tankard, his knuckles white. Under the table, Georgiana pressed her palm against his, threading their fingers together, and he gripped back with zeal. 'Tell us about the man you say was the father?' Georgiana asked Dick. 'Do you know his name?'

'Father and son were both called William Smith. Who am I to say if that was their real name or not? Plenty of Williams and plenty of Smiths in England.'

'Had you seen them before?'

'Don't *think* so,' Dick mused, scratching his head. 'But I'm not certain I'd have paid heed if I had. Besides the boy's limp, they looked like any other swells.'

'And the father's age?' Georgiana enquired. Viscount Wingrove nagged at a corner of her mind, for some reason.

''Bout the same as Sam over there.'

Georgiana glanced at the barman, who wasn't older than fifty. Not the viscount, then. 'You said you saw the girl only on the last day?'

'Aye.' Dick nodded to another tankard. 'D'ye mind? It gets hot, working here.'

Georgiana waved her hand. 'Of course. But please continue.'

After Dick swallowed his second tankard, he leant over the table. 'On Saturday morning, the most terrible scream come from the room. I rushed upstairs with my master and — well, we listened at the door, truth be told. The girl says, "I swear I shan't give you a moment's more trouble if only you take me to the

Vauxhall masquerade on Thursday, like William promised." Now, you'll agree that's odd, eh? First, she screams to wake the dead, and next she's askin' to go to a pleasure garden? There's no rhyme or reason to that already, but then the father's reply was disturbing as all that: said she had no right to ask for anything since she hadn't gone to bed with William, what was supposed to be her brother. Now, Old Sam, he don't have tolerance for perversity in any form, so he whipped out his key and opened that door.'

Dick paused as if for dramatic effect, his eyes bright.

'Dammit, boy,' John said with a snarl. 'Get on with it.'

'A'right.' Dick sulked, taking a third tankard and sucking the foam off the top. 'It was a scene, I can tell you. The boy, he was whimpering and cowering in a corner. The father had your girl by the hair, with his hand raised, as if to strike her. She turned to us when we entered. Had a bloody gash across her forehead, but she didn't miss a beat. "He drugs me," screams she. "Send for—" but the father, he clamped his hand over her mouth and pulled her close so she couldn't do more than wriggle as useless as a fish out of water. Sam, he said he didn't like it. Asked the man to unhand her. Repeated what he always claims 'bout this being a respectable establishment, and said he knew there was something unnatural going on. But the man said, dangerous-like, "You don't want the law any more'n I do." And, well, that's the truth of the matter, so that was the end of it. Thirty minutes later, they left, and the girl was asleep in the man's arms."

'Drugged, you mean,' Tyrold said, his voice ice.

'Who am I to say?' Dick slurped more ale. 'Now that I've told you all I know, you might make it worth my while.'

Tyrold leant forwards, as tense as a crouching tiger. 'If you wanted me to pay to hear how you are a spineless coward who stands by as a girl is hurt,' he said slowly, articulating each word with cut-glass precision, 'you should've demanded the money before you talked. You didn't help her despite knowing she was in danger.'

Dick recoiled nervously, his Adam's apple bobbing. 'See here, man. I helped her now, didn't I? I told you what I know when no one else was willing to speak. Besides, what was I to do? The man said he was her father, and it's up to a father to decide how to manage his child. That's none of my business.'

Tyrold jumped up, grabbing Dick by the coat collar and yanking him half over the table. Dick's chair clattered to the floor and the tankards overturned, spilling their ale. Other patrons stirred, excited by the prospect of a fight. Oblivious to the attention, Tyrold spoke through his teeth, his face inches from Dick's. 'When a man sees someone attack someone weaker, it behoves him to make it his business.'

Georgiana rose. 'Then follow your own good advice and let him go, Jack,' she said softly, stroking Tyrold's arm. 'He's little more than a boy, he's foxed, and fighting with him won't help Flora.'

Tyrold remained frozen, breathing heavily, but, at last, he released Dick, letting the boy tumble to the ale-sloshed tabletop. As Dick scrambled away, Tyrold turned to Georgiana. 'How can we help Flora, then?' he asked, distraught. 'The devil only knows what she's been subjected to, and now the trail is cold yet again.'

'Not entirely cold,' Georgiana reassured him. 'Get yourself a domino and we'll attend Vauxhall on Thursday. Additionally, ask Edward to design a placard tomorrow. It should feature a line drawing of Flora, accompanied by lettering stating her name, her eye and hair colour, and offering a fortune for her safe return – twenty thousand, if you can, and I know you can. We must make the reward irresistibly inciting, ensuring that anyone who finds her will hand her over immediately without attempting to extort more. Once Edward completes the placard, take it to an etcher you trust and have him ready the plate. We won't print them *yet*, but possessing a prepared plate will save us time if the situation becomes urgent.'

Tyrold exhaled, rubbing his powdered temples. 'If at all possible, I want to keep her abduction secret, but I see the wisdom in preparedness. I'll do as you say during the day. Where shall we search tomorrow night?'

'*We* aren't searching anywhere tomorrow, I'm sorry to say. I promised the duchess I'd attend the first assembly of the Season at Almack's, and I'm afraid it's something I must do,' she explained, the weight of the creditors' bills still on her mind.

Tyrold stared at her. Then – quite unexpectedly – he snorted.

Georgiana bristled. 'I can't help that I have obligations to others besides you, sir.'

'That's not what I was thinking.'

Georgiana raised a sceptical brow. 'Then why did you make that derisive sound?'

'Not derisive,' Tyrold said, shaking his head. 'I was astonished, yet again. You are a chameleon. You stand before me wearing the most hideous attire, having just disengaged me from a tavern brawl, yet tomorrow evening you'll dance at Almack's in a duchess's company.'

Georgiana couldn't help but smile. 'And the night following, I shall be scouring a Vauxhall masquerade on the arm of Jack, rogue and scoundrel.'

'Yes,' Tyrold said, and his smile faded as his gaze locked with Georgiana's.

Once more, Georgiana felt the magnetic pull between them, but she'd not moved more than an inch in his direction before she recalled, with a shake of her head, that she *couldn't* kiss him. So she stepped back immediately, nearly stumbling over a fallen tankard, but catching herself on the table edge before she fell.

'Let's go,' she said hurriedly. After kicking the tankard away – for once *not* feeling inclined to tidy – she crossed the overheated room. The crisp night air provided refreshing respite as she stepped onto the street and began to walk home.

Though concerns about Flora swirled like a tempest in John's mind, one thing anchored him: the slight form of Miss Georgiana Bailey walking ahead, draped in a hideous, shapeless woollen blanket.

With her, he didn't feel alone. She was wisdom, she was calmness, she was patience, all attributes John admired immensely – and yet, she was something unsettling as well. Something that set him aflame with yearning, and by no means entirely sexual yearning. Her proximity comforted him and tortured him. Gave him peace and threw him in turmoil. Expanded his chest with tender feelings, heated his body with desire.

Twice, they'd come close to sharing a kiss. A kiss she seemed to want as much as he did. A kiss she could justifiably use to insist he marry her, according to the rules of their class – and John now doubted he'd resist if she tried such a ploy.

She walked several yards ahead and John made no attempt to catch up. He intended to ensure her safe return to Monica House, unlike the night before when she'd got away, but he let her lead, understanding her desire for independence. She clung to the shadows along Maiden Lane and Chandos Street before turning up St Martins Lane, and in her bag of a gown and hideous white cap, she might as well have been invisible to everyone but John. Pedestrians passed her by, utterly unaware that the most fascinating woman in London strode in their presence.

She was some distance ahead when, at a public house past New Street, a man stumbled out of the tavern door, spilled down the steps on unsteady legs, and nearly fell on top of her. John immediately sprinted towards them; it was a dangerous area, uncomfortably close to the St Giles Rookery, and, indeed, by the time he arrived, the man – a portly specimen with bushy grey sideburns – held Georgiana tightly, staring at her with obvious lust.

'Are ye sure I didn't hurt you, lamb?' the lecher asked. 'I thought you a robust serving woman, but I see now you're just a sweet slip of a wench, and a comely one at that.'

'I'm perfectly unharmed.' Georgiana pulled against the man's clasp, but he didn't release her.

John's blood boiled. How dare the man lay his hands on her and continue to touch her when she struggled against him? 'Let her go immediately,' he demanded, looming over his adversary.

The man shifted his attention to John, his drunken gaze struggling to focus. 'Here, who are you to tell me what to do? As I saw her first, I consider it my duty and honour to escort her now.'

'That is my honour,' John said, clenching his fists. 'Unhand her or I'll forcibly remove you, and then you'll find my boot up your arse.'

Georgiana's eyes twinkled, as if she were more amused than perturbed by her predicament. 'I'm quite capable of taking care of myself, but I *would* prefer *his* company,' she nodded her head towards John, 'so if you will please release me, sir—'

'Shh, my sweet little lamb.' The drunken lout breathed against her cheek. 'You've not given me a chance. Why don't you and I have a lovely drink somewhere?'

'She doesn't want to give you a chance.' John grabbed the back of the man's coat, yanked him off Georgiana and tossed him towards the railing. But recognising the man was some years his senior and worse off for drink, he didn't make good his threat of further violence.

Instead, he did something else.

Something he really *oughtn't* do, but driven by a fierce desire to protect Georgiana, he wrapped her securely in his arms and bowed his head over hers. 'Just to warn him off,' he whispered in explanation. 'A chaste kiss — if you have no objection . . .'

She tilted her head back and rose, as if on tiptoes. 'No objection,' she said, her breath on his lips as her arms flew around his neck and her fingers threaded into his hair.

And she kissed him with fervent passion.

Then there was only them, and their kiss, their mouths joined, her tongue reaching for his without hesitation, the taste of her like honey mixed with their ale. John lifted her hard against him; she was delicate in his arms, so small but so *alive* with fever and fire and feeling, and he clung to her as if she and she alone could anchor him. She belonged in his embrace. She fitted. It fitted. Everything. This, them, the comfort and security and wisdom of her. Her soft femininity under which ran the strength of steel. John's body burned with desire; he was alive to her sensuality, her scent heady, her taste sublime, her proximity everything he lacked and needed in his life.

She broke the kiss but didn't pull away.

'By God, Georgiana.' He spoke against her lips, wet with his own taste, and his heart ached with the beauty of the moment. 'Loveliest Georgiana.'

The man from the tavern grunted, reminding John of his presence. 'Well, then. Have him if you want, girl. Plenty more like you.'

As the lout stumbled off, John kissed Georgiana with the tenderness he'd intended earlier, although there was nothing chaste now. 'A bigger lie was never spoken, for there's no one even remotely like you.'

'Oh, release me, please,' she cried suddenly, passionately, and John, although surprised, did as he was told.

Without a moment's hesitation or another word, she walked swiftly up the street, and John's spirits plummeted. He hadn't meant to offend her. He'd thought she'd wanted the kiss, but maybe she didn't, and his compliment compounded her discomfort.

John jogged to catch up. 'Georgiana,' he said when he was by her side. 'Please forgive me.'

Her eyes grew large. 'For what?'

'Let's speak over there,' John suggested, and together they walked to a nearby alley, out of the way of pedestrians. 'I had no right to kiss you like that,' he said when they were alone. 'In truth, I oughtn't have suggested we kiss at all – there were other ways I could have warned him off. I've offended you and I'm earnestly sorry.'

The shadows were murky, but enough light emanated from the streetlamps for John to witness her tender expression. 'No, no, you misunderstand why I needed you to release me. I assure you, I'm not offended by the kiss. We both know we've been wanting it since last night.'

So there *was* something between them, a genuine attraction, which had nothing to do with his money. Of that John was now certain, and the knowledge nearly deprived him of the ability to breathe, because an unconquerable mutual attraction with Georgiana meant one thing, and one thing only.

Marriage.

A surprisingly pleasant thought.

Could John have been hoping for this sort of thing all these lonely years, without even knowing he wanted it? How else could this sudden and fierce connection feel so *right*, so much like something his heart recognised? Did he truly crave a complete transformation of his life, or was his distress over Flora muddling his mind?

'Still,' he said, somewhat shakily. 'I shouldn't have suggested the kiss without . . .' He hesitated, licking his lips, wondering how he could say what he felt. 'Without knowing my intentions.'

She took his hands in hers. 'Your *intentions*? Jack, I have no expectation of intentions,' she responded with sincerity. 'I believed you when you said you were a confirmed bachelor. Two days is hardly likely to change a lifetime's conviction, merely because we desire each other. It was simply a kiss. A wonderful kiss, but nothing more.'

John rubbed his thumbs over the soft pads of her palms as he considered what she'd said, but his truth was, the two days they'd spent together *had*

244

already changed him – in ways he didn't completely understand.

'I don't usually find myself unable to think clearly,' he began hesitantly. 'But the past two weeks – and *especially* the four-and-thirty hours since you and I began our partnership – have been such a jumble of confused emotion and questioning myself and decisions I made years ago and decisions I make now and wondering where the deuce I went so wrong and if, in fact, I've ever done *anything* right. So, yes, I feel it was extremely wrong indeed to act upon my desire to kiss you when I'm in this condition. Yet I've unabashedly wanted to do so since last night, and I want to do it again so badly it's all I can do not to take you in my arms right now—'

Georgiana put her hand over his mouth, silencing him. 'Once more then.' She smiled. She raised on her tiptoes, grasped his shoulders and kissed him again. Rational thought fled as John kissed her back, lifting her from the ground and holding her against him, using the brick side of the laneway to help support her.

Although John could feel nothing of her body's shape through the rough wool of her gown, as they kissed this time, ever deeper, ever hungrier, his cock hardened into throbbing steel. Their mutual desire was tangible as their tongues vied for control and their embrace tightened. John wanted to take Georgiana against the wall; she tilted her pelvis towards him, as if she felt the same desperate urge, and the increase of pressure on his shaft made John break the kiss to moan against her cheek. 'Goddamnit, Georgiana. I don't have gentlemanly thoughts right now.'

'I know.' Georgiana chuckled, her lips at his ear, and John nestled his nose into her silky, floral-scented hair. He couldn't get enough of her. He wanted her more than he'd ever wanted anything in all his life, and he couldn't even fully comprehend why, other than that she seemed to have appeared exactly when he needed her, as if she were an angel.

'You mustn't distress yourself, John,' she whispered, calling him by his real name for the first time. 'I can't speak to everything you feel, but I can set your mind at rest that you aren't taking advantage of me.' She loosened her hold, and John let her feet slide to the ground, the absence of her a vast void. 'In fact, it's all I can do not to take advantage of you.'

'Ha!' He laughed through his desire. 'The last thing you've done is set my mind at rest.'

She grinned, her teeth flashing white in the shadows. 'That's not your mind troubling you. I know because I feel the same. My thoughts aren't very ladylike right now.' She brushed his cheek with her fingertips. 'You needn't worry that I'll misinterpret matters; I'm not an innocent with a vulnerable heart. I'm a woman who's already lived a full life, who understands a great deal about the ways of the world. *However*, as lovely as those kisses were, we can't repeat them. Not here, not in England where you are who you are, and I must maintain a spotless reputation and conceal the fact that I'm sullied goods.'

John frowned. 'Sullied goods?'

'I'm not a virgin,' she said quietly. 'Which is one of many reasons I'm only *pretending* to be a debutante. I'm not marriageable, although my father and the duchess don't know.'

Her revelation didn't particularly surprise John, knowing her as he now did, but her implication that her lack of virginity sullied her did. She treated prostitutes with the same loving care she bestowed upon society widows. She acted as if Flora might yet have a second chance, despite what had likely happened. 'You cannot mean to suggest a woman's value lies in her virginity? I know you don't believe that.'

She blinked, paused, seemed to hesitate. 'I . . . I don't, but . . . well, what I believe is immaterial against society's convictions, which decree that a woman's value lies in her virtue, in her parentage, and in her fortune. In all of which, I'm afraid, I'm sorely lacking.'

'But then what about Flora—'

'Flora possesses a vast fortune. I squandered mine, remember?'

John shook his head, not understanding how she could view herself so poorly when in general she didn't lack self-confidence. 'Only a fool would question either your value or your virtue.'

She smiled wistfully. 'That's kind of you to say, Jack—'

'I liked it when you called me John.'

'Kind of you to say, John, but you don't know the whole story.'

John thought of her locket and his imagination filled in the gaps. She had, of course, given herself to the man for whom she wrote the song, but where there was love the union between two bodies was the most beautiful and natural thing in the world, conventions be damned. At least, that's how it had been for John and Helen, so many years ago.

'Georgiana, I would never, under any circumstances, question your virtue because you gave yourself to a man you loved.'

Her brows drew together as her expression slowly altered, but John couldn't interpret its meaning. 'How kind of you,' she repeated, without a trace of sarcasm, yet John suspected he'd somehow upset her. 'But others would and if my virtue is questioned, my work at Monica House will be as well.' She dusted her skirts in a businesslike manner. 'Now, I truly must return home, because I barely slept yesterday. Unless I rest well tonight, I shan't be in a fit condition for Almack's tomorrow. See me home, John, as I know you wish to do, and then get sleep yourself. Two days' separation will do us both good, and we shall search again for Flora on Thursday. Remember, have Edward draw the placard and get it to an etcher to ready the plate. I'll dwell on other options as often as I can spare time for thought. I'm behind on countless urgent tasks for Monica House, but Flora will be foremost in my mind.'

John considered her words as he escorted her towards Soho Square. He hadn't slept well for the last two nights. Perhaps lack of sleep *had* muddled his emotions. She was wise – she could be correct on this matter.

Or perhaps . . .

Perhaps he was, indeed and at long last, falling in love again, because with alarming rapidity, Georgiana was becoming the focus of his thoughts and his hopes – and the prospect of life without her felt bleak, even if it meant Flora would be found.

Whichever it was, he decided as she vanished behind the metal door, he couldn't wait until Thursday to find out. He'd sleep tonight, and he'd see Georgiana tomorrow.

John took a hackney to Half Moon Street, where Jolly greeted him with a wagging tail in the entrance vestibule. But rather than go directly to his bedchamber, John climbed an extra flight of stairs, a candle in hand, and eased open the door to his housemate's room.

'Edward?' he whispered, shielding the flickering flame to prevent beeswax dripping on the recumbent form of his friend, who was tangled nude in the bedsheets, cuddling his buxom model. When Edward didn't budge, John poked him. 'Psst, Edward. Wake up.'

Edward blinked open unfocused eyes. His brow furrowed when he saw John; then he sat up like a bolt of lightning as his woman murmured and rolled away. 'What's the matter? Who's died?'

'Nothing and no one. I have a question.'

Edward narrowed his eyes. 'What the devil kind of question?'

John shifted his weight. 'Er, how does one get a voucher for Almack's?'

There was a moment of stillness; then Edward ran his hands through his chestnut curls. 'You woke me to ask how to get a voucher for Almack's?'

'Yes, I need one for tomorrow night.'

Edward fell back on his feather mattress and took his woman in his arms again. 'You'll need to speak with my Aunt Agatha, and she won't thank you if you wake *her* in the middle of the night. Go to sleep and we'll talk in the morning.'

John hesitated. 'So it can be done?'

Edward shrugged against his pillows. 'Will the dragon-keepers of Almack's relinquish a voucher for the richest bachelor in London? Who can say? Perhaps if you assure them you intend to look for a wife this Season . . . but that would be a lie, wouldn't it?'

John cleared his throat. 'Not necessarily.'

'Well, well.' Edward chuckled. 'How interesting. But go to bed. We'll scheme at breakfast.'

John rubbed the back of his head. 'One more thing. Could you design a reward placard with a line drawing of Flora? Georgiana thinks an etcher should ready a plate.'

'Whatever you need, my friend,' Edward said, his voice turning sombre.

John felt an odd tickle in his throat. 'Thank you, Edward. Knew there was a reason I keep you around, despite your despicable habits.'

With that, John crossed the room, intending to get what sleep he could. As active as his mind was, he didn't anticipate much success.

Edward's voice stopped him at the door. 'Oh, John?'

John turned, his hand on the handle. 'What?'

'I heartily approve, old man. She's a diamond.'

John's pulse quickened. 'If you're referring to Georgiana, I thought you wanted her for yourself?'

Edward's sleepy laughter filled the room.

14

Almack's plain brick façade, fronting on King Street off St James's Square, housed the central marriage mart of the *haut ton*, but courting held no place in Georgiana's thoughts as she waited in the arriving carriage queue with her father and Fanny.

Despite her intentions, she hadn't slept much the night before, for her thoughts had dwelt on her conversation with Tyrold. At first, he'd reacted to her lack of virginity so exceedingly well that it had left her breathless and pondering why she'd felt something akin to joy, as if Tyrold's opinion on the matter was of consequence. But then he'd said, 'I wouldn't question your virtue because you gave yourself to a man you loved,' and she'd known his acceptance would vanish if he discovered the truth: Georgiana had had two lovers, but she'd never been in love. She didn't even know what romantic love felt like.

Eventually, she'd abandoned hope of sleep and passed the remainder of the dark hours in her study, hunched over her ledger, reviewing the finances by flickering candlelight. Now, arriving at Almack's, she was resolved: tonight she'd succeed in deflecting gossip about Tyrold *and* in securing fifty additional pounds of monthly subscriptions. The five hundred in arrears was also an urgent matter, but ending the accumulation of additional debt was critical.

Failure wasn't an option.

Besides, this was a manageable task. She possessed all that was required for success. Her debut hadn't got off to a good start, but Georgiana could still take control. As the now-recognised daughter of the Duke of Amesbury, she *did* have a place amongst these oft-scornful but extremely influential people; as long as she kept her reputation intact, they wouldn't spurn her completely, as the girls at school had. Surely she could catch the attention of some generous souls. Those who listened would understand that she possessed no motive other than a desire to do good.

And Edward would help deflect gossip by continuing their charade. Georgiana disliked the deception, but it was necessary to remedy the mishaps of the week. Thank goodness Tyrold wouldn't be at Almack's, reclusive confirmed bachelor that he was.

At last, her father's carriage pulled to a stop. The duke alighted first, assisted Fanny out, and then reached for Georgiana. She laid her hand lightly in his and disembarked with a resolved step. She was ready to succeed, to push forwards into the dazzling crowds and get her sponsorships.

But her father pulled her back, tightening his hold on her hand and drawing her close. 'How are you, Georgiana?' he asked, a note of urgency in his voice. 'Are you not sleeping well?'

Georgiana fought back a childish scowl. If he cared about her sleep, why hadn't he asked earlier? Why ask now, in front of the fashionable crowds? He could so easily destroy her composure. It was always difficult to be around him, but when he pretended to care, it hurt profoundly.

She pulled her hand until he loosened his hold slightly. She didn't like standing so close to him; his bergamot scent evoked those early, happy memories, which she'd later learnt were lies. 'I am well . . .' She faltered, as she often did when she tried to name him. If she said 'Your Grace' or 'Duke', his dark eyes would grow unbearably sad, but 'Father' stuck in her throat, and the days of squealing a naïve 'Papa' were long gone. 'I am well, sir,' she concluded, feigning a composure she was quickly losing. 'Thank you for asking.'

His brow furrowed. 'Are you quite certain, my daughter?'

'She can't be,' Fanny chimed in, clinging to the duke's other arm. 'She's too thin, too serious, and she works too hard. You must have *fun*, Georgiana.'

Georgiana dodged their gazes as she fought to suppress the rage and hurt that threatened to well up. 'I'm here now, aren't I? This isn't work,' she lied, extracting her hand.

She stepped into the blue-and-gold entrance hall of Almack's, illuminated by dozens of candles that glittered from a bell-shaped beaded chandelier. Music, gaiety and conversation floated down the sweeping, twinned staircases leading to the first-floor rooms.

Edward waited by a gilded newel post. He wore the knee breeches and stockings required by the Almack's patronesses – his pale grey, paired with a silver-and-pink shot-silk tailcoat – and was impeccably groomed from his chestnut curls to his dancing slippers.

He bowed low, greeted Georgiana's father and the duchess with all his easy charm, and then displayed a small cluster of champagne-coloured blooms tied to a gold ribbon. 'Will you do me the honour of wearing these, Miss Bailey?'

'Thank you, my lord,' Georgiana said, employing formal manners.

Fanny fastened the posy to Georgiana's bodice. 'Loveliest girl,' she cooed, observing her handiwork with watery eyes. She kissed both of Georgiana's cheeks, leaving behind her sugary vanilla scent before returning to the duke.

Georgiana avoided her father's gaze, although it bore into her. Instead, she gratefully accepted Edward's offered arm, relieved she needn't return to the duke's side. She sensed he was attempting to discern her senti-ments and the motives behind her actions at Almack's, and she didn't like it. 'The flowers match my gown beautifully, Edward,' she said with a smile.

Fanny had chosen the gold silk of Georgiana's ball-dress, claiming it would be 'heavenly with your complexion, dearest'. The result was burnished and elegant, and Georgiana felt beautiful wearing it, espe-cially with Fanny's pearls threaded in her hair. But she reminded herself that her appearance mattered only in how it presented her to the *ton*.

'I confess,' Edward said as they followed the duke and duchess up the carpeted stairs, 'I'm indebted to your stepmother for my information regarding your attire. I suspect she's either hoping I shall propose *or* that I'll make a certain someone jealous tonight.'

'Make who jealous?' Georgiana enquired, baffled.

Edward's eyes twinkled. 'Surely you know?'

'Surely I *don't*, Edward,' Georgiana exclaimed, with sudden realisation. 'If you impertinently speak of your friend, it's utter nonsense for many reasons – not least of which is the fact that he won't be here tonight.'

Properly chastised, Edward bowed his head and said no more, and Georgiana didn't enquire further because they'd reached the top of the stairs. Her skin prickled as she entered the cavernous Almack's Assembly Room for the first time. From the towering ceilings hung tiered crystal chandeliers; the brilliant candlelight caught the dazzling glitter of countless diamonds. Dancing hadn't yet begun, but the musicians in the balcony played Mozart over the murmur of conversation.

This was the beating heart of her father's society.

This was Georgiana's chance.

'Edward.' She tugged her friend's arm. 'Don't be excessively attentive tonight. I appreciate our game, as you know, but a *little* flirtation will go a long way. I worry about the scandal if it's rumoured I jilted you.'

Edward grinned. 'My love, I've a feeling that after this evening you can end your part of the charade and no one, even my Aunt Agatha, will blame you.'

'Why, Edward? Why are you speaking in riddles tonight?'

But Edward just laughed. 'Never mind. Sit with Aunt Agatha while I fetch you both some lemonade.'

Since that wasn't a terrible idea – Lady Agatha Matlock had always liked Georgiana and she might be willing to give substantially to Monica House – Georgiana crossed the ballroom on Edward's arm. She smiled at the few familiar faces that were kind until she arrived before the stately octogenarian.

Lady Agatha possessed bright-blue Matlock eyes that peered keenly from beneath thick false eyebrows. She wore a white wig topped with a ruby-strewn turban. Her vast skirts cascaded around her gilded chair like a jonquil waterfall. A lifelong spinster, she clearly didn't favour the muted colours worn by most women her age.

'Georgiana Marinetti,' she exclaimed in her cut-glass accent, extending a red-gloved hand. Gemstones dazzled on each finger. 'How I've missed you.'

Georgiana curtsied. 'Georgiana Bailey now, my lady.'

'And not that for long. A handsome, talented girl like you will soon be snapped up.' She glared pointedly at her great-nephew before smiling at Georgiana again. 'Sit by me, my dear, while Edward fetches refreshment. Tell me where you've been all these years. I was vastly disappointed when you stopped passing the summers with us at Deancombe. But I understand you spent time in Italy? To study voice, I assume?'

Georgiana arranged herself next to her ladyship, although she felt the full weight of her deception. By pretending to be a debutante in search of a husband, she misled kind people like Lady Agatha, who hoped Georgiana would domesticate her rakish but loveable favourite nephew, and Fanny, who just wanted to see Georgiana happily wed. To the duchess, doting upon a husband and sons was the epitome of womanhood. She would never understand why Georgiana couldn't feel the same way.

But Monica House needed her, so Georgiana smiled. 'I studied voice, yes.' Not like she'd intended to in her youth, when she'd dreamed of being a prima donna of the London opera, but a little. Once the dark despair lifted ever so slightly, Georgiana had learnt to value her talent again for the joy it brought others. 'But since returning to England I've given my time to a different and very worthy cause. May I tell your ladyship about it?'

Lady Agatha's encouraging smile fortified Georgiana's hopes.

But before Georgiana could speak more, Lady Frampton slithered up. 'Why, Lady Agatha, I see you are being entertained by London's newest ministering angel. She'll talk your ear off about her good deeds, but she's a sly puss.' Lady Frampton smiled indulgently, as if she were merely teasing Georgiana, but her eyes were flinty. '*Some* wonder if she's pitting one friend against the other.' Her gaze ran up and down Georgiana. 'What an interesting gown, my dear. It's as if you've turned yourself into a golden statue.'

As the baroness's meaning sank in, the rose-coloured walls of Almack's seemed to close in on Georgiana. Oh, heavens! *Why* had she worn a gold gown, when London called Tyrold 'Midas' behind his back? The colour was a coincidence – Fanny had ordered it weeks ago – but *now* Georgiana realised how bold it might appear.

The only saving grace was that Tyrold wouldn't be at Almack's. Regardless, Georgiana's throat felt thick as Lady Frampton sauntered off. She certainly couldn't look Lady Agatha in the eye.

The ancient lady grunted. 'It's anyone's guess what that harpy was screeching about. *I* say, speak plainly if one wishes to be understood. And so I shall do with you right now, Georgiana. Frankly, my dear, I want you for a great-niece. Your influence is exactly what my nephew needs. There's a good man inside him somewhere and not this devil-may-care buck. He needs to settle down, and as I mean for him to do so before the year changes, I shall set you both up extremely well indeed . . .'

Mortified, Georgiana listened, knowing she couldn't ask Lady Agatha for a donation to Monica House now. Not when she was already deceiving the sweet old lady. A nascent pain flared at her temples, and Georgiana regretted her lack of sleep. She was equally miserable and relieved when Edward claimed her for the opening quadrille. Perhaps Fanny would be so pleased by Georgiana's dance with Edward that she'd introduce her to other potential sponsors.

The orchestra grew silent as Georgiana and Edward took their places in the formation of four couples. A pregnant pause lingered as the room readied itself for the first strike of the bows, and from her position to

Edward's right, Georgiana had a perfect view of the entrance to the Assembly Rooms . . . which meant that she was likely one of the first to notice John Tyrold when he entered, looking astonishingly handsome in immaculately tailored evening wear, all black but for his crisp white linen and a gold waistcoat.

A gold waistcoat the *very shade* of Georgiana's gown, as if they'd planned to match . . .

Everyone was noticing now; whispers filled the silence. Lady Frampton swept into action, converging on the millionaire like a hound on a fox. Yet through it all, Tyrold stood frozen, gazing at Georgiana with that heart-wrenchingly sweet smile he seemed to save just for staring at her from across crowded rooms.

Georgiana's headache flared. She sensed the vitriol of others. She could taste defeat. Why would anyone donate money to Monica House when it looked very much as if she and Britain's wealthiest man were involved in something they shouldn't be? If Georgiana spread her legs to Tyrold and his millions – the *ton* would say – her charity certainly didn't need *their* money.

John knew himself to be at the point of surrender as he watched Georgiana dancing with Edward.

She was stunningly beautiful gowned in gold, which highlighted the luscious tones of her tanned skin. She shimmered like a gilded statue, her hair twisted with ribbons and pearls, her poise effortlessly elegant. Had she attired herself thusly in reference to John? King Midas's golden debutante . . .

John dismissed the brief fancy. Her gown fitted her like a glove from the low-cut bodice to the ankle-grazing hem. It was the product of countless hours' work; therefore, its colour was a coincidence. She hadn't shelled out the appalling seventy pounds that he'd *paid* to have an evening suit made for him in a day, complete with the gold silk waistcoat Edward had suggested.

John skirted the multitude of dancers, who were arranged in nearly two dozen swirling, four-sided groups of eight, and watched as Georgiana and Edward moved through the steps like cogs on a Geneva clock. It had been an age since John had danced, and he longed to partner with Georgiana, to glide with her across the chalked floorboards in the age-old ritual of courtship.

To declare to society that she was his object. And that he longed to be hers.

In any other man, such rapid decision-making would be ludicrous, but John wasn't any man. He trusted his instincts with weighing pros and cons, and there were many advantages to making Georgiana Bailey society's long-anticipated Mrs Tyrold.

First and foremost, John valued her wisdom. In fact, he valued it more than her beauty, which spoke to the nobleness of his sentiments. True, her business sense was abysmal, and she was wasteful with money, but she had an awareness of the feelings and emotions of others that mesmerised and mystified him, and which was utterly lacking in his own character. He readily admitted (to himself, at least) that he'd benefit from her guidance.

John had fallen asleep the night before envisioning their future married life, and he'd thought about it as he went about his business that day. He'd decided he'd renovate one of his new houses on Oxford Street for them. Georgiana would make it a comfortable home; her singing would infuse John's day as she glided about, managing this and that, gently reminding him to eat, pouring his coffee, running her fingers through his hair as he worked, taking care of him. And when they found Flora, she'd know what to do. She'd help John become the loving guardian Flora needed.

After years of a lonely existence, John's life would have comfort and warmth.

And the nurturing wouldn't be one-sided. Not in the least. John would protect her. Provide for her. He would generously fund her charity. With his money (and with his assistance in its management), she could have everything her heart dreamed of. Do all the good she wanted.

And although John had elevated his mind to think first of her wisdom, he acknowledged how sweet a reward it would be to hold Georgiana against him every night. He longed to worship and explore her body while her velvet-warm voice moaned to his ministrations. He'd even dreamed about this as he slept; as a result, he woke with a raging erection, which required an ice-cold bath and a great deal of willpower to calm down. He didn't want to pleasure himself to the thought of her yet. Not before he'd proposed.

And proposing was precisely what he planned to do.

Tonight.

There was no reason to wait now that he was decided. At last, he'd found a woman who challenged him in exactly the manner he required. One who scolded him when he deserved it but was yet kind and gentle. Who was intelligent and wise and gave generously of her heart and time. Who was fiercely talented. One who wasn't after his fortune, or, at least, not after it for selfish reasons.

He'd always acted with lightning speed when he spotted a stellar opportunity. This would be no exception. Georgiana would make him happy. At last, he'd experience domestic joy like Nick and Sidney. As Meggy and Kitty had done for his friends, Georgiana would make John a better man.

And lastly – but *not* least – John would be free from the matchmaking mamas, like Lady Frampton who currently followed him about the room.

The baroness trapped him in a corner. 'Mr Tyrold,' she said, simpering. 'What an unexpected pleasure to see you at Almack's. If you're looking for a partner, my Lettice, whom you see there dancing with the young Duke of Gillingham, is currently unclaimed for the next set. But she's such a favourite with the gentlemen – after all, who wouldn't admire her beauty? – that I doubt she'll stay—'

'I suggest you put your efforts into Gillingham, madam,' John interrupted. He didn't have time for matrons peddling their daughters when his only aim was Georgiana, and it was a waste of Lady Frampton's energies as well, since John's mind was decided. 'I assure you the young duke's finances are sound, though naturally not equal to my own. But surely a duchess's coronet is worth more than my millions?'

Lady Frampton's cheeks flushed scarlet.

'Do heed what I say.' John smiled munificently, untroubled by her fury. The mild-mannered young duke and Miss Frampton would make a lovely match, after all. 'My advice is always excellent. Ask your husband; I saved him twenty thousand once. Ah, that's the conclusion of the dance.'

The dancers clapped for the musicians, the sets fell apart, and men led their partners to chairs or to the refreshment rooms. John stalked across the floor, ignoring the horde of matrons who circled him, evidently awaiting their daughters' return before pouncing.

Now was his chance to show *everyone* there was only one young lady for him.

Georgiana laughed on Edward's arm, seemingly intentionally avoiding John's gaze. Jealousy twinged until he remembered she'd professed desire for *him*, not for Edward. Her avoidance must be because – as she'd said the night before – she hadn't yet perceived that he intended to renounce bachelorhood.

John held out his hand when he arrived at her side. 'Georgiana, dance with me.'

She whipped around, her dark eyes flashing with a fire he hadn't seen since their arguments in Covent Garden two days earlier.

She didn't take his hand.

Damn, no wonder! He'd accidentally called her by her forename, which was the only way he thought of her now, and they were in a crowded space where others might overhear. Others *had* overheard, he realised, for the couples in her quadrille were near, and shot covert glances their way.

John tried again. 'Miss Bailey, may I have the honour of the next dance?'

'I'm engaged to Lord Edward for the second set, Mr Tyrold.' Her words were clipped and she still didn't take his hand. 'You will have to dance with someone else until then.'

John glared at his friend, who hid a smile behind his pink-gloved hand. 'Edward won't mind if I cut in,' he said pointedly.

Georgiana's colour heightened. 'But I do, Mr Tyrold.'

Whispering broke out amongst the other couples. Clearly, John and Georgiana were objects of speculation. But all would be well, soon enough. John wasn't subjecting Georgiana to malicious gossip. His intentions were entirely honourable. He'd explain as they danced.

The musicians struck up a note. Other couples returned to the floor and Edward offered his hand.

'The next set, then?' John asked, as Georgiana smiled at Edward. 'I must speak with you.'

There, he couldn't be any more obvious, could he?

Her eyes darted to his, and then she spoke in a low voice, with a kinder tone. 'Only if you dance this second part of the set with someone else. Choose from any of the many young ladies who haven't got partners.'

With that, she let Edward lead her onto the floor. The couples arranged themselves in long rows, and the orchestra struck up a reel from their balcony, and everyone fell into the swirls and casting and allemandes of an English country dance.

John didn't look for a partner. He thought it bizarre that Georgiana had asked it of him. Why should he dance with others when he was there to propose to *her*? Instead, his eyes followed the shimmering gold gown.

A fluttery hand landed on his arm. He turned, blinked at the face of Lady Jersey – a patroness of Almack's and wife to the many-time cuckolded Earl of Jersey – and stepped back against the wall.

The countess laughed merrily. 'You look positively terrified, my dear Mr Tyrold.' She tucked a glossy black curl behind her ear. 'I haven't come to bite you, but only to insist you mustn't stand about. When Lady Agatha requested your voucher, she assured me you're here to dance. Allow me to present you to whichever lady you choose, and join the bottom of the shortest set, for they are in need of couples.'

'No, thank you,' John replied. 'My partner dances right now.'

'But, Mr Tyrold, there are many young ladies in need of partners.' Lady Jersey discreetly moved her fan in the direction of several white-clad debutantes against the wall. 'Lovely girls, all of them.'

'I shan't raise hopes that I have no intentions of fulfilling; therefore, I shall await my partner.'

Lady Jersey whipped her fan open and fluttered it aggressively. 'Do you think so ill of my sex, Mr Tyrold, that you suppose we have no end besides matrimony? Ladies enjoy dancing because it is *fun*.'

'I am not here to provide amusement for young ladies I don't know.'

Lady Jersey sniffed, her nose in the air, but thankfully she then left him alone, crossing the room and joining a collection of plumed matrons who clustered together while John returned his attention to the dance. When the set ended, he approached Georgiana and again offered his arm. 'I shall take her for refreshments, Edward,' he told his friend firmly.

But Georgiana didn't place her hand in the crook of his elbow. 'I shan't dance the next set with you, Mr Tyrold, because you didn't do as I asked.'

John let his arm drop. Clearly, he needed to explain *before* they danced. 'Edward, fetch Miss Bailey a drink.'

Edward bowed and departed readily.

And John readied himself to make his intentions clear. 'Georgiana—'

'*Miss Bailey*.'

John inhaled, steadying a flicker of frustration. 'Miss Bailey,' he said, keeping his voice low. 'I didn't attend Almack's tonight to dance with other young ladies. I want to dance with you. No other lady holds a candle to your talent, to your beauty, to your sweetness of temper—'

Her dark eyes flashed, belying John's words. 'Unless you leave my side this moment and dance with a dozen other ladies before you speak to me again, you will discover that my temper isn't always sweet, Mr Tyrold.'

'Why on earth should I do that?' he asked, appalled.

'Because I am not here to dance tonight—'

'You danced with Edward.'

She held up a hand to silence him. 'Don't interrupt. I'm here to secure sponsorships for Monica House. That is, as I have told you countless times, the *only* reason I at last agreed to let the duchess parade me around in society. All I ever wanted was to go quietly through this Season becoming acquainted with ladies and gentlemen who might sponsor Monica House. *Your* actions, however, have prevented the success of my plan. Three times now in full view of society, you have singled me out for recognition – *you* who never say a kind word to anyone – insulting other young ladies in the process. Now the gossipmongers' – she waved her hand around the room – 'are enjoying destroying my reputation. Saying I'm setting my cap for you – oh, and worse than that, I assure you. That I'm pitting Edward and you against each other or even that I . . . but never mind.'

She clamped her mouth shut, pursing her lips together.

'When you dance with Edward and not with me, it *does* give the impression that you wish to make me jealous.'

She gasped, eyes wide. 'Why! How *dare* you, Mr Tyrold! I'm not a child playing at silly games. This courtship pretence Edward and I have is the only thing protecting me from cruelty much worse than what I experienced at school, and, this time, with devastating consequences for Monica House. If you turn all the ladies with marriageable daughters against me, I shall never be able to repay my debts, much less keep Monica House running . . .'

John huffed, his frustration getting the better of him. It seemed he must dismiss these concerns by promising money before he was even allowed to speak – so much for nobler sentiments. 'Are these financial concerns all that troubles you?'

She seemed to shimmer with anger. '*All* that troubles me? No! Every aspect of this hurting world troubles me. But at the moment, I am bent on acquiring the donations needed to help the women and children of Monica House, who matter more to me than anything else.'

Again, that little prickle of jealousy, but John dismissed it. In time, he could make himself matter to Georgiana, if indeed he did want it, for misgivings plagued him suddenly. She was being combative and unreasonable tonight. 'How much do you need?'

'Fifty pounds a month in additional sponsorships, Mr Tyrold. Immediately. Tonight. Plus an additional five hundred to settle my debts. Now do you understand how dire the situation is?'

'Done,' John snapped. 'I shall send over five hundred and fifty pounds tomorrow and give you fifty a month after that – devil take it, I'll make it sixty. Regardless of whether you find Flora.' It was always about money. He cared for this woman and felt she'd be the helpmeet he hadn't even realised he'd needed, but she just wanted money, like almost everyone else. He wouldn't propose tonight after all, he decided – but at least he'd negated her reason for not dancing with him. 'Now you needn't care what people think of you, and I believe I've earned my dance.'

Before, Georgiana's eyes flashed, but now they turned colder than ice. 'You think you can buy my acquiescence. What else do you think you can buy from me?'

John curled his lip, taking her sordid meaning. 'Come, don't sully this. You know I respect you.'

'*Do* you?' she asked. 'I see no evidence of it. I won't dance with you, Mr Tyrold. I don't know how to put it to you more plainly, regardless now of whether you dance with others. In fact, don't speak to me again. We have already caused enough of a scene tonight.'

She turned on her heel and anger flared in John's chest. The tenderness and passion he thought they'd shared the night before meant nothing to her. It had been a figment of his imagination. Clearly some part of him still hoped that one day, a woman would love him – truly love him – for him, and not tolerate him for his wealth, but that wasn't the case.

He spoke to her retreating back. 'Miss Bailey, am I to understand that you have no interest in my money for Monica House?'

She froze mid-step, and the seconds passed like ages.

When she turned, her eyes were downcast. 'No, that is incorrect. I am immensely grateful for your offer, which will benefit the women and children of Moni—'

'Oh, enough.' John seethed. It was a bitter victory to see her contrite before him. 'So will you dance with me after all?'

Time passed even more slowly, but, at last, Georgiana lifted her chin and looked him in the eyes. 'I'd be honoured, sir.'

The quiet devastation of her manner cut John to the quick. He'd been unnecessarily cruel, and she was now *letting* him behave badly. She wasn't correcting him, as she had several times before. She was no longer trying to help him be a better man, now that money was involved.

'I find myself disinclined to dance now, Miss Bailey,' John said, hoping the words hurt her as much as she'd hurt him. 'So I shall bid you a good night instead. I'll bring a hackney to Maria DeRosa's tomorrow at seven, as we discussed.'

And with barely another glance at her face – he couldn't abide seeing her aversion – he walked out of Almack's without dancing with a goddamn soul.

15

As Georgiana stepped out of Maria DeRosa's coffee-house the next evening, she wrapped herself tightly in her red wool domino. The day had been rainy and although the darkening sky had cleared, a chill dampness hung in the musty air.

Behind her scarlet mask, Georgiana's eyes darted over the busy square. When she spotted a tall, masked man in a black domino standing beside a hackney, her blood boiled anew. After Tyrold had left Almack's the night before, she'd had to muster all her resilience to pretend she didn't notice the smirks and glares. It had been miserable, though. No one but Edward, his aunt, Georgiana's father and the duchess had spoken to her for the rest of the evening. Even hideous Sir Ambrose Pratley-Finch had sneered when she'd walked past and he'd said in an overly loud voice to his companion, 'When Tyrold could marry anyone, one wonders what his intentions are with an opera singer's bastard. Shameful of Amesbury to parade around such a brazen little piece.'

Fanny had fretted incessantly, twisting her hands and crumpling her pretty face, which had no doubt fuelled more gossip. She'd burst into tears the moment the footman had closed the ducal carriage door, sobbing onto Georgiana's father's shoulder, 'Oh, that dreadful man! Making a scene of Georgiana and then not even dancing with her!'

'I mean to speak with Tyrold again,' the duke said, his normally kind voice laced with vitriol as he rubbed Fanny's back. 'He's an insolent ass if ever there was one, but I'll make him hear me this time. What can he mean by soiling Georgiana's reputation, other than cruelty?'

'I beg you do no such thing, sir!' Georgiana pleaded, aghast. 'Least said, soonest mended most certainly applies here.' Not that she believed that – gossip involving the moralist Duke of Amesbury, his bastard daughter by a famous long-dead soprano, and the ever-fascinating Tyrold would fuel imaginations for a long time.

Without question, Georgiana's reputation was already in tatters. Most people would assess the situation as Sir Ambrose had, and that angered Georgiana. She didn't care about the lack of suitors, since marriage wasn't her goal, but she *had* wanted societal acceptance at last. And, she admitted ruefully to herself, not *just* for the sake of Monica House.

But perhaps most hurtful of all, Georgiana had begun to care for Tyrold – no! – to care *about* Tyrold. To want better things for him, to desire his happiness. And just as she'd begun to think him a true gentleman, he'd turned horrid again.

Georgiana picked up the skirts of her domino and marched fuming across the rain-slicked cobbles to the hackney. She didn't take Tyrold's offered hand when she arrived and, after jumping up the steps, she sat on the far side of the bench with her arms crossed. The coach swayed with Tyrold's weight as he climbed up and sat beside her, but Georgiana looked resolutely out the window.

Silence reigned.

Some time later, when the driver turned towards Whitehall at Charing Cross, Tyrold spoke at last, rather brusquely. 'With masked people swarming Vauxhall's opening night, how do you suppose we'll recognise Flora *if* she's there?'

The sound of his voice infuriated Georgiana. 'I don't know, but it's worth the effort to try, is it not? Unless your oh-so-brilliant brain has a better plan, that is.'

He said nothing, and they passed between Westminster Hall and the Abbey in more silence.

The ripe-fruit smell of a brewery south of Parliament, intermingled with the dusty odour of the whiting factory and the stench of the river, penetrated the hackney before Tyrold spoke again. 'Did you receive my five hundred and sixty pounds?'

Georgiana clenched her fists as she relived the humiliation of the night before. 'Yes,' she said when she'd mustered some control over her voice, although she remained furious. 'Perhaps you wish for evidence of my gratitude, but last night you cut short my efforts, so I shan't bother. Yet no doubt you'll eventually think of a new way to humiliate me.'

He didn't answer at once; when he did, he sounded miserable rather than angry. 'I did not ask for a dance to humiliate you. *Nothing* was further from my intention.'

His palpable hurt managed to dispel some of Georgiana's fury. She faced him, although the hood of his domino shadowed his masked features. 'If that were true,' she replied, softening her tone, 'you would've danced with other ladies, as I requested. It's not raising hopes, it's *polite behaviour*.'

'It is, I suppose, inconceivable to you that I might be capable of polite behaviour *without* your guidance. That I might have had a worthy reason for . . . but never mind.'

He looked out his window.

The remainder of Georgiana's anger slipped away. He was deeply unhappy and he was distressed about Flora. While these facts didn't excuse hurtful behaviour, Georgiana acknowledged she'd made no effort to see events from his perspective; therefore, after taking another a moment to calm herself, she reached for Tyrold's hand.

He snatched his away.

'John, I apologise for what I said,' she said gently. 'But you should apologise for your behaviour last night.'

There was a pause as the hackney turned onto the new Vauxhall Bridge. 'If an apology is what you want,' Tyrold said at last, 'then I shall say I'm sorry. But I confess I don't understand my transgression. I wished to demonstrate that you – and you *alone* of all the ladies at Almack's – mean something to me. Something significant.'

Naturally, it was impossible for such a speech from the great Tyrold not to affect Georgiana. She wasn't immune to compliments, and her heart went fluttery as she absorbed his declaration. But it appeared he genuinely didn't comprehend how harmful a public display of their mutual attraction and burgeoning friendship was, and that was dangerous. He didn't realise that outside of marriage, which neither of them wanted, they could be friends only in secret, and *even then* only with the utmost care. Tyrold was too famous, too enigmatic, too much a figure of speculation and fascination in London – and Georgiana too immersed in scandal by birth alone – for anything else.

But there was no time for explanation now because the hackney neared Vauxhall. In the few remaining minutes, Georgiana wished to re-establish the *bon accord* they'd enjoyed on the evening they'd questioned Lucy and Dick. A harmonious partnership was the best way to find Flora.

'May I take your hand, John?'

Without turning, he gave it, and Georgiana edged closer and brought it to her mouth. When she pressed her lips against the veins crossing its back, his fingers closed tightly around hers. He smelled pleasantly of soap, and Georgiana leant against his shoulder, savouring their closeness. 'You're understandably anxious, so let us not dissect our behaviour now, John. No doubt further conversation would reveal poor conduct on both our parts, but, for now, let us focus on Flora instead. I shall help until we find her. And we *will* find her.'

'What has she suffered, though?' he asked quietly. 'And will she ever forgive me?'

John's breath caught when he walked into the vast Rotunda of Vauxhall. From the soaring conical ceiling hung a vast array of birds, a veritable flock of intricate, highly realistic paper puppets with wings that fluttered in the draughts. As roaming flautists mimicked bird-song and calls, a crowd of masked viewers pointed and exclaimed.

He hadn't expected *this*.

'Flora loves birds,' John said to Georgiana, whose hand was tucked into the crook of his elbow over his domino's drapery. A quiet companionship had developed between them and, for now, it was enough. 'She must have known these puppets would be here.'

Georgiana gazed thoughtfully at the ceiling. 'Yes. She must've asked William to take her, and he promised he would. She referred to that when Dick was eavesdropping. Perhaps that's how the discussion of elopement began.'

John's stomach knotted. 'She could've asked *me* to bring her here.'

'And would you have said yes?' Georgiana's voice was gentle, no longer accusatory and angry as she'd been in the hackney.

John looked at the birds. What would he have said if she'd asked? When was he going to announce Flora publicly? He'd told himself he kept her identity secret to protect her from fortune hunters, but the truth was he didn't know how to tell his friends about what had happened with Helen, and he couldn't bear to discuss the possibility that had plagued him since he first met Flora . . .

'I would've said yes,' he said at last, his voice ragged. 'But only because this is a masquerade, where we could've appeared in public without anyone recognising us, so don't think well of me. It's no wonder she didn't ask. My behaviour over the years forced her to trust a stranger.'

Georgiana leant a comforting cheek against his arm. 'When we find her, John, you'll have a second chance to build a relationship. Dwell on the mistakes of the past only enough to let them inspire you to be a better person.'

'That is what you do.' He gazed down at her, his chest aching with longing. 'But perhaps there isn't a better person inside me, Georgiana.'

'Of course there is. There's good and bad within us all. You must merely put your mind to cultivating the good. Spend fewer hours stacking and restacking your piles of gold, and instead learn to value other humans. *Talk* to people. Hear their stories. Their hopes and dreams. Their memories, the joyful and the sorrowful. You're clever enough to build the greatest fortune in Britain, so you're clever enough to build friendships. But enough talk. Now we must circulate through this crowd and see if we can find Flora.'

John felt himself again on the cusp of a declaration. Words floated in his head, wanting to take form: *be my teacher; be beside me always; call me mad if you will, but now that I know you, I know I can't be without you.*

But it wasn't the right time or place for a proposal. Last night, at Almack's, would have been one thing, but, at this masquerade, Flora was the priority. Georgiana was correct, as always.

With Georgiana on his arm, John weaved through the throng of revellers, studying each masked face as it stared at the birds, hoping he'd see a copper curl under a domino hood or that he'd recognise the shape of Flora's lips and the curve of her chin. But with the multitude of people and the dimness, everything was a blur of movement in shadow.

'This is impossible,' he said half an hour later.

Georgiana stared straight ahead, her lips pressed into a line. 'Look at that man in the parakeet mask. He walks with a limp.'

John narrowed his eyes. The man in question wasn't wearing a domino over his bright green suit, but a feathered mask with a hooked beak covered most of his face. He was slim but straight-backed and walked elegantly with an expensive gilded walking stick.

'He's not limping,' John said. 'Besides, he's alone, and we're looking for a limping man in company with Flora.'

Georgiana shook her head. 'I've been watching him for some time and he does limp. Granted, it's barely discernible, but it's exactly as Lucy described: he presses rather too heavily on his walking stick for a person of his age. He's very young – you can tell by his smooth cheeks and lack of sideburns – yet he keeps that walking stick close to his leg and clenches its handle. Furthermore, I believe the sole of one shoe is built up higher, as if to accommodate for a shortened leg. Note too the colour of his hair visible under his hat – light brown, as Lucy described. Lean build, neither tall nor short. John, he might really and truly be Flora's young man.'

John peered again. Everything Georgiana said proved correct on further inspection. 'Well, then goddamn him,' he said, fuming. 'And what the devil has he done with Flora?'

'I don't know,' Georgiana responded slowly. 'But we must be careful how we approach him. Remember Lucy said he's a boy. Besides, we don't know for certain that he is Flora's Will—'

'There's only one way to find out,' John interrupted. He disengaged himself from Georgiana and closed in on his target in no time at all, seizing the boy's arm and yanking him against his chest. 'You have something of mine, you damned reptile,' he hissed. 'And I'll see you hang if she's not returned to me at once.'

The boy squirmed to no avail, for John held him tightly. Behind the parakeet mask, pale eyes darted wildly, and a high-pitched whine emanated, his desperation declaring his guilt.

'Where is she?' John demanded, confident he had his villain.

But the boy knocked him a powerful blow to the abdomen from the hilt of his walking stick, and John flinched, loosening his hold enough that the scoundrel wriggled away and fled with surprisingly agility though the crowds. Within moments, the bright green back was on the other side of the Rotunda, dodging around masked revellers as he fled towards the pillared foyer.

Fortunately, John was fast as well. He shoved forwards with ,no regard for anything but the retreating form ahead, and thundered out of the Rotunda. There he paused, glancing frantically over the masked people in shadowy paths. Laughter and music pierced the damp, chilly air, and, for a moment, John thought he'd lost his quarry. Then he caught a flash of green going against the crowd emerging from the water-gate entrance.

John pounded the gravel, running faster than ever, dismissing shrill cries and admonitions from those he inadvertently knocked against. He couldn't lose the boy. *He couldn't lose the boy*.

Once he emerged from Vauxhall, the crowds thinned, and despite a haze rolling in from the river, John spotted the green suit running down a narrow street heading towards the Thames. In the open, John was extremely fast and the sound of his footfalls echoed like thunderclaps.

Repeatedly, the boy looked over his shoulder, and on one such occasion, in front of the Vauxhall Vinegar Distillery, he stumbled and fell flat on the pavement, but managed to crawl through a crack in the distillery gate before John reached him. Perhaps he thought John couldn't fit, or that he could hide amongst the barrels in the courtyard, heavy with the scent of yeast, or that he'd flee to the loading dock on the Thames, but John easily kicked the gate open wider. He grabbed the boy's arm before he'd progressed halfway through the yard and yanked him to his feet.

Only then did John become aware of Georgiana's presence. She appeared at his side, slightly out of breath, and took hold of the boy's other arm. John ripped off the parakeet mask, exposing a tear-streaked face that appeared no older than Flora herself.

'Forgive me, Mr Tyrold,' the boy said, blubbering. 'I didn't want any of this to happen. I love her. Truly, I do.'

John pushed the boy against the brick wall of the distillery building, next to stacks of wooden barrels on their sides. 'One doesn't abduct the people one loves, you wretch. Now tell me where she is, William – if that's your true name.'

The boy's blubbering intensified. 'I don't know where she is. That's why I went to see the birds tonight. I hoped she might come. I thought I might find her again and—'

John's throat constricted. 'What do you mean "find her again"?'

'She escaped on Sunday, bless her, and I'm glad she did because Father was cruel. I never intended that. I wanted to explain tonight and ask for a second chance, just the two of us managing it properly this time. I swear I never lifted a hand to her. I never defiled her. No one did. I want to ask you honourably for her hand.'

'I'd sooner let her marry a snake.' John didn't permit his hopes to rise at William's claim no one had violated Flora. He'd wait to hear the same from Flora before he believed it. 'You let your father hurt her, so you are every bit as culpable. Who is your damnable father?

282

He'll hang for this. You both will.' In his anger, John shoved the boy harder against the wall.

William whimpered. 'Please, sir, you're hurting me.'

John clamped his free hand round the boy's neck. 'No worse than your father hurt Flora, and not nearly as badly as that noose will hurt—'

'John.' It was Georgiana's soft voice at his side. 'Be gentle. Remember your own words: when a man sees someone attack someone weaker, it behoves him to make it his business. I'm not a man, but I'm making this my business. He's a child. No matter what he or his father did, you mustn't retaliate with more of the same.'

Realisation washed over John as he looked into William's terrified eyes. 'You're correct, of course.' He relaxed his grip, but he still held the boy against the wall. 'Don't try to flee, boy,' he cautioned. 'Tell me, how old are you?'

William sniffled. 'Seventeen.'

John spat out a curse. 'Well, seventeen is old enough to know better, but likely your father *is* primarily responsible. Come with me to Bow Street, make a statement against him, and, in return, I shall ensure your life is spared.'

'I can't report my own father,' William responded, scowling now. 'Besides, Flora's better off without you. She told me you're a selfish, horrible man who doesn't care for anything but your fortune.'

The impact of those words – more confirmation that Flora hated him, believed him to be cold and selfish – far surpassed the boy's earlier physical assault. John inadvertently loosened his hold and William seized the opportunity to break free from both John and Georgiana, and sprint towards the distillery gate. John's response was delayed, but Georgiana leapt into pursuit and managed to restrain the boy again, which allowed John the moment he needed to regain his presence of mind.

However, before John could reach them, William extracted himself from Georgiana's hold with a shove that sent her tumbling against a wooden barrel.

A primal yell tore from John's throat as he pursued William with heighten zeal – by God, he'd drag the boy to Bow Street – but consumed by seething rage, John failed to perceive the glint of metal in William's hand until it was too late.

The deafening crack of a pistol resonated through the night; a crimson blur ploughed into John, and Georgiana yelped, short, quick, anguished. The impact of her body sent John crashing onto the cobblestones, with Georgiana collapsing atop him, and by the time John regained his bearings, a second or a minute or two minutes later, the two of them were alone in the distillery yard, with the pungent odour of gunpowder scorching the night.

As his gaze sought the top of Georgiana's head, resting upon his chest as if she were asleep, terror gripped him. She must have ploughed into him to save him from the bullet and been hit in the process . . .

'Speak to me, Georgiana,' he urged, sitting up and taking her in his arms, cradling her to his chest. 'For the love of God, speak to me! Speak to me!'

Her eyes blinked open behind her mask. 'Very well.' The corners of her lips lifted. 'What do you wish to speak about, John?'

Too overcome with relief to answer, John clasped her tighter, but she flinched and sucked in a sharp breath. 'By God, you *are* hurt,' he said, terror filling him again.

'Not *very* hurt.' She began to fiddle with the folds of her domino, attempting to access her left arm. 'Only a graze, I think. I may need your cravat, however.'

Eager to help, he arranged her in his lap so his legs supported her while he loosened the knot of his cravat. 'Where is the wound?'

'Just here, near my shoulder.' She wrestled out of her domino, exposing her plain frock, greyish in the dim light. A dark, viscous stain was spreading over her upper arm.

Blood.

And with a rush of feeling – fury at William, fear for Georgiana, and gratitude that whatever had happened to her arm, the bullet hadn't hit her chest, mere inches over – John felt something else, something deep, something profound, something certain: without a shadow of a doubt, his heart belonged to Georgiana Bailey, and he'd do anything in the world to save her. He might've botched many things in his life, but he wouldn't fail a woman he loved, ever again.

He wouldn't fail Georgiana. He wouldn't fail Flora.

As John unwound his cravat, there was no question of seeking William again tonight or returning to Vauxhall to search for Flora amongst the paper birds.

John doubted she'd be there, anyway. A girl who'd fled her captors wasn't likely to return to a place they expected her to be, no matter how much she wanted to see the puppets. Wherever Flora was, she was at least free from her abductors. Searching for her was a matter for tomorrow – and when John found her, he'd arrange for another display of the paper birds for her alone, cost be damned.

'I shall tie up your wound,' he said, having decided upon the best course of action. 'And then I suggest we call upon my friend Alexander Mitchell.'

Georgiana studied her arm. 'I'm fairly certain it's only a scratch, but I confess I'm no expert on bullet wounds, and I know and trust Dr Mitchell, so I agree with your plan.'

John wrapped his cravat securely around her arm. 'I'm so sorry if this hurts, my sweet darling.'

'The pain is subsiding, truly. Make it tight, and I think the bleeding will stop.'

When John finished applying the makeshift bandage, he tucked Georgiana's domino loosely over her, like a blanket, and then gathered her in his arms, her body delicate under the folds of wool.

She smiled up at him as he stood. 'You needn't carry me. I can walk.'

'I want to, if I may.' Providing secure arms so she could rest and conserve her energy was one small thing he could do.

In response, she nestled close, her head resting on his shoulder, her fingers clinging to his lapel, and William's parakeet mask in her other hand. John hitched her securely against him and looked about cautiously as he left the yard. There was no visible sign of a green suit on the relatively deserted street. William had likely long since fled, but John was concerned he might return – perhaps with his father – to finish what he'd begun (or conceal evidence of what he might well think was a murder). Rapidly, then, John strode down the street towards the milling crowds emerging from the water stairs. On the corner shone the gaslights of the timber-framed White Lion inn, and John headed there, grateful he hadn't removed his mask, for he drew curious stares as he progressed.

He whistled to catch the attention of a hackney, but the driver looked askance. 'What's wrong with 'er? Too much drink? I won't have vomiting in my cab.'

'Take me to the Mayfair Maternity Hospital at Park Lane and Stanhope,' John growled. 'And for the love of God, have someone open this bloody door. Can't you see my arms are full?'

The driver nodded to an inn boy. 'You, whelp. Open the door for this gentleman; his lady is having a baby. And hurry. I don't want it born in my cab.'

Georgiana stiffened in John's arms. No doubt the implication embarrassed her, but it had been unintentional on John's part and served the purpose well. The driver would make haste in the belief that otherwise his cab would be soiled even more heavily than vomit.

Within the hackney, John arranged Georgiana carefully in his lap before tossing the boy a coin. As the coach swayed into motion, her dark eyes met his gaze.

And John's chest swelled with love. 'How are you, Georgiana?'

Her lips quirked. 'You're making a fuss over nothing, John, but I don't dislike it.'

He cupped her soft cheek, caressing her chin with his thumb. 'That bullet was meant for me, not for you.'

She crinkled her nose. 'I doubt it was meant for either of us. He was terrified.'

'As well he should be, for he's destined for the gallows.'

Georgiana rested her head on his shoulder. 'He's just a boy.'

'A boy that kidnaps, drugs and shoots women,' John replied. 'He doesn't deserve your defence.'

'Since you don't know the whole story,' she murmured sleepily, 'you must reserve judgement.'

John stared in disbelief. 'He *shot* you, Georgiana,' he said, brushing loose strands of her hair back from her forehead. 'What gentle madness possesses your sweet mind, that you feel pity for him?'

'I can't help it. I sensed his fear, as I feel your anger and fear now. Somehow, I absorb the emotions of others. So much so, my friend, that I must ask you not to argue with me any more tonight, because my arm already hurts enough.'

She smiled as she spoke, and John could've melted at her feet. 'Your wish is my command.'

A declaration he meant with all his heart.

Her smile broadened, although her eyelids were heavy. 'That's from *The Arabian Nights*. I like that, because I want you to tell me a story tonight. Not now, but later.' She snuggled into his chest and sighed drowsily.

'Stay awake, darling,' John urged. She *must* stay alert, in case the wound was more severe than either of them realised.

'Then sing to me.'

So John did. He sang while cradling this remarkable woman, protecting her from every jolt and jostle of the hackney as they sped towards Mayfair. He sang about the sentiment which reigned in his heart.

He sang about love.

16

As the hackney crossed the Vauxhall Bridge, the initial shock subsided for Georgiana. Her strength returned, but she still let herself be cradled within Tyrold's embrace, savouring the silky tenor tones of his voice. His breath caressed her cheek as he sang; her body moved with the rise and fall of his chest.

A woman could get used to this, she thought dreamily.

Well, some *other* woman could.

Georgiana couldn't.

But *still* . . .

It would be utterly foolish not to enjoy the proximity while it lasted.

She nestled her nose into Tyrold's loosened shirt collar, as she'd yearned to do for days, and drew his scent into her. It settled deep in her core; his skin against hers made her want to forget her concerns and fill her senses with him instead. Sheltered in his arms in the hackney, it was impossible to ignore how much she desired him, and how much she ached to experience his desire for her. She'd wanted that ever since he'd held her outside Galatea's establishment . . .

'I've realised something about you, John Tyrold,' she whispered into his neck when his love song finished.

A pause. A tilt of his head, his cheek pressed against her. And then, 'What have you realised, Georgiana?'

She trailed her fingertips through the short hair at the back of his head and thought the better of saying aloud what she was thinking: that all the cocksure bluster he'd built around himself was the thinnest of veneers, and that she had the power to brush it away with a sweep of her hand. That the real John Tyrold was tender-hearted and generous, but something held him back from showing it . . .

He wasn't ready to hear that.

So, instead, she placed her lips on the faintly pulsing vein of his neck. 'Only that you are such a man.'

His breath stilled, then resumed. 'Such a *man*?' he queried after a moment. 'Or *such* a man?'

Georgiana smiled against his skin. 'Both.'

He didn't speak, and yet Georgiana knew something had changed between them, because she felt it in the softening of his shoulders, the easing of his tension, a gentler and yet closer cradling of his arms.

Deep within her chest, her heart did the oddest little flip.

The butler who answered Tyrold's knock on Dr Mitchell's door first confused them for a couple in need of the neighbouring maternity hospital, but after Tyrold removed his mask, they were led to the doctor's study, a cosy room with cabinetry and bookshelves, a crackling fire, and a faintly herbal smell.

'Dr Mitchell is attending to a birth, Mr Tyrold,' the butler said as he urged them to seat themselves on the sofa or armchairs near the hearth. 'Is the matter urgent, sir?'

Georgiana answered for Tyrold by insisting that Dr Mitchell should most definitely not leave his patient early.

'We may have to wait for hours,' Tyrold said after the butler closed the door and left them alone. 'Alexander loses track of time with his patients.'

Georgiana settled herself on the sofa, placing her mask and the parakeet mask on a side table. 'Then we will wait.' She loosened her domino and studied Tyrold's cravat-bandage. Some blood had soaked through, but it was a small amount and already turning a dull brownish red. 'The bleeding has stopped, so there's no urgency. Have a seat and you can tell me a story.'

Tyrold placed his mask on top of hers. 'Do you want a drink?' he asked, indicating a decanter on Dr Mitchell's desk, which was laden with books, documents, and various professional accoutrements, including a leather uterus model with a baby in the womb. 'It'll be whisky, knowing Alexander.'

Georgiana smiled. 'Yes, I could use a drink.'

As he poured, she examined the parakeet mask for clues, but sadly there was nothing obvious on it — not even a maker's mark — so she returned it to the side table when Tyrold approached.

'What sort of story do you want?' he asked, handing her a whisky. Georgiana patted the sofa beside her and he sank down on the upholstery. 'I can speak rather eloquently about the benefits of diversifying one's investments.'

She sipped her drink, savouring the peaty flavour and the warmth that ran down her throat. 'That wouldn't be very useful to me, because I haven't any investments to diversify. I spend money the moment it's in my hand. In fact, I spent the entirety of my ten thousand pound fortune in two years.'

He cocked an eyebrow over his glass rim. 'But not carelessly, as I unfairly assumed when we met at the park.'

'I'm glad you realise how unwarranted your accusation was.' She rested her hand on his upper thigh and his gaze felt to his lap, but he said nothing, so she left it resting there. 'That ten thousand pounds accomplished a great deal, but I was astonished how swiftly it disappeared.'

He adjusted his leg so it pressed against Georgiana's skirts. Her hand slid farther into his inner thigh as he slipped an arm over her shoulders. 'What did you do with the money?' he asked, his voice rather huskier than before.

Georgiana melted into his half-embrace. Between the whisky and the feel of his body, she was delightfully warm and tingly. 'First, I absorbed the lease on Monica House. Then I purchased and furnished a cottage in Kent for the aging former owners, who were exhausted after decades of service. I also leased Maria DeRosa her coffee shop and started businesses for about two dozen other past residents. Next, I thoroughly renovated Monica House, which was in desperate need. Now it has gas lighting and flushing close stools and a beautiful kitchen and thirty separate chambers, both individual and family units. That and . . . oh, I don't know, John. So many other things. Money poured out of my hand every time I'd go amongst the suffering and soon enough, I had nothing left. For the first year after that, my lack of fortune didn't matter much, because I had a generous sponsor. But when she died in the summer and her son contested her will successfully – he *claimed* she was afflicted with dementia, but she wasn't – everything began to fall apart.'

'But what you describe isn't spending, Georgiana. It's giving. Giving sacrificially, as a matter of fact, which is the most generous, if not the wisest, type of charity there is. I shan't fault you for it, but, sometime, should you wish to hear, I could help you formulate a budget – although I suspect you'll say that's not what you want.'

Georgiana smiled. 'Oh, I might, in theory, *want* to give sensibly, but in practice, I'm not capable of it. You weren't wrong two weeks ago when you said I shouldn't oversee charity subscriptions. That's why you angered me so terribly.'

Tyrold grimaced. 'Oh, Lord, Georgiana. Please forgive me for everything I said during our initial meeting. You deserved none of it, and I'm heartily ashamed of myself.'

He captured her hand as it lay on his thigh. 'But you wanted a story. Since you don't want me to speak of investments, what shall I tell you instead?'

Georgiana squeezed his palm. 'Please tell me about Flora's mother.'

Something flickered in his eyes. 'I'm afraid that's not a happy story.'

'I know, but I want to hear regardless. Did you love her very much?'

'I thought I did,' he said, studying his drink. 'But in the end, I didn't act like a man in love.'

Georgiana tilted her head. 'Why not?'

He paused, gathered a breath, and then spoke, his voice resigned. 'Perhaps I should start at the very beginning, for the circumstances of my youth are relevant to the story. I'm an only child, born more than twenty years into my parents' marriage. As you can perhaps imagine, they rejoiced at my birth. I believe they thought me the embodiment of a miracle, after so many childless years, and, as I grew, I could do no wrong in their minds. They indulged me excessively; I was king of their household. I shan't pretend I didn't think extremely well of myself.'

Georgiana laughed. How perfectly she could imagine a tiny, tyrannical John Tyrold spouting dictates as he toddled about on dimpled feet. 'You still think well of yourself, John.'

He sipped his whisky. 'Not lately, I don't.'

She sobered. He wasn't laughing, so she wouldn't either. 'Go on. When did you meet Flora's mother?'

'Helen.' He quaffed the remainder of his drink and put down his glass. 'Her name was Helen Jennings.'

'Helen,' Georgiana repeated, because it seemed important to do so.

'My mother brought a substantial fortune into her marriage, but my parents have always lived a simple life by choice. During my childhood, they resided in the dower house on the Tyrold estate of Oakwood, which was then owned by my father's elder brother. My uncle was a widower with only one child as well – my cousin, Arthur, ten years my senior – but shortly before my eighth birthday, his orphaned niece through marriage fell to his guardianship and came to live at Oakwood Hall. Since my uncle was nearly sixty years old, my own mother very happily took on the bulk of her care – and that is how Helen, with her copper curls and big blue eyes, came into my life.

'She was two months my senior; we were barely eight when we first met, and from the beginning, we were always, *always* together. Except for my uncle, who closeted himself in his library most of the time, everyone on the estate encouraged our friendship. And for good reasons: Helen was genuinely happy around me – and she'd had such a sorrowful childhood – and I was less overbearing when she was about. She was always kind and gentle, and I *need* gentle people around me. They calm and soothe me. No doubt they are the only people who can tolerate me,' he growled, looking down at their joined hands, still on his thigh. 'At any rate, without such people, my mind has a tendency to become overactive and restless. That's why I set up the household on Half Moon Street to live with my friends. Sidney especially has a soothing presence, which I've missed terribly since he married. Edward, on his good days, can have the same, but his way of life irritates me.' Tyrold scowled. 'Unprincipled scoundrel.'

'That's not quite fair, John.' Georgiana couldn't help defending her old friend. 'Edward does have principles. Yet I'll grant you, he *is* a scoundrel. But go on – please tell me more about Helen.'

Tyrold frowned, still studying their hands. 'One day soon after Helen arrived, I watched her care for her dolls, and she said, "Come, Johnny, sing our babies a lullaby so they can fall asleep." After I did so, she asked me if I'd marry her when we were older. I responded that I'd be honoured, and that seemed to settle matters between us. She kissed me for the first time when we were ten, and shortly after my four-teenth birthday, we . . .'

He faltered.

'Bedded together?' Georgiana offered.

He sighed heavily, squeezing his eyes tight. 'It felt like the most natural thing in the world, something we both wanted, but of course I knew my mistake afterwards. I hadn't behaved like a gentleman, and, though Helen wasn't upset, I got down on one knee and formally proposed, promising I'd marry her as soon as our uncle granted permission for the license. She accepted at once and later that same day, I marched into my uncle's library and announced that she and I were engaged to be married. Naturally, I did *not* tell him what had occurred between us.'

'And how did that go?' Georgiana asked.

His jaw tightened. 'Not well. Not that I blame him, in the least. He saw me for what I was: an impudent pup who barked orders to his own parents and thought the world of himself. He leant over his desk and said, "John, Helen is a beautiful young lady with a large fortune. When she's old enough to marry, she can have her pick of good and honourable men. There is nothing in the world that would induce me to let her throw herself away on an impertinent jackanapes who is neither good nor, I fear, honourable." That alone was a dreadful blow; it rang bitterly true to how I felt about what had transpired earlier that day. But he wasn't finished. He proceeded to reel off a devastating list of my faults, concluding with the declaration that despite being "not an idiot", as he said, I was disrespectful to my masters at Eton and lazy in my lessons. It was all true, but the more he spoke, the more furious I became. He didn't understand me, I told myself. He didn't respect my genius, didn't realise I was far cleverer than my teachers. But I could force him to take notice, I knew. I stormed to my parents' house and – prepare yourself, for I warned you I was a brat – I demanded my father immediately relinquish my portion of my mother's fortune so I could invest it.'

Georgiana widened her eyes. 'And he gave it to you?'

'He never refused me anything. Besides, he was confident of my success. It's true I didn't do my lessons at school, but my mind wasn't inactive during Greek and philosophy. I was constantly pursuing financial, agricultural and industrial reports and doing figures. Since I was nine, I'd advised my parents on investments with tremendous success. And, anyway, I wouldn't have settled for a *no* from my father; I would've left home to scrabble for my fortune if he'd refused, and he knew that. After my uncle's lecture, I was determined to prove myself worthy of Helen.'

He paused.

'I know you made your fortune,' Georgiana said. 'But was your uncle impressed?'

Tyrold looked up. 'I'm not certain, Georgiana. When I was fifteen, I left school and took up lodging in London. I quickly achieved such unprecedented success that my parents gave me control of the remainder of my mother's fortune and, from then, there was no stopping me. I became thoroughly obsessed with money, but I still relished Helen's letters, which were frequent at first. She claimed to love me devotedly and I certainly considered myself bound to her. I told myself everything I did, I did for her. By the time I was sixteen, I'd increased my mother's fortune tremendously and Helen urged me to come home permanently; she had an aversion to London, which is where she lived as a young child, before her mother died. Instead, I returned to Yorkshire only for a month, during which time she begged me to speak to our uncle again, to settle down, to purchase an estate nearby, but I didn't. It was the only time we argued, but we resolved it, I thought, by agreeing that when my investments reached a million pounds in value, I'd purchase a house in town and we'd be wed. But after that, her letters grew less frequent, and when I returned to her the last time, the summer when we were seventeen, she was different. She'd bid me to come up, she seemed eager to be with me, and yet I later learnt from my mother that even before that visit, my cousin had been courting her. Mere weeks after I returned to London, my uncle gladly relinquished Helen and her fortune to his own son.'

'Oh, I see!' Georgiana exclaimed, the blood relation between Tyrold and Flora crystallising at last. 'Helen married your cousin; *that* is why Flora is a Tyrold.'

Several long moments passed before Tyrold spoke again. 'When Helen rejected me in favour of Arthur,' he said slowly, 'I thought my heart was broken. Flora was born eight months later, a strong and healthy baby, apparently. Naturally, I assumed she was Arthur's child – until I met her for the first time, days after Helen's death. From the moment I saw the colour of Flora's eyes, so much like my own, I wondered if she might be my daughter – and a much more intense heartache began. As the years have passed, I've perceived many similarities in our natures – things that aren't like either Helen or Arthur – and every time I notice something new, the heartache begins again. The thing is, Georgiana, Helen and I were always careful . . . but we *weren't* those last few times, at Helen's request, which I granted because . . . well, because I think a childish part of me wanted the decision to be made for us. If I got Helen with child, my uncle would grant permission for the marriage, Helen would move to London and there would be an end to the matter. When Helen married Arthur, I was far too upset, too heartbroken for the possibility to occur to me that she might've carried my child – and although Flora was born short of nine months into their marriage, I was too absorbed in my own concerns to contemplate that Helen might've betrayed my trust in such a manner. In fact, to this day, I can't fathom what she was thinking if she did indeed knowingly carry my child and yet chose Arthur to be the father. What could have motivated her to make such a choice? Was I so . . .' He paused, sighed, and rubbed his temples. 'It torments me, Georgiana. It has tormented me for years. Did Helen, after all we shared, truly not trust me enough to allow me an opportunity to do right by her? Was I that despicable to her, in the end?'

'It might not have been anything of the kind,' Georgiana said, seeking to reassure him. Although she could guess at what Helen might've done, loving John but perceiving their values too diverse for a happy union, it was useless to dwell upon something that could never be answered, and Georgiana would be a hypocrite to judge the desperate decisions of a lonely young woman. There was nothing to do now but ease Tyrold's unhappiness and remind him that Flora's future was the most important thing. 'Besides, even if Helen was with child, she might not have known yet.'

'I have attempted to console myself with such thoughts for many years, but it doesn't help. The possibility that she is my daughter and yet I can never claim her pains me . . . *here*.' He placed his hand over his heart, drawing a ragged breath before steadying himself. 'I don't have the privilege or the right to tell Flora that I love her . . . that I love her differently from how I would love my cousin. I feel, in my heart of hearts, that she is my daughter, but I can never tell her that.'

Georgiana ached for him. 'Oh, John. This will be extremely hard, but you must cease this wondering. Release your hurts, perceived or otherwise. No good can come of them. Instead, focus on this: you are the man raising Flora. She relies on you for love, guidance, support and protection. Nothing else can matter.'

'You are without doubt correct, but that doesn't make it easier.' He studied their clasped hands for a moment before continuing, his voice resigned. 'Well, and so there's the story you wanted: the tale of my not-so-great love affair. I didn't return home for years, so I never saw Helen again, even when the deaths began. First my cousin, Arthur, quite suddenly, not long after Flora's birth – his health had sometimes been indifferent, though no one expected such an early death. My poor, devastated uncle succumbed to an attack of the heart not long after. My father then inherited Oakwood and my parents moved to the big house to help Helen. My mother urged me to return and marry her, but I had hardened my heart by then. Whatever her reason for marrying Arthur, I couldn't forgive her, and, besides, she didn't encourage me to renew my addresses. She never wrote, for example . . .' He paused, working his jaw, gazing across the room as if lost in thought and memory. 'She wrote *once*, but by then it was too late. When she died, she assigned me guardianship of Flora, with no explanation other than a brief letter, which said she'd "left me her doll" and in my "heart of hearts", I should know why. Those words have added to my torment. Tell me, what did she mean by them, if not to say Flora is my daughter?'

Georgiana squeezed his hand. 'Stop allowing them to torment you and let them inspire you, instead,' she advised. 'Helen entrusted her precious child to your care. It was like when she asked you to sing lullabies to her dolls as they drifted off to sleep.'

He sighed. 'I've failed miserably. I told myself I placed Flora at school to protect her, but, of course, I've only been protecting myself so I needn't admit the truth. Helen believed I loved money more than her, and, even worse, might've believed I love money more than my own child. And now perhaps it's too late to right my wrongs.'

'It's not too late, John. You'll find Flora and you'll correct the mistakes of the past, but now I think the time for secret searches is over. Flora escaped her captors four days ago, yet she still hasn't returned to you, which worries me more every moment I think of it.' She spoke from experience, remembering her own foolish determination to flee those who could've helped her. 'You must inform the Runners first thing in the morning, so an extensive search can begin.'

'I expect my investigator Starmer to return tomorrow,' Tyrold said, somewhat hesitantly. 'Shall I have him organise a sweep of London?'

'Yes, that's an excellent plan. But the Runners as well, John. Additionally, print the placards and have them posted from Tower Hill to Kensington, in order to alert everyone about Flora. With the incentive of twenty thousand pounds, someone will find and return her.'

'And then?' Tyrold peaked his brows. 'What do I do then, Georgiana? How do I make amends for how I've failed her?'

Georgiana tightened her hold on his hand. 'By loving her fiercely, firmly, and unconditionally, no matter how much time and care she requires to heal.'

'She won't trust me.'

Georgiana's own experience with her father spoke to the validity of John's concern, but if they worked hard enough, hopefully they could recover Flora before the child's heart and spirit were as irreparably broken as Georgiana's were.

'Regardless,' she said, 'you must never stop trying to win her trust. I was once a high-spirited, lonely girl too. Not an orphan, exactly, but I might as well have been, and I *craved* love to the point where I daydreamed obsessively about possessing the admiration of others. Not unlike Flora, I sought attention in impulsive ways, when all I truly needed was my fa—' Georgiana stopped; she didn't want to discuss the duke right now. She couldn't complete the sentence, anyway. The words 'all I truly needed was my father's love and acceptance, before it was too late' stuck in her throat. 'Never mind. This isn't about me. This is about Flora, who needs you, whether you're prepared to be a father to her or not.' Georgiana brought Tyrold's hand to her heart. 'Did you and she ever have good times together?'

Tyrold's gaze followed their clasped hands and Georgiana realised she'd nestled them between her breasts, but she didn't move. Nor did Tyrold reclaim his hand, but he did eventually turn his eyes away until they came to rest on the crackling fire.

'Flora used to love it when I visited,' he then continued. 'But that changed one day, when we went to the fields north of the Paddington Road to look for birds—'

He was interrupted by the door opening. In unison, she and Tyrold released their joined hands and created space between them on the sofa as Dr Mitchell entered.

The auburn-haired physician was a familiar sight to Georgiana, and he recognised her at once. 'Why, Miss Marinetti! And with you, John?' he queried in his soft Scottish accent, clearly bewildered.

Georgiana smiled brightly, as if there were nothing at all odd about calling upon the physician late at night in the company of John Tyrold. 'I'm called Miss Bailey now, Doctor.'

'Ah, yes,' Dr Mitchell said, returning her grin. 'I knew that, in fact – my dear friend Lady Rose Edwards told me. You've made quite the impression on her, and then she was very pleased with me when I informed her that I've called in at Monica House for years.'

'Sweet Lady Rose,' Georgiana said, relieved to hear someone still thought well of her after the Almack's disaster. 'So kind, though she suffers greatly.'

Dr Mitchell's brow furrowed, but, before he responded, Tyrold interjected, informing him of the nature of Georgiana's injury.

'Shot! Where?' Dr Mitchell exclaimed, dashing to Georgiana's side, which Tyrold vacated. She held out her wounded arm for his inspection, and his face calmed the moment he loosened the cravat and exposed the wound, a shallow gash, red and raw but no longer bleeding. 'The bullet grazed the arm without any fragment lodging,' he said, sounding relieved. 'Only the most superficial of damage, but, by God, you've had a close shave, Miss Bailey! Was the perpetrator apprehended?'

'He will be,' Tyrold growled, his voice lethal.

Georgiana glanced at his tight jaw and decided to turn the subject. 'Shall I wash and bind the wound then, Doctor?'

'I shall do so now,' Dr Mitchell replied. 'It will allow me to verify my initial assessment.'

A flurry of activity followed. The butler was summoned to bring hot water and soap. Dr Mitchell rummaged through his cabinetry and returned to the sofa with an assortment of bottles and bandages. He asked and was granted permission to cut away the sleeve of her gown, to best expose the entire limb for inspection.

As the wound was cleaned, Georgiana distracted herself from the sharp sting of soapy water by thinking over the story Tyrold had told.

It hadn't dampened her desire for him one bit. Certainly, he'd made mistakes, but they were the mistakes of a man whose pride and conceit had been indulged all his life. Georgiana knew he wanted to change.

He really was *such* a man . . . and, perhaps, well, *perhaps* being shot while trying to do good justified a single self-indulgent night? If Georgiana gave herself a few hours to bask in one of the great pleasures of life, wouldn't she continue her work tomorrow with renewed vigour?

Yes, she decided as Dr Mitchell bound her wound in fresh linen. Yes, yes, and yes.

She deserved this.

She deserved to give in to her desire for Tyrold, *just this once*. The pleasure would be fleeting, of course, but perhaps all the sweeter for it. In fact, before she left Dr Mitchell's house, she'd ask the physician for some of the dense sea sponges in netted bags Monica House residents made for him to sell to his patients . . . and then she and Tyrold could indulge in *complete* enjoyment.

Georgiana wanted it to be a night they'd both remember, with no repercussions at all.

17

John wasn't a religious man, but as he watched Alexander clean Georgiana's gunshot wound he thanked whatever higher power had spared her. More than thanked – he wanted to prostrate himself in gratitude.

His parents would be pleased if they could see him now, thoroughly aware of life's preciousness and beside himself with appreciation for second chances. He should write to them, or visit, and tell them of his newfound conviction. How he finally realised he'd valued the wrong thing for too long and was determined to change. He could – and he would – make everything right for Georgiana and for Flora, no matter the emotional or financial cost.

Somehow.

'There might be slight discomfort as I apply this benzoin.' Alexander dabbed the wound with the amber fluid, but not only did Georgiana not flinch, she also wore a smile as she watched Alexander work. 'Ah, I see you are stoic, my brave Miss Bailey,' Alexander said, recorking the flask. 'I'm not surprised, for I've had the privilege of witnessing your superhuman feats for four years now.'

'She's remarkable,' John agreed, fully accepting he wore his heart on his sleeve.

Georgiana's eyes danced, as if she were as giddy with relief as he was sombre with it. 'Remarkable, am I?' She laughed. 'Well, there's a change from earlier this week. To imagine, I only had to take a bullet for you to make you perfectly agreeable.'

Alexander's gaze shifted from Georgiana to John and slowly back again, but if he sensed the sentiment between them, he didn't remark upon it. Instead, he made himself busy with his rolls of linen. 'I'll just wrap your arm in clean bandages, and you're free to go. Infection of the wound is the only concern, so I shall check in daily, beginning first thing in the morning. John, will you see Miss Bailey to Monica House safely?'

'Of course.'

Once Alexander had bandaged her arm, John wrapped Georgiana in her domino. He intended to ensure her safe transportation home and advise her to ask one of the women at Monica House to bring her tea and sustenance before she went to bed. It was reassuring that Alexander would check on her in just a few hours' time.

Alexander rummaged in his cabinets. 'I'll package some fresh bandages and some tincture of willow bark, in case there is either bleeding or pain.'

Georgiana tied on her mask. 'Thank you – and could you add three or four of those items we make at Monica House? Along with the accompanying tincture?'

At his shelves, Alexander froze. Slowly, he looked over his shoulder, glancing again between John and

Georgiana, but, this time, his brow was heavy. 'Forgive me, Miss Bailey,' he said, his manner rigid. 'But it behoves me to enquire if you *truly* wish Mr Tyrold to take you home? My carriage is at your disposal. I will myself accompany you safely to Monica House's gate. You needn't feel any sort of pressure—'

'Oh, I don't, I assure you,' Georgiana said, laughter in her words. 'No pressure in the least.'

Alexander shot John a narrow-eyed scowl of abhorrence.

Startled and utterly bewildered, John lifted his hands, palms out. 'What?'

But Alexander showed him the cold shoulder and continued his work without a reply.

Once his back was turned, Georgiana shook with silent laughter, her lips pressed together but her eyes sparkling. When John raised a quizzical eyebrow, she shook her head, revealing nothing, and picked up the parakeet mask, readying herself to leave.

John dismissed the matter. Women's concerns, he supposed, as he tied on his own domino and mask, although that didn't explain why Alexander's displeasure seemed directed at him. Or perhaps the physician considered John responsible for Georgiana's injury – in which case, John certainly deserved his censure. But Alexander would soon see that John intended to make it right.

Georgiana had mustered control over her amusement by the time a still-silent Alexander handed her a brown paper parcel, which she tucked into a pocket of her domino.

John reached into his own pocket. 'How much?'

Alexander waved his hand. 'Forget it.'

'No, come, my friend.' John extended some gold coins. 'Two guineas at least.'

But Alexander crossed his arms over his chest. 'John, you are the Maternity Hospital's most generous benefactor, and Miss Bailey performs the work of a saint at Monica House. Neither of you will ever pay a penny for my services.' He looked pointedly at Georgiana. 'By the by, Miss Bailey, I can guarantee nothing with those items—'

She flashed a smile. 'Truly, don't trouble yourself, Doctor. I know what I'm about.'

Alexander studied her, nodded, and bid her a good night.

But after Georgiana had proceeded into the corridor, Alexander blocked John's path. 'Miss Bailey is an angel, John,' he said fiercely, his voice low. 'She lives and breathes for the women and children at Monica House. She saves and changes lives. I won't stand by and watch a friend of mine not treat her like the lady she is.'

John frowned, taken aback. 'Good God, Alexander. Isn't it obvious I realise her worth?' He almost confessed the full extent of his sentiments, before recalling he wasn't at liberty to do so until he'd spoken to Georgiana.

Alexander held his gaze, as if searching John's eyes for the truth. Then nodded, clearly much relieved. 'Yes, I see that now, and I'm glad of it.' Slowly, he smiled his crooked grin. 'Enjoy your night, my friend.'

Still baffled, but relieved Alexander had decided not to dig out swords (as there'd been enough injury for

311

one evening), John caught up with Georgiana, who awaited him at the door.

She slipped her hand in the crook of his offered elbow, and they proceeded out and onto the pavement. A night fog was settling, and ghostlike mists curled around the streetlamps.

'John,' Georgiana said quietly, leaning her cheek against his upper arm, her body warm at his side. 'Is it true you sponsor the Maternity Hospital?'

'I do,' he responded simply, feeling shy about drawing attention to what was hardly sacrificial giving, even though he funded it to the tune of a couple of thousand a year. 'Alexander relies on sponsors so he can provide care to every woman who comes to him, regardless of her ability to pay.'

'Oh, I know. I just didn't realise you donated.' She beamed at him. 'As it happens, you've been indirectly supporting Monica House without either of us knowing it, because Dr Mitchell considers the maternity needs of my residents to fall under his hospital's expenses. So, thank you, John. The more I learn about you, the more I admire.'

John's chest swelled. 'Thank you for the compliment, but I must return it to you a thousand times over. You and Alexander are the true heroes.'

They proceeded to the corner of Park Lane, where John hailed a hackney.

After John lifted Georgiana into the cab and settled himself beside her, she turned to him. 'I shall pay you a *second* compliment tonight.' She laid her hand on his cheek. 'You have the most beautiful eyes, John Tyrold. I've wanted to tell you so since first I met you, but you wouldn't have believed in my sincerity before. I think you will now.'

Her words seemed so close to a declaration of affection that John's pulse raced. It would be a perfect time to declare his own sentiments, but his throat was suddenly too tight to speak. Like earlier, during their cab ride to Alexander's, she seemed to be inviting physical intimacy, but John wasn't yet certain.

Georgiana watched him during the ensuing silence, while grazing her nails over his jaw, down his neck, and along his arm, until entwining her hand with his. 'Would you mind terribly coming inside Monica House?' she asked, casting an intense gaze through her lashes. 'With my wounded arm, I need assistance in readying myself for bed.'

Perhaps John was unsure of Georgiana's intentions, but his cock didn't have the same doubts. It was half hard and aching already. 'What sort of assistance?' he managed to enquire, his voice thick.

Georgiana smiled slowly, her gaze unwavering. She raised his hand to her mouth and her lips brushed the tip of his index finger. 'All sorts, really.' Her tongue circled his fingertip, leaving a trail of wet heat that drove a jolt of electricity straight to his cock, so that it rose, ready, insistent, throbbing. 'My needs could consume the rest of your night, if you are willing.'

John no longer questioned her intentions. She was seducing him.

And he was damned well going to let her.

'You did take a bullet for me.' It hurt like the devil to talk, as if the rigidity of his erection had rendered even his vocal cords stiff. 'Perhaps I ought to comply.'

Georgiana laughed, a delighted, delightful sound. 'Do you recall on Monday evening, when you suggested I wanted you to tuck me in? I confess I didn't want it then, but *tonight* . . . well, John, I think it would be immensely satisfying tonight. I hope you'll be more agreeable to the prospect now than you were then.'

John cast a grimace in her direction. 'Can you ever forgive me for the foolish things I said at the beginning of our acquaintance?'

She grinned. 'I *do* forgive you. But making you eat your condescending words lessens the agony of that gunshot I took for you.'

She laughed again, entirely aware of her power over John. Delighting in it, in fact, and it was all he could do not to kiss her cheekiness away with bruising passion. But the driver pulled up his hack, and there was other business to attend to first.

John controlled himself as he paid for the ride and assisted Georgiana from the carriage. But the moment they were in the dark and misty alley, he caught her in his arms, careful of her wound, and leant over her, one hand supporting the back of her head.

Then – masks be damned – he kissed her.

Hard.

He showed no mercy as he parted her lips and claimed her honeyed mouth, plunging his tongue to drink deep.

She moaned into him; he growled in response but gave no quarter because she asked for none. Instead, she threaded her fingers around his neck and attacked him back vigorously, her own tongue jousting with his for control.

John released her mouth at last, his erection hard between them, his fist knotted in her thick hair. 'You want me to eat my words, woman?' His voice was ragged, tearing from his chest. 'Then I shall, dammit. Georgiana, you bewitched me from the moment of our first meeting. Every protest I have uttered against you, every disagreeable action on my part, every time I scolded or chastised you, I did because I was peeved that you enchanted me so wholly and completely. But then you defeated my grumpiness with your wisdom, your kindness, your gentle and generous heart, until I stand before you now a conquered man, with you my victrix.'

She blinked, her eyes wide and glistening. 'It was never my intention to conquer you. I only wanted you to donate to Monica House.'

John drew her to him and kissed the top of her head. 'But what do you want now, darling?' he asked, his lips pressed against her hair. 'More of my money? If so, it's yours for the asking.'

'No, John,' she murmured into his chest. 'I want only you.'

Her words pierced him. 'And you're well enough? Your arm, your injury?'

'You can distract me from the little pain that lingers.'

'Then, yes,' he said, full of feeling. 'I'll tuck you in. As many times as you desire.'

They wasted no more moments embracing in the alley; Georgiana took his hand and guided him swiftly through the swirling fog.

Inside the Monica House yard, Ben the grounds-keeper scowled at John, his lantern held high, tendrils of mist reaching fingers into its golden glow. His scowl only deepened when Georgiana hastily dismissed his pointed offer to show John out. He looked very much as if he wished to disregard Georgiana's wishes, but Georgiana pulled John across the yard and all thoughts of Ben vanished.

Georgiana was John's sole focus.

He desired her with an unrelenting passion such as he'd never felt for anyone else, and as she led him up the narrow flight of stairs, he knew the sentiments of his mind and the hopes of heart with perfect clarity. He loved her. He would now *make* love to her, since she had asked it of him, and afterwards, he'd ask her to be his wife.

John luxuriated in those thoughts as he entered Georgiana's bedchamber, but uncertain now how to proceed, he removed his hat and stood holding it by the brim as she lit candles in sconces. It would be best to follow her lead so he didn't misstep as he had at Almack's.

'Remove your domino and your coat, John,' she said quietly, extinguishing the lighting stick with a shake of her wrist. 'I want you to be comfortable.'

John tossed aside his hat and did as she requested, throwing the discarded items to the floor. His erection was clearly visible under his trouser fall, but she looked instead at the clothes crumpled on the floorboards.

'Tsk, tsk.' She shook her head. 'Fold those neatly and put them on the trunk.'

As John followed her request to the best of his rather pathetic abilities, she looked him up and down appraisingly.

She tapped a finger to her chin. 'Take off your waistcoat, too, I think,' she said, as if advising him on fashion, as Edward had done two days earlier.

Her mock seriousness amused him. 'Shirt as well, I suppose?'

Her lips twisted. 'Why not? And your boots. They look stiff and uncomfortable.'

John snorted as he unbuttoned his waistcoat. Of course, she intended the double entendre. 'I worry about your own comfort, Georgiana. Perhaps I ought to assist you in removing some layers.'

She lifted her nose haughtily. 'Fold it,' she scolded, as he'd been about to drop his waistcoat to the floor. 'And there will be time enough for my layers later. First, you'll pour us both a drink.'

After crumpling his waistcoat into a ball, John pulled his shirt over his head.

With her nose still aloft, Georgiana's eyes trailed slowly over his torso. John was too thin, perhaps – he'd never been able to put on an ounce of fat – but he was otherwise confident of his physique. Frequent sport with his friends and long rides with Thunder and Jolly in Hyde Park had given definition to his lean muscles.

After her inspection, Georgiana met his gaze, her dark eyes flashing. 'Boots off,' she ordered, none too kindly.

John obeyed.

'There.' He stood in his trousers and stockinged feet. 'Satisfied?'

She grinned slowly. Rather wickedly, in fact, which thrilled John. 'Not yet, but what I see raises my hopes. I'll take wine, and so will you. There's a decanter in the antechamber behind my screen. When you've poured our drinks, make us a fire. I don't want you to get cold. I appreciate the size of things as they are now.'

Oh, good *God*. She was a bold little exactress.

He loved it, and judging by the throbbing state of affairs in his trousers, his cock was desperate to be her whip-boy.

John bowed. 'As you wish, madam.'

She seated herself in an armchair by the hearth, and John set about fulfilling her orders. As she'd said, behind the screen was an orderly antechamber with a small table on the far wall, upon which rested a decanter of wine. But John didn't cross the plain wool carpet immediately. He allowed himself to linger in this intimate space, drawing out his anticipation.

Linger, but not pry. He didn't investigate the closed wardrobe or disturb the tidy stack of hat boxes, but he did brush his fingers against the gold satin folds of the gown she'd worn the night before, which was airing on a cedar clothes-horse. Then his eyes were drawn to a row of pegs, upon which hung dainty underclothes. A pair of cream-coloured stays . . . a chemise so tiny it looked impossible for an adult to wear . . . delicate silk stockings, hanging by pink garter ribbons. Everything smelled of Georgiana, and John let his nose and fingers trail through them on his way to the decanter.

Because her scent was headier than strong spirits, he had no need of wine, but Georgiana had asked for it, so he poured and emerged.

'Thank you.' She took her glass and sipped, looking over the rim. 'Now the fire.'

John swallowed a mouthful of wine to moisten his throat and set his glass aside, not wanting more. He knelt before the metal hearth and built up a bed of kindling.

A rustle from behind drew his attention over his shoulder. Georgiana had arisen and was heading towards her screen, holding the package from Alexander.

'Focus on your task, John,' she admonished before disappearing into her antechamber.

John laid the coal and sparked the firelighter. As the flames rose, he fed them until the coal caught and eventually glowed, and heat radiated over the hearth. After ten minutes, the fire was healthy and the smoke rising properly, so that only the warmth, the crackle, and the pleasing aroma of burning coal penetrated the room.

John fitted the fireguard and rose, expecting new instructions.

Georgiana was again seated in the armchair, sipping her wine. 'I'm impressed. I didn't think you'd know how to make a fire.'

'What skills shall I demonstrate next, madam?' John asked, wiping his hands on his thighs.

She grimaced. 'I intended for us to enjoy our wine together, but you mayn't sit on my armchair in those dirty trousers, so take them off. They look . . . constricting, anyway.'

John lifted an eyebrow. '*You're* sitting on an armchair in a blood-splattered domino.'

She blanched, leaping to her feet to examine the green upholstery. 'Thank goodness.' She exhaled in relief. 'Not a mark.'

John laughed, thoroughly touched by her excessive concern over her chair. Even now, she remained adorably wide-eyed, her thick hair tousled deliciously with silky strands falling about her heart-shaped face. 'The blood dried a long time ago, my silly girl.'

'Yes. I . . . knew that.'

She blinked, long lashes over those dark eyes, playing at being timid now, and John knew she wanted him to assume charge.

'Come to me,' he directed her firmly, and she obeyed, inching closer. He caught her chin in his hand and lifted her head until she met his gaze. 'I'm going to undress you, Georgiana.'

She nodded, nibbling her bottom lip.

With his free hand, John loosened the knot of her domino. The red fabric pooled around her feet.

'Fold it?' she suggested.

John shook his head. 'No. Not now. We're going to leave it crumpled on the floor, and you aren't going to worry about it or about anything else, my darling.' He pressed his lips to her forehead until she relaxed, closing her eyes with a sigh. 'There, my love. There. Let me take care of you.'

John kissed down her forehead, and over the curve of her lids. 'You're exquisite, Georgiana,' he murmured, grazing his fingertips over her jaw, down her neck, and to the peach-soft skin of her upper back until his hands arrived at her gown's laces.

John tugged, but the knot didn't yield, so he hooked his fingers into the seam and, grabbing the fabric securely, he ripped the gown down the back.

Georgiana gasped, her eyes flying open. Then she grinned. 'For shame, John Tyrold! What a wanton waste of a perfectly good frock.'

John let the gown drop to the floor. 'It's bloodstained and one sleeve is cut off,' he said huskily as he took in the breath-stealing sight before him.

She wore a knee-length white chemise with a blue ribbon gathering its scooped neckline. The glow of the candles and the fire flickered through the thin fabric; her gently rounded breasts swelled the chemise, hard nipples peaking the cotton.

'Let down your hair,' John ordered, his voice thick.

Georgiana extracted her hairpins and shook out her profuse mane, which fell over her shoulders and down her back like a dark river, every bit as lush as John had imagined.

'Drop your hairpins on the floor now.'

'Utterly horrid man,' she teased, her gaze smouldering

at him from under her lashes, but she complied, reaching out a slender arm and dropping the hairpins one by one onto her crumpled domino.

'Magnificent.' John wrapped his hand around a thick segment of her hair, clasping her at the nape of her neck, and claiming her mouth. She yielded to him, and he pulled her against him and drank deep, her body filling every void.

'My stockings,' she said when they paused for breath, lips still touching. 'Kneel down and take them off me, John Tyrold.'

He kissed her again first, capturing her bottom lip between his teeth. 'As you wish, enchantress.'

When he knelt on the floorboards, Georgiana pulled him so close, his cheek rested on the cotton covering her abdomen. He knew what she really wanted. He closed his eyes, luxuriating in her proximity, his hands gliding down her back and over the curve of her bottom. His nose lingered at the apex of her legs, the smell of her sex spiking his desire.

He sat on his heels and lifted her chemise to expose her ribbon garters. He kissed one at the bow, holding his lips to it as he untied and slid the stocking down the curve of her calf until it pooled about her foot.

He moved to the other side. As he mirrored his actions, Georgiana ran her fingers through his hair, massaging his scalp as she'd done at the coffeehouse. Inching the hem of her chemise higher, John kissed up her thighs, slowly, agonisingly, wanting to draw out his anticipation and hers, wanting to make these moments last for ever. She was as soft and sweet-smelling as the petal of a flower, and, as he worked higher, he slid his hand up to grasp her firm bottom, skin on skin. When his lips arrived where they longed to be, he kissed her feathery dark triangle of curls.

She made a sound – a whisper, a whimper – and John lifted his eyes, asking silent permission to continue.

Her face was flushed, her lips soft. 'Please.'

John parted her with his fingers and put his mouth over her, drinking in her hot taste, finer than brandy. He slid his tongue into her folds, around the centre of her pleasure, nipping, sucking, licking at her nub, taking her in as if she were an oasis in the desert and he a parched man.

Which he had been, hadn't he? Alone for years. Unwilling to submit to anyone, for anything, until he was faced with a challenge that he could neither ignore nor surmount alone, and then somehow, Georgiana had appeared, an answer to prayers he hadn't even uttered. An angel in his time of need, there to soothe him, comfort him, help him, guide him.

John's heart burst with yearning far greater than his sexual desire, though his cock was so hard it strained tight against his trousers.

God help him, he loved her so much, and he'd do anything for her.

He was fully vulnerable and in her power.

Desperate to call her his own. Desperate to protect and provide for her, to give her everything her heart desired. To make all her dreams come true.

And to please her . . . which he seemed to be succeeding at, because her breathing quickened as her abdomen rose and fell against his forehead. She tilted her hips to allow him better access, and her nails dug into his scalp. John slid a finger into her hot, slick opening, wet and luscious. When she released an agonised moan, he slid in another and stroked her on the inside. He increased the intensity of his licking, her scent in his nose, her taste in his mouth, and, still, he didn't have enough of her. He wanted her to feel the intense torture of longing but more than that, he wanted to bring her exquisite pleasure. He sucked harder. Sobbing out a moan, she wrapped a leg around his neck and thrust her quim forwards so he could cover her even more fully. She was sloppy and wet on his chin as he fingered – faster and harder – that sensitive place inside the vagina which he knew could drive her to intense climax.

Then she came hard, forceful pulses against his tongue and hand. With his mouth still on her sex, John glanced up to witness her ecstasy, thrilling in his success as she threw back her head and whimpered, long and low.

He'd done that. He'd satiated this lush and passionate woman.

At least for now.

Georgiana disengaged, covering her face with her hair and hands. 'Damn,' she said, and it was the first time John had heard her swear. 'That was very good.'

John wiped his mouth and chin as he stood. 'There's more where it came from.'

She peeked from under her curtain of hair, looking more beautiful than ever, flush faced and tousled. 'Soon – it's a bit sensitive right now.'

'It's primed. This is too.' John rubbed the tortured bulge in his trousers; his cock was like iron, and his swollen balls ached. 'You've made me impossibly hard, woman.'

She tucked her hair behind one ear. 'In that case, you'd better remove your trousers.'

John unfastened the buttons at his waist. 'Chemise off.'

He held his waistband until she complied. As she crossed her arms to pull the fabric over her head, exposing her body, John released his trousers and stepped out from where they fell on the floor.

They faced each other, entirely nude in the firelight.

As her eyes trailed over him, John hoped she liked what she saw even a fraction as much as she delighted him, for she was utter perfection. She held her hands against her abdomen, as if in modesty, but it tantalised John, for her fingers were positioned towards her heavenly triangle. Her skin was smooth and tanned, and her waist impossibly tiny. Her breasts were half-hidden under her curtain of lustrous hair, but what he could see drove John wild. They were small and firm, the perfect size to cup in his palm as he thumbed and suckled her nipples.

The gold locket about her neck raised a flicker of envy before John could stop himself. She'd implied it contained a memento of her lost love, and, whoever that man had been, John might yet have to reckon with the hold he retained over Georgiana's heart. But John laid his jealousy aside. He didn't know much of love, but he knew that what he felt for Georgiana wouldn't alter because she'd already lived a full life. Her former loves were in the past, just as Helen was in John's past. Here and now, Georgiana was joined with him in desire, if not yet in love.

She *wanted* him. Not his money, but *him*.

None too gently, John cupped his hand around the nape of her neck. When he kissed her, she tasted of wine and her own carnal pleasure, still on his lips. She embraced him, her nipples brushing the bare skin of his chest. She curved her leg around one of his and grazed her wet quim against his thigh, too low for him to plunge into.

Without pausing their kiss, John lifted her from the floor, bringing her to his hips. She wrapped both legs about his waist and when he pushed her up against the wall, her sex spread wet and open against him.

Georgiana broke their kiss. 'I want you in me, John Tyrold. I'm dripping for you.'

John closed his eyes. She *was* dripping, and as she slid herself slick and hot along his length she brought him close to the cusp, which reminded him there were practical matters to consider – ones he now realised he should've addressed earlier. 'I don't have a condom, Georgiana. I could try to withdraw, but I'm so primed I don't trust myself, so as much as I want to, I shouldn't enter you. Not this first time, anyway, when I feel like I'll come as soon as I thrust.'

She squeezed her legs tighter around his waist, her vulva tight on his aching shaft. 'While you made the fire, I inserted a sponge and tincture from Dr Mitchell, to prevent pregnancy. They aren't guarantees, but I also know my cycle. Enter me, finish in me; you won't get me with child tonight.'

'So *that's* what you asked Alexander for,' John said, understanding at last, a chuckle breaking through his desire. 'No wonder he looked as if he wanted to challenge me. He thought I intended to take advantage of a wounded lady.'

'Whereas in truth, *I'm* the seductress,' she purred. 'But you wanted to be seduced so badly you could taste it, John.' She kissed him again, drawing his bottom lip into her mouth and sucking it as she released. 'Now take me against this wall, like I wanted you to do in that alley on Wednesday.'

The reminder of their frustrated desire on the night of their first kiss drove John over the edge. He pulled his hips back enough to let his cock fall into position at her opening, hovered there a moment, steeling himself, and then he plunged into her vagina, molten lava tight against his swollen shaft. A moan tore from his throat as he gripped Georgiana, every nerve in his body alive to the intense pleasure of being inside of her, the smell and feel of her something he wanted to drown in.

She answered him with a sharp whimper. A most exquisite sound of female pleasure.

John's eyes teared – he wanted to fucking *cry*, his feelings for Georgiana were so powerful. He held her hard against his chest, melded her body to his as he moved within her, rubbing his cock along the length of her passage, stroking her with calculated concentration. Of all the beautiful sounds she made – her singing, her speaking voice, her musical laughter – nothing was lovelier than her sounds of bliss when *he* was the goddamned lucky man who got to drive her to them.

Only by focusing on her pleasure did John hold himself back from orgasm. He drove into her, kissing her bare shoulder, her neck, her tangled hair, and she clung tight, squeezing her legs around his waist, her arms encircling his neck, her hands in his hair, until his second triumph came and she bit into his shoulder, barely stifling a cry, scraped her nails into his skin, and pulsed on his cock.

John gazed into her hazy dark eyes as she melted like butter in his arms, looking every bit like a woman thoroughly fucked.

Only not thoroughly enough yet, because he hadn't finished with her.

He grinned. 'You liked that, my sweet love.'

'It was luscious,' she said, her voice husky and lazy.

'No resting yet, darling.' John withdrew, scooped her into his arms, and crossed the room to her narrow box bed. He laid her down crossways, with her bottom at the edge of the mattress and her legs off the side, mindful of her wounded arm, and stood, devouring her with his eyes. Her dark hair fanned out over the green counterpane, her lips were red with his kisses, her eyes dilated and dark. One hand lay across her abdomen.

John knelt at the side of the bed and parted her sex. Now he could see her well, glistening, wet, still vaguely pulsing. 'So pretty,' he said, putting his fingers into her and breathing in her musk as he licked up though the folds until she squirmed on the bed and fisted her counterpane. She was so passionate and alive to her own pleasure that it took John little time to bring her back to a whimpering mess.

'Come with me this next time,' she gasped, stopping him before she climaxed. 'Come deep, deep inside me, and let me hear it when you do. No one else's sleeping quarters are near.'

As John moved his kisses towards her navel, she pulled him higher. 'My breasts,' she urged. 'But get on the bed.'

She slithered lengthwise on the mattress and placed a pillow under her hips so when John lay above her, her pelvis tilted into his. With the fingers of one hand back in her quim, he cupped a perfect palm-sized breast and flicked his tongue over its hard nipple. When he drew her into his mouth and suckled, she rocked her hips and called out.

'Stop,' she said at last, reaching back and seizing the posts of the narrow headboard, as if to brace herself. 'I want your cock, *now.*'

John plunged into her so deeply he had to grab the headboard himself, wrapping his hand over hers, their fingers entwining as they gripped the post. The pillow allowed a depth of penetration he hadn't been expecting. 'By God, Georgiana,' he called out, thrusting again. It was heaven, sheer paradise, the most exquisitely beautiful torture. When he pulled back and plunged a third time, she lifted herself up to meet him.

'More, you delicious man,' she cried.

And John obliged, thrusting again and again until there was nothing but the flames of his passion, consuming his body, his senses, his mind. He thrust with single-minded determination to bring her to climax a third time. When at last she arched against him, called out and throbbed on his cock, he clutched the bedpost with his other hand and gave her one last pounding, which sent him exploding inside her, groaning her name as pleasure peaked with every pulse of his cock and of her quim, over and over and over again until at last he collapsed, racked, wasted, shattered, and rolled to his side, taking into his arms the spent form of the woman he loved and cradling her to his chest.

18

Georgiana awoke to her wound throbbing. Wrapped in snug covers, she was cuddled against Tyrold – against John, rather, as she'd come to think of him. His arms encircled her to prevent a tumble from her narrow bed, and his chest rose and fell with slow, steady breaths.

Untroubled and unguarded in sleep, and with his dishevelled black hair falling over his forehead, John looked adorably boyish, and Georgiana couldn't resist an urge to kiss the tip of his nose. His eyelashes fluttered when her lips touched his skin, but he didn't awaken.

How perfect a man he was, she thought with a surge of warm feeling in her chest. Gentle yet passionate. Virile yet considerate. Conceited, yes – but endearingly so once one understood him.

Oh, how lovely it would be to grow accustomed to this. To him. To them. How wonderful it would be to take John as her lover for however long their passion endured. To owe nothing to society, to be allowed to luxuriate in his embrace as she slept, to spend time with him, to let their intimacy develop, just the two of them, with no one judging, no one paying them any mind.

But Georgiana couldn't, of course. After tonight, she must return to her life's purpose, and a love affair with a famous millionaire held no place in the existence of a virtuous charity worker. Quite apart from the disastrous scandal, it would also distract her, muddle her, make her yearn for things to which she'd long since forfeited her rights . . .

But her throbbing wound reminded Georgiana she deserved this one hedonistic night. She shifted her head on the pillow. The mantel clock above the low-burning fire showed two in the morning. Georgiana didn't know how long she'd slept, because she wasn't certain what time she and John had concluded their marvellous lovemaking. She hadn't looked at the clock then; she hadn't had energy for anything other than extracting the sponge before crawling next to him beneath the covers. They'd snuggled together, utterly spent, their limbs entwined as they fell into near-instant oblivion.

But although the sleep couldn't have been long, it had been solid and satisfying. As solid and satisfying as John's prowess; he'd given Georgiana the best sex of her life, and she was ready for more.

If she was only going to have one night of pleasure, she'd make the best of it.

She just needed some willow-bark infusion and a second sponge first.

She slithered out of his arms, crossed the room, and slipped behind the screen into her dressing room where she cleaned herself before inserting a fresh, tincture-soaked sponge. Her mouth quirked as she rubbed her swollen quim, feeling its heightened sensitivity and pleasant soreness. What a fantastically energetic and attentive lover John was. The remembrance made her squirm and squeeze her inner muscles, which ached in anticipation. She was so ready for him.

But first, some willow-bark tincture, best mixed with the remainder of her wine to alleviate the bitterness. When she emerged from behind the screen, flask in hand, John was awake, propped on an elbow as she crossed the room.

'Everything well, my darling?'

The tender way he uttered terms of endearment melted Georgiana's heart.

She uncorked the flask and poured a generous portion into her leftover wine. 'My arm hurts a little.'

John jumped out of the bed, tall, lean, masculine in the firelight. His body was beautiful, his muscles smoothly defined, with dark curls on his forearms, on his legs, across his upper chest, and trailing in an enticing line down his abdomen to his cock.

A cock that was hard again, standing long and erect, although it hadn't been a moment earlier in the bed.

Georgiana thrilled. It was reacting to her nudity, which provided oh-so-solid evidence that John Tyrold's cock liked her. It was a heady, if silly, realisation. *Take that, every rapacious, fortune-hungry, gold-lusting lady in London*, she thought. *John Tyrold desires me, nobody that I am.*

John followed her gaze downwards. 'Excuse him. He has no manners. Shall I take you back to Alexander?'

Georgiana shook her head and quaffed her wine and willow-bark, shuddering as she swallowed the disgusting draught. 'I needed more tincture to stop the throbbing in my arm' – she placed down her empty glass – 'so I can take another pounding from your cock.'

John started, then laughed. 'You never stop delighting me,' he said, his gaze growing tender in the firelight. 'Do you realise that, loveliest Georgiana? You delight me, body, mind, and heart.'

Georgiana's own heart twisted. She suddenly suspected that, in bringing John to her bed, she'd given him the impression that she wanted to be his new lover. He even knew that she knew he was looking for one – and that she was aware he wanted someone who met him with equal desire and mutual respect.

But Georgiana wasn't like her godmother. Betty ran a rowdy theatre in Covent Garden; she could make her own decisions about whom to bed and on what terms. Whereas although Georgiana wasn't accepted by her father's world, she also wasn't free from its constraints. Not when she depended upon its generosity. Not when her actions reflected on Monica House, and therefore affected the lives of everyone in her care.

She needed to explain to John why she couldn't be his lover, and perhaps the gentlest way was through song.

With that purpose, she opened her leather guitar case and took up her instrument. 'I hope my injury hasn't affected my ability to play. Come back to bed; I shall sing to you.'

He reclined on the blanket-jumbled mattress, one leg cocked, an arm thrown over his pillowed head, and she perched cross-legged beside him. He rested his other hand on her knee, stroking her thigh with his thumb, and Georgiana strummed an opening motif.

'Do you know this one?' she asked over the music.

'*Plaisir d'amour*,' he replied, his lips slightly turned down.

She nodded, and then began the song, a tale of the fleeting nature of love's pleasures.

He watched until she faded the last note and silenced the guitar strings with her palm.

For a time, the only sound was the crackle of the coal, and then two faint lines creased his brow. 'This pleasure between us needn't be fleeting, Georgiana. Nor need it cause pain.'

Georgiana propped the guitar against her bedside table. 'It must be fleeting, John, or it will have the potential to cause one or both of us considerable pain. I admit I'm tempted, but we mustn't continue as lovers past tonight.' He opened his mouth, as if to say something, but she held up her hand. 'No, stop.' If he attempted to persuade her on this magical evening, with those green eyes full of tenderness, she might surrender and promise him another tryst. And while she could revoke that promise, of course, she had no wish to raise false hopes. She could face saying no tomorrow, in the harsh light of day, but tonight she was weak. Lord only knew what she'd succumb to at this vulnerable moment; she might agree to be his *publicly acknowledged* mistress, so heady was their intimacy and so unfairly tattered was her reputation already.

But, of course, she couldn't. Not when she'd pledged her life to Monica House, in atonement for her selfish past.

'Say no more on this subject right now because it will spoil the magic.' She stroked his cheek, already rough with stubble though he'd been clean-shaven at Vauxhall. 'Tonight, John Tyrold and the debutante daughter of the Duke of Amesbury get to surrender to desire as if we really *were* Jack and Georgie, rogue and bawd. No consequences, only pleasure.'

John studied her, forehead knotted. 'If that's what you prefer, I shan't speak tonight on the matter of our' – he appeared to hunt for a word – 'connection.' His eyes fell to her lap as he grazed the back of his fingers up and down her inner thigh. 'But let me say one thing about myself, please. People . . .' He hesitated. 'People call me "King Midas" behind my back. Did you know that?'

Georgiana smiled, hoping to ease his solemnity. 'Of course. You're a legend.'

He met her gaze, his fingers tantalising as their repetitive strokes trailed her sensitive skin. 'But I'm a tragic legend. Midas valued gold above all else and in the end, everything but gold was lost to him. That's been my story for nearly twenty years. Georgiana, I don't want that any more. You – and our search for Flora – have made me hope I can change.'

'Yes, and you've changed already, John.' Georgiana straddled him, leaning forwards to shadow her lower belly, hiding the fine white lines that crossed her abdomen, and placed his hand over one of her breasts.

336

He massaged gently and she ground herself against his cock, which had softened but now swiftly rose to readiness. 'Look – you're touching *me*, and I'm not turning to gold.'

'You're already more precious than gold,' he said, with a gaze that made Georgiana's insides puddle.

Rather breathless, Georgiana teased in return. 'Listen to you, you silver-tongued charmer.'

'Golden-tongued, surely?' He stuck out the tip of his, as if for her inspection.

'Whether it's gold, silver or pink,' she said, laughing, 'I can think of better uses for it than talking.' Wiggling forwards, she brought her breast to his mouth, sighing in contentment the moment he caught her nipple, kissing, licking, suckling. Ripples of pleasure coursed through her and when the urgency reached higher peaks, she lifted herself up – not letting him kiss her abdomen – until she knelt on either side of his shoulders, her quim at his mouth.

He parted those lips and applied himself diligently, and fire shot through Georgiana's veins as she let his ministrations consume her. He was so good at love-making, she thought, just before a shattering orgasm evoked the *petite mort*, that blissful near loss of consciousness. She shuddered over him, clasping the bedposts so the waves couldn't sweep her away.

As her orgasm ebbed, she sat on John's upper chest, her legs folded on either side of his neck, unable to speak.

He blew lightly on her clitoris, sending delightful shivers throughout her body.

'Mmmm,' she moaned.

'Why do you taste like brandy?' he asked, matter-of-factly.

The question surprised Georgiana out of her ecstasy-induced stupor, and she laughed. She'd noticed the brandy smell when she'd first uncorked *that* tincture from Dr Mitchell, so she'd read the ingredients on the label: brandy, quinine and various herbal infusions. 'It's the pregnancy-preventing tincture on the sponge. Apparently, Dr Mitchell puts brandy in it.'

'Clever.' Tyrold lifted her bottom, bringing her quim back to his mouth and licking through her folds again. 'I'd give him my compliments, but the best nectar is your own taste.'

He sucked her clitoris with so much renewed vigour Georgiana had to seize the bedposts again. But as tempting as it was, she didn't let herself climax. It was her turn to demonstrate that she could elicit pleasure he'd never forget.

'I want your cock to do the job next time, John.' She slid down his body and brought her lips to his and kissed him passionately, her brandied, musky taste in his mouth. He made as if to roll her over, with him on top, but she pushed her hand, splay-fingered, against his chest until he relaxed into the rumpled bedding again. 'First something else.'

She worked her way down, kissing along his firm jaw and his gorgeous neck – the neck she couldn't stop lusting over. Then she kissed the length of his chest, and he sighed, a man contented.

Time for some torture.

Georgiana positioned herself between his legs until his cock was at her mouth. With her hand, she manipulated it until his breath grew ragged. As she traced its satin-smooth head with her tongue, tasting the salty fluid that beaded at the tip, he moaned and tangled his fingers in her hair.

She plunged her mouth over him, taking him deep and sucking hard, and he released a guttural groan. Georgiana triumphed in her success. She'd reduced him to the same moaning mess he'd made of her, and she was going to suck him until he couldn't take any more.

He tasted of their lovemaking – sex, brandy, passion – and the smell that infused her senses was the scent of triumph and pleasure. Hedonism, but with a man unlike any other Georgiana had ever known.

She didn't understand exactly what she felt for John, but she knew it was different from her previous lovers. Her first lover . . . but, no, it was best not to call him a lover. It was best not to think of him at all. And as for her Italian lover, rakish Domenico . . . well, he'd been something Georgiana had needed at the time, a way to reclaim her body as her own. But he'd never encouraged anything beyond sex, and she hadn't wanted it. She didn't believe they'd ever said more than half a dozen words to each other during any of their encounters, and she'd certainly never slept in his arms.

With John, everything was completely different, and she couldn't even determine why, other than it felt as if she stood on a precipice before an abyss, and if she allowed herself to fall forwards, there might be no end to what she could feel, what she could receive, and what she'd want to give in return.

But of course, it couldn't stay that way. Not just because of society. Not just because she already had too many claims on her time and attention. Not just because she'd relinquished her right to think of her own desires . . .

But because John didn't know the real Georgiana.

What would he say if he discovered her dark secrets? If he learnt she'd once been selfish and vain, abandoning her only friend to pursue a reckless flirtation with that friend's brother? And how would John react if he knew that later, in the ensuing loneliness after losing Henrietta, Georgiana had given herself not to someone she *loved*, but to a vile man? A villain whom she hadn't even liked. A man who'd made her feel sordid.

John would be disgusted if he learnt that although Georgiana hated her seducer, she'd returned to him repeatedly, because being used by him was preferable to the cruelty of the girls at school. John wouldn't still think Georgiana clever and wise if he knew she'd been foolish enough to believe it when the man had said he'd taken precautions – so much so that she'd been shocked when her monthly courses had stopped, her breasts had grown tender and her abdomen had begun to harden.

And that wasn't even the worst of it.

If John knew the truth, he'd think her utterly despicable.

Tears welled up, burning the back of her eyes, but she couldn't and wouldn't let John see them. She couldn't bear to ruin this perfect night when he thought so highly of her.

She pulled away from his cock, wiping her eyes quickly before he could notice, and sat up to straddle him. She'd ride him like a stallion – ride him until no thoughts were left in her head. Until she collapsed in utter exhaustion and could lose herself in sleep at his side again.

She impaled herself on his cock and tugged the blanket over her abdomen, although she needn't have bothered because he was gazing deep into her eyes as he grabbed her hips and helped her rock. She rose and fell, each stroke along her vagina enflaming her passion, each time his pelvis pounded against her clitoris bringing her to toe-curling peaks. She told him to hammer her, she praised him, she gasped his name – and he answered with rough, raw passion, calling her beautiful, calling her his Georgiana, saying he could make love to her for ever, and he'd never, ever have enough of her.

Faster she moved as she locked gazes with him. Faster they gasped in unison.

The bed creaked and the headboard slammed.

She'd never, ever, ever achieved gratification like this. It was too good, she suddenly realised, and she wanted it *too* much. She'd have to pay for her greedy indulgence later, somehow. Selfishness was always punished. But then John fondled her clitoris, and at last Georgiana achieved the obliteration of thought that she'd desired. Waves built until she drove herself deep on his shaft, letting him fill her completely, and she climaxed in a white blaze of ecstasy.

The power of her orgasm brought him over the edge. He bucked his hips, pumping his seed deep into her, moaning her name, squeezing her bottom, his head thrown back on the pillow and his eyes closed. In perfect ecstasy because of *her*.

As the last waves of Georgiana's orgasm ebbed, she kissed his sweat-damp forehead. 'You liked that,' she said with a laugh, throwing his own teasing words back at him.

He enveloped her in his embrace and smothered her face in kisses. 'I *loved* that. And,' he whispered into her neck, 'I love *you*, Georgiana. I love you so very, very much.'

Georgiana stiffened in his arms, unable to believe her ears.

He *loved* her? Could John, not really knowing her, truly imagine he had feelings *that* powerful? And if so, how had she not sensed it, with her innate awareness of the sentiments of others? Oh, certainly, she perceived he admired her. That he desired her. That he took pleasure in her company, enjoyed their companion-ship, respected her opinion and her wisdom, and that he trusted her, but she hadn't sensed that he *loved* her.

'I . . . John, I . . .' She stumbled over her words, unsure. What did romantic love feel like, even?

He folded her tight against his chest, kissing her tangled hair. 'Shh, darling. In the passion of the moment, I spoke too soon. I remember now that you asked me not to talk of this tonight, so we won't. Let's sleep now, but if you need another shag, awaken me and I'll oblige.'

342

Georgiana managed a little chuckle and kissed his forearm, but she did so with an aching heart. Let it not be true that he believed himself in love, she thought, squeezing her eyes tight. Let him have mistaken his sentiments.

Because if John *truly* loved her, tomorrow's conversation would break his heart.

And Georgiana realised she cared a great deal about John's heart . . .

343

19

Sunlight bore through John's closed eyelids as a resounding knock startled him from deep sleep.

But it was Georgiana's insistent shaking that made him bolt upright, fully alert.

She shoved clothes in his arms. 'Dress yourself.'

John sat on the mattress, drinking in the sight of her wearing a simple dressing gown, with her dark hair cascading down her back, but, evidently, he gaped too long, for she thrust his shirt over his head.

'Make haste, John! I meant for you to leave before dawn.'

John crawled out of bed and shook out his trousers.

The knock sounded again. 'Georgiana?' a female voice called. 'Dr Mitchell is in the parlour, requesting an audience with you.'

'Thank you, Amanda,' Georgiana responded, raising her voice to be heard. 'But please have him visit Lily before he discusses business with me. She's near her time.'

As the knocker's footsteps receded, Georgiana waved her arms. 'Swiftly. You must depart before breakfast finishes, or someone might see you in the yard.'

John didn't share her urgency. To eliminate risk to her reputation, he simply needed to declare himself and be accepted. Preferring not to propose nude, he struggled into his trousers. 'Georgiana, may I ask you something?'

She opened the door to the back stairs and stood with her hand on the knob, as if ready for him to leave. 'Not now.'

He fastened his waistband. 'When, then?'

'Not today.'

'Georgiana, please—'

She shook her head violently. 'You have too much to do to organise the search for Flora and, unfortunately, I cannot help today, for I must pay the debts you so generously provided for, and I'm behind in other duties. The children are in need of new shoes, and at last I possess the funds to purchase them, along with countless other essential supplies. *And* Fanny insists I attend her soirée tonight. She and my father intend it to be,' she waved her hand, 'oh, a silly coming-out event for me, I suppose. Not that anyone will attend after . . .'

She said no more, but John knew she referred to Almack's.

Soon enough, he'd make amends for that disaster.

He wrestled into his coat, hopes elevated. The soirée was perfect for his purpose. If his proposal was successful, it could be announced that evening, erasing negative gossip about Georgiana in one swoop. Also, to do things properly, John must speak to Amesbury as well as Georgiana, and both she and her father would conveniently be in the same place tonight.

John grimaced as he pulled on his boots, dreading the conversation with the duke. After insulting the nobleman at the garden party, John suspected he'd need to eat rather copious amounts of rue-pie before his proposal received Amesbury's blessing. No doubt with many fathers, the marriage settlements John intended would instantly dismiss any paternal reservations about John himself, but Amesbury had a reputation as a man of integrity.

Never mind, Georgiana was worth it a million times over.

'May I attend the soirée so we can talk then?' John asked.

She knotted her brow. 'It never ends well when we see each other in company.'

He tenderly caught her hand, hoping she sensed how he'd changed since almost losing her. Now he possessed a clarity that he'd lacked at Almack's. 'Georgiana, I'll stay away if you insist, but if you can trust me, I promise I shan't make a scene. I shall speak to everyone in the room before you, and I'll take only a few minutes of your time. What I have to say won't take long.'

All he needed was permission to request her hand from her father. After he settled matters with the duke, a formal announcement would allow John and Georgiana to be alone together, with no need for concealment as they searched for Flora or planned and directed the school renovations. Under John's protection, gossip couldn't hurt her, nor would she need to rely on good public opinion to support Monica House. John could easily absorb the entirety of the charity's expenses.

Her eyebrows drew together. 'You need to search for Flora, John. I worried less when she was with her kidnappers, because at least I knew they wouldn't . . .' She hesitated. 'Well, William's objective was to marry her. On her own, with her identity unknown, Flora is vulnerable to a different sort of kidnapper altogether – and she's vulnerable to the torture of her own mind. She is the priority now, not our conversation.'

John agreed, almost. Flora and Georgiana were *both* priorities. 'I understand and share your concerns. I assure you I shall make Flora the primary business of my *day*, but this evening I'd like to speak with you, if you will permit it.'

A bell rang and she jumped. 'Truly, you must leave. Breakfast will be over as soon as the tables are cleared.'

'Please answer me first. May I come to the soirée or not?'

She hesitated, eyes cast down, and then nodded. 'Yes, yes. I think it for the best, actually. You're correct, we *do* need to talk.'

'Thank you, my sweet.'

He stooped to kiss her, but she darted away, dashing down her stairs, urging him to follow. He obeyed, though he was bedraggled – cravatless, hatless, and in wrinkled clothes. He'd left behind his domino and mask so he couldn't cover himself, but, fortunately, London was accustomed to seeing him dishevelled. No one would think anything of it.

At the bottom of the stairs, Georgiana flung open the door and pushed him over the threshold. Unfortunately, Ben the groundskeeper knelt on hands and knees not three yards away, investigating something in the Monica House wall.

Ben spoke without looking up from his work. 'This here is how the mice are entering the parlour, Georgiana. I'll patch it today, but what d'ye think of getting a Monica House cat? It'd thrill the children—'

He turned, grinning, but both his smile and his words vanished the moment he saw John, and his expression turned to steel.

'Why, good morning, Ben,' Georgiana exclaimed, with what seemed to be forced cheer. 'You're just the person I hoped to see. Would you be so good as to see Mr Tyro—' She stopped, evidently realising she'd revealed John's identity. 'Please see my guest out, Ben. And yes, a cat is a lovely idea.'

Then she closed her door, leaving John with the murderous-looking groundskeeper.

To engage the boy further risked making a scene best avoided, so John bid Ben a good day and crossed the yard alone, only to discover that the gate required a key to open, so he was forced to wait as Ben stalked over with narrowed eyes and fisted hands.

As soon as the scowling boy unlocked the gate, John stepped into the alley, but Ben followed and thrust him against the wall.

'Unhand me at *once*.' John spoke with severe authority. Nobody manhandled John Tyrold, and yet within twelve hours, two boys had assaulted him.

Instead of complying, Ben shoved his face in John's. 'I thought you looked familiar the other night, but I couldn't quite place you. I suppose with your pockets lined in gold, you think you can use anyone however you want with no consequences. But Georgiana is a *lady*. A good and generous one. What are your intentions towards her?'

'My intentions are Miss Bailey's and my business,' John snapped. He wasn't about to discuss his intentions with Ben before he'd discussed them with Georgiana herself. 'I owe you no explanation.'

Ben drew back with a snarl, but he released John's arm. 'Aye. I reckon you're right. You don't owe an explanation to *me*.'

John considered offering some reassurance as he straightened his coat, since the boy obviously believed himself to act in Georgiana's best interests. But he didn't want to appear to capitulate any more than he wished to discuss Georgiana without permission, so he squared his shoulders and walked away without further conversation.

Besides, soon all of London would know his intentions.

Dismissing Ben from his thoughts, John focused on what must be accomplished before the evening. Bow Street. A meeting with Starmer. Organising the printing and posting of the placards.

And there was much to do on Georgiana's account as well. John must settle business with Lord Oxford regarding the row of terraces, so they could be officially in John's ownership as soon as possible. The one he'd already absorbed the lease on would be for Georgiana's school, of course. But another – likely the seven-bay one on the corner, whose current resident seemed keen to relinquish his leasehold – John would refit elegantly, sparing no expense.

He smiled. With Georgiana by his side, he could make a loving home for Flora.

And, lastly, John decided he'd visit Rundell and Bridge before the soirée. He wanted to purchase Georgiana a ring to bind their engagement. An exquisite piece of jewellery, tasteful yet unquestionably of the highest quality. A hint of the luxury he'd lay at her feet. A tangible promise that his love would be everlasting and generous.

But first, John needed a bath and to walk his poor dog.

He emerged from the alleys and set off towards Half Moon Street.

The moment Georgiana closed the door, abandoning John in the yard with Ben, she knew with ice-cold certainty that the beautiful night was a dreadful mistake. Not because Ben would gossip – he wouldn't – but because her unintentional engagement of John's heart would ruin everything she hadn't already spoiled.

If John thought himself in love with her, he'd be devastated when she refused to continue their affair. As a result, he wouldn't want her help finding Flora, which meant Georgiana would lose her dream of the school. She would hurt John as well as fail Flora and the Monica House children. And, as if that weren't catastrophe enough, Georgiana hadn't even managed to be accepted into society to raise funds for Monica House, her primary objective for the Season. If John ever revoked his sponsorship, she'd be insolvent.

The sense of her failure weighed heavy, accompanied by regret and self-disgust.

She should've known better. Every time she was even the least bit selfish, there were terrible consequences.

Georgiana's sorrow felt overwhelming as she went about the morning tasks: paying the overdue bills; ordering clothes and other dry goods (all supplies, from soap to flour, were low); enquiring with a local tailor about an apprenticeship for twelve-year-old Frank Martin, who was eager to get out into the world. She was no cheerier in the afternoon as she sang for the women while they worked at their crafts and sewing. She could barely bring herself to smile when the newest member of the community – the bruised prostitute she'd met outside the bagnio on Monday – gave her a lung-crushing embrace and told Georgiana she was happy for the first time in years.

But Georgiana's depressed spirits sank even further as she walked about Amesbury House that evening, her gloved hand on her father's arm, navigating the crowd of elegant attendees. Judging by the cuts direct she'd received when her father wasn't looking, she suspected many guests had attended only because they hoped for another spectacle.

And there was a spectacle, but it wasn't coming from Tyrold. Though John was there, he was being true to his word and speaking to everyone but Georgiana.

His manners appeared as exquisite as his eveningwear; currently, he bowed his head to listen attentively to Edward's Aunt Agatha. He looked every inch the refined gentleman, with a signet ring on the littlest finger of his right hand, a simple gold chain at his fob pocket, and, evidently, a jewelled cravat pin, based on the sparkle emanating from the crisp linen at his neck when struck by candlelight. More than one quizzing glass was raised in his direction, but he certainly wasn't making a scene.

No, Fanny was the one inciting whispers and malicious smiles tonight. The duchess had behaved fretfully all evening, her large blue eyes brimming with tears. Currently, she was seated, deep in weepy conversation with Georgiana's Aunt Clarissa, who periodically held a flask of restorative vinaigrette to her sister-in-law's nose. It seemed the duchess had finally realised the shame of having to host her husband's bastard daughter's coming out. The cruelty was that since Georgiana knew she wasn't likely to get any sponsorships, she'd only attended the event because she didn't want to disappoint Fanny, who'd planned it for weeks. Now, the duchess appeared not to care that Georgiana was there – and it was the duke who insisted Georgiana remain until midnight, which meant she must pass an additional two hours before she could sink into a bed that would feel lonelier than ever without John's presence.

Fanny's excessive sensibility seemed to have made Georgiana's father steadfastly determined to put on a cheerful face. He seemed positively proud, in fact, with the way he escorted Georgiana on his arm through his guests, and Georgiana acknowledged that had this come years earlier, her life might've been very different indeed. If she'd been raised at Amesbury House on South Audley Street, the recognised daughter of the Duke of Amesbury, she would've perhaps never longed for anything beyond this gilded splendour. She would've been a debutante years ago, making her curtsy at eighteen to Queen Charlotte, and she would've demurely accepted whatever gentleman the duke and duchess suggested. Then she would've promoted her husband's interests by hosting dinners and raising his children, in the manner of Fanny, who showered the duke with devotion. Georgiana wouldn't have desperately craved attention to her own detriment because her childhood would've been safe, loved, and secure.

'Happy, my daughter?' Georgiana's father asked, patting her gloved hand where it lay on his forearm.

A lump thickened in Georgiana's throat. No, she wasn't happy. It was years too late for her to find happiness here, with him. But she wasn't about to explain that to her father.

She merely said, 'The duchess outdid herself.'

It was true. All the receiving rooms on the ground and first floors had been opened to guests. Profuse flower arrangements perfumed the air. Beeswax candles twinkled like stars from chandeliers. A string quartet played in a drawing room set aside for conversation. In another chamber, guests played high stakes at whist. A pianist performed jigs for two dozen couples in the ballroom. The dining room was filled with linen-covered tables, around which people ate ices and confectionary. And everywhere, liveried footmen bustled about with endless silver platters of fluted champagne.

'But are you happy, my daughter?' the duke repeated, evidently unsatisfied with Georgiana's avoidant reply.

'Oh, Pa—' she began, then stopped, appalled that she'd almost addressed him by the name she hadn't used in years. 'Sir, I'm immensely grateful for the kindness you and the duchess bestow on me, but please don't ask me to be happy in the way you mean. The only peace I receive is through my work at Monica House.'

The duke opened his mouth to reply, but a gentleman approached with a bow, and both Georgiana and her father were required to make small talk.

'Perhaps you'll sing for us later, Miss Bailey?' asked the gentleman, an MP named Harrison with fine dark eyes that he cast up and down Georgiana's figure. Evidently, she passed muster, for he oozed closer. 'I've heard your voice is unequalled.'

He was clearly attempting to curry Georgiana's favour despite her tattered reputation. No doubt a personal connection to the Duke of Amesbury would further his political career.

Georgiana's stomach coiled, but she forced a smile for the sake of Monica House. 'It would be a pleasure, sir – and while I have your attention, may I inform you of a charity dear to my heart? It's called Monica House, and it supports women who have seen great hardship, trying to provide for them a new, safe start in life.' Mr Harrison's smile became rather stiff, so

Georgiana concluded quickly. 'We're ever in need of new sponsors, and even the smallest donation—'

'Supports the noblest of causes, Mr Harrison.'

It was Tyrold's voice, firm yet gentle, sounding behind Georgiana's shoulder, depriving her of breath, filling her with warmth.

'I myself am a proud sponsor,' he continued. 'Surely Miss Bailey can count upon five guineas a month from you, considering your recent good fortune with the canal venture?'

Harrison issued a polite but noncommittal reply before turning his shoulder to engage the duke in a discussion on the wheat bill. Georgiana took the opportunity to slip her hand from her father's arm and face John, tilting her head back to meet his gaze.

'Thank you for trying,' she said with a small smile.

He spoke in a low voice, his eyes twinkling conspiratorially. 'I have been here for two hours, speaking with dozens of people – and with some success. Lady Agatha is keen to sponsor Monica House; she promised twenty guineas quarterly.'

'You were soliciting subscriptions?' Georgiana asked, clasping her locket, for her heart performed that odd little flip again. Of course, such an action would only elevate gossip, but the fact that John cared about Monica House gave Georgiana a decidedly pleasant – though strangely achy – feeling.

'A few,' he admitted, rather sheepishly. Then he leant closer and spoke under his breath. 'I'd do anything for you, my darling.'

Georgiana's temporary elevation of spirits evaporated, leaving devastation in its wake as she remembered she'd soon break his heart. These were the last few minutes in which he'd think of her with admiration and tender affection. She probably wouldn't even get those subscriptions. He'd forget all about them the moment she hurt him – and likely Lady Agatha had only donated because she believed Georgiana would soon be her great-niece.

'Oh, John.' She sighed, wishing she could run back to the safety of Monica House, rather than hurt him. Why had she been so stupid the night before? She'd known he was looking for a lover – why had she not realised he would naturally interpret her behaviour as her inviting him to have an affair? She'd been inconsiderate, impulsive and selfish, and now she must face the consequences.

'May I escort you into your father's conservatory?' he asked, his manner heart-wrenchingly sweet. 'I went through all the rooms, and it's the best for a secluded conversation. It's busy enough that we won't incite gossip, but quiet enough that we'll not be easily be overheard.'

Knowing it was best over with, Georgiana agreed. She laid a hand upon her father's sleeve, interrupting his conversation. 'Sir, Mr Tyrold has expressed an interest in observing the palms, so I shall escort him to the conservatory.'

Her father's usually kind expression darkened.

John inclined his head. 'With your permission, sir.'

The two men locked gazes, and the duke's eyes narrowed, but then he glanced at a longcase clock and nodded curtly. 'Very well, but I shall come and find you in precisely fifteen minutes, Georgiana.' He kissed her cheek and bestowed another threatening glare on John. 'The conservatory, Mr Tyrold. I have your word as a *gentleman*?'

John's lips pressed together, but he spoke with good grace. 'Naturally, sir.'

Georgiana flushed with embarrassment, so evident was her father's strong disapproval and mistrust. As she quit the drawing room with John, crossing into the long gallery at the back of the house and walking amongst rows and columns of painted ancestors she felt no connection to, she felt compelled to explain. 'My father is upset over what happened at Almack's.'

'Yes, and about something else,' John said, casting a rueful smile. 'I confess I've given your father reason to dislike me. I owe him an apology, which I shall issue after I speak with you.'

'Did you have any luck with Flora?' Georgiana asked as a footman opened the door into the back ante-chamber, a circular room with marble statuary and a stained-glass rotunda, which led into the conservatory and into the gardens.

'Not yet,' John responded. 'But I've notified the Runners and organised the private search. The placards will be hung overnight, and notifications printed in the morning newspapers, so all of London will soon know.'

Realising the moment of truth had arrived when they entered the humid conservatory with its arched glass ceiling and towering palms, Georgiana led John towards an open alcove with shelves of orchids, where they'd be within sight of the other meandering guests, but their conversation could be private.

'John, please allow me to speak first.' She closed her eyes, the better to focus on forcing out the horrid words. 'You said some lovely things last night, and I'm aware you want a continuation of our . . . affair, but it is out of the question. I meant it when I said one night only. I cannot risk such a thing, ever again.'

Having said her piece, she met his gaze, expecting to see pain or frustration.

But his eyes shone with amusement. 'For an immensely intelligent woman, you are being exceptionally wattle-headed, Georgiana. What on earth makes you suppose I'd ask such a thing of you?'

She blinked. He *didn't* want to continue their affair? 'Why . . .' Her cheeks warmed. 'I thought . . . well, it seemed as if you enjoyed . . .' She put a hand to her mouth, feeling very sick indeed, although she *ought* to be relieved his sentiments weren't as strong as he'd supposed in a moment of post-climatic bliss. 'Perhaps I've made a fool of myself.'

'My darling Georgiana,' he said with unbearable tenderness. 'You truly possess the most astonishing combination of self-confidence and humility. I would never ask you to conduct an affair with me, when I love you with every fibre of my being.' He paused, looking at her in such a way that she was forced to steady herself against the shelves. 'Indeed, I love you as I never imagined I could love anyone. We haven't known each other long, but I know my mind. I always have, I always shall. Georgiana, I am not asking for something fleeting. I am offering you my heart and my hand, my future and my fortune. All that is mine, I lay at your feet. My darling, will you do me the great honour of becoming my wife?'

Georgiana's knees buckled from shock. John attempted to catch her forearms, trying to steady her, but she pulled away so no one would see them in a half-embrace and leant her shoulder against the edge of the alcove, her emotions swirling.

Did John Tyrold really and truly want to *marry her*? On Monday, when she'd believed him ill-tempered and controlling, the thought of him as a husband had repelled her.

But she knew differently now.

She would have *such* a life as John's wife. With access to his protection, his power, the influence of his name and position and his unparalleled fortune, Georgiana could do such a profusion of good that it was almost too tempting to refuse. And so much about him was appealing – his kindness, his gentleness, his companionship, the way he needed her . . .

But that thought grounded her. She *couldn't* marry him, she couldn't belong to a man when she needed to belong to Monica House. Besides, he knew nothing about her past. He thought she'd always been virtuous and selfless.

He wouldn't want her if he knew the truth.

'I am deeply, deeply honoured,' she said at last. 'Truly I am. But I cannot accept your proposal.'

His smile faded slowly, replaced by a furrowed brow. 'May I ask why not?'

Georgiana pressed a hand to her coiling abdomen. 'That question has a many-layered response, which I'm not able to explain fully. But I think it will suffice to remind you that I told you on Monday that I am a confirmed spinster, and I meant it.'

'Georgiana, on Monday I was a confirmed bachelor. But you, and this week, changed me. My heart. My purpose.'

Georgiana struggled to catch her breath. Oh, if only it could be so simple. 'John, that is incredibly kind, and I am exceedingly aware of the great honour you do me, but – and I speak frankly because you deserve my honesty – you haven't changed my heart and purpose.'

Then his expression reflected pain, and it was agonising to witness the transformation. She wished she could lessen it, but, at the same time, she wondered if now that she'd been so blunt, he would lose his temper or behave like the spoilt boy who occasionally emerged.

He did neither.

Instead, he was devastatingly kind.

'Georgiana, I wish to support your purpose, not change it,' he said gently. 'I'm asking to journey through life with you, sharing its joys and challenges, each of us strengthening the other. I believe we are quite marvellous together, my love.'

Those sweet words certainly didn't make it easy for Georgiana to stick to her convictions, but she knew what she must do. 'I cannot marry you, John.' She pressed both hands to her abdomen, certain she'd soon be sick. 'I simply cannot.'

'I see.' His voice was measured. 'Yet perhaps with time?'

She shook her head.

He studied her, frowning. 'Do you not care for me even the slightest bit? Because last night it seemed that—'

'I beg you not to speak of last night,' Georgiana exclaimed, for the memory hurt too much. 'Of course, I care for you. I . . . more than care. I . . . I hold you in the highest esteem.'

Her words didn't really encompass her sentiments, but she didn't understand her feelings towards him, so how could she possibly express them?

'A happy marriage can be built on esteem,' John responded, ever so tenderly. 'I'm not perfect, but I shan't ever deny you any request.'

'Then please grant this request and say no more!' Georgiana cried, holding up a hand, for it was becoming increasingly difficult to stick to her resolve. She folded her arms over her chest, hugging herself as if it could hold together the shattering bits of her heart. 'There is so much you don't know about me. I'm a broken woman with a cleft in my heart too great be your wife . . .' She faltered, struggling to hold back tears, tightening her hold on her body. She wondered if she should tell him the truth, but she dismissed the idea almost immediately; there were eyes upon them even now and she couldn't bear to sob before an audience. All she could do was make her decision clear in a way where he'd understand the finality, so he wouldn't tempt her into a life she couldn't accept. 'John, once and only once, my heart belonged to another, and I was responsible for my beloved's death. Guilt eats away at that wound unless I work ceaselessly and tirelessly for the good of others. The only thing that ever softens the grief, the only thing that makes me stop wishing I also were covered in soil, returning to dust alongside my darling, the *only* thing that keeps me from utter despair is living every moment of every day in service to those less fortunate. That and that alone convinces me there's purpose to my existence. For the sake of my beloved, every life I can save—'

'You give whatever you must, to the last penny in your pocket.' His voice was raw as he quoted her words back to her.

She nodded. 'Yes.'

He closed his eyes. 'I understand now.'

'I'm sorry, John,' she said, meaning it. 'I value your friendship, but even that I cannot continue in any meaningful way. Even now, we've whispered together too long – and there *will* be repercussions—'

'If there are repercussions, I can make them right,' he said wearily, rubbing his temples, his eyes still squeezed tightly shut, pain etched in their corners. 'I could marry you in name only. You can have half of my fortune to distribute as you wish, and I shan't make any demand on you . . .'

'No, I couldn't, John. That's no life for you. You have a generous heart, and you will make a fine husband and father. Don't throw yourself away on a woman who can't return your love wholeheartedly.'

He didn't speak for a long time.

But then he nodded and opened his eyes at last. 'Very well. Your father will arrive shortly.' He reached into his pocket and removed a tiny box. 'This is for you, and your answer doesn't change that. Keep it as a testament of my regard or sell it back to Rundell and Bridge's. If you choose the latter, I shall ensure they refund the purchase price in full, and you may do as you wish with the money. Additionally, I'll have the deeds to your school delivered tomorrow. Don't worry, I shan't come with them myself. I don't wish to cause you any more pain, and I apologise for that which I have caused. It was most unintentionally done.'

Georgiana opened the box, exposing the loveliest ring she'd ever seen, a filigree gold band sparkling with diamonds. 'Oh, no, John,' she said, breathless as she latched the box again. 'I can't accept this.'

'Sell it for Monica House then.'

For the first time, she discerned a hard edge to his voice. But she knew it wasn't anger. It was hurt – he was trying to repress evidence of it, but she'd broken his heart.

She returned the jewellery box, squeezing his fingers. 'The house I thank you for, but *this* is different. This I can't accept, John.'

A throat cleared directly behind her. Horrified she might have been overheard, she pivoted to see who stood nearby.

Her father and the duchess were at the edge of the alcove. Fanny looked much improved, her cheeks rosy and her blue eyes bright, but the duke wore a thundercloud on his brow. Georgiana released Tyrold's hand; her father's eyes darted to the jewellery box before John slipped it in his pocket.

When the duke lifted his gaze again, he simmered with fury.

Georgiana stretched her lips into a bright smile, hoping to distract him with fake cheer, since earlier he'd longed for her happiness. 'Mr Tyrold and I were about to return, sir.'

Fanny released the duke's arm and took Georgiana's instead, drawing it close to her bosom. 'Good, for so *many* people have asked for you to sing tonight, dearest, and they can't wait another moment. Come, let's you and I go in together.'

As Georgiana allowed Fanny to pull her from the alcove, she cast John a beseeching gaze. 'Mr Tyrold, please remember the urgency of Flora. I can't express that enough.'

He nodded, his jaw set, but he didn't make eye contact.

That was as it must be, now.

Resigned but miserable, Georgiana's feet fell like lead as she made her way through the conservatory paths, winding past palms and citrus trees. The humid air was heavy, but it was nothing compared to the emotional weight pressing hard upon her chest.

Fanny leant her blonde curls against Georgiana's head. 'Dearest, I apologise for being out of sorts earlier. I'm much better now, for I've had a chat with your father, and he's to make everything right, as he always does. Silly me, not to go to him the moment I . . . but never mind that now, for soon all will be well.'

Fanny was mistaken.

Nothing would be well for a long time, because Georgiana's already broken heart was shattering into a million new pieces.

20

As Georgiana walked away, John stared at the orchids, attempting to master his broken heart and shattered hopes.

He'd known she didn't return his love equally, but he'd thought – no, arrogantly assumed – his proposal would please her. Even after her initial refusal, he'd believed patience and generosity could convince her, but her speech about her lost love had decimated John's hopes. A tragedy held her heart and her happiness captive, and she was too honourable to marry without the ability to give both to her husband.

But he had a single comfort: he possessed the means to ease her pain by supporting the work that brought her peace. In time, he told himself, perhaps it would be enough; at the moment, it stemmed his sorrow sufficiently for the task at hand, which was to leave Amesbury House with no outward evidence of his turmoil. He'd think more at home, in his study with Jolly for company. Thus bolstered, he dragged in a deep breath to steady himself and turned, ready to stroll with apparent nonchalance from the conservatory.

The Duke of Amesbury still stood at the edge of the alcove.

And he was clearly after John's blood.

Knowing he hadn't mastered his emotions enough for a conversation with an irate father, John gave a stiff head bow. 'Thank you for a pleasant evening, sir. I shall take my leave now.'

'You're not leaving yet, Mr Tyrold,' the duke replied. 'You and I are going converse together in private, and you won't dismiss me like you did at Holbrook's garden party.'

John didn't appreciate the duke's patronising manner, but for Georgiana's sake he'd accept whatever chastisement Amesbury felt the need to deliver – and then he'd go home to blissful solitude. 'Well, lead on, then,' he said, resigned.

He followed Amesbury out of the conservatory and through a succession of rooms, up a flight of stairs and into a dark corridor, where a footman stood on guard.

'These are my private rooms,' the duke said at last, opening the door to a small library with dark leather furniture, illuminated by a blazing fire and two candelabra on the mantlepiece. 'My footman will ensure we aren't disturbed here.' The duke lifted one candelabrum and gestured towards another door. 'Come with me into my study.'

The study contained a fine marquetry writing desk, two armchairs, and a number of Italianate landscapes hanging on dark damask walls. There was a small fireplace, not currently in use.

'Leave the door open and it will warm soon enough.' The duke sat in the desk chair, settled the branched candlestick beside his writing instruments, and steepled his fingers. 'Have a seat, Tyrold, for you will be here a while. We have a great deal of business to conduct.'

Amesbury's cool assuredness reminded John of his uncle's scolds, an irritation he wasn't in the mood for. If Georgiana had agreed to be his wife, John would've done whatever necessary to placate the duke. As it was, he simply wanted to go home.

He sat, but he did so with an impatient air, stretching out his legs and steepling his own damn fingers. 'Say what you wish and be done with it, Amesbury.'

'I shall take as much time as I please, Tyrold. Firstly, why did you offer my daughter jewellery?'

Damn – it was too bad the duke had seen that, but John wasn't about to explain without Georgiana's authorisation. 'I haven't your daughter's permission to discuss her business with her father.'

Amesbury tightened his jaw. 'When a man defames my daughter, it's *my* business. Tell me: did you offer Georgiana an arrangement, which she very rightly refused?'

The duke's baseless accusation infuriated John. In her humility, Georgiana had first supposed the same thing – but it was quite a different matter when another gentleman thought John capable of dishonouring a young lady.

'You slight my honour by suggesting I'd do such a thing, Amesbury,' he said, a warning in his voice. 'My character is well enough known that you can have no reason to suppose I'd make Georgiana an illicit offer.'

The duke's face reddened, as if he were as angry as John. 'In fact, I have excellent reason to question your character and your honour. After you departed for the conservatory in my daughter's company, my wife told me a most disturbing tale, which she'd not wished to trouble me with earlier. Tyrold, late yesterday evening the Monica House groundskeeper saw you and my daughter entering her private quarters together. You remained overnight and emerged from the same door this morning in a state of dishabille. I conclude from this tale that you seduced a virtuous young lady, which is utterly reprehensible; furthermore, you are *quite* mistaken about the way to treat my daughter. So now you and I shall write out the marriage settlements and an announcement for tomorrow's papers. I dislike marrying her to a man whom I consider impudent and conceited, but you must have more redeeming qualities than you reveal, or Holbrook and Eden wouldn't think so highly of you. *Now* what have you to say?'

John tapped his steepled fingers together, considering how to respond. If he were as dishonourable a man as the duke supposed, this would be his golden opportunity to make Georgiana his wife. But naturally, he'd never force her hand in such a way; it turned his stomach to think of it.

Yet he also wouldn't subject Georgiana to her father's disapprobation by informing the duke that she'd refused John's proposal after spending a night in his company. Thus, as badly as it sat with John, he must absorb the blame.

'I shan't marry your daughter, Amesbury,' he said at last.

The duke rose, nearly tipping over his desk chair. 'How dare you, you impudent ass!'

'How dare *I*?' John retorted, furious. Although he ought to control his temper, there were limits to what he could stand. Yes, he was *acting* a despicable part, but the duke had *actually done* what he (falsely) accused John of doing. 'A bit rich, coming from you. Tell me, why is Anna Marinetti not the Duchess of Amesbury?'

Amesbury deflated at once, his face losing its colour as he sank heavily into his leather chair. 'Ah, I see. You suppose you can seduce Georgiana without repercussions because she's merely the by-blow of a callous liaison.'

In fact, John had never seduced anyone, but he'd betray Georgiana if he told her father she'd initiated the night of passion, just as Helen had every time he'd lain with her, just as Galatea had, when she first led him to her bed. 'You made assumptions based on the groundskeeper's tale, so allow me the same licence. You got Anna Marinetti with child and, although you were a bachelor at the time, you didn't wed her. If that's not callous, what is?'

'Your facts are correct but incomplete, thus your interpretation is flawed.'

'So is yours, regarding Georgiana and me.'

The duke drummed his fingers against his desk. 'If I prove my love for Anna was honourable, will you make right your own transgression against our daughter?'

'I can't do that for reasons you must accept without my explanation. Your daughter is a woman grown, and what transpired between us is not something I'm comfortable discussing with her father without her permission. If you insist on pursuing this line of inquiry, you should invite Georgiana to partake in the conversation, but I warn you I have reason to suspect it would cause her significant unhappiness.'

The duke didn't answer for several moments as he searched John's face. When he spoke at last, his voice was soft and even. 'Georgiana is extremely unhappy this evening, and I don't wish to trouble her further. I shall explain my relationship with Anna Marinetti, and perhaps my tale will move you to return the favour as regards you and my daughter.'

'It won't, so don't trouble yourself,' John replied, although, in truth, he was exceedingly curious to hear Amesbury's account of his affair with the soprano.

'I want to.' Amesbury studied his folded hands. 'I first took my seat in the Upper House in February of seventeen eighty-eight, during the same season in which Anna debuted at the King's Theatre and captivated London. Despite her fame and beauty, she maintained a reputation for unimpeachable virtue, which only increased everyone's admiration. My mother was enchanted with her and invited her to perform at a musical evening she hosted in March. By the by, you can – should you wish – apply to Anna's maid for the veracity of everything I am about to tell you. She is the proprietress of a coffeehouse on Soho Square—'

'Signora DeRosa?' John asked, surprised.

The duke lifted his brows. 'Ah, you've met Maria. Perhaps you've had more interactions with Georgiana than I supposed?'

Since Flora's abduction was no longer a secret, John decided to explain. 'Georgiana has been advising me in my search for my fifteen-year-old ward.' Without revealing the extent of Georgiana's assistance, he briefly relayed the details of Flora's abduction.

When he concluded, the duke furrowed his forehead. 'That does bring a fresh perspective to matters. Your anxiety must be great. Please tell me if I can aid your search in any way.'

John inclined his head. 'Thank you, but I have ample resources and friends who will assist. I shall find her.' He spoke with more confidence than he felt. 'Please, continue your story,' he said, abandoning his pretended indifference. 'I shall take you at your word, rather than applying to Signora DeRosa for veracity.'

'All the same, Maria *can* verify my account. Anna never went anywhere without her as a companion and chaperone. From our first meeting, Maria was privy to all our conversations, which were plentiful, because once I realised Anna enjoyed my company, I found reason to encounter her as frequently as possible. I was madly in love with her, of course, but so was most of London. Why she liked me puzzled me exceedingly at first. She later told me she fell in love with my kindness, which I initially discounted, but no longer do.'

John said nothing, but silently acknowledged the words rang true. It wasn't far off from his own experience falling in love with the duke's daughter.

'After many months of chaste but passionate devotion,' the duke continued, 'I asked Anna to be my wife, standing next to Maria DeRosa all the while. I knew my family and society expected otherwise, but I loved Anna. I was prepared to weather the storm of ill-opinion and demand everyone respect my choice, much like your admirable friend Lord Eden did recently.

'But Anna refused, citing our different spheres as her reason. I tried to convince her. I was the head of my family, a man of fortune, a man of sense. I knew what I wanted, and I knew what I felt was no passing fancy. But still, she refused me, and I had no choice but to respect her decision.

'Not a month later, however – and this was by now the early spring of seventeen eighty-nine, more than a year into our acquaintanceship – Maria DeRosa brought me a letter. All it said was: *I cannot be your wife, but, if you will have me, I long to be your lover.*' The duke peered at John. 'Tell me, Tyrold, you who spent last night with my daughter, what would you have done upon receipt of such a note?'

John shifted in his seat. 'Touché, sir. Please continue.'

'What Anna and I did never felt like sin. It was love. Equal love with mutual respect. And with Maria's help, we were able to keep the affair a secret.' The duke paused, looking at John keenly before continuing. 'We were exceedingly happy in those months, but they didn't last long. In early June, my sister married the Duke of Gillingham. I had some misgivings about the match, but Clarissa was determined. She believed herself in love, and I wasn't yet confident enough to question the character of a man my equal in rank but my superior in age and experience, so I consented. At Clarissa's request, Anna sang at the wedding breakfast. That evening, when I visited Anna, she was in tears. "He will not be good to her, George," she said repeatedly. "There's cruelty in his eyes. I could see it."

'I reassured Anna I would protect my sister, and eventually she calmed. "Never stop your vigilance," she told me. "When a woman is married to an unkind man, she needs the support of her family more than ever. Let Gillingham know you are always watching. Be certain your sister knows you are there for her if ever she needs you. If you must fetch her in the middle of the night, do it, George. If you must kill him to protect her, then kill him."

'I confess I thought her a bit excessive at that point, but I assured her I'd do as she said. She insisted I follow Clarissa on her wedding trip and, although I did not relish the idea, I acquiesced that point as well.' The duke rested his head on his hands, cradling his scalp, his fingers entangled in his silvering hair. 'Looking back now, I cannot believe my blindness. But at the time, I thought only that Anna was tender-hearted and nervous for my young sister, with whom she had a friendship. So after that night – it would be our last together – I left for Switzerland and didn't return until the end of September.

'Upon my arrival in London, I went at once to Anna, but she received me coldly. Viciously, in fact. She demanded I leave and never return, she claimed she was returning to Italy at once. When I begged to make amends for whatever wrong I'd done, she called me a villain who'd coerced her. Who'd forced her to abandon her virtue, which was so vastly far from the truth I grew outraged.' The duke paused. 'God, Tyrold, if only I'd had half a wit about me! If I'd calmed my anger and thought to question why Anna was acting so wildly different, perhaps . . .' He sighed. 'But there's no benefit in retrospection of that nature. If such thoughts could bring her back, they would've done so six-and-twenty years hence. Suffice to say, I left her lodgings devastated and furious.

'With my great love affair ended and my heart broken, I turned my mind to duty and courted the young lady my family expected me to marry. That autumn, Fanny was eighteen, all sweet innocence, happy when she'd pleased me, distressed if I seemed sad. After Anna's cruelty – her *perceived* cruelty, I should say – Fanny was precisely the balm I needed. What she lacked in sen— in anything, she made up for a thousand times over in her genuine love for me. I married her at Christmas, and I've never regretted that decision. I dearly love my wife.'

The duke looked pointedly at John, as if expecting him to question the statement.

'I have no doubt of that, sir,' John said, since it seemed important to Amesbury.

'Good. I shall let Anna tell the next part.' Amesbury slid open a drawer, extracted a small box inlaid with the same marquetry patterns as the desk, and reverently withdrew a letter. 'Just over five months after my wedding, I received this, which had been written some weeks earlier. Read it, please. It is in Anna's hand.'

He offered it across the desk to John, who took and unfolded the parchment, revealing an elegant but fading script, marred in places by what looked like long-dried tears.

Monica House
1st May 1790

My beloved George,

I begin by begging your forgiveness. I wronged you when you visited me in September, but I did so to protect you, myself, my dear Maria, and the precious and innocent life I carried inside me.

Next, I wish to inform you that our daughter was born on the first of March, a fine baby with dark hair and a powerful set of lungs. I've named her Georgiana, for she is the embodiment of our love. George and his Anna.

I was always your Anna. I remain your Anna. I shall be your Anna for the rest of my life. I write this without guilt, although you rightfully belong to another now, because I suspect my life will be over before you receive this letter.

Let me tell you now what I was ever too scared to confess before. When I was five-and twenty, after performing on stage for more than fifteen years, I married a wealthy man from Florence. I was content with the time I'd spent singing, and I wanted a family and a home. But on my wedding night, I learnt I'd married a cruel man. I shan't describe what he did to me.

He held me captive for a year, isolated from my family and friends, and in that time I prayed God would not give me a child with that monster. With the help of Maria DeRosa, I prevented it. When Maria and I finally escaped, we fled at once to England, because my husband is terrified of water. I thought I could begin a new life using my maiden name and for two years, I succeeded. George, when you asked me to be your wife, I longed to accept, but I couldn't deceive you into a bigamous union any more than I could bring myself to tell you the terrible truth.

My husband found me the day before you returned from Switzerland. He was there, in my apartments, the afternoon you arrived, and by then he'd discovered I was four months pregnant with your child. It was all I could do to keep him from killing you – I explained who you were, and that he would hang for it. He told me to get rid of you in a way that ensured you'd never return and to inform you I intended to travel to Italy immediately. I believe he told me to say this because he meant to kill me the moment you left. He is too cruel, too jealous to let me bear another man's child.

But I outwitted him again. I had heard of Monica
House from a chorus girl at the theatre, and Maria
and I fled not half a minute after you left my
lodgings. For months, I have been safe here, but not
any more.

Today I ventured out with Georgiana, so she
might experience nature for the first time – it was a
magnificent day and the thought of fresh air filtering
through the trees, with their new leaves and sweet
blossoms, was too tempting to ignore, and Monica
House has no garden of its own. But I was punished
for my foolishness, for my husband found me,
recognising me though my face was veiled. This time,
he saw where I fled. That is why I write this letter,
for tonight I leave my beloved Georgiana with Maria
and return to him. If I do not, he won't rest until he
has killed our daughter.

God forgive me, I shall do whatever I must to
protect my child, though it means I shall never see her
again in this lifetime.

I've instructed Maria DeRosa to wait a month
before she gives you this note, because you must not
attempt to find me. I depend upon you to care for our
daughter. Because I know you will do that, I shan't
mind anything that happens.

George, I treasure the memory of our time together.
I regret nothing, and I love you and Georgiana,
always.

Ever your Anna

John looked up from reading, his heart heavy. 'What happened to her?' he asked, dreading the answer.

Amesbury's shoulders sagged. 'Maria delivered the note in the beginning of June. From the onset, I didn't follow Anna's instructions. The first thing I did was search for her. Not for a continuance of our affair – I always have been and always shall be faithful to my wife – but to save Anna from her husband. I imagined I could set her and Georgiana up in the country and ensure their protection.

'I discovered her fate with little difficulty – or, at least, I discovered as much as I ever shall. A trip to Dover and some enquiries at the harbour revealed that Anna and . . . that monster vanished in the middle of their Channel crossing, miles from land. I spoke to the ship captain himself; all his lifeboats were accounted for and, although he attempted a search as soon as their absence was noted, nothing was found. There can be no doubt they both perished. We will never know more about it than that.

'I was devastated. Maria and I grieved together, and only Georgiana eased our despair. She was simply the most beautiful baby, Tyrold. So fine-boned and delicate, but as her mother had said, with a powerful set of lungs. I couldn't believe the wonder of her, and I should've taken her home at once and confessed all to Fanny. But I didn't.'

The duke paused.

John released a breath he hadn't realised he'd been holding. 'No?' he queried to encourage Amesbury to continue. Why the duke hadn't immediately claimed Georgiana was a vital piece of the puzzle that still made no sense. Amesbury was honourable. He'd loved Anna. How could he deny his only daughter in such a way, when, unlike John, he was entitled to the claim of father? 'May I ask why not?'

'Yes, yes. Of course, you wonder.' Amesbury picked at the edge of his desk, his lips turned down. 'That same summer, my wife was in the midst of an exceedingly difficult first pregnancy, which left her mind exhausted, her body weak and her spirits fragile. For the sake of Fanny's health, I decided I'd tell her about Georgiana after our baby was born, once she'd recovered. But, once again, tragedy struck first.

'My second daughter was born six months after my first, but my second daughter lived only two weeks. Fanny was *devastated*; her health was already so feeble I thought she would die of grief. I was little better myself. Two terrible losses, in addition to my concern for my young wife and for my sister, whose husband was every bit the monster Anna suspected, took their toll on me as well. Meanwhile, Georgiana was safe and loved at Monica House in the care of devoted Maria, so I delayed telling Fanny. Every time I'd gather the courage to do it, I'd see new evidence of how she still mourned our poor Charlotte, and I thought the knowledge that I had a healthy daughter by another woman would destroy her. By the time the eldest of our sons was born four years later, I'd lost my nerve entirely. In those days, it seemed as if all my wife's happiness depended upon evidence of my devotion; therefore, I couldn't bring myself to inform her she wasn't my first and only love. But in thinking so, I gravely underestimated Fanny. The first thing she did when she at last learnt of Georgiana's existence was gaze at me with sorrowful, tear-filled eyes and say, "George, why did you keep her from me when you know I've longed for a daughter?"'

The duke clutched his head, shaking it as if in frustration. 'Do you see what a fool I was? I deprived her and Fanny both. Fanny wants so much for Georgiana to love her, for we shall never have a daughter of our own now, but Georgiana doesn't let us into her life. She's not unpleasant, mind you – no, if anything, she's *too* pleasant. She has every right to be furious at me, but she says nothing. Instead, she works herself to the bone, never a thought for her own wellbeing, as if nothing she does is ever good enough, and I don't understand why.'

John knew. At least, he knew a *little*. But he kept his thoughts to himself, as Georgiana hadn't given him leave to discuss what he knew of her tragedy with her father.

'I'm very sorry, sir,' he offered instead. The story was heartbreaking – heartbreaking to imagine Anna Marinetti's anguish and tragic death, and heartbreaking to think how much happier Georgiana, the duchess, and the duke might've been for years, if only Amesbury hadn't kept truths from his wife. 'Have you tried explaining your actions to Georgiana?'

'No.' Amesbury sighed. 'She knows nothing of what I've told you other than that her mother died shortly after giving birth. I'm too much of a coward to tell her; I worry she might despise me more than she already does. Believe it or not, Tyrold, you are the first person besides my wife to whom I've told the entirety of this story. I can't fully imagine why I did so, other than to help you understand that however it might appear, I honoured Anna, and I expect our daughter to be honoured as well. And you've dishonoured her and yet refuse to marry her. It grieves me deeply.'

John folded his hands in his lap. Despite his earlier protestation that his resolve wouldn't alter, the duke's story moved him to tell the truth, although he'd also explain why Georgiana must be allowed to make her own decisions in life. Miscommunications and concealed truths had caused enough damage to Amesbury and Georgiana's relationship; he wouldn't participate in furthering the harm already done. 'Sir, I do honour Georgiana. In fact, I love her. The jewellery you saw her return was a betrothal ring. I asked her to be my wife, but she declined to accept my proposal.'

A sharp cry of fury was the first thing that alerted John to Georgiana's presence.

Dammit, he thought, turning towards the door just as Georgiana emerged around the corner of the open entrance from the library.

She was positively fuming, her dark eyes piercing John like knives.

21

Throughout Georgiana's performance in the music room, she looked about unsuccessfully for her father. Sometimes when she sang, he got a pained expression that she liked to fancy was some residual feeling for his discarded mistress. It was one of the few times she imagined a connection between them.

But tonight he hadn't even bothered to listen.

When she'd performed an adequate amount of time, she relinquished the Broadwood grand to another young lady and accepted scattered praise on her way to the duchess, intending to inform Fanny she wished to return home.

Fanny, perched on a snow-white upholstered chaise, flashed a dimpled smile and patted the empty space to her right, so Georgiana sat obediently. She could chat for a moment in return for Fanny's kindness. The debut had been a disaster, but it wasn't for lack of effort on the duchess's part.

Fanny's gown rustled as she snuggled near, as sweet-scented as a cake. 'You've had a difficult week, dearest.'

'That's an understatement,' Georgiana replied, unable to curtail her testiness. The week had been a nightmare, and, now, on top of everything else, John's proposal had awoken a yearning in her breast. She'd never expected to want a husband, so it shocked her that the prospect of being Tyrold's wife was so heartachingly enticing, and not simply for the money and position. If she'd accepted John in the conservatory, he'd be at her side right now, offering his arm for support and comfort. Insult and injury wouldn't hurt any more. Even the duke's indifference wouldn't cut so deeply, with John holding her.

'Poor love.' Fanny wiggled closer, inadvertently pressing against Georgiana's wound and sending a stabbing pain up her arm. 'But soon all will be well, as I said in the conservatory.'

Georgiana shifted within the duchess's hold to ease her wound's ache. 'If you don't mind, ma'am, I shall return home.'

'Oh, no, dearest. You must stay, for we shall have the announcement tonight, after your father has made everything right.'

Georgiana's skin prickled unaccountably. 'What announcement?'

The rosy glow of Fanny's cheeks heightened. 'The announcement of your engagement to Mr Tyrold,' she whispered under her breath.

Georgiana's blood went cold. 'Wh-what?'

Fanny giggled softly. 'I told you your father would fix everything. Oh, I do understand what you're feeling, dearest. I was ever so upset when Ben told me what happened, and at first far too terrified to tell your father.

Mr Tyrold *oughtn't* have behaved in such a manner, but a conversation with your Aunt Clarissa set me right. She assures me her friends Lord and Lady Eden have the highest opinion of his overall goodness, so I have no more doubts that he will be kind to you. I shall tell you a secret, my love: husbands perhaps aren't *always* wholly perfect, but they make up for it in other lovely ways. And I can tell you like him, so you'll be ever so happy . . .'

Georgiana's inertia dissolved and warmth returned to her veins — more than warmth, in fact. Blood-boiling rage. She could forgive Ben's misguided but undoubtedly well-intended interference, but that her father felt he had any right to involve himself in her life's intimate details was too much to be borne. Only the certain knowledge that John would never betray her blunted her fury.

Still, he couldn't be left to defend himself against attack without reinforcement.

Georgiana wrestled from Fanny's embrace. 'Where is my father?'

Fanny tilted her head, her blonde curls bobbing. 'Why! You're not angry at him, are you, dearest?'

'Where is my father?' Georgiana repeated through her teeth.

Fanny's lips trembled, but she capitulated. 'Likely in his private rooms, in the north-eastern wing . . .'

Georgiana didn't wait to hear more. She marched resolutely out of the music room, knowing precisely the chambers Fanny referred to. It's where she'd sat with the duke, prim and proper and businesslike after her return from Italy four years earlier and asked, with the utmost politeness and coolness, for her ten thousand pounds so she could resurrect Monica House's waning fortunes.

Georgiana nodded to the footman guarding the darkened corridor. 'Good evening, Timothy,' she said without slowing her determined pace. Naturally, he didn't deter her progress.

She opened the door to her father's library. At first, the room appeared deserted. But John's muffled voice over the crackle of the fire told her they were in the duke's study. Her slippers glided soundlessly across the carpet and as she approached, John's words became decipherable. 'I asked her to be my wife, but she declined to accept my proposal.'

Georgiana couldn't contain a sharp exclamation of rage, for it sounded as if John was attempting to secure her father's assistance in pressuring her into marriage.

She rounded the door, her fists clenched as John turned to meet her gaze. 'You collaborate with *him* behind my back? I never imagined you'd betray me, John Tyrold!'

'I didn't betray you, Georgiana,' he responded, his voice gentle. 'Please don't barge in here, having overheard only the end of a long conversation, and imagine you know everything that happened, and I won't have an argument about a miscommunication that can be easily settled. I mentioned a tiny part of what transpired between us in the conservatory only because your father and the duchess know we spent the night together—'

'I know they know,' Georgiana retorted.

'Then you understand why they are justifiably upset and demand I wed you. I only wanted to explain to your father that your wishes against our marriage must and will be respected, without revealing any details of what you told me.'

Georgiana calmed. John's story rang true, which was a tremendous relief. She didn't want to think badly of him. Not when he'd become so special. Not now that her heart sometimes did that curious little flip when he was nearby. Not when she'd lain in his arms the night before, and it had felt like heaven. She never wanted to think badly of him, ever again.

'Very well, John. I acquit you of wrongdoing.' She spoke those words serenely, but when she turned to her father, who sat so grandly behind his desk, she shed her calmness. 'But *you*, sir? What have *you* to say for yourself? What right do you imagine you have to interfere in any part of my life?'

The duke raised his eyebrows, likely surprised by her harsh tone, for she'd never been anything but painfully even-tempered around him. 'Georgiana, as your father, it is both my right and my honour to—'

'No,' Georgiana snapped. 'Absolutely, irrefutably no. I confess I've lapped eagerly enough at the scraps you've thrown over the years, but don't confuse my needful acceptance of financial assistance with an acceptance that you are a true father to me.'

The colour drained from the duke's face, and, for a moment, Georgiana's resolve faltered.

But then she lifted her chin. She would make a stand. Tonight, finally. John's generosity had freed her from an obligation to ingratiate herself to her father and his society, and the *ton* refused to accept her anyway. What did she gain now by pretending to be something she wasn't?

Besides, she was tired. Tired of pretence. Tired of masquerading in a life that it was too late for her to live, and which she hadn't been offered when she might've lived it. And the sooner she revealed her true selfish, despicable, reckless nature, the more rapidly Tyrold could forget his infatuation and focus on the only thing that was important: Flora.

'Let Mr Tyrold be, sir. He didn't seduce me. I seduced him. Because that's the kind of wanton woman I am.'

Her father drew back in his seat, clearly surprised.

John stiffened. 'Georgiana, that isn't—'

'Allow me to speak, John,' Georgiana said defiantly. 'It's time both of you knew the truth about me, for you seem to have inflated notions of my virtue. I admit I'm good at pretending, when necessary, that I'm a virtuous spinster of mature years—'

Tyrold positively snorted.

'Stop it.' She scowled. 'I *am* good at it when I want to be – you believed it yourself at Lady Holbrook's garden party.'

John sobered. 'Forgive me. I was laughing at the "mature years", Georgiana. Your virtue I'd never question, as I've said before.'

She raised her eyebrows. 'Oh, you should. You think you're only the second lover I ever took, and that the first was a mysterious true love who died. But you're mistaken. My first lo—' Georgiana's throat thickened, and she found the word stuck. 'No, he wasn't that. I have twice taken lovers of my own free will – once with you, John, and once a meaningless affair I conducted in Italy. But with the first man, it wasn't by choice. Not really . . .' Her eyes stung. Why was it so difficult to clarify what had happened? At times, she had come to the music master at Miss Shirley's Seminary willingly, but, at the same time, it had never felt like a choice. While the other girls had been so cruel, Mr Jasper had listened to her dreams. He'd told her she needed worldly experience only he could give her if she hoped to be an opera singer one day; he'd used his fingers to make her feel good, and then, one day, he'd unbuttoned his breeches and taken her virginity. Not violently, but suddenly, so that it had been over almost before she'd known it had begun. And then he'd done it again, and again, every time she'd had a lesson, telling her he'd taken precautions when all the while his aim had been to get her with child so her father would consent to their marriage. 'Oh, it has always confused me. He was my music master, and one day he just took me before I knew what had happened.'

'If he acted without your permission,' John said in a level voice, as if he weren't disgusted by what she'd revealed, 'he violated you, Georgiana.'

She stepped back, putting a hand to the door frame. 'But it wasn't violent. I let him kiss me, I let him touch me, so . . .' She trailed off, trying to sort bewildering memories, trying to view what had happened from a different perspective, but ultimately failing. 'I flirted with him. I permitted him to flirt with me. I put myself forwards to him without a chaperone present. These actions naturally incited his desire . . .' Again, she faltered, because even as she described her actions, she began to realise that she had been young, innocent, and alone, and he had been her teacher, and he had known she was vulnerable . . .

'Oh, my darling.' John's voice was tender and sorrowful. 'A freely offered kiss is nothing more than a freely offered kiss. The same is true of touch, no matter how intimate. If you didn't grant him permission for more, then anything he took was a violation. And I'm so terribly sorry that happened to you.'

Then the past slipped fully into focus, and Georgiana trembled involuntarily. She recognised predatory behaviour when it happened to others, so why had she denied herself the same compassion? Yes, sometimes rape was a violent offence; her music teacher had performed it upon the sly, like a pickpocket gliding past and stealing a treasure without a rustle of fabric, but it was no less a rape.

'But I don't suppose it really matters what happened,' she said stiffly as she recovered her resolve. Her words were more a response to her own thoughts than to John's statement, for she had a task to perform, and she couldn't allow herself to be sidetracked. 'Or, at least, it doesn't change the fact that while I've been with three men, I've never loved any of them. So you *should* doubt my virtue, John.' She turned away from him, unwilling to witness his admiration turn to disgust, as it no doubt would.

She locked eyes with her father, who still sat at his desk, although he no longer appeared grand. His shoulders slumped and his eyes had lost their vigour. His face was ashen, greyer than his hair, and, for the first time, he looked old to Georgiana.

But that didn't soften her heart.

She wanted him to know the truth. How she'd made selfish choices, yes, but that he'd driven her to them. 'You . . .' Her voice broke, but she continued. '*You* are the only man I've ever loved, Papa, but you weren't there for me when I needed you.' She turned back to Tyrold, her pain so raw it didn't matter any more if she saw disgust in his eyes. 'Do you know why I worry for Flora? Because when I was seventeen, that man you said violated me got me with child. It turned out his objective had always been to force me into marriage. You can perhaps imagine my surprise when he informed me my father wasn't a prosperous businessman frequently travelling as I'd been led to believe, but in fact, the Duke of Amesbury, who had a grand home in Mayfair and countless estates all over England, though I'd never seen any of them. Yet even upon first learning of this deception, I had faith in my papa. He'd help me, I thought. He'd save me, love me, protect me, provide for me. So, innocent and trusting as a babe myself, I fled to London.' She paused her story only long enough to draw in a deep breath and face her father again, setting her heart against his crumpling expression. 'But what did I find when I arrived at my papa's house? At this house, whose precious floors I'd never before walked on? First, I found a butler reluctant to admit me. Who wanted to turn me out on the streets. I doubted things then . . . and perhaps all yet might have been well if I'd left at that moment because I would have gone to Monica House and sought Maria's help. Perhaps, amongst a community of women who'd been betrayed, I could've absorbed the truth better. But that's not what happened. Instead, I heard a laugh. A joyful laugh that I would've recognised anywhere because it was my papa's laugh. So I ran past your butler, sir, as you know. I ran right past him, towards the laugh, certain that all would soon be well – but instead . . .'

Georgiana hugged and rocked herself, temporarily unable to continue.

'My daughter, please.' Her father's voice sought to mollify her. 'I never meant—'

'No!' Georgiana yelled. 'I don't care what you meant or didn't mean. You'll listen to me tell this. I want you to feel, in as much as you ever could, what it was like to be a motherless, friendless girl who'd longed her entire life for a family to run with a hopeful, loving heart towards her father's arms . . . only to find his arms already full of his *real* family. His golden-haired sons, his beautiful wife, carrying a child herself, all clustered together laughing over some private joke or family tale or something else to which I wasn't privy. In one horrible second, I understood everything. I realised the boys you held were the children you loved. The children who knew you intimately, to whom you read and with whom you played. The children who shared your home, with whom you passed every precious day, rather than the bastard you visited a few times a year, and even then always in secret. Meanwhile, Papa, during all the years you hid me away, I'd thought the sun rose and set with you. My greatest dream was to make you proud by becoming a great soprano, like my mother, whom I'd thought you loved. But you didn't love either of us.' Georgiana's eyes were so hot with unshed tears that she could barely make out the form of her father hunched over his desk, his head in his hands. 'You broke my heart, Papa,' she said, her voice cracking. 'I saw myself for the embarrassment I was to you, I saw your beautiful wife nearly faint, and your perfect children – the little *lords* – look up in wide-eyed horror at the bedraggled hideous monster who'd dared to enter their home and I saw disgust in your eyes. You *knew* I came to you in trouble – and what trouble but one would I be in? – but you let me go. You let me flee. And I had only ten pounds in my pocket and a baby in my belly when I sailed for Calais.'

Georgiana rubbed her eyes, wiping away her burning tears.

Her father's cheeks were wet, and his eyes red-rimmed. 'I wasn't disgusted at *you*, Georgiana. I was disgusted at myself. It was a dreadful, unforgivable mistake not to raise you with your brothers. I regret it every day of my life. But I swear to you, I had no notion you were with child. Why did you not go to Monica House? Why did you leave England?'

'Because of *pride*.' Georgiana slid down the door frame and landed on her bottom in a skirt-crumpling heap, her anger sinking into despair. 'Selfish pride. And now you'll hear of *my* dreadful, unforgivable mistake – the one *I* regret every day of my life. After realising how you'd betrayed me, I never wanted to see you again. If I'd fled to Maria at Monica House, you would've found me in a moment, if you'd bothered. I didn't know if you *would* search – if you cared enough to search – but I knew whether you didn't come or did, I couldn't bear it either way. My only alternative was to try to seek my mother's family in Italy.' Georgiana stroked her locket, her mind's eye full of the only person who'd ever belonged to her. 'My sin was worse than yours, Papa, because my selfish choice cost my baby her life. Without adequate money for the journey, I was forced to sing for coin, which delayed my progress through Europe. By the time my delivery was near, I'd travelled only as far as Piedmont-Sardinia, where I was grateful to find shelter with an elderly woman in a small hamlet in the Alps, out of the way. I bore Annie, and I thought my happiness complete. I loved her so much,' she said, her throat aching and tears falling at will. She closed her eyes, squeezing her hand around her locket, almost able to feel the warm, solid weight of Annie's body, the pull of the baby's mouth on her breasts, the little hands that kneaded for their milk, and the dark

394

blue eyes that had stared at Georgiana. She remembered how Annie would periodically stop nursing and detach from the nipple with a toothless, milky smile, sometimes accompanied by a giggle. Georgiana had been Annie's whole world, and Annie had been Georgiana's everything. Together, they had been enough. A love more profound than Georgiana ever could have imagined.

Georgiana crumpled over her heaped skirts, embracing herself to keep from shattering. 'I loved Annie so much. For six months, I knew happiness like no other . . . and then . . . and then she died and I've never, ever, ever been the same.'

And covering her face with both hands, Georgiana wept.

A hand touched her, and she knew it was John. She could feel him sitting on the floor beside her as he rubbed her hunched back and murmured something, but his gentleness only made her cry harder. He must scorn her now that he knew her for what she truly was. How thrilled he must be that she'd refused him. That the future Mrs Tyrold wouldn't be a disgraced woman of loose morals whose stupid selfishness had cost her baby her life.

Then John's fingers were on the clasp of her locket, and Georgiana gasped as he slipped the chain from her neck. 'Why do you take it?' She sat up, her face tear-streaked, but the moment she registered the deep compassion in his eyes – without a trace of disgust – she knew why he'd taken the necklace. 'You want to see her? You want to see my Annie?'

'May I?'

She nodded, wiping her nose with her wrist. 'It's not a proper portrait,' she explained as she unlatched it. 'It's only the best I could do with a bit of pencil. I simply couldn't let her pass from this earth without some record of her little face. But' – Georgiana's voice squeaked as the tears began again – 'it doesn't show her sweet smile. That was already lost, and now exists only in my memory . . .'

'She was beautiful.' Tyrold's eyes glistened as he studied the locket. 'And I shall imagine her smile. Do you want to tell us how she died?'

And Georgiana suddenly realised she *did*. She'd never talked to anyone about Annie, and something tight around her heart was loosening. 'Scarlet fever in the hamlet. The old lady I lived with died first, although a third of the hamlet followed her. One of the men travelled for help, but he brought back a priest, not a doctor. My throat ached so badly with illness, I couldn't even swallow water, and . . . I suppose my milk dried because Annie would try to nurse only to fall off my breast, whimpering. I attempted to feed her on goat's milk and grain – one of the other women helped – but . . . I don't know. She grew ill with such terrible swiftness, as if she had no reserve in her tiny body. She stopped trying to eat. She ceased laughing, her eyes lost their shine. And then she was dead, and, at first, I couldn't believe it. I held her in shock.'

John stood, leant across the duke's desk and handed the locket to her father. 'Your granddaughter, sir.'

The duke held the locket in his palm, gazing at it with teary eyes. 'Did you name her Anna?'

'Yes,' Georgiana said, fresh tears welling. 'After Mama.'

John returned to Georgiana's side, settling himself on the floor next to her crumpled skirts. He cupped her chin, lifting her head until she met his gaze, and, still, his eyes revealed only compassion – no shock, no repulsion, no disgust. 'Georgiana, I can only begin to imagine how dreadful it must've been to lose Annie. How dreadful it must still be to recall your helplessness and your fear. How much you must long for things to have happened differently, and how desperately you wish she were alive. But you need to understand it isn't your fault Annie died. Children can die of scarlet fever even with the best medical care.'

'But she didn't get *any* medical care,' Georgiana said. 'She depended on me, and I failed her.'

Tyrold enfolded her hands with his. 'No, you fought for her life as best as you could under the circumstances, which is all anyone can ever do. Annie's death was a tragedy and you'll always feel the grief of her loss. But don't add blame to your agony, my sweet love.'

'I know what you are trying to do,' Georgiana said through her sorrow. 'I even realise there's probably truth to what you say. But I can't *feel* the truth. I think only about how I ought not have acted out with selfish pride when I discovered the truth about Papa. If I'd gone to Monica House for help, Annie would be alive. She'd be eight now. She'd have a favourite story. A favourite animal. She'd have a voice, and words, and thoughts and hopes and dreams. My foolishness deprived her of all of that.' The swirling nightmarish images of the forlorn dead began to swarm Georgiana's mind, as always happened in the depths of her despair, and she rocked to keep the anguish from consuming her. 'At times, grief possesses me like a madness, and the only thing that alleviates it is to try to save as many lives as I can. But the truth is, even if I saved a hundred thousand lives, it wouldn't bring back Annie. It wouldn't change how my selfishness destroyed her chance at life.'

John pressed her hand. 'You are the least selfish person I've ever known, Georgiana.'

'Perhaps I am *now*, but I wasn't *then*. Don't you understand my selflessness now – and everything you think good in me – is because I *must* be? For the rest of my life, I must be. I cannot think of my own happiness any more. I had the most exquisite joy once, in the form of Annie, and I put her in danger, and she died. I don't deserve to ever have it again.'

'That is simply not true. You deserve the best of everything, my love. If your mind won't let you believe my words, then feel the sentiment in my heart.'

He brought her hand to his chest and for the first time, Georgiana sensed his genuine love for her, something as unconditional as her own love for Annie. And she knew then – beyond all doubt – that Tyrold's love wasn't tied to how society viewed her or even how she viewed herself, but instead to something inherently *her*, which even she couldn't sense.

Oh, yes, a woman could get used to this, but John's goodness was all the more reason why she couldn't marry him. She couldn't let a man this wonderful throw himself away on a wife who could never love him with a whole heart.

'I feel that you believe it, John. I truly do. And I confess it's tempting to believe it myself. But believing it doesn't bring Annie back to life, so it doesn't change anything. Now do you understand why I can't marry you? No matter how sweet and kind and gentle you are, or how patient, or how generous you are with Monica House, and no matter how pretty the rings you give me are, all you'd get in return is a guilt-ridden woman whose heart lives in the grave.'

'That's a challenge I'm willing to take on, Georgiana.'

Georgiana leant forwards and pressed her lips to his forehead, closing her eyes to breathe in his scent one last time. 'Eventually, you'll feel differently.'

She disengaged herself and stood, empty, exhausted, and approached her father's desk. 'I need my locket back. I can't bear to be without it for long. It has Annie's hair inside, and sometimes I imagine it still carries her smell.'

When her father returned the locket, he squeezed her hand over it. 'Georgiana, I made mistakes, but I love you. I always have, I always shall. Annie was my granddaughter, and I can mourn her with you—'

Georgiana pulled her hand away, too drained to feel anything at his words. She secured the locket around her neck and sighed as the familiar weight fell against her chest.

'It doesn't matter any more, sir. John understands now, and so must you. I buried all thought of myself with Annie. The best thing you can do is to let me be.'

She turned towards the door. She'd leave, she decided. She'd walk out the back, into the mews, to spare the duchess any embarrassment, and then she'd return to the quiet comfort of Monica House, a community filled with women who knew pain on the same scale she did, if not more. A place where she could throw herself into the work that gave sense and purpose to her life. She needn't mingle in society again, because she knew with certainty that John wouldn't renege on his subscription promises. He was too good a man.

At the threshold to the library, she paused.

He was still sitting on the floor, gazing up at her.

'Find Flora,' she said, trailing her fingertips over his cheek. 'For God's sake, John, find Flora and give her the love and support she needs now, before it's too late. Don't let her become like me.'

She left the study, strode across the library, and let herself into the dark corridor.

The library door slammed closed behind her, with an echo utterly forlorn.

22

Edward called at Monica House around noon the next day, bearing a key, a lease agreement and a letter.

He plopped into an armchair across from Georgiana's desk, his gloved hands folded over the ivory handle of his walking stick. 'John says a man rather aptly named Joiner will manage the renovations. You're simply to tell him what you want, never mind the expense. It's to be your school, I understand?'

'Yes.' Georgiana studied the lease, wondering how she could feel so depleted when she held her dream in her hands. Soon, the children of Monica House and the greater community would mingle at a school that would foster love and kindness as much as knowledge, and at long last, Monica House residents would have a safe, secure, private garden, which had always seemed of critical importance to Georgiana. Already, the lilac trees were budding on the other side of the wall. By the time a gate joined the two properties, the children could run amongst purple blossoms while their mothers watched, breathing in the sweet-scented air.

'You look unhappy, Gee.'

Georgiana glanced up; Edward was watching her keenly.

'I'm anxious about Flora,' she said, uttering a partial truth. Her emotions weren't stable, and she longed for Edward to leave. 'Thank you for this delivery, but I don't wish to take any more of your time.'

Edward's mouth quirked. 'Being dismissed, am I? Well, Gee, let me know if you need anything. John's orders, not mine – although I'm happy to fulfil them while he's away.'

'Away?' Georgiana asked, dismayed. 'Where is he going? And what about Flora?'

Edward stood. 'Explained in the letter, I imagine. I'll let you read in peace. Good day, Gee.'

With a tip of his hat, Edward departed.

Georgiana ripped open the seal, revealing John's written hand for the first time. She trailed her fingertips over the bold strokes, none too neat but confident. She pressed the letter to her nose, but it smelled only of paper.

Her eyes stung as she applied herself to his words.

My dear friend,

I am honoured you shared such painful memories with me; your bravery and strength are astounding. You are a survivor, a kind-hearted warrior, who turns her pain into a battle for the good of suffering women. You say you are only selfless now because you must be, and that in your youth you were wont towards selfishness – but I am strongly of the opinion you mistake loneliness, inexperience, and a certain innate self-interest that most children possess, as selfishness when you view your youthful actions.

However, I also understand my opinion doesn't alleviate your grief.

In thinking over your heartbreaking tale, I grew aware of its similarities — as you have often said — to Flora's current situation. I dwelt most frequently upon the actions you took when you felt desperate. You wanted your parents. First, you sought your father. Then you sought to return to your mother, in as much as you were able.

This morning, I finalised organisation of the London searches, which I've now left in my investigator's charge, with Edward overseeing. I've decided to travel to Yorkshire in case Flora slipped past the tollbooth guards, determined to return to a place where Helen's memory and presence linger. I know she hasn't made it to Oakwood or my parents would've sent word, but perhaps she has been depleted of funds on the way, as happened to you. At any rate, I believe it's worth exploring. Together with two of my friends, I shall scour every coaching house, village, and inn between London and York and throughout the North Riding.

All success so far in this search has originated with your wisdom and guidance, and for that I remain ever your grateful

J Tyrold

Georgiana pressed the letter to her heart, put her head upon her desk, and cried.

She cried for Flora, she cried for Annie, and she cried for what could not be between herself and the kindest man in the world.

For the next two weeks, in addition to her regular duties, Georgiana oversaw the renovations to the school. And in every moment she could spare, she searched for Flora, showing the placard to river dockworkers as far east as Limehouse, enquiring at markets from Shadwell to Mary Le Bone, and venturing into the gambling hells, gin houses, and rookeries of Southwark. She visited hospitals, workhouses, and churches.

All to no avail.

She wasn't the only one searching; London buzzed with word of the missing heiress. Flora's face plastered walls and windows, and everyone from paupers to lords sought the twenty thousand pound reward – a fortune by *anyone's* reckoning. Princess Charlotte's wedding on the second of May provided the only other interesting topic of conversation.

On the evening of the wedding, Georgiana threaded through the crowds thronging Pall Mall outside Carlton House, hoping not for a glimpse of the silver-gowned princess on the arm of her handsome Coburg prince, but for green eyes and copper curls, no doubt hidden under a hood or cloak. But if Flora came to view the royal wedding, she remained hidden from everyone's sight.

Two mornings later, Georgiana received an invitation.

Holbrook House, Piccadilly
Saturday, 4th of May

Dear Miss Bailey,
If you aren't otherwise occupied today, please come to
Holbrook House for a noontime luncheon. It will be a
cosy affair — only Rose, and Kitty, and me — as
Holbrook and Eden haven't yet returned from Yorkshire.
We long to hear how renovations for the school progress.

Yours most affectionately,
Meggy Burton

Georgiana hesitated only a moment before deciding to accept. She knew from the brief notes Edward sent daily that the journey to Yorkshire had proved fruitless so far, so there was no news on that front to glean from Meggy. But Georgiana had been inclined towards melancholy and less productive lately; discussing the school with three charitable and benevolent ladies might enliven her and renew her energy for the project.

She attired herself in a white muslin frock sprigged with pink flowers, one of the many gowns Fanny kept sending over, although Georgiana had declined to attend social events or even family dinners with her father and his wife. The weather, warm at the start of spring, had taken a turn for the worse recently, and even with a matching rose-velvet spencer and kid gloves, Georgiana walked swiftly to Piccadilly, the wind whipping at the layers of her skirts. The sun shone, but only weakly, filtered through a high haze.

But she warmed the moment Holbrook's butler ushered her into a feminine sitting room papered in floral print and hung with intimate family portraits. Fresh bouquets burst from vases throughout the chamber, and a cheery fire crackled under a pink-marble mantelpiece.

The three smiling ladies were every bit as welcoming as the room, and, to Georgiana's astonishment, Rose wore a grey-and-lavender shot-silk gown rather than her customary black.

'What a lovely room,' Georgiana said, exchanging handshakes and kisses with her new friends: Meggy with her golden-brown curls and dimpled cheeks; Rose, tall, slender, pale and oh-so-elegant; and exquisite Kitty, with her glossy dark locks arranged under a fine lace cap. 'And what a stunning gown, Lady Rose.'

A hint of pink tinged Rose's cheeks. 'I must be Rose to you, Miss Bailey, for I already count you amongst my favourite people.'

'Then I am Georgiana, please.'

Rose smiled. 'I owe you a debt of gratitude, Georgiana. The song you sang three weeks ago at Kitty's salon had such an impact – "with joy and woe, still forth we must go, whatever befalls us today" – that I ordered new gowns and, ever since, my girls have been much happier. I didn't realise how the black depressed their spirits.'

Meggy embraced her sister-in-law. 'One day our Rose will bloom in every colour, again.'

'Grey and lavender are enough of a change for now.' Rose kissed Meggy's cheek.

Kitty threaded her arm through Georgiana's and gushed about Ada-Marie's interest in the guitar.

'Come, come.' Meggy pulled everyone towards a table set with porcelain plates and gleaming crystal. 'We shall have a decadent luncheon while the children eat in the garden, between rolling about on the lawn like the wild animals they are. This will be our respite from the madness of town lately.'

The luncheon – a veritable feast of lobster cream, lamb and mint with fresh green peas, cold salmon and tongue, pigeon pie, and salads served with French wine – passed in companionable, comfortable conversation. After the meal, Meggy served tea as they sat near the fire.

While Georgiana sipped the restorative beverage – much needed, since she was unaccustomed to large midday meals – a flustered nursemaid entered the sitting room with a sobbing toddler.

She addressed Meggy. 'I'm terribly sorry, m'lady, but Freddy won't settle for his nap, and I know you like me to bring him to you—'

Meggy jumped up from a sofa, where she'd been half reclining against an embroidering Rose, and took her dark-haired son in her arms. 'Of course, Harriet. Think nothing of it. Leave him with me and these ladies; between the four of us we'll smother him in kisses until he can't stay awake a moment longer. Please enjoy a well-deserved rest.'

Harriet smiled, bobbed a curtsy, and departed.

Meggy adjusted her crying son on her hip as she brought him to the sofa. 'Sweet Freddy, you miss Papa,

407

don't you? But he will be home today, to play with you before you go to sleep tonight.'

Either that news or his mother's embrace seemed to settle the toddler, who rested his tear-streaked face against Meggy's shoulder. His sobs reduced to ragged gasps and then to hiccups. At last, he stuck a thumb in his mouth and sucked, his lids falling heavy over his blue eyes.

Meggy rubbed her son's back. 'This last month has been difficult for Freddy because his second set of molars is breaking through. In the past, I've put him to breast when he's teething, but perhaps because of my pregnancy or his age, he's weaned himself.'

The conversation naturally fell into mothering-discourse after that, and, although Georgiana's eyes stung and she frequently touched her locket, she contributed her bit here and there, referencing the Monica House babies and toddlers as the source of her knowledge.

But she allowed the other ladies to dominate the discussion. As Meggy described how her morning sickness was easing, Georgiana sipped a second cup of tea. From her seat in an armchair, she observed the paintings on the wall. Each one was a portrait of a woman or a girl, and Georgiana's interest was most piqued by those of Rose, Meggy, Rose's girls, and Meggy's sister, Sophia, all of whom she recognised.

But the face of a beautiful auburn-haired lady with large grey eyes – exactly like Rose's, but also reminiscent of Lucy – hanging across the room caught her attention. Georgiana narrowed her own eyes to focus better. The portrait was small and intimate. The lady's long hair spilled over the shoulder of a loose muslin gown, in the style called *chemise à la reine* after Marie Antoinette who originated it, and she held a green parakeet on her finger. Georgiana's skin prickled; the thought of Flora's abductor, William, in the parakeet mask was fresh in her mind. Every few days, Georgiana re-examined the beautifully crafted mask, hoping a clue would reveal itself, to no avail. Furthermore, her wound, although healing nicely, still caused her some discomfort. Even now, looking at the painted parakeet, her arm ached.

Yet she couldn't draw her gaze away from the grey-eyed lady. As Georgiana studied the portrait, Meggy answered a question from Kitty about names for the new baby.

'We shall call her Susannah, if it's a girl; we'd already chosen that when I was pregnant with Freddy. And if it's a boy, he'll be Anthony after my father, since Freddy's named Frederick for Nicky's father.'

Georgiana jumped in her seat, rattling her teacup in its saucer. 'Frederick!' she exclaimed, staring at the portrait. Frederick was the name Lucy had given for Wingrove's former lover Rosamunde's husband. And the auburn-haired, parakeet-holding lady resembled Lucy, and was dressed in the clothes of the 1780s, as John said Lucy had worn . . .

Georgiana placed her tea upon a side table and looked keenly at her friends, who stared with quizzical eyes. 'Frederick and Rosamunde, perchance?'

Meggy cocked an eyebrow. 'Oh, I can't name a daughter Rosamunde. That was my husband's mother's name, and I'm afraid she and Nicky had an exceedingly difficult relationship.'

Georgiana shook her head. 'No, forgive me. You misunderstand because I didn't express myself clearly. I was in fact enquiring if your mother-in-law's name was Rosamunde, but you've answered me.' She looked at Rose. 'You were named for her, perhaps?'

Rose lifted her slender shoulders. 'In a way, although I was christened Rose, not Rosamunde.'

Georgiana indicated the lady with the parakeet. 'And that's your mother's portrait, is it not?'

'It is,' Rose said.

Georgiana furrowed her brow, studying the painting. Surely, Rose's mother was the original Rosamunde, the source of horrid old Viscount Wingrove's obsession. But it was the parakeet that particularly fascinated Georgiana, given William's mask. Parakeets were moderately popular pet birds, but the mask was unusual, and, put together, the parakeet link between Rosamunde and William seemed too coincidental not to explore . . .

Meggy's voice aroused Georgiana from her thoughts. 'Something troubles you.'

'Yes . . .' Georgiana wondered if more enquiries would confirm a connection between young William and the old viscount, something that had always nagged her as a possibility. 'Rose, may I presume to ask some difficult questions about your mother?'

'You're not presuming,' Rose said gently. 'You're amongst friends here.'

'Did she . . . did she like parakeets?'

'Oh!' Rose chuckled. 'I thought you intended to ask something quite different. When I was about eight, my mother was given a pair of parakeets by . . . well, she was given a pair of them, and she did like them, yes. Their descendants live in my brother's conservatory in Suffolk to this day.'

Georgiana grimaced. 'My next question is likely more what you were expecting. By any chance, was Viscount Wingrove the friend who gave her the parakeets?'

Rose sobered. 'I cannot say for certain because I was a child when my mother was intimate with the viscount. But as well as memory serves, I believe the birds appeared around the time Wingrove was so frequently in my mother's company.'

Kitty tilted her head, her glossy dark curls bobbing. 'There's a parakeet on the Wingrove heraldry. A reference to exotic shores, I understand. The original source of the fortune – or rather, the fortune that was – was in shipping.' She scrunched her nose at Georgiana. 'Sorry, I'm a fount of inconsequential knowledge. One learns a great deal of rubbish from years of listening attentively to men. On the odd occasion, it proves accurate, and occasionally even useful.'

That was it, then, Georgiana thought as she observed the painting again. Rosamunde, Viscount Wingrove, Lucy, Mother Harris, the boy in the parakeet mask, Flora and her love of birds: the portrait linked them all, albeit superficially. 'Viscount Wingrove – or rather, probably his son and by extension his grandson – abducted Flora Tyrold,' she said, as the ladies drew sharp breaths. 'I could never prove it, but I'm certain nonetheless.' She looked at each of her new friends. 'Can any of you think why a nobleman would take such a risk?'

Meggy repositioned her sleeping son, and the toddler's thumb fell from his mouth. 'The depleted fortune, one would suppose.'

Georgiana shook her head. 'There are simpler ways to marry a fortune. If the boy is the heir to the title, he ought to be able to find a wife with money.'

'Not one with a half a million pounds,' Rose said, snipping a thread. 'And with the prospect of great deal more one day, unless, of course, John marries and has children of his own.'

Georgiana's cheeks flamed, but fortunately her three friends appeared to be looking anywhere but at her.

'It might be revenge motivated,' Kitty said after a moment's silence. 'Revenge against John.' She leant forwards eagerly, her blue-green eyes shining. 'When Sidney and I first married, we lived with John for about a month. During that time, Viscount Wingrove called on two or three occasions. The last time he visited, John chastised him so violently I had to cover Ada-Marie's ears.'

Meggy snorted. 'But John chastises people frequently—' She stopped, drew her lips in a circle, and looked at Georgiana. 'Please don't misunderstand me. John's a sweet man, but sometimes his patience . . .' She sent Kitty a peaked-brow plea, evidently for assistance.

Kitty nodded. 'Meggy's correct. John *is* lovely. He goes to some effort to conceal it—'

'Oh,' Georgiana said, flustered. 'There's no reason to defend your friend's conduct to me.' She was well aware of John's goodness, but she couldn't talk about that. It hurt too much.

The three women exchanged glances.

Kitty continued. 'Well, we wouldn't want to give you the wrong impression. John speaks his mind, but he doesn't grow fierce without great provocation. Later, Sidney discovered what happened. John had left Wingrove in his study and returned to find the old man riffling through his safe, for all the world like a thief.'

Meggy's eyes grew huge. 'Good Lord! Did he steal money?'

Kitty shrugged. 'John couldn't be certain. The oddest thing of all was John had the key on him, and he was certain he hadn't left the safe unlocked, as if Wingrove had picked the lock, or had a second key, but John couldn't see how he could, given that the safe was made especially for him by a craftsman in Yorkshire. But however it happened that Wingrove got in, when John discovered him, the viscount was most certainly perusing a specific document, very much as if that had been his goal.'

'What document?' Georgiana asked eagerly.

Kitty lifted her hands, palms up. 'That's the thing. John never discovered which, because Wingrove then caused a dreadful disarray, spilling papers everywhere, claiming John's advice was rubbish and that he kept the best investments secret so no one else could benefit. All in all, his behaviour was that of a petty and puerile old man, and once John established nothing important was missing, he let the matter go without retribution beyond that vicious scold.'

Georgiana frowned, somewhat surprised. 'He never pursued the matter?'

Kitty shook her head. 'No, but that's not so odd as it may seem. See, on occasion, John's advice upsets his visitors because they don't like to alter their ways. They come to him thinking he can snap his fingers and change their debt to fortune, and they are devastated when they discover otherwise. Sidney took pity on Wingrove, supposing the viscount to have acted out in terrible desperation. John finally agreed to let the matter alone, primarily because he supposed the viscount's mind riddled with madness – and, in this matter, I have to agree with John over my own husband, for if that old rakehell doesn't have the pox, I don't know how he escaped it, and, of course, a virulent case can infect the mind. I know with certainty that no courtesan has been willing to touch him these twenty years, even when he had some fortune left.'

Kitty then sipped her tea as calmly as if she'd been discussing the weather.

Georgiana tapped her fingers against her thighs. 'Perhaps Wingrove discovered Flora's existence then – or he'd somehow *already* discovered her existence and sought more information within Joh— Mr Tyrold's safe.' Puzzle pieces were clicking together, but to what purpose? 'So Wingrove found Flora, and somehow his grandson ingratiated himself with her, a feat easily enough achieved with a lonely young girl. We know who probably abducted her, but we are no closer to finding Flora.' Georgiana looked at her friends, but they simply stared in return. 'Forgive my fruitless musings. I've been attempting to aid Mr Tyrold in his search—'

Kitty smiled. 'We know. John speaks *very* highly of you. I got the distinct impression you and he are on quite . . . excellent terms?'

Georgiana's cheeks warmed again. 'We became rather companionable while scouring London together,' she explained before quickly changing the subject. 'Meggy, you said you expect Lord Holbrook today? Do you know Mr Tyrold's plans, by any chance?'

'Nicky wrote to say that he, John and Sidney will return this afternoon, but he didn't mention a precise time. Do you mean to tell John what you've discovered?'

'I don't know.' Georgiana pressed her lips together. 'More than anything, I want to search his safe for any clue that might prove helpful.' With an apologetic smile, she addressed her hostess. 'Would you think me terribly unmannerly if I take my leave?'

'Not in the least,' the marchioness said. 'Anything to find Flora.'

With one last glimpse at Rosamunde and her parakeet, Georgiana dashed from Holbrook House, hoping the weather remained clear and John made good time.

In the meantime, she'd see if Edward could unlock the safe.

23

It was late afternoon when John arrived at Number Twenty-Nine Half Moon Street, his hands stiff with cold, his body sore. Except for the two days he'd spent comforting his parents, John and his friends had been in the saddle for a fortnight, combing every city, town, village and hamlet along the Great North Road between London and York.

His housekeeper, Mrs Smith, greeted him in the entrance vestibule with her arms crossed under her bosom. 'So you're back,' she stated in a kinder voice than usual. 'And with no word on your girl, eh?'

John removed his gloves. 'Nothing. Some false leads and attempts at deception, but no real news.'

Mrs Smith tsked her tongue. 'Poor poppet.' Then, sympathy evidently over, she reverted to her customary brisk manner. 'Sir, you should know there's a young lady with his lordship.'

John hung his hat on a peg. 'Indeed, Mrs Smith? There must be some significance to this communication, which I'm afraid I don't perceive. I thought we tended not to discuss his lordship's profligate ways?'

'I said a young *lady*, sir. Not like his lordship's usual

trollops and whatnot. What's more, he's let her into your safe. She's up in your study now, with your papers scattered about the floor, and I can't imagine what Lord Edward means by it. He's gone mad, is what I think.'

The words warmed John's cold and aching body better than a fire. There was only one young lady Edward would allow to do such a thing, and whatever Georgiana's reasons for going through John's papers, they were bound to be excellent. Moreover, the thought that she was in his house at that very moment filled John with peace despite his despair. He'd missed her dreadfully.

'Ah. If this young lady is a diminutive brunette with the most striking pair of dark eyes, she's more than welcome to go through whatever of my things she likes.' John quickly checked his reflection in a wall mirror. He desperately needed a shave. With a week's worth of dark stubble, he essentially had a short beard, but he was too eager to see Georgiana to do more than comb his fingers through his hair and adjust the knot of his cravat.

When John faced his housekeeper again, Mrs Smith's eyes had grown as wide as saucers. 'What's this?' she asked, aghast. 'Looking at your reflection? Smoothing your hair and tidying your neckcloth? Does this mean I am to have a mistress at long last? Is that young lady the reason you finally learnt to hang your hat and coat on pegs? And started dressing as befits your status?'

John shoved his hands into his pockets. 'She's the reason, yes.'

Mrs Smith threw her arms in the air. 'The good Lord has heard my prayers. There is to be a Mrs Tyrold, and it'll be her, not me, what has to put up with the worst of you.'

'Don't rush to conclusions, Mrs Smith. I'm afraid there won't be a Mrs Tyrold.'

'And why not, sir?' the housekeeper demanded.

'Because two must come to the altar,' John replied, surprising himself with his candour.

Mrs Smith stumbled in shock, falling against the newel for support. 'Never tell me she declined your offer?' When John didn't reply, Mrs Smith formed her own conclusion. 'She has. I see it in your face, though I scarce credit it. What can she be about, rejecting you, sir? Rejecting tall, handsome Mr Tyrold, with his millions, and with a heart of gold to match?'

John blinked, nearly as shocked as his housekeeper. 'Good Lord! In the many years we've known each other, you've never once said such nice things. I was generally given to understand you thought me the worst sort of callous and parsimonious cad.'

'There's naught wrong with you but what a wife can't set right in a week, and so I'll tell your lady caller, should you give me leave to do so.'

'I'm afraid I must decline your offer, Mrs Smith. It's best if I set *myself* right. Then, if I am ever fortunate enough to win the heart of the lady I love, she will wed an equal partner, rather than a reform project.'

Mrs Smith's eyes went misty. 'Oh, Mr Tyrold. Seems to me you've already set yourself right.'

No, he couldn't do that until he found Flora and became the loving and supportive guardian she needed, at long last. 'Not yet, Mrs Smith. Not yet.' Simultaneously in torment and in hope, he mounted the stairs to discover why Georgiana had decided to scour his papers.

A cosy scene welcomed John when he opened the door to his study. A fire burned cheerfully in his hearth, Edward lounged in a leather chair, his legs thrown over its arm and a sketchbook in his lap, and Georgiana sat on the floor in front of the open safe, her skirts spread like a cloud around her. Jolly rested his head on her lap, gazing up with longing eyes.

John must look much the same, he realised. He stood with his hand on the doorknob, drinking in the sight of her: thick brown hair smoothed into a fat but tidy chignon; slender arms and delicate hands shuffling and sorting his papers into organised stacks; calm radiating from her body.

Jolly peaked his shaggy eyebrows at John and thumped his tail, looking utterly guilty but not moving from Georgiana's side.

'Am I so easily replaced, Jolly?' John put his hand over his heart. 'You cut me to the quick, though I can hardly blame you. But a word of warning, sir: don't become accustomed to her. She's an angel, but I'm afraid we can't keep her.'

Georgiana flushed most becomingly. 'Good afternoon, Mr Tyrold.'

Her velvety voice warmed John's soul. He wanted to kneel at her side, offering his heart and fortune all over again, for every day without her had been agony.

But he wouldn't, of course. John respected and understood her sentiments, and to beg and torment her wasn't fair.

So, he simply replied, 'Good afternoon, Miss Bailey.' With a tiny smile, Georgiana continued perusing his papers, and John turned to Edward. 'Any news?' he asked, although he knew the answer.

''Fraid not, old man.'

'Well, damn.' Exhausted, John collapsed onto his sofa. When Georgiana finished whatever task consumed her attention, he'd ask her advice on what to try next. In the meantime, he'd rest for a few minutes.

Mrs Smith, who'd followed him upstairs, fluttered about him, offering comfort without a single scold about mud-splattered clothes on the upholstery. With her eyes flicking to Georgiana, she murmured, 'My poor master, how tormented your mind must be, as *good* and *generous* as you are. I'm always saying to anyone who'll listen how Mr Tyrold is the best and kindest of souls—'

Edward's hand stilled over his sketchbook. His eyes rounded as he pivoted his head, staring slack-jawed at their housekeeper.

Even Georgiana looked up from John's papers with a quizzical lift to her brow.

Mrs Smith evidently took it as encouragement. 'Indeed I am, miss. Just the other day my sister what

420

works in Grosvenor Square called here and do you know what I said to her? "Sister," says I. "My master is—'

'Your master is extremely desirous of tea, Mrs Smith,' John interrupted, thoroughly embarrassed by his house-keeper's overt praise, and hopeful Georgiana didn't think he'd put her up to it. 'At once.'

But Mrs Smith was clearly enjoying herself. 'He wants tea, bless him! That's another thing I'm always saying. Mr Tyrold is most temperate in his appetites. Tea or coffee, rather than brandy or whisky—'

'Good Lord, woman!' John growled, having had *quite* enough of his housekeeper's meddling. 'Cease your prattle and bring me my blasted tea.'

Mrs Smith's eyebrows drew together, but she turned with an angry swish of her skirts and stomped from the room, muttering, 'Well, blunder my good efforts, why doesn't he . . .' followed by some indecipherable but vicious-sounding words, which only faded once her heels stopped clicking on the stairs.

Edward snorted. 'That's more like it. For a moment, I thought she'd gone a bit . . .' He tapped his temple with his index finger and gave a knowing wink.

Georgiana cracked a half-smile, and continued to peruse her papers.

Peace descended after Mrs Smith's departure. Everything was quiet but for the murmur of the fire, the scratch of Edward's charcoal, the shuffle of papers and the tick of the mantel clock. John propped his head upon his chin, his elbow resting on the sofa's arm as he watched Georgiana. She was reading one of Flora's journals, her finger trailing across each page before rapidly flipping to the next. The fact that she appeared to still have hope brought John immeasurable peace.

His heart twinged. Two weeks' absence hadn't diminished his love one whit. Quite the opposite, in fact. Georgiana had pervaded his thoughts ceaselessly on his travels. He'd longed to have her by his side, advising him, guiding him, comforting him, while he showered her with love and devotion.

'Edward, could you please leave?' he asked kindly, wanting to enjoy Georgiana's soothing presence alone.

Without a word, Edward carefully tore the paper from his book. He stood, stuffed his charcoal in his pocket, and wiped his fingers on his handkerchief. On the way out the door, he placed his sketch on John's lap.

John cast an eye over the beautifully rendered charcoal Georgiana bent pensively over a journal, her eyes downcast and her thick lashes curling towards her cheekbones. Giving the sketch to John was a kind gesture of Edward's but possessing it without Georgiana's permission felt like an invasion of her privacy. Yet John left the paper resting on his knee while Georgiana was occupied.

'Are your parents well, John?' she enquired some minutes later, after Mrs Smith had returned with a tray, then left.

'As well as can be expected.' John sipped his tea. 'But they feel it deeply, and I sensed their condemnation. No word of rebuke passed their lips, but I wasn't greeted with the customary fatted calf, either.'

'Silent censure for the prodigal son.' Georgiana's lips quirked. 'How truly dreadful.'

'Miserable,' John agreed. 'Made me want to put my tail between my legs, like Jolly does when I scold him for chewing my slippers.'

'Scold *this* beastie?' Georgiana asked in mock horror. 'Now you have my censure, John, for how could you ever scold Jolly?' The wolfhound's tail thumped violently against the floorboards as she scratched his neck, kissed his furry head, and called him a good dog.

'Flora named him, you know,' John said softly, after watching this sweet scene.

Georgiana looked up. 'Named Jolly?'

Lost in a memory, John didn't respond immediately. He recalled travelling to Mary Le Bone just over a year after Flora came into his care, excited to show her his new wolfhound pup, who'd been all fuzzy fur and massive paws. Flora had been delighted; she'd let the clumsy creature lick her face while she'd hugged and kissed him, much like Georgiana had just done.

After rolling on the floor in a bundle of fur and child, she'd asked John the pup's name, giggling all the while.

'I was thinking of calling him Lupus,' John had replied, thinking the name would please Flora, who'd apparently been memorising Linnaeus's scientific classifications of animals when she was meant to be studying French conjugations, according to her headmistress.

But Flora shook her head back and forth, her copper curls swishing over her pink cheeks. 'No, for he's *not* a wolf, John.' As if in agreement, the puppy licked her cheek and Flora fell into another bout of giggles. When her laughter finally abated, her green eyes glistened with joy. 'You will call him Jolly,' she declared. 'For that's what you never have enough of, John. You need jolliness.'

John drew himself from the reminiscence. 'Yes, Flora named Jolly,' he said in answer to Georgiana, and he drank more tea, hoping to stave off the ache in his throat, which had arisen with the memory of a moment so beautiful it now hurt to recall.

Georgiana studied him, her expression sombre. 'How *are* you, John?'

John set aside his tea; it hadn't soothed his throat, anyway. 'I visited Helen and Arthur's graves. Apologised for blundering the raising of their daughter.'

'You poor dear,' she murmured, and, casting her eyes down to Jolly, moved the dog's chin off her knee. 'I apologise, sweetheart, but you must let me up so I may sit with your master.'

John's heart lifted as she stood, journal in hand, and closed the distance between them.

'*May* I sit beside you?' she asked. 'As your friend?'

'Please.' John slid over on the sofa, making as much space as possible. He appreciated her clear boundaries. He wanted to take her into his arms, but, even more than that, he wanted to respect her.

As she settled beside him, her gaze fell to the sketch on John's lap. 'Oh! I didn't know Edward was drawing me. It's a good likeness.'

'Edward is extremely talented, and he caught your *outward* loveliness well. But he couldn't catch the brave and generous spirit inside, which is your greatest beauty.' Georgiana's lips pressed together, her face pained, and John's spirits fell again. He'd gone too far and made her uncomfortable. 'I apologise, Georgiana.' He held out the drawing. 'Please, take it. I have no right to keep your likeness – it should be yours.'

'Keep it, John,' she replied, a quiver in her voice. 'I confess there's a part of me that very much wants to imagine you looking at it.'

'Then imagine me looking at it all the time when not in your presence, for that is what I shall do, now that I have your permission.'

She met his gaze, and John could've sworn there was love in her dark eyes . . . But then he recalled she felt the emotions of others, and his nascent hope shattered. She was simply mirroring his own devotion.

He looked away, to master himself, and silence reigned for a moment.

Then the journal pages rustled, and Georgiana spoke. 'John, in October of eighteen thirteen, Flora writes that you took her birdwatching north of Paddington Road. I believe you recall that day, because you started to mention it on the night we visited Dr Mitchell's?'

'I do recall that day, yes,' John said, surprised Georgiana had mentioned it. 'It occurred about a week after Sidney and Kitty moved to the country. In a fit of loneliness, I visited Flora and asked her what she'd most like to do.'

Georgiana glanced at the journal and back at John. 'What more do you remember?'

John considered. 'We packed her field-glass and her bird book, and we went into the fields. It was a fine day, and I read for hours while she amused herself. That part was enjoyable, but I'm afraid the day ended dreadfully.'

Georgiana flipped a page. 'Yes, I assumed something unpleasant occurred for her to write: *Today I have discovered what I long suspected: John hates me.*'

John released a heavy breath. 'She was justified in thinking it, although it isn't true. The trouble started when I told her it was time to return to school. She begged to live with me instead – which I wasn't prepared for – and when I said no, she grew sulky and defiant. When that didn't achieve her purpose, she threw a dreadful fit. By the time she exhausted herself with her screaming, I hadn't an ounce of patience or tolerance left. Desperate to return home and be alone, I half dragged her back to her school. When we arrived, the other girls were queued up, ready for some outing, and several of them began to laugh. Flora – still in a horrid mood – rather cruelly said they laughed at my appearance. I told her I couldn't care less, which was completely true, but my reply seemed to anger her even more. "I care," she told me. "Because they laugh at me too." I discredited her sentiments. What did it matter, I argued, if they laughed? Thanks to me, Flora was wealthier than any of them.'

John stopped talking.

Georgiana put a hand on his knee. 'What did Flora say to that?'

'She said, "They are far richer than I am, for they have people who love them. You were supposed to love me. Before my mama died, she told me you'd love me and take care of me as if I were your very own daughter. But you don't, do you? If you love me, say so now, or I shall know you don't." Georgiana, I didn't tell her what she wanted to hear. I was already in a terrible mood, and Flora's comment about Helen exacerbated my anger. I remembered that declarations of love had meant nothing to her; I wondered what she'd meant by telling Flora I'd love her as if she were my own daughter.' John sighed. 'Unfortunately, my failure to respond that afternoon was a turning point in my relationship with Flora. Every interaction after grew increasingly miserable. Any time I tried to be a better guardian, or attempted to demonstrate my love, she'd say things that seemed designed to hurt me as deeply as possible.' He rubbed his hands in his hair. 'God, how I now wish I could turn back time and say the three words that might have made all the difference.'

'John, regarding Helen . . .' Georgiana looked again at the journal, tapping her finger on some scrawled lines. 'After that bit about you hating her, Flora details some of your greatest offences, including your dreadful brown hat, which shows excellent taste on her part. Then we come to the crux. *But none of that matters so much as the wonderful thing that happened on the birdwatching adventure. I found Mama today, and she smiled at me.* John, I can't help thinking this could be significant. Do you know what Flora might've meant?'

A buried memory surfaced.

'The dovecot,' he recalled, sitting up straight, because even as he said it, he knew Georgiana was correct. It *was* significant. At the time, it was a poignant, sweet moment – but the bad end to the day had eclipsed it, and he'd long since forgotten. 'It happened *before* we began birdwatching. It was her window to heaven . . .'

John had first taken Flora to the farms that skirted the northern edge of Mary Le Bone, and purchased milk, cheese and a loaf of bread from a shop run by a farmer's wife. 'Provisions for the afternoon,' he'd explained to a beaming Flora, who'd held his hand and skipped beside him, her curls bouncing. As they travelled past the farms on the way to the fields, Flora had spotted an ivy-covered, stone dovecot, shaped like an enormous beehive.

She pointed. 'What's that, John?'

He explained its purpose and because she hoped to see doves, he lifted aside a heavy wooden door with a rusty latch. He thought she'd be disappointed when a quick glance over its pigeon-holed walls revealed (per John's suspicions) that it was long-since abandoned, but she clasped her hands to her heart and stared transfixed at the round hole in the roof.

A ray of light shone through, casting a column of sunbeams to the dirt floor.

'It's a window to heaven,' Flora said. 'Mama is smiling down at us. I love it here, John, for it is just us and Mama and no one else exists.'

John gripped Georgiana's hand, for a sudden realisation flooded his mind like that light from the window.

428

The dovecot would provide excellent secret shelter. It was far enough removed from the bustle of Mary Le Bone and the Regent's new park for concealment, and yet it was close enough to farms that a cunning scamp like Flora could procure food and water.

Furthermore, if a desperate, frightened, lonely Flora had indeed wanted to flee to a place where she felt close to Helen . . .

'By God, Georgiana. I know where she might've sheltered.'

Georgiana's lips parted into a beaming smile. 'That is precisely what I hoped to hear.'

'Come with me, please?' John beseeched her. 'I know I must learn to be the guardian she needs on my own, but—'

Georgiana squeezed his hand. 'Of *course*, I'll come, John. I wouldn't be elsewhere for the world.'

24

On the pavement outside Number Twenty-Nine Half Moon Street, Georgiana accepted John's assistance into a hackney in full view of anyone who wished to see.

She settled herself on the bench seat, her hopes of finding Flora elevated. With a folded paper clasped in one hand, she gazed confidently at passers-by who eyed her askance. Let them think whatever poisonous thoughts they wished about the Duke of Amesbury's unmarried bastard travelling unchaperoned with the kingdom's wealthiest bachelor. Flora and John's well-being was worth it.

Of course, John had given Georgiana the financial independence not to care about the opinions of others, but it wasn't merely money which provided her freedom. An afternoon of collaborations to solve – Georgiana *hoped* – the mysteries of Flora's disappearance had brought a new awareness. Even John, with his millions of pounds, couldn't do everything alone. Nor could Meggy and Rose with their birth, breeding, and loving family, or Kitty, with her astonishing beauty and worldly experience. Why had Georgiana tried to bear *her* burdens by herself for so long? Why had she persisted in believing her father and Fanny didn't care for her based on the experiences of her childhood, when recent years had proven their consistency and thoughtfulness, just as John was proving his love for Flora after many mistakes?

Perhaps Georgiana *should* let the duke share her grief for Annie, as he'd offered . . .

The thought of grief moved Georgiana to take John's hand. 'We mustn't give up hope if we don't find her even yet, my friend,' she said as the hackney driver called to his nag and the coach swayed north over the cobbles. 'There is another course of action we can take if this one fails. Rather, we need to take it whether we fail *or* succeed in finding Flora right now.'

As Georgiana relayed her suspicions regarding Viscount Wingrove, John clamped his bearded jaw, and she tightened her hold on his hand. 'Please stay calm. If Flora isn't at the dovecot, we shall go immediately to the Runners with our suspicions. It won't help find Flora, but perhaps we can bring the Wingroves to justice. At first, I thought I'd never be able to prove it, but I've adjusted my thinking on that matter. You and I can identify the boy, as can that lad, Dick, at the King's Head.' She opened the folded paper she held. 'Additionally, I found this love poem to which he indirectly gives his name.'

'The poem amongst Flora's things?' John scowled. 'That rubbish doesn't identify him. I searched and found nothing. Not even a watermark to ascertain where he purchased the paper.'

'Well, it's tenuous evidence, but, along with a hand-writing match, I believe it would support our case.' Georgiana pointed with the tip of her finger. 'Look more carefully at this beginning: *I will when in a grove with my Flora meet; and take her hand as our hearts greet.* Utterly dreadful, of course, but he's attempting to be clever: I, Will Wingrove with my Flora meet and take her, et cetera.'

John grabbed the paper and held it near the window, his eyes running over the lines. 'You're a genius to catch this, Georgiana,' he said, speaking through clenched teeth. 'We'll see how clever the fucking little slug is when he's put before the magistrate for the abduction of Flora and attempting to murder you. As you said, it won't find Flora, but it'll be *some* justice, and it will prevent them finding a new victim.'

'I don't like the thought of a boy hanging, though, John.'

John merely grunted.

That was a matter for another day, Georgiana decided. She entwined her fingers with his and leant against the back of the seat. Despite her worries, it was invigorating to follow a trail again, and it felt good to be with her friend. John's nearness was inexplicably comforting.

The days were lengthening, so there was still much sunlight as they travelled north of Mary Le Bone and west of the Regent's new parks, where roads were being laid and terraces were rising in rows. Though it neared seven, workers still hammered, wagons hauled brick and timber, and the smell of cut wood infused the air.

North of the park, construction gave way to open fields. Further yet, half a dozen ancient wattle-and-daub farmhouses clustered together, relics from centuries earlier, likely not long to remain standing, with the way London was expanding.

After asking the driver to wait, John assisted Georgiana down. Hands clasped, they passed the farmhouses without pause, although two kerchiefed goodwives and several barefooted children gave them quizzical stares. At the edge of a rising field, John hopped over a stile and reached out to assist Georgiana.

She allowed him to lift her down, briefly delighting in the feel of being in his arms, and she took his hand again as they traversed the incline, their feet falling softly on the carpet of shorn grass. A cluster of cows watched their progress, chewing cud as their spindly-legged calves nursed.

The ivy-covered dovecot stood atop the hill, and Georgiana issued frantic prayers – *let her be here, let us find this child* – while John raised the rusty latch and pushed open the wooden door.

'Flora?' he called as they stepped into the dim interior. 'Flora?'

Silence.

Georgiana's heart plunged – until she heard a rustle from the shadows, followed by a cough.

Then: 'John.'

A statement, not a question.

Georgiana squinted into the darkness until she deciphered a bundle of fabric, lying unmoving upon the floor. 'She's ill,' she said, dread enveloping her.

John edged closer, as if the bundle was a wild animal about to dart away. 'Little one?'

The bundle sat up, revealing big eyes in a smudged, too-thin face. 'You remembered this place,' Flora said, her voice sounding stronger now, though listless and flat. 'I didn't think you would.'

John knelt on the dirt floor. 'I recalled that I have some unfinished business from that day. You know I don't like unfinished business, so I thought I should rectify it at once.' He leant closer and tentatively put an arm around the child, and tears prickled at the back of Georgiana's eyelids. 'Flora,' he said. 'The day we found this dovecot, you asked me if I love you, and I was too bitter over something that happened before your birth to tell you what I felt in my heart. I *do* love you, little one. I l–lov . . .' He faltered, his words wavering, until, with a deep breath, he continued. 'Flora, I loved your mother very much indeed. She was the best friend of my childhood. And loved your . . . your father, my cousin. And I love *you*, their brilliant, wonderful daughter.'

'Their *stupid*, *ruined* daughter.' Flora's words were bitter, rife with shame and pain. 'All I wanted was a real home, away from that horrid dull school, and I thought William was the answer to my dreams. He said you'd approve the match because he's heir to a title. He said I'd be hostess for his father and grandfather as well. That there would be parties, and the theatre, and trips to Vauxhall, and loads of birds at their estate. I thought he'd take me to Scotland to be married, and he did mean to, but when I got into the hackney, his father and grandfather were there as well, and they insisted on a change of plans. First to a boarding house, they said, until William got your permission, John . . . they acted like their purpose was honourable, but I soon learnt the truth. They wanted to *force* you to relinquish my fortune, by whatever means worked. William's father is a villainous worm, his grandfather is a vile old corpse, and William is a spineless little scab.' She coughed, a rough, barking sound, indicating an irritation of the lungs. 'I hate them all.'

Georgiana's heart ached as she tiptoed into the dovecot. Near the door was a small collection of food. A hard loaf of bread, some onions, a few withered apples. Flora hadn't had proper care in weeks. Then and there, Georgiana decided that – if John were agreeable – she'd take the child to Monica House for recuperation, so she could have a woman's care. Flora needed a steamy bath to bring moisture to her lungs as well as cleanse and soothe her body. Then a bowl of soup, wholesome but not too rich, and warm bread with butter. Tea infused with lemon and honey. A clean nightdress and soft bed. If Flora would permit it, Georgiana would tuck the feather bolster around the girl's neck herself and sing as she fell asleep. Flora needed to know she was safe, loved and cared for; Georgiana suspected that for *now*, she and Monica House could provide that better than John.

Only until the child healed, of course.

As Georgiana's thoughts were thusly occupied, John adjusted himself from kneeling to sitting beside Flora, their backs against the latticed wooden walls. He took her in his arms and she leant her head on his shoulder. 'Damned clever of you to escape, little one. But why didn't you come to *me*?'

Flora sniffled. 'Primarily because I thought they'd be watching the door to your house, ready to steal me again. But also because I thought you'd be furious. I thought you'd lock me up in a convent for the rest of my life, and I'd have to take a vow of silence and live in a dark cell and grow whiskers on my chin like an old crone.'

Georgiana pressed her lips between her teeth to repress a bubble of laughter. What spirit Flora had, even after all she'd been through!

'And thirdly,' Flora continued. 'Because I stole twenty guineas from William's father when I left, and I will hang if I'm caught.'

John pulled her closer. 'You won't hang for stealing money from those villains. They are going to feel the wrath of John Tyrold, but you won't.' He kissed the girl's filthy head, bless him. 'Flora, I haven't been a good guardian so far, but if you'll grant me a second chance, I'll give you a proper home at last. And there will be parties if you like that sort of thing, and trips to the theatre and to Vauxhall, and sometimes I shall let you drag me to Yorkshire so you and I can search for owl pellets all day. And there will be friends, and love, and no vows of silence nor whiskers on your chin.'

'You might as well lock me up, instead,' Flora said. 'No one will be my friend now, with my reputation destroyed.'

John rested his chin on her head. 'To the right sort of people, your reputation won't matter. And let's only be friends with the right sorts, eh, little one?'

Georgiana sniffed; her nose dripped from the evening chill. No, she was crying. Her thoughts had been so absorbed by the scene before her, with John doing and saying all the right things, without even needing to look to Georgiana for prompting, that she hadn't noticed her damp cheeks. Hastily, she wiped her tears.

Her actions drew Flora's attention, for the girl asked, 'Who's she, John?'

'She's one of the right sort, little one. In fact, she's an angel. Her name is Miss Bailey. She's the reason I found you, and she's helped me understand some secrets I've kept locked away for far too long – most importantly, how much I love my Flora.'

'Oh, John,' Georgiana breathed, too overcome to say more.

Flora's gaze darted between them. 'Did *she* get you to cut your dreadful hair?' she asked at last, rubbing her nose.

'She cut it herself,' John replied.

Flora snorted, sounding very much like John. 'In that case, you *must* be an angel indeed, Miss Bailey.'

But the words instigated a strong emotional reaction within Flora even as she said them, for the moment she'd uttered 'Miss Bailey', her face began to rapidly crumple and her lips turn down, and she flung out her arms, stretching them towards Georgiana, silently asking for an embrace in much the same way Freddy had reached for Meggy hours earlier.

She needed a mother's hug, and Georgiana, who had those sorts of embraces bottled up inside, dashed forwards, falling to her knees and drawing Flora close. She rocked and swayed the girl as one would rock a babe in arms, and Flora's sobs began, her body shaking with the release of weeks of torment and fear. 'You poor love,' Georgiana murmured, her own tears falling freely. 'Poor, sweet, darling girl. Let it all out. Let it all go. You're safe with people who love you. John and I won't let anyone hurt you now.'

Flora clutched tighter, fisting a chunk of Georgiana's spencer as if holding on for dear life. The girl's finger caught on the back of Georgiana's locket, bringing Annie to mind with full force. Then grief gushed forth from Georgiana like waters over a collapsed dam, and her own sobs grew as raw as Flora's, but warm arms enveloped them both, and John offered soothing comfort. He kissed Georgiana's head as well as Flora's, and Georgiana let him, relishing the security he provided, savouring the solace of his embrace. And for the first time in years, the thought of Annie didn't hurt *quite* as much. Or it did, but it wasn't accompanied by oppressive guilt and overwhelming horror.

Her heart filled, because she knew then what bound their embrace was love, wholehearted in giving, wholehearted in receiving, and there was no place for guilt in love like that.

25

John agreed with Georgiana that it was best for Flora to move to Monica House for her recuperation for the rest of May and June. Although he was eager to prove his good intentions to himself and Flora, a sheltered community of loving women who'd experienced hurts of their own was much more conducive to healing than a bachelor abode. Besides, London was astir with the gossip that the heiress had been found, and at Monica House, Flora was protected. The gawkers and newspaper reporters lining Half Moon Street, hoping to catch a glimpse of Flora, were disappointed.

The only thing that marred John's reunion with his ward was the realisation – the same evening that he'd found her – that the Wingroves had fled the country a fortnight earlier, on the very night of the Vauxhall masquerade. The viscount and his son must've realised the moment young William returned that it was only a matter of time before John discovered their identity and had the boy arrested.

Investigator Starmer went after the Wingroves; from the investigator, John soon learnt that the viscount, his son and his grandson had sailed first to Portugal

439

and then for South America. John directed Starmer to follow them to Brazil. Even though there would be no jurisdiction to arrest them, the investigator could ensure the villains realised if they ever set foot on British soil again, John and the law would be waiting.

It was cold comfort, but at least they couldn't hurt Flora any more.

Meanwhile, John assisted Georgiana in overseeing the renovations to the school, and directed renovations to the corner house beside it, which he'd selected as his future home.

He approached the matter of his move with Georgiana one evening in mid-May while they toured the interior of the school after the workers had left, their footsteps and voices echoing in the empty rooms. 'Will you mind if Flora and I are your neighbours?'

She stood near the window of an upstairs classroom, gazing down to Oxford Street below, the evening light casting a lavender-gold hue on her tanned skin. 'You're the school's sole benefactor, John. Naturally you may live next door if you like.'

'My dearest friend,' John said tenderly. 'I'm enquiring what you would like. If you prefer I be farther away, I—'

'No.' She spoke quickly, sharply, still not returning his gaze, but her cheeks now looked decidedly flushed. When she spoke again, her voice was barely a whisper. 'I don't want you farther away, John. I want you close to me.'

Hope swept over John, but he didn't press her for more. He'd wait patiently for Georgiana to come to him when or if she was ready. In the meantime, he'd be her devoted friend and supporter.

He joined her at the window. 'Then Flora and I shall move next door this summer. We'll create a second gate from the Monica House yard, and our garden will be available to your residents as well.' His gaze fell to Jolly, who sat at Georgiana's feet, his tail sweeping sawdust flakes on the newly hewn floorboards. 'As long as they don't mind the presence of Mr Wolf there.'

Georgiana smiled, scratched Jolly's ears, and they said no more on the matter.

Throughout May, John's most important occupation were the hours he spent every afternoon in the company of Flora, and often Georgiana, in a small bedchamber in Monica House. It was a private room, simply furnished with a wooden bed, a dressing table, and a chair. A sash window with ruffled white curtains and a geranium-filled jardinière lent a fresh and feminine air, further enhanced by the arrangements of roses and peonies John brought every few days. After a wagon-load of books and other possessions arrived from Flora's room at school, the chamber grew crowded, but all the cosier for it. The mechanical swan had a place of honour beside Flora's bed; she'd passed her sixteenth birthday alone in the dovecot, but John promised her a party when she was fully recovered.

'William never ruined me, you know,' Flora said one afternoon. John sat in the chair near the window, open only a crack because of the weather's persistent, hazy chill. Jolly snored at his feet. Georgiana perched on the mattress beside Flora, her legs tucked under her blue cotton skirts, and Flora's head resting in her lap. She played with the girl's curls, wrapping them around her finger, brushing them back from her forehead. Meanwhile, Flora fiddled with the chains of Georgiana's chatelaine.

'Of *course*, he didn't ruin you, sweet girl,' Georgiana said. '*You* ruined *him* with your indomitable spirit. You bested three men all on your own.'

Flora smiled weakly. 'I mean he didn't ruin me in *that* way, although I suppose it doesn't matter because everyone will assume he did.' A flush tainted her cheeks. 'His father tried to make him, but . . . but it didn't happen. They never hurt me worse than a slap. Once I fell against a wardrobe, which is how I got this scar on my forehead, but that's because my legs wobbled from the laudanum.'

Georgiana lifted Flora's chin. 'Listen to me, Flora,' she said firmly. 'Everything that happened to you – every touch, every angry word, every dose of laudanum – was an assault to your body and to your spirit, and you may grieve it as such. That's something I realised about myself recently, and,' her dark eyes raised to meet John's, 'it's helped.'

John smiled at her before offering his resounding agreement.

But Flora said no more as she played with Georgiana's chatelaine, a wistful look in her eyes, and John doubted they'd convinced her. The child was different now – subdued and quiet rather than boisterous and animated – and John longed for a return of her high spirits.

'I doubt they will ever return exactly the same, John,' Georgiana told him when they discussed the encounter over tea in her study later. 'Scars remain though wounds heal. But, one day, Flora will be happy again. I didn't believe that until recently, but I do now, even though I don't *feel* it yet. Not *quite*. But soon, I think. Perhaps very soon, indeed.'

Little hints like that raised John's hopes, but he never pushed for more.

In early June, the cold Flora had developed in the dovecot worsened. John and Georgiana were both frantic with worry, considering Helen's long illness and early death, but Alexander reassured them Flora's lungs were strong. All the same, John didn't rest easily until the middle of the month, when the flush on Flora's cheeks returned to the bloom of youth rather than the red-stained violence of fever, and Alexander stated his firm opinion that Flora's recovery would now progress swiftly and thoroughly.

On a visit one day towards the end of June, as John was reaching to knock upon Flora's door, he overheard Georgiana's muffled voice say Annie's name. He pressed his ear to the door, intending only to ascertain if his presence would be welcome, but what Georgiana said caught his attention so wholly that he remained listening.

'I keep her drawing here in my locket, with this knot of hair. So, you see, I truly *did* lose my virtue, and, yet, I have friends who don't care about that.'

'Like John,' Flora said. 'He doesn't care.'

443

'Yes, like John, the dear man,' Georgiana replied tenderly.

'Whatever happened to that music master, Mr Jasper?' Flora queried. 'To Annie's father, I mean?'

John pressed his ear closer.

'When I returned to England four years ago,' Georgiana's muffled voice said, 'I employed someone to seek him out. I intended to ensure he never worked in a school by writing to every headmistress where he attempted to teach, if necessary. But my investigator discovered he was arrested for debt not long after I fled from him – he'd lived a duplicitous life for many years, and owed hundreds of pounds, which is no doubt why he sought my fortune. As he has no family or friends to pay his debt, he has been at the Marshalsea all this time.'

And there he shall stay, John thought to himself. *I shall personally ensure it.*

Georgiana sighed before she spoke again, her voice urgent. 'Flora, remember that your past won't matter to the right people, so don't give up on any of your dreams, whether they are having a family of your own, or travelling the world to study birds, or something else you haven't even thought of yet.'

Suddenly recalling, to his shame, that he was eavesdropping, John threw open the door to the room and spread his arms wide. 'Definitely don't give up on your dreams, Flora, because I am the dream-granter. Tell me what you long for, and I shall snap my fingers and make it come true, to the best of my abilities.'

Flora grinned, looking truly happy for the first time in years, and patted the bed beside her. 'Come here, please.' When John complied, she threw her arms around him and Georgiana. 'I have everything I want for now.'

John kissed Flora's curls.

She released the embrace. 'When may I see our new house?'

'Whenever you feel strong enough,' John replied. 'And when you do, you can advise me on wall colours. Otherwise, I shall be forced to capitulate to Mrs Smith's wishes, and she's already had her way on everything from bell pulls to moulding.'

Flora shook her head. 'No, no, I can't. *Georgiana* must choose the colours.'

John hesitated, considering how to reply. Naturally, if Georgiana were to become his wife, it made sense for her to decorate their home, but it would be inexcusably presumptuous to ask that of her, and her current silence in no way encouraged him. 'Georgiana is busy with the school renovations, Flora,' he said, perhaps too firmly. 'We can't ask her to take on more.'

Flora's bottom lip jutted, reminiscent of her childhood scowls. 'Very well,' she said sulkily. 'Maybe I shall want to see the house tomorrow, but now I wish to be alone to read my book.'

Georgiana whispered something in Flora's ear, and John stepped away to give them privacy.

When he bid Flora farewell a few moments later, he noted that the girl's expression had brightened, so, once outside Flora's room, he couldn't help but enquire what Georgiana had told her.

Georgiana said nothing in reply as they progressed down the corridor together. The silence hung between them, eased only by their footsteps on the plank floor.

'Forgive me,' John said at last, his hopes fading. 'I shouldn't have asked.'

Georgiana halted, seizing his forearm. 'John, I—'

But a woman turned the corner of the corridor, advancing towards them, and Georgiana stepped aside to allow her to pass. They greeted each other, and only once the other woman walked on did Georgiana speak again to John. 'The ledger is in my study, Mr Tyrold, if now is a convenient time to review the finances.'

'Oh! Er, indeed,' he said, understanding. 'Now is a most convenient time, Miss Bailey.'

He followed Georgiana to the study, an oak-panelled room on the ground floor. The moment John entered, Georgiana closed the door behind them and locked it with a key from her chatelaine. She proceeded to close the windows and draw the drapes, dimming the room, and then she crossed to John and grabbed his lapels. 'I need you, but we must be quiet.'

John's cock hardened at once, instantly comprehending. 'I can be quiet.' He caught her in his arms, wasting no time. She yielded to him, and he kissed the curve of her neck, inhaling her intoxicating scent, her taste sweet on his lips, her body filling the void of eight weeks' longing.

She whimpered her need, her throat vibrating as she tilted her head back, offering herself wholly, and John trailed kisses to the neckline of her gown, pulling away her fichu and grazing her breast through the cotton. As usual, she wore no stays, and he cupped the weight of her, thumbing her nipple through the layers of fabric until it hardened, showering hot kisses upon the soft curve above her neckline, his cock throbbing with anticipation. She was everything he yearned for, everything he desired, everything he required for perfect happiness.

'My love, you undo me,' he said, bringing his mouth to her nipple, which strained against her gown. He suckled her through the fabric until her breath grew ragged. 'I want to learn every inch of your body,' he murmured against her peach-soft skin as he slid a finger under her neckline and released her sweet breast from its prison. 'I want to worship you, Georgiana.' He licked the rosy tip, hard and wanting, and she gasped. 'To make love to you until you feel nothing but mind-shattering ecstasy.' With those words, he took her in his mouth and suckled until she filled him. Only when she was writhing, her nails clawing at his scalp did he do the same to her other breast, his cock heavy with need.

'Kiss me,' she demanded, and he cupped his hand round her neck and drank deeply as she answered back. Her fingers worked the buttons at his waistband until she'd released his fall, although his braces still held his trousers. While yanking up his shirt with one hand, she grasped and manipulated his aching shaft, her thumb flicking over its agonisingly sensitive head, slick with his essence, until John had to pull away from her mouth and smother a groan against her hair.

He scooped her by the bottom, lifting her to him. She wrapped her legs around his waist, her skirts bunched between them.

'I want you, John,' she purred into his neck.

'Show me,' he said, carrying her to a sofa. Once he laid her down gently, he slid her skirts over her hips and spread her legs until her sex was exposed before him. 'Show me how much you want me. Show me how wet you are.'

She rubbed herself, her head thrown against the armrest, her fingers gliding over her quim. 'So wet, John.'

'Have you been doing that these last eight weeks, my sweet love?' he asked, aiding her efforts by slipping two fingers into her opening.

She released a sharp cry of pleasure, turning her face into the upholstery to smother it. 'Yes.'

He fingered her passage faster and teased her clitoris with his thumb. She was hot, engorged, slick with arousal, and his desire reached a fevered pitch. 'My God, woman.' He groaned as she squirmed and whimpered. He was bringing her close with hardly any effort. 'And what do you think about when you make yourself come, Georgiana?'

'You,' she cried. 'Always you, and how good you made me feel.'

'You're not wearing a sponge, are you?' John's words emerged as a growl. 'I ask because—'

448

'No sponge,' she gasped. 'Can you withdraw before you spend?'

John was on fire, but he replied levelly. 'Anything for you.' It was true. He'd walk barefoot over hot coals for her. *Of course* he'd pull out if she asked it of him. He knelt over her on the sofa, positioned himself at her opening, and steeled himself to mount her hard, without coming too soon. Then he plunged, fire into fire.

'Oh, my love.' He groaned again, fully engulfed. She bucked, squeezing his cock with her inner muscles, and John grabbed her hips. Still half upright, he braced himself, he braced her . . .

And then he withdrew . . .

Only to plunge again, deeper, harder.

Georgiana smothered a scream of pleasure.

'Again,' she panted.

John withdrew and thrust, and withdrew and thrust, a smile curving his lips as she whimpered on the sofa, her skirts spread around her, her chignon loose in a tangled mass, her face flushed with desire.

He withdrew, but this time he didn't plunge again.

She opened her dark eyes. 'Don't stop.'

'Tell me what you desire, Georgiana,' he said, his voice thick, his heart aching, 'so that I can make your dreams come true.'

Her gaze grew hazy. 'I desire you, John. You, and only you.'

And so he gave himself to her completely, leaning forwards to cover her with his body, enveloping her in his embrace and his protection, one hand knotted in her hair, the other clasped with hers, as he serviced her with rapid, all-consuming thrusts. When she lifted her bottom to meet him in her climax, she grabbed the fabric of his coat and bit his shoulder, moaning her pleasure as she pulsed on his shaft.

Only sheer willpower provided him the wherewithal to wait until her waves receded, pull out, and spill himself in exquisite release on her abdomen.

After, he cradled her against him, lying together on the sofa, blissfully expended, their breath rising and falling in tandem. She rested her head on his chest, her tousled hair falling on his shoulder, her skirts still bunched at her waist. John extracted his handkerchief and cleaned her stomach. 'Sorry about that, my love. I know you don't like a mess.'

'I loved *that* mess,' she responded drowsily.

Faint white lines, the marks of a pregnancy, etched her otherwise smooth stomach. Realising they were the reason she'd hidden her abdomen when they made love before – and recognising the honour of her no longer covering herself before him – John traced them tenderly with his fingertip. 'Thank you for trusting me, Georgiana.'

'Those scars appeared when I carried my Annie,' she said in a whisper. 'And they've never gone away.'

'They are beautiful.' John tucked her skirts around her legs, for she had begun to shiver. 'As are you. Inherently beautiful, through and through.'

Tears welled in her dark eyes. 'I love you,' she exclaimed, abruptly and fervently, as if the words had been locked up inside her and now burst free from their shackles. 'I'm wholly and completely in love with you, John Tyrold, and I'd love you even if you lost every penny of your fortune tomorrow.'

'And I love you too,' John said, his heart full, for she had given him the world with that declaration, although now that he heard it, he realised it came less as a surprise and more as a confirmation. Perhaps a little of Georgiana's intuitiveness was rubbing off on him, after all. 'But the only way I'd lose my fortune is if my Georgiana gave it all away.'

She laughed through her tears and kissed him, and he kissed her back, and everything was as John had desired, ever since he had first realised Georgiana was the woman of his heart. When they came up for air, she smiled against his lips. 'Would you let me give your fortune away?'

'Naturally,' John replied, and he kissed her nose.

Her smile broadened. 'I never imagined you would make such a great sacrifice for me.'

'Not as great a sacrifice as you imagine.' He winked. 'I should make it back soon enough.'

She laughed, but her laughter soon turned to tears, and she lay her head upon his chest, sobbing. 'I love you so much and yet it seems as if I love you more every day, and it frightens me to feel this much joy after so much grief.'

John held her, murmuring comfort and reassurance.

'When did you fall in love with me, my darling?' he asked when her sobs lessened, hoping to lighten her heart by basking together in their happiness.

'I can't say because I don't know when it began. I first *realised* it in the dovecot, when you embraced me as I held Flora, because at that moment, for the first time since Annie died, I felt like I was with my family. And every day we are together, I feel that more and more. I believe the three of us belong together, and I think, John, that Flora feels the same . . .'

'Of course Flora feels the same,' John said tenderly, rubbing her back. 'Georgiana, I will be content with whatever relationship you choose for us, but if you ever decide you could marry me, I shan't ask you to change anything. You will always be your own woman. I merely wish to share your life.'

'I know.' She sniffled, her tears abating as she stroked his waistcoat. 'But I must warn you, Fanny will demand a massive celebration if we marry. You won't be able to tolerate it.'

John grinned. 'You underestimate me. I intend for our wedding to surpass the grandeur of Princess Charlotte's.'

Georgiana's teary eyes twinkled. 'Then I'm afraid I shall disappoint both you and Fanny, with regards to the ceremony itself. I want a simple wedding. Here, in St Anne's parish, with only the women of Monica House and our dearest friends in attendance. But if you and Fanny wish, there can be a grand breakfast afterwards, to be followed by a ball and other celebrations, and Fanny can gloat to all her friends about how *she* brought out the debutante who secured the elusive Midas.'

John cradled her head and smudged away her tears with the back of his thumb. 'Just to be clear, my love – do I understand correctly that you accept my proposal?'

'*Soon*,' Georgiana said. 'There is one thing I must do first. Over the last several weeks, I've realised I haven't forgiven myself for Annie's death in part because I've never celebrated her life. John, would you mind if others know your soon-to-be wife once bore another man's child out of wedlock? Because I'd like to invite our friends to celebrate my daughter's life with me.'

John cocked an eyebrow. 'Georgiana, are you truly asking me if I care what others think?'

She held his gaze. Then, with the softest of laughs, her body eased into his arms. 'My John, you are the most perfect of men.'

Epilogue

A vibrant sunset streaked the mid-July sky as guests gathered around the pianoforte in the Monica House gardens, celebrating both Flora's sixteenth birthday and the imminent opening of Anna Marinetti's Seminary for Boys and Girls. Georgiana and John's dearest friends and family were present, including most of the residents of Monica House, attired in new silk gowns John had financed.

Because the weather was unseasonably cool, everyone stood close together, sipping negus, with the smell of brandy, sherry and sweet lemon scenting the air. Flora was radiant in an emerald-green gown, looking every inch the young lady. At her side stood John's parents, who'd come down from Yorkshire, and together the trio stared towards the sky, their eyes shining.

Above the grounds, the paper bird puppets of Vauxhall fluttered in the evening breeze. John had done that, as well.

Georgiana's heart was full as she observed Flora's joy. Near the girl stood other children who were fast becoming Flora's friends: auburn-haired Tess Preece, the same age as Flora; slightly younger Lady Sophia Fairchild, with copious honey-coloured curls; the three red-haired daughters of Lady Rose, ranging in age from five to thirteen; sweet Ada-Marie Wakefield, clasping Tess's hand, and the freckled young Lord Berksleigh, better known as Harry. *He* ignored the cluster of girls and was locked into conversation with Ben, who'd scrubbed up nicely for the occasion. No doubt they discussed steam engines or the like.

John moved amongst everyone, a perfect host wearing his exquisite eveningwear, dark blue coat with tails falling to his knees, cream-coloured breeches, which fit like a second skin, and crisp shirt linen. So handsome Georgiana had difficulty prying her eyes from him.

But take her eyes from him she must, for now, for there were friends to talk to. Embraces to receive and give, cheeks to kiss, pleasantries to exchange – and all of it sincere, for the guest list was exclusive. Only *true friends*, the sort that stuck by one through thick and thin, were present tonight.

Later, Georgiana intended to let herself into John's new house with the key he'd given her and creep up the stairs to his room. If Mr or Mrs Smith or any of the other servants heard her whispering footsteps, they'd keep her secret. Everyone knew what hadn't yet been officially announced: before autumn painted the leaves gold, King Midas would take a wife.

A vanilla-scented presence nestled beside Georgiana. 'Dearest one,' Fanny whispered in her ear. 'May I show you something?'

Georgiana smiled at her father's wife. She owed a debt of gratitude to the duchess, for Fanny had undertaken most of the planning for tonight's event. 'Of course, ma'am.'

Fanny slipped an opal ring off her littlest finger. 'I wear this for my sweet Lottie. I couldn't keep her hair, for she had only the finest blonde down upon her little head, but her name is inscribed on the inside, and the opal holds all the colours of the rainbow, and when I see that, it helps.'

Deeply moved, Georgiana touched the milky gemstone. John had told her about Fanny's daughter some weeks earlier. 'Lottie was my sister.'

'She was, yes.' Fanny's lip wavered as she returned the ring to her finger. She looked at Georgiana with tear-filled eyes. 'My Lottie is in Heaven, but I like to think that I still have a daughter here on Earth. Dearest Georgiana, I know I can never be a mama to you, but I wondered if perhaps you might call me Mother, rather than ma'am, as you always do?'

The words pierced Georgiana's heart. Oh, how she'd underestimated the purity of this sweet lady.

'No, no,' she exclaimed. 'Not "Mother".' Fanny's blue eyes rounded like a kicked puppy, and Georgiana gasped, realising her mistake. 'I only said no because . . . because I want to call you *Mama*, if I may.'

Then Fanny looked as if she'd been given the world, and she embraced Georgiana, sobbing, and whatever fragments of walls remained between them dissolved then and there, when Georgiana fully accepted a mother's love and gave a daughter's back in return.

It was a powerful moment, yet similar to some she'd shared recently with Flora, as they'd forged their

456

relationship, as well. Years of longing for her mother had worn at Flora much as years of longing for her daughter had worn at Georgiana. When they'd found each other, they'd clicked together like two puzzle pieces. Earlier that very evening, as she'd helped Flora dress, the child had slipped her arms around Georgiana's neck, kissed her, and whispered, 'It's lovely to have a mother again.'

And now Fanny had said what she'd said, and suddenly Georgiana was both daughter and mother, after yearning for so very long for both.

Only the chime of metal upon crystal and the subsequent quietening of murmured conversation drew Georgiana and Fanny apart, although they remained side by side, their arms around each other's waists and their heads pressed together as they turned their attention to John.

He tapped his crystal glass. When the remaining conversation stilled, he smiled at the company. 'I'm afraid I must demand your attention briefly. Edward?' he asked, glancing towards their friend who stood nearby, next to an easel covered in purple velvet.

Edward lifted the cover. As Georgiana's gaze fell to the gold-framed portrait, she clasped Fanny even tighter, because Edward had painted *La Grande Bellezza* cradling a blonde-haired baby, and that baby was Annie, smiling at her grandmother.

'Oh, Edward,' Georgiana breathed, too overcome to say more.

She didn't need to. Edward returned her gaze, his expression sombre. 'Something for you to hang in the school, Gee. John and I conceived the notion together. As you know, he borrowed your locket for a short time, and I owe a debt to Sir Joshua's portrait and' – he looked at Georgiana's father, who stood alone, a glass of negus in his hand – 'to others to catch your mother's likeness.'

Georgiana squeezed her locket. 'It's perfect, Edward.'

And it was.

John addressed the company again. 'If you can bear with my singing and playing, I'd like to perform the song Georgiana wrote for Annie. I think it will resonate in the hearts of all who have suffered loss – and who amongst us hasn't? For what is life, but a journey of joy and grief woven together so finely as to be inseparable?'

He took his place on the piano bench, flicking his tailcoat behind him, his back straight and his wrists upright, as he began to play.

'With joy and woe, still forth we must go,
Whatever befalls us today.
Of grief is born purpose, of gladness comes pain,
'Twas ever and always the way.'

In that magical moment, Georgiana could at last fully decipher the threads of silken joy from the blanket of grief that had surrounded her for so long. They had always been there, even when she hadn't seen them, but now they shone with the lustre of gold. Her fingers traced the etching on Annie's locket; she gazed at the portrait of the two Annas, she pressed closer to Fanny, and, for the first time in years, guilt didn't weigh her down.

'They are at peace,' she said.

'Yes, dearest daughter. They are. We shall always love them, but we shall also live.'

'I believe that now, at last.'

Georgiana's heart swelled as John finished playing and walked towards her.

'I think he has something he wishes to ask you,' Fanny whispered excitedly, her breath tickling Georgiana's ear. 'I shan't say I told you so, but I did!'

Georgiana rolled her eyes and laughed. 'I suspect you'll never let me forget, Mama.'

'Mr Tyrold,' Fanny said, bouncing slightly when John neared. 'May I introduce you to my . . . to my *daughter*?'

John's eyes twinkled as he made a formal bow. 'Thank you, ma'am. May I ask your permission for a few moments of conversation with your beautiful daughter?'

Fanny's dimples deepened. 'Indeed,' she said, almost squealing. She gave Georgiana another kiss and fluttered away with a rustle of sweet-scented silk.

John brought Georgiana's hand to his lips. 'Do you wish to say a few words about Annie?'

'Yes, but later, when I have something else to announce.'

'Truly, my love?' he asked, with boyish delight. 'Tonight?'

'Well, as my wise John said minutes ago, grief and joy are interwoven – and so they shall be in my speech.'

He smiled his eye-crinkling grin. 'Shall I get down on one knee before all these people?'

'Not now,' she said with a naughty smile. 'Get down on your knees later tonight, when I visit you.'

He waggled his brows. 'It will be my *pleasure*, enchantress. And so this is it, at last? All is settled between us? I shall take on the yoke, and you will become a matron of mature years, as you would say?'

'All of that shall come to pass, yes.' Georgiana squeezed John's hand as she surveyed the company. Most guests were talking in clusters, paying John and Georgiana no obvious mind, but the Duke of Amesbury studied them intently. Georgiana's eyes locked with her father's, and she felt his sorrow and his regret. It was time for those things to be buried, and for there to be only love in their place. 'But first, John, ask for my papa's permission. I want his blessing to marry.'

John tucked her hand into the crook of his elbow. 'Let us go to him together.'

'Yes,' Georgiana agreed. 'Let's do that.'

She nestled next to her love as he led her through the fairy-tale night, the birds fluttering overhead below indigo-purple skies. She leant her head against his upper arm, safe in the knowledge that she was with the best of all men, the granter of her dreams, the epitome of her heart's desire.

Yes, a woman could get used to this.

Acknowledgements

A novel never comes into existence without a support team, and I truly have the best. My tremendous thanks to my brilliant editor, Sanah Ahmed, and my ever-supportive agent, Kate Nash, and to a host of other people: to Jessica R, my dear friend who happens to be an opera singer, for her musical expertise and her poetry; to Jessica Bull, a brilliant author and wonderful critique partner; to fellow Regency romance author, Emma Orchard, and to my Twitter friend, Lady Tarleton, for answering questions about Italy and Italian; to every single one of my lovely friends, whose presences are blessings in my life; to my extended family and to my wider community, and to Tim, Benjamin, and Susannah, my dearest loves.

And, always, my thanks to you, my readers. I hope this novel brought you joy.

Credits

Felicity George and Orion Fiction would like to thank everyone at Orion who worked on the publication of *A Debutante's Desire* in the UK.

Editorial
Sanah Ahmed

Copyeditor
Suzanne Clarke

Proofreader
Sally Partington

Audio
Paul Stark
Jake Alderson

Contracts
Dan Herron
Ellie Bowker
Alyx Hurst

Design
Rosanne Cooper
Joanne Ridley
Rachael Hum
Anna Egelstaff
Sinead White
Georgina Cutler

Operations
Jo Jacobs
Sharon Willis

Editorial Management
Charlie Panayiotou
Jane Hughes
Bartley Shaw
Tamara Morriss

Finance
Jasdip Nandra
Nick Gibson
Sue Baker

Production
Ruth Sharvell

Sales
Jen Wilson
Esther Waters
Victoria Laws
Toluwalope Ayo-Ajala

Don't miss the next hilarious, heartwarming and unputdownable Regency from Felicity George . . .

In Pursuit of a Duchess

Two sworn enemies. One inconvenient truce. What could possibly go wrong?

When the beloved Duke of Severn passes away under suspicious circumstances, rumours are alight that it was because of his young, rebellious, and outspoken wife, Henrietta. Especially once she goes on the run . . .

But she's not alone.

Theodore Hawke, a ruthless journalist and her sworn enemy, shortly follows behind – determined to be the first to get the scoop.

With no other option, Henrietta presents a truce: if he helps her uncover the true identity of her late husband's killer, he can publish whatever he likes.

So when their inconvenient truce begins to cause inconvenient feelings, it's not just Henrietta's reputation at stake – but her heart too . . .

<u>Available to pre-order now!</u>

'A heart-warming and richly emotional debut that shines with sparkling wit, passion and fun' **NICOLA CORNICK**

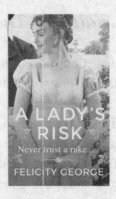

Never trust a rake . . .

Lady Margaret has devoted herself to taking care of her young siblings and the estate while her half-brother fritters away the family fortune. Upon Edwin's death, she learns he has left them destitute and, worst of all, at the mercy of a notorious and cruel rake.

Lord Nicholas would much rather be pursing women for quick sport rather than taking care of a headstrong debutante without any prospects, as well as her siblings. But Edwin saved his life once, and now he owes him a debt. Fortunately, all he has to do is find Meggy a husband, and his debt will be paid.

There's just one issue: Meggy is *nothing* like what he'd imagined. And the more time he spends in her company, the more he begins to wonder whether he's met his match . . .

466

'A gorgeous, captivating Regency romance'
SOPHIE IRWIN

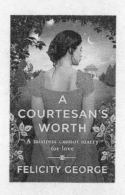

A mistress cannot marry for love . . .

As one of the famous Preece sisters, Kitty is the most sought-after courtesan in London. But with the vicious Duke of Gillingham scaring away any man who looks her way, securing a new arrangement with a wealthy gentleman will be no easy feat. Kitty's only hope to find someone suitable is through her loyal and cherished friend, the Reverend Sidney Wakefield.

Sidney has devoted his life to the church, but it was never by choice. He is a writer and Kitty his muse. As he is roped into Kitty's plotting, he begins to realise that protecting her from the malevolent Duke comes at a price – and it might mean losing Kitty to someone else entirely.

As Kitty and Sidney try to find a way out, it becomes clear that years of friendship have developed into something deeper. Except that they are from different worlds and Kitty's heart has never been hers to give away . . .